Defenseman

A Hockey Player's Story

By

Michael J. Maloni

Strategic Book Publishing and Rights Co.

Strategic Book Publishing and Rights Co.
12620 FM 1960, Suite A4-507
Houston TX 77065
www.sbpra.com

Hardcover version published in 2009.
Softcover version published in 2012.

ISBN: 978-1-61897-748-9

Book Design: Roger Hayes

Dedication

To my friend Leo Sagan and his family who never told me to get a real job.

To my agent who suffered through countless dumb jokes over the e-mail.

To my publisher who is getting used to my dumb jokes!

The most important contributions during this time in my life: to my families, the Maloni family, my church family, and the Commonwealth of Massachusetts who supported me with disability.

Acknowledgements

Before there was BU, there was my family and as much as I love BU, the family has some merit. My dad, Pete, mom, Marie, my brother Chris and the Dyjak gang, Jim, Joyce, and Delaney along with the Mangos, Grandma Yolanda, and Aunt Nikki! Also, the late, Joe Mango, my grandfather!

Also, to whom it may concern anywhere from Junior High to College. It could've been better but I must have learned something. I really don't know what to say except just enjoy the book and the other's coming down the Pike.

I want to include, the people at Romito's and Starbuck's in East Longmeadow, they helped me with writer's block and writer's contortion.

The folks at the Pizza Makers let me write like crazy and I am grateful for them!

Barb Perry at *The Reminder*. Who helped get **AmericanView Photo** off the ground.

Chapter 1

Steve Thompson was standing on the corner of Baystate Rd. in Boston, MA reading a copy of the Freep, short for Boston University's *Daily Free Press.*

"Hey! Hot Shot!"

He looked up from the paper to find a girl about his age smiling.

"Hello," he said, startled.

"So, you're going to lead us to the Promised Land," she giggled again.

"I'm reading the paper," he said.

"Everybody's reading about you. You're even reading about you."

"Who are you?"

"I have class," she winked at him and spun around books in hand.

"That's what you think!" He hollered.

She laughed.

"I'll see you around hot shot."

"Hey! You're pretty cute! What's your name?"

"Hot shot!"

She stuck her tongue out, turned her head and kept walking.

"Damn. If you really had some stuff, you would've had her name and number."

Steve's roommate was standing a few paces away.

"Nate. What am I doing wrong?" Steve asked.

Nate Williams was Steve's defensive partner on the Boston University Terrier hockey team. Nate was about 6-2, 200 pounds, dark haired, the captain, and a Rhodes Scholar candidate. Steve felt like a neophyte next to him in many areas including this one.

"She's cute," Nate smiled, "Hang in there kid."

"I have to go to class," Steve said. "Beginning Photography."

"Hit your classes and I mean all of them. Then we have practice and then we have study hall. This is not cup cake U. Do your job."

"Yes, sir."

"Hey! Opening night is Friday! They gave you a nice write up. You seemed to have some stuff."

"Meaning?"

"Meaning, you didn't make an fool of yourself. Good job. Your parents coming?"

"And about a third of the Commonwealth."

"Good. Always remember. We're the best."

"Right."

"Go to class."

"When I figure out how to do this photography thing, I'll get you some nice photos for your Karen."

"You know, as seniors, it's our team..."

"I know."

"Stay awake in class."

Steve had to laugh and hurried off to the big gray building that was the Communication school. Steve had come from a fairly affluent suburb in Western Massachusetts and had some life experiences through family vacations and such where he thought he had some sort of education about the world. He really didn't know the complexities or the opportunities that awaiting him at BU when he was a freshman. And now that he was a senior he was much more, savvy about the world around him. The school was run like the hockey program in that it expected you to win immediately without any hesitation. Their attitude was that if you put your time in then you could accomplish your goals.

Boston was much different than back home. In East Longmeadow, you needed a car to go anywhere. In Boston, you hopped on the 'T.' The population was much more dense in Boston and you had to be more careful but the cultural opportunities were more vast and the possibility for enhancement was greater.

Like many young people his age, at times he was very much a supporter of his hometown and sometimes he was a detractor but at least he made his criticisms make sense. Steve was happy and excited to be a part of the Boston University tradition and he was working as hard as he had ever worked in his life. He didn't want to be left behind by successful people so he just picked up and forged his own identity. It was only the first week of senior year and he was wondering just who that girl was who was made him react that way. She had a fun personality and she was cute.

After classes that day, Steve headed over to Harry Agganis Arena. Harry Agganis was BU's most famous athlete. Multi-sport the "Golden Greek" excelled at all of them. Steve would get to play there but that wasn't on his mind at practice, surviving the drills were.

The college game was more complicated than the high school game. In high school, all Steve had to do was skate through the opposition. Now he had to think and pressure smartly instead of pressuring constantly and dangerously. Steve had grown accustomed to wheeling up ice in high school mostly because he scored or assisted on seventy per cent of his team's points. Now he was in Division I College Hockey playing against some of the best amateur players in North America and the world.

As in the classroom, the learning never stopped on the hockey rink. Today, Coach Bricker, was teaching the guys how to break a defensive trap with quick short passes. Steve was having trouble with his positioning and the Coach let him know it.

"Steve, I know you're intelligent. BU doesn't accept dummies. Skate your zone. That's all you have to do. Don't make the situation more than it is. Skate your zone. Use your head. I'm telling you nicely now but if you don't understand what I'm saying, it seems to me that you're glory grabbing and that can't be with the Terriers. It's not going to happen. We're a team here. We play as a team. All right! Let's hit it again."

Steve played desperate. Coach Bricker was a legend. He had known Steve since he was in mite hockey and travelling with junior clubs. This was Steve's first choice to come to school and he worked as hard as he could to impress his coach—sometimes too hard. Finally, Steve finished the drill satisfactorily and practice was finished a short while later.

After study hall a bunch of the guys went to Shelton Hall to eat dinner. Steve was kind of quiet at the table.

"Don't worry about it man," Tony Buck a right wing said.

"Coach is like that," Paul St. Croix smiled.

"It's not that. I know what he's worried about," Nate grinned.

"What?" Tony asked.

"Oh! He went down in flames with some girl today—right on Baystate," Nate laughed.

"I did not go down in flames. She said and I quote 'I'll see you around hot shot!'"

"He didn't get her number or her name," Nate said flatly, "All who think he struck out say 'Aye!'"

"Aye!" The other players chorused.

"Drop dead."

"You're a senior. You can't say that." Paul said.

"It's a democracy." Steve said.

"This hockey club is the Boston University Terriers. We had an off year last year and we didn't win the Bean Pot, which is ours by the way. We're not here to shoot our mouths off. It's just good-natured ribbing. It's fun. We like winning. That's all. You are the best defenseman in college hockey but you're way too serious," Nate said.

"Right. I'm sorry."

"Are you going to miss this college food?" Tony asked.

Steve laughed.

"That's about the size of it," Paul grinned.

"Next year you'll be playing for the Bruins," Tony said.

"Yeah. The NHL," Steve said quietly.

"I think I may take my year, enjoy the hell out of it, take the walk and sign my contract. After we win the National Championship and the Pot; that is how I want it to end," Nate said.

"Well, to our year," Paul said.

"To the best defenseman in college hockey," Tony toasted him with his water.

"Yeah, all hail the Terriers." Steve smiled.

"You just keep that in your head and you'll be fine in life," Nate smiled.

"Well, we start with them right off. The toughest team in Hockey East besides us," Steve said.

"We can take them at Conte Forum. I know it," Paul smiled.

"Then we take them when we get back," Steve said.

"They're big and they're fast. They play hard. We joke around a lot but they have quality players. You have to play hard, skate, and get in the corners with them. It's a toughness test against the Eagles," Nate said.

"What about Harvard, or Northeastern?" Paul asked.

"They're tough. It's Division I College hockey. They're all out to win a National Championship—at least the ones worth playing against are," Steve answered.

"Why did you come here?" Tony persisted with another question directed toward Steve.

"I want my degree to go along with my National Title," Steve smiled.

"Titles. Don't forget the Beanpot," Nate smiled.

"Clean sweep. I want my senior title," Steve grinned.

"Well, we had that forever," Paul grinned.

"Why not?" Steve asked.

"Well, we have to win this one," Nate said.

"Yes, we do," Paul said.

They ate for a while and Steve listened to war stories about the Beanpot and the NCAA play-offs and then they went back to the room to study. At about eleven o'clock, Steve took a break to go upstairs to watch the full moon from the ballroom window that set atop Shelton Hall.

Along came roses and sunshine almost in the middle of the night.

"Hello," An innocent voice called. He turned to see that girl from this morning.

"I'm not talking to you unless you tell me your name," he grinned.

"It's Susan. Why so snotty?"

"Because you embarrassed the hell out of me in front of our team captain."

"It's my job. If you listen to the *Freep* telling you how great you are, you'll get a swelled head."

"Would you like to sit down?"

"Does that mean you like me?"

"It means I want to chew you out."

She laughed and so did he.

"You're easy to talk to even when I'm trying to bait you," he smiled.

"Thank you. Thank you very much," she blushed.

"So? What's your story? What possible function do you have here?"

"I'm pre-med."

"You have to be kidding."

"I want to be an ER doctor like on television."

"Are you serious?"

"Oh! Yes!"

"Oh! Yes!"

"Uh! Huh!"

"So? You could possibly be more intelligent than me?" He smiled innocently.

"I'm trying to be nice."

"Yes but can you pull it off."

"Hey!"

"Ah-Hah! I got you."

"Very funny!"

"Why aren't you nervous? I'm running on adrenaline"

"I'm not."

"Why?"

"You're easy to talk to. You can find people right off and for the record, I don't do this with everybody. I like you and you're going to pay for it for the rest of your born days."

"Well, thanks very much."

"Well, isn't this nice," he looked away.

"You're getting shy on me now."

"Maybe."

"Turn back to me."

"Do me a favor. Sit down next to me. I'll clear the sports page off the sofa."

"Aren't you the sport?"

"Hey, it beats reading and seeing pictures of cadavers."

"It's not all cadavers."

She sat down next to him as he cleared out the newspaper.

"Then what is it?" He asked.

"I like it. I like helping people. Just between us. It's well worth it. You can help most and most is enough for me. For some docs it's not. They want to help every one and nobody's perfect. Mostly right now, we're loading up on science courses. It's tough."

"Intimidated?"

"No. I'm just a realist. It takes effort."

"What's your last name?"

"Baker, Susan . I'm from Springfield."

"You're kidding."

"Springfield's not Boston but it's nice."

"I'm from East Longmeadow. Ten minutes away from Springfield."

"Spartan?"

He nodded his head.

"Golden Eagle?"

"Yes. Pretty much."

"I am very much interested in you," he said.

"I am very much amazed by your maturity."

"Well, it took me four years."

"I don't know. All the hockey players I knew in high school cared more about Bourque than SAT's."

"Yet, you like me. I was one of those by the way."

"Why are you here? I heard those stories about the draft and the Bruins. Why come to Boston University? The press will filet you."

"The only thing the press has filet my so far is what I'm so solely dedicated to get out of the locker room expediently. Besides the real reason why I'm here is my degree. I always wanted this. College and everything mean a lot to people. It's more than just hockey games. I lied. I was trying to make you laugh about the SAT's. I want my degree and I like Business Management. It will make me mentally to get my degree. It'll be easier to live because I stuck it out. I don't know. People have all kinds of hypothesis about life. That's mine."

"You passed up all that money."

"Yes. I did. In the future with my degree and my abilities I'd have a successful life anyway. I still wanted my degree in the end. Why are you here?"

"I wanted to be a doctor since forever. When I was young, I was mystified by getting strep throat and then having the doctor proscribing the cough medicine to cure it. Medicine fascinated me from an early age. I mean, you want to help people anyway. Medicine just seemed like my way. Why Business?"

"I like leading and using a group of people to overcome challenges."

"Materialist," She teased.

"Not quite. Builder! "

"You're a hockey player."

"Not permanently; it's got to end sometime."

"It's not that bad."

"I beg to differ. It stinks. I'd play until I was one hundred."

"You're pointed."

"I have tact. I just don't show it unless I need it."

"All right but still; you think sometimes."

"Hazard of college***"

"Of course, I'm serious. Why come to college—especially one like this? It's important that I win. In the NHL, and back home it's important to win. A school like BU just doesn't happen and they accepted me. I have a chance. What about you? What are your dreams? Besides medicine?"

"I want to be an ER doc like I said. To tell you the truth, I've been here three years and I'm hooked on cities. I love everything being five minutes away from each other or at least you hop on the 'T' and you're there."

"What neighborhood are you from?"

"Behind Kiley. Near Veterans Golf Course."

"Keep talking."

She blushed but continued on.

"I have a lot of the same feelings as you. I like Springfield but Northampton is a drive and the city for the most part shuts down at five o'clock. I love the Big E. All my friends do. It's just that people are in love with their houses. You buy a house and it's the center of your universe. I'm a condo person myself—especially in a city. Boston doesn't shut down at five o'clock.

"Okay. Tough guy," she smiled quietly.

"It's sort of important to me that I graduate," he said quietly.

"Hey," she squeezed his hand. "It's okay."

"I get very competitive. I'm sorry," he apologized.

"Me too."

"I can't see you as competitive. Cool under fire yes but not very competitive."

"I'm liking this."

"I can also see you as really caring. I can see you as my friend."

She blushed and turned away.

"How are you?" he asked quietly.

She held his hand tightly and he watched her brown hair fall to her shoulders.

"Hey brown eyes. Turn around," he ordered gently.

She turned toward him.

"I could kiss you right now," he said.

"Go easy with me."

"I have a big mouth. I'm only teasing you. It's okay. May I?"

She moved gently toward him and he finished the motion softly. Their lips touched.

Chapter 2

"You said I struck out," Steve gloated when he arrived back at the dorm.

"Excuse me," Nate was reading above the fold with a story about the Bruins.

"Name, room, number and a kiss."

Nate put the paper down.

"Well, you're all right!"

"Yes! I am!"

"Tell me about her."

"Man, she's great. Her name's Susan Baker—room 306. Nice girl. Med student from Springfield—ten minutes from my house."

"She kissed you."

"Don't look so surprised."

"Is she coming to the game?"

"Of course, we have a rendezvous on the roof later."

"Aren't you smooth? I'm impressed."

"Me too! This girl is so easy to talk to. I came all the way to Boston and fall for a girl ten minutes from my house."

"You didn't tell her that. Maybe you should cool down about falling for her. Hockey players attract shoe flies like nothing."

"Never mind what I told her but 'no' I didn't. She likes me so you have to take back everything you said."

"She wants to be what kind of doctor."

"ER—like on TV. I sprained my ankle playing scrub football in gym in junior high and had to go to the emergency ward. It's a pretty wild place. All the doctors do is careen around from one patient to the next. It's chaos. You have to have nerves of steel and a lot of brains. I admire her."

"Well, you're growing up."

"Stop that please."

"Hah!"

"Hah! Yourself!"

"Speak politely in front of your captain."

"I'm going to bed."

"Don't throw a temper tantrum. Talk to me about her."

"It's private."

"You kissed her."

"That's uncalled for."

"I don't care."

"Once," Steve blushed.

"You stud!"

"Very funny! Anyway, she's somewhat delicate. She said to go easy on her."

"What do you think that means?"

"I don't know. She's definitely a nice girl though."

"Bring her home to mamma."

"Not yet. She's kind of like me."

"A flake?"

"Sort of but she's a really smart flake. Laughs come easy to her. She likes to have fun."

"Sweet."

"Oh yeah."

"Well, Sparky, you are just the boss."

"Why do you always make me feel like I'm in junior high school."

"My job is to keep you from getting a big head."

Steve flopped on the bed and then rolled over face the captain.

"Yes?" Nate asked.

"It's about my brother."

"He would admit to having you as a brother."

"I'm worried about him. He's older than I am. He wants to come to the game on Friday."

"So?"

"He's mentally ill. He has bipolar disease. When he gets in places with a lot of noise the voices in his head gets worse. He also has mood swings but not to the degree he did without medication. He really wants to come and I don't know what to do."

"Geeze. I thought you were going to say something about his car or something."

"He's tough. He actually graduated from this place before he was diagnosed. Tony's doing okay. He's working with the mentally ill now besides his job at a department store . I'm just worried about him.

"Every Christmas, my parents have a party. We have about 20-25 people over the house. Sometimes Tony has to go in his room by himself to take breaks from the noise. He says he wants to go. The doctors say it's okay. So it's okay. Right?"

"Yeah, right. How bad is it?"

"Pretty bad when he isn't taking medication but better now. The resources out there are vast. The trouble is peoples' perceptions'. Some people think he's evil and he's not. He's the nicest guy. He's married and they're saving for a condo."

"He has guts," Nate said.

"More than me: Everybody accepts me right off because I am a hockey player but he went through a time when he was first diagnosed that he told people he was mentally ill and besides the family virtually nobody accepted him. He became more involved with mentally ill people and they became his friends. His fiancee is normal as the saying goes."

"Does he try with 'regular people?"

"Not as much as he did. I try and pump him up but he can't talk about his disease because sometimes you know he has it anyway."

"Does he like people?'

"Sometimes he forgets that he has it and he just relaxes but sometimes he is wary. He is always watching himself.

"You have to understand that my brother when he was young was a paper boy, was a Cub Scout, and organized a wiffle ball game for Jerry's Kids. He's like that and then it happened and he changed. He had friends in school and then he didn't. He didn't want them and they thought he was weird for alienating them. You know junior high school. Everyone is at that age where your shirt has to be the cool shirt. It's the beginning of materialism or sophistication depending on how you look at it. My brother was special.—different but special.

"He's the brother I don't know and the brother I do. It's tough sometimes. I get angry for him having the disease and I get angry with him for taking so long to accept it. He doesn't get angry though—at least outwardly. He hasn't said anything to me. Tony has a good heart. His natural inclination is to help other people. He's very happy now because the medicine and the therapy are working. It was the worst for him when he wasn't working. To Tony, a man worked and it was demeaning but he's happy and that's good."

"Do you tell him you're angry?"

"He knows. You can't miss it. He's my older brother and it's not fair to him. My brother wasn't exceptionally fast on the ice nor talented before the illness but there was something about him. I think his life is good now but I think he became afraid and gravitates toward people who are mentally ill. He should try normal settings with 'regular people' but he likes his life. Then again, what's more normal than a hockey game? I'm worried."

"Did it ever happen before?"

"No. I've never seen him this excited before either. When I pull on that number seven for BU, his emotions will be flying."

"You can pray."

"I do. I call it the 'standard desperation prayer.'"

"Which is?"

"'God, please help my brother.' It's not much but you really don't need much more."

"Does he need a lot."

"He took a long time to accept. He kept waving his degree in everyone's face saying, 'If I graduate from a school like BU without meds, how can I be crazy?' He doesn't think of himself as crazy anymore. He just considers it a regular medical condition and that's what it is—a simple chemical imbalance in the brain."

"Did it cause a lot of problems for him?"

"There were credit card debts after college and the emotional toll it took on all of us but we made it through and so did he. He's a good guy. I wish he would come up and watch the game in the hotel room and then we could go out or get room service or something."

"If the doctor said it was okay…"

"I know. Still though."

"You're worrying."

"I think I've made that clear."

"Look, you have to be rational about this. The doctors said it's good. He's looking forward to it. From what I heard, you may make him depressed just talking about it. Just let it ride. Take them out to dinner after the game and relax. How old is he anyway?"

"He's older than me—thirty—but he's smart and he works really hard for those people he represents. He sort of fell into the job; Tony wanted to learn more about NAMI in WMASS so he started hanging around the office, which was good, because he wasn't alone so much but then he enjoyed answering phones and helping people out. He was able to be like an ombudsman in a paper for the center. He sort of is a liaison to the community. At thirty-five, he is much different than twenty-one or even twenty-three. He's making it in America and I'm proud of him. I just get angry some times but it passes. He makes it pass because I'm so proud of him."

"I never have been exposed to someone on a consistent basis who was mentally ill," Nate said.

"Tony's obviously really bright. This guy has a resolve to him that defies imagination. When it is good, it's very good but if he's off his meds he's a load. He can be real tough case."

"That's better."

"He's still my big brother and we laugh, especially at Christmas. Tony's the instigator. He gets up every Christmas morning before the sun comes up and rouses everyone out of bed. We all know it is coming and we all tell him to go back to bed and he feigns disappointment but it works and we tease him about it all day and he laughs. I love Christmas. It happens every year. Tony really gets excited about it."

"Look man, no matter, I go around sometimes with my brother too. It's just different personalities. Maybe it's not all the illness. It sounds like you're both strong personalities."

"Yes, we are. I just worry. His life is going so well. I think what bugs me is what he went through. The first time it happened, he lost all of his friends and that adversely affected him. He associated not ever having friends with the disease so he rebelled against the diagnosis. It took him a long time to recover. I don't know if he can face that again. He's reasonably sure, in fact he's told me that he's sure these people would stand by him because they are more mature and know the risks but I'm not so sure."

"Well, aren't you the optimist?"

"Yeah, you're right. I have to study."

"I'd like to meet Tony after the game."

"Later. Mom is here. Get it? They are staying the weekend so we'll go out next weekend."

"You're afraid of your mother," Nate said.

"Yes I am!"

"We could. It's definitely something but don't say much in front of the guys until its square."

"Why?"

"If she squashes me, it'll suck! I have to study."

"How can you be such a pessimist?"

"It's what life taught me."

Chapter 3

The next day at lunch, Susan blew the whole thing wide open. Steve was sitting with the guys and they were acting juvenile like usual and she walked by with her girlfriends and waved to him with a big smile on her face. Steve waved back and the jokes came.

"What the heck is she waving at you for? She's too good looking. She should be waving at me," Rico Barrini, a tough left wing said.

"She must like ugly guys," Dan Fredricks, a slick center said.

"She thinks I'm cute. She said so."

"She must be blind," Rico teased.

"Twenty—Twenty," Steve said.

"As far as you know," John Mark said.

"As far as you say," Rico said.

"Look guys, you can lay it on me all you want but you be respectful around her. She's a good person. She's a nice girl."

The guys took full advantage of his remark and teased him some more before lunch was over. Steve skirted through the rest of the day and then knocked on Susan's door after study hall. She was out and he left a note on her door to come see him. Steve turned around and she stood before him.

"I guess you need my phone number," She said.

"I guess so."

"Let me put my stuff away. We can go for a walk," she said.

"Where've you been?" Steve asked as the walked to the elevator.

"Working at the bookstore; It's cool. There's a neat sweatshirt that I have my eye on."

"I washed dishes in a pizza shop to earn money for college," he smiled.

"That's hard work."

"It makes you tough. It makes you mentally tough. We had fun though. The owner was a real die hard Red Sox fan and he used to die in agony every fall."

"Which one was it?" She asked as they walked out onto Baystate Rd.

"The old one on Shaker Rd. Not the new one started by the other family. The old one."

"I know the one you are talking about. The pan pizza place."

"Right. How's the pre-doctor business going?"

"Okay. There is a lot of science like I said. How's Management?"

"I like it."

"Good."

"There's a tremendous opportunity in business to make a difference."

"Specifically?"

"You'll laugh."

"I won't laugh. You're my friend."

"Well, I always thought about owning a restaurant sometime. "

"You are kidding. Right! You break your back for four years in this place and you're going to own a restaurant?"

"Well, what I was going to say was I having second thoughts."

"Well, you better."

"Well, it's just that all jocks own restaurants and bars. Even Jack Dempsey did."

"Who the hell is Jack Dempsey?"

"'Smiling Jack.' The champion boxer; you've never heard of him."

"No."

"God help us all."

"What about your parents?"

"I haven't spoken to them yet. The truth is I have another plan. I just know how I'm going to pull it together. It is after all BU and I have to find a good way to succeed. The trouble is the more I think about it, the more it seems plausible."

"Well, take you degree, start to make it happen and be happy. By the way? What is it?"

"What I really want to do is put a sports photography museum in Springfield. That's a bit ambitious. Yes, but if you don't get rambunctious once in a while life with get stale. It will be good for the city and good for me. I can't wait until May. Finally, I'll be able to take the walk and then I can sign my contract and get going."

"Same with me."

"I like doctoring because you push yourself hard but you are convinced that it's not intrinsic—not just for you. You have to give something back. It's the nature of the business."

"Yeah, I've met some like you."

"Oh really? Get the hiccups?"

"No. But I can hiccup if you want?"

"Thanks anyway. Where did you meet them like me?"

"My brother's bipolar. I've seen some docs in my time and they all cared about him. I've seen some."

"Older or younger?"

"My brother or the doctors?"

"Don't be a wise guy."

"It occupies my mind too much. I worry about it every waking moment. I have to stop this or I'll go crazy. I love him but ninety per cent of my conversations are about him. Even my parents tell me to stop talking about it. In short I don't want to talk about it."

"If you say so."

"I'm sorry. I don't mean to be evasive. It's just that my parents are right. It's in God's hands and you can pray and beg God to help you but in the end it's in His hands. I just want to talk about something else."

"The one thing that bothers me is that his friends vaporized. Everybody liked Tony and then when the mental illness hit they parted like the Red Sea. All of a sudden he was loser. He went from nice guy to bum in six months to a year. Tony hangs out with mentally ill people mostly because he feels safe around them. It's good I guess but I wish he would try again with quote unquote 'normal' people."

"It's rough on people being in relationships with mentally ill people."

"It didn't seem rough on them sweetheart. They adjusted well. There were winners and losers in life and Tony was judged to be the latter. Life moved on really quickly. Nobody batted an eye. Tony didn't deserve that."

"You're bitter."

"It is part of the reason why I went away I guess. I don't know. I'm just really nervous about this weekend. I feel something bad is about to happen."

"We have a good deal not to worry about you know."

"I just don't want to see my brother go through that again. The mental illness part was bad but the part where he lost his friends. He spent some time in prison because of his credit cards and in prison there was a phone and the worst people he had ever encountered, car thieves, pimps, drug dealers, and larcenists to name a few called their friends and he had nobody to call. I don't want that to happen again."

"Well, does he have friends now?"

"He has a wife. They live in an apartment and are saving for a condo. Maybe I'm projecting or I'm afraid for myself, which makes me a rat for using my brother as an excuse but his experience has made me more cautious about friends and girls—particularly a possible wife. I am more leery now. Before it was just like—hey whatever! Now I'm not so sure."

"Are you afraid it may happen to you?"

"Sometimes I get scared but it blows over. Mostly I just want him to keep his friends again. You don't know what it's like to have your big brother ask you if he was a bad person because he had no friends when at one time he did."

"How does he feel about it?"

"He feels that I worry too much. He feels that people are more mature and because most of his friends have mental illness now they would stick with him if something happened. I hope he's right."

"I think you should worry about the game to be honest with you. You have about one hundred things in your head."

"We could get a cup of coffee in Sherman. We could talk about something else."

"Like what?"

"I don't know. How about where we're going to take my family Saturday afternoon before the game? Saturday night I can't see you."

"Why the heck not?"

"Brother's night out. I'm seeing him Friday night."

"You're lucky you have a good reason."

They opened the door to George Sherman Union, Boston University's Student Union, and found the coffee bar. Steve ordered a mocha latte and Susan ordered a decaf.

"You're healthy," he teased.

"You're such a jerk," she giggled.

"You can't even insult people," he smiled.

"No, I can't. I thought you were a good conversationalist. What happened?"

"I'm sorry dear. What would you like to talk about?"

"Well, this thing you have in your head about a museum."

"Ah! My thing! It's an idea, miss. I have had it since I was probably fourteen or fifteen. The thing is even though I grew up there, I'm an outsider."

"Why?"

"Because I went out of Western Mass to go to school; It's not like WMASS is the only community to think that way but it's a royal pain in the butt when you try to get things done. They're busy throwing stupid little comments out when work could be getting done. "Well, I didn't go to BU. I only went to Springfield College." If I was spending all that money on tuition and my kid came home with an attitude like that, I'd be really angry. Geeze, I'm trying to do something good here and they aren't even making difficult tasks more difficult by asking logical questions. They're just being stupid."

"How do you know this?"

"It is like good is never good enough. If I want to do something for my church then, why shouldn't I do it for five other places?"

"When I arrived here, I wanted to do something really important. Huge! After all it was BU! But I enjoyed part of my pre-college life and maybe I fully haven't explored this dream. Maybe it isn't limited to one place maybe. I'm going to be splitting my time between Boston and WMASS."

"I think you worry like nobody I've ever seen. Relax and concentrate on the business end of it. Things are changing in Springfield. There's a lot more college students in WMASS that have gone away to college. To change the subject before the horse gets beat; I have a question for you. Do you think a physician in her own private practice is too soft a job for someone like me?"

"I can see you being very good at it. In private practice I mean. I can even see you in the psych side of medicine."

"Really?"

"Take it as a compliment. I wasn't being a wise guy. What brought this discussion on?"

"I've had a myriad of thoughts lately. I'm so excited to be here and the thoughts have grown recently—everywhere from private practice to medical research. The medical field grows every day and there's so much out there to study. It's hard sometimes to decide."

"You're twenty-one years old. Why should it be easy?"

"Medical research fascinates me. Curing cancer; working for the Jimmy Fund. I don't know. There's a lot of personal reward no matter what kind of doctoring you do. It's tough."

"What do you like about ER doctoring?"

"You help people in severe distress. The fast pace. The mental challenge of performing under pressure."

"What do you like about private practice?"

"You get more in depth with the patients. You have more time to talk to them. You find out about their families and such."

"What about medical research?"

"You practice science for the benefit of people."

"Boy! I wouldn't like to be in your shoes."

"Thanks a lot."

"I like on getting on your nerves."

"You're my friend but you're such a jerk. What's your middle name?"

"Michael. Why?"

"Good solid name."

"I don't understand how everything is so… You're so…"

"Thank you."

"Thank me. Why am I thanking you?"

"Because you think I'm attractive and this is beyond friendship."

"We already discussed this."

"You're being dense. If you want to see me that means you like me more than average. Right?"

"Okay. You have me on that one."

He finished off his mocha latte. Her decaf was half finished.

"Nervous?" She asked.

"A little."

"I'm still me."

"I was talking about Friday night."

"I'm sure you were."

"You should be a shrink."

"So now what do we do?"

"We're friends. That's the best I can do for now. I've seen too much in my life. I'm definitely interested but I don't know."

"Well, how are you going to get more interested?"

"Keep seeing each other. Look, you're a nice girl but I've been involved with nice people who did the proverbial 'I can't take it routine.' First impression I like you a lot. Second impression is wait and see, if she can hang in there for right now we're good friends. Okay?"

"Maybe we can be good friends tonight at about eleven on the roof."

"That's possible."

"Good because I have to go home and study like a demon."

"Supper first—I'll buy."

"What a sport!"

"I told you were my good friend. You alleviate the whole problem."

"Which was?"

"The whole woman thing; where you wanted me in a relationship right away. It takes me a week to pick out a tie for a social engagement. Let's just be good friends for now."

"You're okay."

"You're really think I'm going for the idea that hard huh!"

"Maybe."

"It's a big decision. There's a lot to it with many factors that can be weighed in on all sides. You have to do what makes you happy. Nobody has the perfect life where every decision they make goes perfectly and every job is not perfect but if you're happy at it then it's worth it."

"You're pretty smart—sort of."

"Dinner with you is going to be a real trip."

"It must be the caffeine."

"I'm sure that's what it is."

"Come one. I'm trying to lighten things up. You're very different from most of them."

"Who's them?"

"The bubble heads. That's what I call them. They want to go out with a hockey player and won't tell him their own opinion if it kills them—as long as they have a hockey player."

"And you know this?"

"Since junior high."

"I didn't need to know that."

"I didn't fall madly in love. It's just that you're young and stupid. Well, you have a big head because you are after all a 'hockey player.'"

"What brought you down to earth."

"I don't know specifically but I like you because you speak to me straight away without any pretenses and you aren't argumentative getting your point across. You're easy to be with."

She blushed a little bit and then recovered.

"I think my parents would think I was crazy. Some wet nose twenty one-year-old trying to organize this."

"Maybe."

"Let's have dinner."

"Let's head to the salad bar."

"Health nut."

"What do you want?"

"Pasta—good carbs."

They picked up their dinners and sat down. Steve felt she was holding something back so he asked.

"What's going on? You're awfully quiet."

"I'm thinking that I'm going to go for it. For a near vegetarian, you're a nice person."

"Just near dear," she smiled.

"You just eat healthy stuff around me because you want to impress me."

"Oh, my God! You have such a swelled head."

"Have pity on me. I'm breaking a code."

"What code would that be?"

"I'm going to tell you something Susan. I'm so freakin' nervous about playing BC it's unbelievable."

"Why is that breaking a code?"

"Because you never tell anyone you are nervous about an opponent. Ever."

"Not even your close friends?" She asked skeptically.

"Especially not them."

"Why not?"

"The best side of it is you are supposed to show mental toughness. On the worst, it's a curse."

"You're an idiot. There are no such things as curses."

"Well, thank you very much. I let you delve into a personal part of me and you call me an idiot."

"It's a hockey game. I will still like you if you lose."

"Thank you but I won't like me if I lose."

"Look, you go out there, you play until you're exhausted and if you win or lose I know you still have morals. That's what I care about," she said.

"Geeze, you almost make me feel good. Do you know that?"

"It wasn't planned."

"Thanks all the same."

"Don't mention it."

"Why do you pump me up and then hit me in the crosshairs with a different opinion?" He asked.

"I want to test your conviction. I don't care what you do as long as you're happy but I'm going to tell you right now, you're pizza shop will be a credit to the community around it. If you do it, you'll be involved in local charities. I can tell. You have that kind of motivation. You're civic minded."

"Guilty."

"Not guilty—very true and very good."

"You could've taken summer classes."

"Then I would've never been able to have a real college experience. Everybody thinks the pros are so glamorous right off but you give up your youth. College gives you a transition. You give up the money sure but there's something to college. There's something to it. I like it. I have no regrets. I have grown immensely.."

"I like talking to you. If you walk me home, so I can study, I don't want to flunk out of this place I'd be grateful."

"Only if you meet me on the roof at eleven o'clock, sir."

"Would you hold my hand?" She asked.

"I'd like that very much."

"It's getting chilly," he said when they were out the door.

"Yes, I like the fall."

"I like the leaves. All my time is taken up with hockey but what a great way to take up your time."

"Even raking them."

He squeezed her hand tightly and she looked down at her shoe tops and stopped.

"Just friends, huh?" She asked.

"Yes. Very good friends."

"How many adjectives do you have to put before it before I'm your girlfriend?" She asked.

"Let it just be for a while."

She started walking again very quickly and then she stopped.

"I'm pulling out all my stops with you. I'm kind. I'm considerate. I'm sensitive. What's the problem?"

"It's not you. It's me and I'm not dangling or angling you."

"It sure feels like it."

"Can I have your hand? We'll walk normal pace together."

They walked for a short while and she asked.

"So?"

"I saw how my brother was treated. Everybody liked him—like me now. Big hockey player—everyone likes you. If I stink, that's something else."

"We already covered that. Try again."

"In a weird way; the elite athlete wants the pressure on him. And then something like that happens too Tony and you understand what pressure is. Anyway, an athlete wants the last shot of the game."

She stopped in the middle of the road as a gentle rain began to fall.

"Please kiss me," she said.

"I really care about you," he whispered before touching his lips to hers.

She pulled away after a moment and looked at him.

"Are you okay?" He asked softly.

"I'm fine," she smiled gently, "we'd better get home. I, um, have lots of studying. I want to see you tonight."

"Okay. That was really beautiful."

"Yes it was."

They walked the rest of the way in silence. He held her hand tightly so, she wouldn't let go—maybe even too tightly but she didn't flinch. Susan held on just as tightly and he could see the trace of tears in her eyes. He walked her up to her room and gave her a gentle along with a peck on the cheek before they retired to study.

Steve went into his room but Nate wasn't there so, he studied until eleven o'clock.

Chapter 4

They had boys night out after practice and the fun and frolic of the evening turned at least semi-serious when Rico looked over at Steve and asked.

"Are you going to tell them?"

"Yes. I think it's time."

"Gentleman, please. Can we have quiet?" Rico called out.

"What for?" Dan Fredricks asked.

"It's important," Rico said.

"Gentlemen, we've all sweated it out in school. We've worked hard on the ice and in the classroom. Now we have a test that I have concocted to see if we really are up to real world standards."

"Are you going to feed us to the lions?" Rick Barnes asked.

"It could seem like that sometimes."

"What are you offering us?" Ben Garvin asked.

"Well, about an hour and a half west is where I come from. It's a city called Springfield. It houses the Basketball Hall of Fame, which you should go see because it is cool. What I would like to do is place an International Sports Photography Museum damn close to it. That's what this meeting is about."

"How can we help?" Steve Carmichael asked.

"The first two projects are primarily my ball. I have to write a mission statement and a business plan and then you guys get to review them.

"You don't have to sign up for this. I don't expect you all to sign up for this. We will still be teammates and friends if you do not sign up for this. Think it over. Take three days to think about it. Relax. I would really appreciate it if you guys took it seriously.

"I have a few friends at UMASS-Amherst that have already signed on. I'm looking for about a dozen, driven, and well-qualified people. Anyway, finish your pizza. It's getting cold."

Instead of being raucous, as most of the meetings were, this one ended quietly.

"Well, it's on," Steve whispered to Rico.

"You did well."

"Thanks, I'm going for a walk to clear my head. I finally said it to a group of people without being scared that I would be laughed out of the room."

"I think you got the boys roaring. I don't know if anybody else thought that way but it was my opinion."

"Well, the next step is wait and see. Hopefully a few of the boys will come a long."

"You made a strong impression. Relax and have a good time."

"I don't mean to be rude but what's your major?"

"Poly-sci. I get to help you out with the political types and the unions."

"How do you plan to do this?"

"Just give them the situation and the benefits it would bring to Springfield."

"Talk to them."

"If they have a brain in their head they'll know it's a good idea."

"Now we have to do it without the animosity. No 'brains in their heads speeches.'"

"Yes, sir."

"All right look, I know this sacrilege but I'm going to take a jaunt over to Harvard pretty soon just to see what I can see. It may lead to something. It may not. We'll see."

"Fair enough! You know they are a little upset that we own the Bean Pot."

"Commerce shall overcome."

"You're going to need lawyers," Rico said.

"Yeah, I know. I'd have to do some research on that because I'm still not sure who'll dot the 'iii's and cross the 'ttt's.'"

"Architects?"

"Part of the plan to be explained in two weeks."

"What about UMASS? Do you think they'll mix with us?"

"Yeah, it will be okay. They're college kids or almost grads. At least we're going to be young. Most importantly they believe in the project."

"What about East meets West?"

"Well if they act like they're in junior high, they'll be walking. I'm trying to build a family atmosphere here. I have no time for foolishness."

"Any girls?"

"Two of the five from WMASS***"

"Good, it will help us sell better."

"Geeze, that's cold. You could at least ask if they were cute."

"Are they?"

"To a man's eye—definitely."

"Also good."

"Do you think we should work outside the team?"

"Not yet but we should stay in touch with alumni contacts."

"Why the team first?"

"Because I know them and they have a unique resource. I also know their work ethic."

"This is my job. Hockey is just really fun. The museum is something I can hand down to my kids."

"Do you ever stop thinking?"

"It doesn't seems so."

"See you at practice tomorrow."

"See you Rico."

Steve walking home that night his mind blurred with thoughts—good and bad. He needed a mental break so he called Tony.

"Hey, it's me!" Steve said.

"How are you?"

"I did something magical tonight."

"You're going to keep me guessing?"

"Well, I presented a plan to my teammates about building an international sports photography museum in Springfield."

"Can you do it?"

"With a little help from my friends sure."

"I don't know that's a pretty tall order. How are you going to do it?"

"I'm going to draw up a preliminary plan and send my people to finish their assigned tasks."

"You're either a brave or a crazy man."

"I don't think I'm either. I just keep thinking how cool it would be to have it finished."

"I don't know man. That's a lot to do. You have to get a lot of people rowing in the right direction. I don't know if you can do it."

"Tony, America wasn't built by people who say I can't. There will be challenges sure but Springfield if dying for something. It would be a great catalyst to renovate other parts of the city. Don't be negative.

"I had this idea in my head since high school. The Lord wouldn't have left it there for nothing."

"What are you going to do?"

"I'm going to have the 'family' solve their assigned challenges and tasks,"

"Who may I ask is the family?"

"They're my staff."

"What are you paying your staff?"

"Pizza and beer at the meetings; I'll pay them when I sign my contract. I'll hire you if you keep that negative crap out."

"Dedicated staff***"

"I was serious about that job offer. Are you interested?"

"Hey, it's free pizza. I'm in. What do I do?"

"I was thinking Marketing. You're definitely creative. It would get you talking to people. It would be good for you and the company."

"You're the weirdest boss I ever heard of."

"Why?"

"Nobody gives a damn whether it's good for you or not. They just want performance."

"If you give employees room to grow and expand their horizons, they will work harder for you."

"And you pay them."

"That'll come when the contract gets signed."

"What do you think?

"What do you think?"

"That's not bad."

"Mostly it's my ball but I rely heavily on advice from the staff."

"I really can't believe you are doing this."

"Look, you want to give back because I'm going to be making millions. Why not be creative?"

"I'm impressed little brother."

"I'm honestly chomping at the bit to get out of this place and get into some action."

"I thought you were Mr. Hail BU."

"I am. I just want to put my education to work. I am getting itchy."

"What about getting Springfield to back you?"

"That's where marketing and sales come in."

"What if I don't do a good job because of my mental illness?"

"We'll work something out. On Saturday the 20th, I want you to be here at ten am."

"Yes, sir."

"Just come with an open mind."

"I'll tell mom and dad."

"Not yet. They'll think I'm crazy."

"If you insist***"

"We have to jell more as a team."

Chapter 5

The next day after practice, Steve sat in the locker room quietly while the other guys joked around. For some reason, he picked himself up and knocked on Coach Benson's door.

"Hello," the Coach smiled.

"Hi coach. I think I need all kinds of advice."

"Sit down boy. I'm full of it."

The Coach was a big, tall, rangy, ex-goalie for BU who had played in the nineteen seventies for two national championship teams. His own record as a coach was impressive with many Beanpots and three National Titles. Steve sat down in the chair.

Steve told the coach about his plan for a museum.

"That's pretty ambitious."

"I asked some of the guys if they'd like to be a part of it and I feel kind of weird because I'm their boss now."

"I don't need you to fit in. I need you to be a leader. Sometimes leaders do different things.

"All right, let's just say you are right. Nate's the Captain. I don't want to have a cat fight in the middle of the middle of next week. I am his stand in."

"Look, kid, everyone knows that Nate is Nate but if you didn't keep his feet nailed to the floor, he'd be in Sweden or somewhere exploring life."

"What does that mean? Coach I came to school for they not so average life and I'm getting it and it's weird like I'm stepping through a time warp or something. One day I was doodling out the plans for this in study hall during high school and now I'm doing it. It's different when people believe in you. I was the best player in high school but there was a ton of resentment. You assembled the most unselfish guys and that's why we win. It's not because I am a leader and there are followers but because we know our personal talents get better when we are together. I like school but I think I am ready in some ways for the imaginary, 'real world.'"

"Well, my advice to you is keep doing it. Talk to an expert. Sit down with your favorite professor and ask them about your options. Personally, I think it's the first week and you're more concerned with your performance against BC."

"Well, I want to win. My family's coming up for the weekend. You know about my brother. He's all excited and he's bringing his girl. She's from

Springfield. Here at BU. I want to win for him. I think they will have a good story to tell their friends when they get back. Besides half my high school rented out a bar to watch the game; the pressure is on. I can feel it."

"Son," the coach scratched his thinning, white crew cut, and played with the lanyard of his whistle, which was still around his neck. The coach looked down at his red sweat suit with the BU logo on the right breast, "I've seen players, real live, big time college hockey players in my time and you're one of them specifically because you play to win."

"I hate losing coach. It's terrible. In high school it was easy. I was supposed to score every chance I got. Push it! Push it! Push it! But here there's so much talent. Now as a senior, I look to take control of the game. To let the opposition know they can't ever beat you—especially in your house. It doesn't matter how you beat them as long as you beat them. Beat the trap, play wide open, play physical. Win where you're at."

"You will but you worry man. I'm going to start calling you the 'Hen'—short for 'Old mother hen.'"

Steve smiled.

"If I were you, I'd go to study hall. Have some dinner. See that magnificent girl you've been talking about and relax. Tomorrow is the show. It's fun tomorrow. We're on television both nights. Your family's here. Just live it up. It's college hockey."

"Yes, coach."

"But shower first, will you? You stink!"

"Coach," Steve smiled, "do you really think I'll do all right?"

"That's not advice. You're sucking up for a compliment. Get out."

The next night, he was on the ice at Conte Forum and he was more nervous than he'd ever been in his hockey life. For some reason, he was a step slower than the play and he wasn't finishing off his checks. At one point, near the end of the first period, Nate skated over to him during a TV timeout and chastised him.

"Hey, if you don't want to break your glass slipper before the ball, that's your business but we have a hockey game to win. Hit someone. Will you please?"

"Sorry. It won't get any worse," Steve replied.

But it did. Steve was playing not to embarrass himself any more and his mistakes mounted and then "it" happened. He was skating up behind the play and at center ice, during a two-two tie; he tripped and fell flat on his face. Not like a senior at all.

Angrily he pounded the ice with his padded glove hand and jumped up. He raced blindly into the offensive zone and suddenly the puck was on his stick. He deked left and then cut over right to blast a slap shot at the net. The goalie flailed helplessly with his oversized blocker glove and his stick but the puck sailed past into the net.

Steve felt like a million dollars. The goal did wonders for his confidence and he felt a member of the Boston University hockey program for the first time that season.. When his teammates mobbed him and they went to sit on the bench for the line change, Steve confessed to Nate.

"I didn't even see where the puck came from."

"I passed it to you moron. Who do you think is looking after you?" Nate smiled.

"You. Man, we did good. We're having a good time now."

"Just relax. It's hockey. You've been playing it since you were a kid. Have a little fun. Get a little goofy. We all do it. It's for fun."

Steve had fun the rest of the game. Soon, he was banging, skating, and passing with the rest of the guys. He even helped Nate out with an insurance goal late in the third period. The Terriers took the away game in their red and white uniforms 4-2 and then Steve had to go into the locker room afterwards.

"Hey, are they making a new Superman movie?" Steve Carmichael, the second line center asked.

"You could play the lead. Making an idiot of yourself all game and then poof! You take one pratfall and everything's beautiful," Dan Fredrick smiled.

"He's not Superman. He's Chevy Chase," Rick Barnes joked.

"I think we should all keep in perspective that we won the game," Steve blushed.

"Yes, but it was the way we won—so much humor!" Tony Banks smiled.

"You guys are idiots! Absolute idiots!"

"Hey clumsy! Do you want to come out? We'll go crazy. " Rico told him.

"I have a very hot date. Thanks very much," Steve winked.

"Hey, forget the date, she'll be here when you get back. Let's go have some fun," He grinned.

"You're right." Steve said.

She ran up to him and gave him a big hug.

"Look the guys want me to go out with them. A kind of guys night out; I'm sorry but I'm going to have to take a pass."

"Thanks a lot. What am I going to do?"

"Come on. Please this important."

"You're a jerk."

"Please."

She turned and walked on.

The team ended up going to Burger King in the Student Union. They were all very happy. A win over BC did that for a person. Steve felt good that the guys accepted him even though he would be boss to some of them.

"Hey, you know. I was thinking," Rico said.

"Did you hurt yourself?" Steve asked.

"I'm serious man. Did you ever think you were more than a museum?"

"Yeah, actually I have but I have to have verifiable facts that this is true.

I'll go with the museum project first—get my feet wet and then explore other opportunities later."

"Good. I just didn't want you to get bored."

"What are you thinking about?" Peter asked.

"Well, the way I figure it. It's going to take some time, if it comes to fruition at all. I have too much to learn to even have it formulate into a plan. I'm going to keep my mouth shut so I don't jinx myself."

Chapter 6

Afterwards he found her sitting on the sofa on the roof.

"You mad at me?"

"Pretty much. You're a jerk you know."

"Look, the guys wanted me to discuss something important. I don't think it's so bad a sacrifice. I've been spending all my free time with you. You can cut me slack one night. If we're going to fight, I'll go downstairs."

"What would you like to talk about?"

"Tell me about your family," Steve said as they gazed over the Charles in the dark with the streetlights up and running and reveling students also upstairs.

"Hey! Steve! You recover nicely!" One guy yelled.

"Shoot! It was a good thing I scored," he said sheepishly.

She laughed.

"Anyway, about your family."

"Well, my dad is a former sergeant in the Marines. He still keeps up with his buddies and he's a foreman at Lenox. My mom is a homemaker but she went to work at Filene's so I could go to school and I am in every sense of the word their little girl. Let's get upstairs. I have a story to tell you about college and what it means to my father."

"Fire away," Steve said.

"Every day my father would come home from work and ask me if I did my homework. I mean every day. One day I decided to test him just to see what kind of a reaction I'd get. I said no. I watched television—even though I studied.

"He blew as only as Marine can blow. He was furious. Except for the language, I thought I had joined the Marines. Finally, he calmed down and I told him I was just teasing. I told him I studied. I was in junior high at the time and I asked him why college was so important."

"Well," he said, "You'll be able to have a much more fulfilled life. I see people in the factory making more money than a lot of people in society but their outlook on life is such that they don't see how lucky they are. They are not in firefights. They don't see their buddies die but to them life is just the same old, same old. Life isn't that and the more educated you are gives you and your family the ability to enjoy life more. That's why it's important to study.'"

"I never heard my father talk like that. I thought he was going to keep yelling."

"He's right. My dad didn't go to college either but he's really smart. He's in industrial sales—packaging. He always gave us a choice but I knew he hoped secretly wanted us to go to further our education. My mom was the same way."

"Team dinner is at four. My brother wants us to spend some time together. He says he needs my opinion about something. I don't know what it is. He won't let on."

Steve found out at breakfast the next morning.

"I want to go into car sales," Tony said.

"You're telling me this," Steve said.

Tony was a strong guy, mentally and physically but not very tall only about five feet seven inches.

"Why?" Steve asked.

"You're pretty snide."

"Well, your life is going so well."

"I can't tell you because I feel like a heel for saying what I want to say."

"Do you want to kill anybody?"

"Of course not."

"I'm open then."

"Working in retail isn't challenging enough. I went into a shell. You were right. I'm looking the challenge of leading people someday. "

"Is it the money?" Steve asked.

"Sometimes. I know Annie wants a house but she's biting the bullet because of my pay scale and I've finally released that fear of having my own children. I'm also not volunteering at the clinic.

"All you do all day in the mental illness field is talk about mental illness in one form or another and that can get really heavy. I don't have the mentality for it."

"The people around you say you're really good."

"That's not aptitude. That's desperation. When you are released from the hospital, your world is upside down. You don't know about anything. You grab at straws and I think I didn't grab the right straw."

"So, what do you do? How? What about sales and cars?"

"Are you kidding me? Cars?"

"All right, that was stupid. What about sales? There's a lot of rejection."

"I know. I like talking to people and if you look at sales—all you really do is that. If you have a product you can stand behind, it's easy to introduce it to a person without feeling like you sold them a mine with no gold."

"You're still an idealist."

"So are you? What's up?"

"What do you mean?"

"You're different. You seem not so sure of yourself."

Steve told Tony about his travails with his life's plan.

"Brother, you probably don't want to tell mom and dad at this point so, I'm going to say talk to some professors and your academic advisor and then get some things straight in your head."

"Tony, I hope you make it in car sales. It's just that you're doing so well. Any little changes freaks me out."

"I can't be afraid of this damned disease my whole life. I don't want to end up alone with a bunch of people around me feeling sorry for me."

"Is that what it's like?"

"It is as if you're not challenging yourself. I have to do this. I tell people every day to go out into the world and do the best they can. It's about time I did. I've been clear for a while. Just minor interruptions but the fact is junior, illness or no, it's my job to take care of my family and that means sending kids to college and giving the family a father who isn't afraid to go out into the world."

"Man, I was so scared when you were sick. I really was. I wish I could've done it like you if I ever got sick. You fight so hard. Hockey's nothing."

"No. That's where you are wrong. Hockey is part of you and you'll find the other parts. It'll be okay. You'll be happy."

"I want to thank you for being my brother. I, well, when you were sick you said that you could never compete with me because I'm a hockey player. That's not true. You leave me in the dust. I'll support you whatever you do. You have my word."

"Not everything is a major disaster you know. It'll be all right. What are going to do until lunch with mom and dad?"

"We are going to experience culture. We're going to the MFA. They have an impressionist exhibit that's supposed to be out of the world."

"You need any money."

"Not yet. Don't worry about it."

"Do you know something that I don't?"

"No. Why?"

"You have this look of doom on your face. You had that same look no matter what happened after my diagnosis. Why?"

"I was just trying to anticipate any problems."

"Over breakfast? Listen buddy, there's a chance it could happen again but it gets smaller every day and I have tremendous support from my therapists. I have a right to be happy and I have a wife to think about."

"Yes sir."

"Well you forced me to pull rank."

"Hmm***"

"Look mental illness is what you make it. People that are totally healthy either have made it or given up. It's the same thing with mental illness. I've talked over with Annie, mom, dad, and of course the therapists and it all came out clear. It's a better life for us so, I'm going to do it," Tony said.

"All right*** What can I do to help you?"

"This one I have to do on my own."

"No you don't. We can figure it out together," Steve said.

"Okay. I'll buy that," Tony answered.

"Do you think I'm a jock head?"

"In some ways yes but so what?"

"Well, you always hear about jocks opening restaurants, bars, or car dealerships."

"Another plan of mine was to open a car dealership."

"Why are you so afraid of what other people think of you? Those kinds of people aren't half as perfect as they think they are. Do what makes you happy. If you're happy selling cars then do it. If you are sad selling cars, get involved with something else. How's your writing coming along?"

"It's easier on the medicine—by far. I get little pockets of mental illness and I have to go straighten them out. It's strenuous to keep my temper down during these times. It's really weird. My writing is sort of a moat to keep the mental illness away from my castle. It's just good to write to produce ideas on paper. Except there are many writers that don't care if they get published; I do. And I want to reach a mass audience."

"Can I ask you a question? Why don't you do what you do best? That's right. Don't feel guilty about it. In a few months I sign my contract and I can take care of you. Get a little job for a the next 3 ½ months and you'll be set."

"You think."

"Sure."

"Do you really think you'll be happy selling cars?"

"No. I was going to make money selling cars."

"I'll have the money in three and a half months. After the season, we'll think about what to do.""Stay in school. It won't matter if you win the Stanley Cup every year. Your degree will need something for you beyond hockey."

"So, it does make you a better person."

"If you have a good heart, It's like mental illness. The medicine can sharpen your mind but it's not a morality pill. A good person can be helped tremendously in their desire to live but a bum is still a bum and that's the way life is."

"When you were in the hospital, did the staff see this and keep the A team away from the B team?"

"Not really, the theory being that we all good be on the Yellow Submarine and learn together. I learned how to punch better. I ended up duking it out a few times."

"Great! I'll tell mom!"

"The staff tries but you should see the animal factory that comes through there. Drug dealers and so forth. The patients say that the regular drugs don't work and the cocaine or whatever does. You feel for those people. I never tried the stuff. I'll tell you truthfully I am afraid.

"They think they feel better but you should see them or hear them I guess. Staying up for days at a time yelling for more coke; it's terrible. Half of you wants to kill them and the other half cries for them."

"What about you? What do you do when it gets bad?"

"I read *Sports Illustrated* or anything that's fun! I write too although afterwards, I edit a lot," He smiled.

"Well, you keep writing. It's what you love. I wish I could do that man. You're the writer in the family. You make us all proud."

"What if I got published?"

"I don't know. What do writer's do when they get published?"

"Go to church and pray that it sells."

Steve laughed.

"I hate those damned hospitals. Those drug dealers own it, like they own a street corner block. There are like lice, all over the place. They are called 'frequent flyers,' they come in every few days sell some drugs, go outside sell some drugs, when the police get wind of it, they come back in the hospital and do the same thing."

"There's no racial discrimination because white people talk to white people and so on down the line. It makes them worse. There isn't one symptom but multi-faceted. For regular patients like me; it is horrifying. Also it is dangerous, in a weak moment, you may try it. I don't know how the doctors get me diagnosed right in the hospital because I am a mean guy. You have to be to survive. I've threatened and come to fisticuffs with those lice and I'd do it again. God help me if my sister was in there."

"What's the disease like?"

"Exactly like it sounds. When you're manic, you feel invincible. Nothing can harm you ever. You can do anything. It's like to the moon."

"What's the rest of it like?"

"It's like not having enough gas to get back. You're terribly depressed. I've never been suicidal but I've helped people that have been."

"You've never been suicidal?" Steve asked skeptically.

"I was afraid of God. It would be my luck they'd cure the damned disease the day after."

They laughed.

"I can't believe we're laughing," Steve said.

"It beats crying."

"It's going to be hard you know. Car sales ain't easy."

"Nothing worth having is easy. Did you ever here that expression? You have to stop worrying about me little brother. Mentally, I'm okay. I have a good team behind me just like you do. If you want to talk, you can call me on the cell. You have a lot of growing up to do."

"I just want to say one thing. You are over qualified so don't be surprised if you don't get hired."

"Maybe, maybe not but you just can't stay in a comfort zone your whole life. Sometimes you have to be good and afraid to motivate you. Annie's been great. She supports me one hundred per cent. She grilled me even worse than you are."

"What about your writing project?"

"I am slowly getting back into it. I was afraid to do it because I was afraid it would make me manic but my therapist said it was okay. It wasn't mania. It was a dream. Dad's for it. Mom's like you. A million in one questions. She's afraid I'll break my hitting streak up."

"Are you for it?"

"Yeah, I feel like I have to write this one. It's about me really. I don't want to buy cars or paintings or cameras. I want to write."

"Then get an easy job for three months and cool it."

"It's embarrassing. A BU grad stacking cans in a grocery store."

"What do you feel? Are you blinded by the possibility of bigger paychecks? In the short term."

"It would be nice but really, what would be really nice is getting the albatross off my back that I've been living with the last nine months."

"Which is?"

"Mental illness can beat you many ways. You can be functioning fine. Nobody could know the difference except you. You would know you settled. You would know that you were afraid to live the life you want. Some people can live with it. I can't. I must try this."

"All right, now I'm satisfied. Let's square up and go get mom and dad."

The brothers went up to the hotel room and met Anthony Sr. and Patty Stevenson.

"How was breakfast?" His mother asked.

She was a petite woman in her mid-forties with black hair and black eyes. Tony Sr. looked like Steve. He was the same age as his wife but lithe and muscular. He was decked out in a BU sweatshirt, blue jeans and athletic shoes.

"Tony's doing good mom," Steve said, "He doing really good."

"Good" His mother smiled.

"Steven, how are you?" His father asked.

"Good and you?""

"Just don't trip over the damn ice next time," Tony junior teased.

"Well, I scored any ways," Steve grinned sheepishly.

"We're all so proud of you," Patti smiled.

His mother pinched his cheeks and then threw her arms around him.

"Mom, get this all out of your system because the guys can't see me like this," Steve grinned.

"Where are we going?" His father asked.

"Fanueil Hall," Steve answered, "We'll hop on the T."

The underground subway was packed with people and when the train came and whooshed them down the tracks Steve took great delight in his father's attempts to stay balanced amidst the bobbing heads of other passengers. When it came time to disembark at the Government Station stop, there was an orderly rush for the door but all got out safe and sound.

"Where do we go first?" His father asked.

"Mom, where do you want to go?" Steve asked.

"Let's go to the water. We'll shop later. It's so beautiful," Mrs. Johnson said.

"Mom doesn't want to shop first. That is a first!" Tony teased.

"She's saving up for something expensive," his father quipped.

"I can't hear you guys. I'm having too nice a day."

They crossed the busy, snarl of traffic and went past the Grande Hotel that dotted the pier with it's large arch leading to a beautiful look at Boston Harbor. The pleasure boats of the affluent dotted the pier and harbor.

"Wow!" Steve said.

"Maybe I should sell boats," Tony made a supposition.

"They're yachts," his father said.

"I think he can get used to selling them," Steve said.

"Damn straight," Tony answered.

"The seagulls are so beautiful," she said.

"Let's feed them. I'll go to the convenience store and get a bag of popcorn," Steve said.

"Get a big one," Tony said.

They laughed until lunch as the sea gulls swooped in and snapped up the popcorn. It always amazed Steve how those few little medications helped his brother lead a full and happy life. Tony caught his younger brother looking at him once and the older brother smiled gently.

"This is why you went to college," Tony said.

"This is why I came to Boston," Steve said, "A guy can go to college anywhere."

"I know what you mean bro."

"I hope you went to college for your studies too," his father smiled uneasily.

"Oh, well, speaking of which. Your youngest son has an interesting story about his studies," Tony said.

"Spit it out," his father said flatly.

Steve glared at Tony, who winked.

"Idgit!" Steve mumbled.

"No Idgit! Just tell us about your studies," his mother prodded.

"I like my business major but I'm not quite sure what to do with the knowledge I've acquired. It's a good amount."

"What is it? Exactly what is it?" His father demanded.

"Well, my plan to open up a restaurant just doesn't seem to balance the hard work I did at school."

"What's your plan?" His father asked.

"I'm developing it."

"Well, I'm going to talk to my favorite Prof. And I'm going to ask around but basically I'm a senior. I'll make the decision myself. I have a good, solid education. I can accomplish my goals."

"And?" His mother said.

"And what? That's a pretty solid plan mom," Steve said.

"I think she means… and you can talk to us," his father said.

"I have to do some of this on my own though. It's part of growing up," Steve said.

"Yes I know but you always have a family," she choked up when saying.

"I just have to figure things out. There are so many ways to make a living," Steve said.

"Including professional hockey player," Tony said.

"Someday, hockey will end besides there is the off-season," Steve said.

"Talk to people with experience. Talk to a bunch of them. If anything sounds positive talk to a person in that field," his father said.

"We're almost out of popcorn," Tony said.

"Should I get another one?" Steve asked.

"It's time for shopping!" Their mother smiled.

"Why don't you get another bag?" His father said semi-innocently.

"Come on cheapskate," their mother frowned.

"She's mean dad. I wouldn't mess with her," Tony teased.

"Come on dad. We'll get it over with," Steve promised.

The rest of the afternoon was spent shopping in Fanueil Hall and in the North End but as the time drew later in the day,

Steve closed his mouth and began to concentrate on the game. Coach Parlon had stressed after the game the previous night to step up the physical contact, which was part of the game that Steve enjoyed anyway. Coach was determined to wear out the opposing team's energy. He would bang and bang and bang tonight.

Soon he was standing for the National Anthem in front of the home crowd. Agganis Arena was new and shiny. Steve would be one of the first players to hold up the Terrier hockey tradition in that building. He felt extremely proud to wear the red and white of Boston University.

For as proud as he was, he was just a bit nervous. It was the first home game ever at Agganis arena and the Boston press corps was there in full force. The Terriers took the ice with one standing order—put a body on your check.

"I want you guys to bang them. Wear them down. Get the crowd into it. Set a tempo. Let them know they will have to pay to be invited into our house," Coach Benson exhorted.

"You guys go out there and be disciplined. You bang but you bang clean.

You keep the sticks down and the elbows down," the coach said.

That's what the Terriers did. Bodies rattled against the boards and rolled to the ice. The teams were trying to out hit each other. The end result was large amount of hitting and no goals. The first period ended in a 0-0 tie.

"Keep driving at them. They'll lose their composure. They think they have the Hockey East Championship locked up. They read the same paper as you do. They're conceded. Take them twice this weekend and they'll begin to second-guess. We can shake their confidence," Coach Benson preached.

With three minutes left in the second period, there was heavy action in the BU zone. Steve was shadowing his man and eye checking another because BC was on the power play.

One of the Eagles said something to Jeff Brantley, the BU goalie. Jeff, using his BU education and command of the English language told the Eagle to "go screw himself." The Eagle responded by spearing Jeff in the chest.

Steve lunged at the Eagle and punched the player's mask calling the Eagle a fanciful adjective in the process. Sticks dropped and everyone paired off. The referee and the linesmen piled in to restore order.

When the physical altercation was over, Steve and the BC player went to the box. The Eagle was tagged for spearing and Steve went for roughing. On the way to the box, Steve let the other player have it.

"Hey, weasel. You try that stuff in my house and I'll knock your head off."

"You're over rated," was the only thing the Eagle said.

Steve joined Peter Lute in the penalty box for the final thirty seconds of Peter's tripping penalty. Steve was still angry at the spear of his goalie in his house.

"So? You have some guts. Maybe you aren't entirely useless," The big forward cackled.

"Thanks a lot," Steve laughed.

"It's Danke in German."

"How do you say 'stick it' in German?"

"Aren't you touchy?"

"Do you realize that I'm the only sap on this hockey club?"

"Look at the bright side. It means that you're the best."

"Danke."

The penalty expired and Peter jumped over the boards.

"Time to go kick their butts!" Steve yelled over the boards.

After the altercation, the game got nasty. Both sides forgot their discipline and many questionable hits were let go because if the referees called everything, there would be nobody to play the game. It was definitely college hockey at it's worst.

With four minutes left in the third period and the teams playing four on four, Nate lugged the puck up ice and fired it into the right wing corner. Andy Miller, the undersized BU center raced in. Rico Barrini headed for the slot.

Andy was undersized but he was quick. And he squeaked past the Eagle defenseman. Andy turned and slid a crisp pass to Rico who redirected the puck right between the goalie's legs.

The goal pumped the BU fans up but the teams still had to play the last four minutes. Boston College threw temper tantrums and slammed Terriers at will with stick sticks and elbows. The referees put their whistles away.

Nate stopped it all with fifteen seconds left in the game. He caught the Eagle captain racing up the ice with his head down in a desperate attempt to tie the game. Nate leveled him. The Eagle captain was sent rolling to the ice and had to be helped off by the BC trainer. The wind went out of Boston College's sail's after that and Barrini"s goal held up.

Because of the type of victory it was, the Terrier locker room had plenty of comments about how the victory was won.

"That number two. He swings his stick like a baseball bat. I should've broke it over his head," Rich Wilson muttered.

"Number two. Number six is who you have to worry about. He goes after peoples' knee," Normande Jocque snapped.

"That's enough with the complaining," Coach Benson hollered and immediately the room fell quiet.

"You gentlemen represent your school and you better remember that. I don't care what you do to get rid of those impulses—take a cold shower—stand on your head! When you get dressed and walk out of this locker room, you better be gentlemen."

"Sinners," Steve hissed.

"You played well. You conduct yourselves accordingly. Those are the rules. Thompson, in my office."

When the coach stepped out of the picture, Nate leaned over and said.

"You quite possibly could be the stupidest person I ever met."

"Did I do bad?"

"Yes. Go take your medicine and shut up."

Steve finished tying his tie and went into the office.

"Close the door," the coach said flatly.

"You're mad."

"What possessed you to open your mouth?" The coach asked.

"I thought it would lighten the guys up."

"Did you ever think I was trying to teach them something?"

"Coach, we were just letting off steam. None of us would embarrass the program."

"It's not a sometimes thing. You are who you are and we ain't that. Got it?"

"Yes, coach."

"Use your head before you speak. That's not our program."

"I understand."

Chapter 7

The next morning, Steve had breakfast with his older brother Tony at a café in Kenmore Square.

"Are you afraid?" Steve asked.

"Well, yes, I guess I am. Changing jobs is nerve wracking enough for a normal person. You see, people learn to live with what they have from the Man Upstairs as they grow up. They get a job. They get married. They buy a house. With mental illness it's exactly the same—except it is skewed."

"Are you scared enough to quit."

"I don't have a choice. I'm unhappy to the point of distraction now and I'm married. I know it'll affect my marriage. So, I don't have a choice. I have to take a chance."

"Are you sure you want to sell cars?"

"I don't know. I've been working retail and volunteering with the mentally ill so long I don't know. I just need a change."

"Please tell me you have a plan," Steve smiled uncomfortably.

"Well, there's this place in Holyoke. It's a career building place. They have counselors and they have this psychological profiling test that helps you pick out a career path based on your personality. I have been working with them and all the psych profiles came up sales and marketing."

"I'm hoping they'll help me find an employer who will be sensitive to my mental illness."

"What's your mental illness like? I keep asking to see if the symptoms are the same."

"It's like interference in the brain. Stray thoughts tell you things. People hate you or at the very least they dislike you. It tells you that you can't do what everyone else does or it tells you that you can do things so much better than everyone else. It can tell you that you're invincible or helpless. It's not a fun disease."

"I wish I could help you. Are you hearing those voices now?"

"Way back in the back of my mind, I always hear them. The trick is not listening. I've learned to ignore them over the years but sometimes my brain won't allow it."

"Geeze, you drive a car. Is it okay driving?"

"Yes, it is. I only hear the voices when I'm around people. It mostly happens at parties or social functions. That's how I met Annie. She was standing on the steps of the church in the spring during one of the socials. She was shy and didn't have anyone to go in with. She was working her nerve up. We struck up a conversation. I don't know who was clinging to who hardest when we went in," Tony smiled.

"Damned, she told me you were a stud."

"Well, I was, in a mental illness sort of way."

They both laughed.

"Do you think it will happen to me?" Steve asked.

"I didn't think it would happen to me. Heck, I didn't know what it was until it happened to me. All I can tell you is that the doctors are not the enemy. Some of them even get to care about you pretty deeply. I hope there is a cure. Maybe it will. I'm not God. I don't know if it will but you remember what your big brother said. Okay?"

"Yeah, okay. You remember what your little brother said."

"Which is?"

"Brothers forever."

They shook hands across the table in a hammerlock.

"Don't be afraid for me. I have to take risks to get a better life. It's like real life."

"Except it ain't," Steve answered.

"You know. You don't have to be so negative. It's hard enough facing it without your brother telling you how lousy it can get."

"That's only because—only a few years back your mental illness put this family in the blackest hole in the universe. My heart wants to tell you to do it, to trip the light fantastic. Get a new job. Risk all that you worked for. What if you get sick? What if you can't handle the stress? What is something crazy happens?"

"I talked to my doctors and they said it wouldn't because of the way I handle my treatment. The doctors trust me and I trust them. They get everything from me no matter how frightening or embarrassing it might be."

"Do they help all the time?"

"No. Nobody does."

"That's their job."

"Yeah, well, they are human—sue 'em!"

"I don't know what I was thinking. Sorry."

"I just have to risk it."

"What do the doctors say? And don't lie to me."

"They think it's a life happiness issue. People face that at one time in their life—maybe more. Being in that hospital is no fun but waiting for a future that will never come is worse," Tony explained.

"Do mom and dad know?"

"A little; they aren't happy in some ways but are in others."

"Dammit! Why'd you have to get sick?"

"I don't know. God hasn't told me yet. I ask him every day. No answer. I'll guess I'll have to wait or cure it or something. It'll be all right you know."

"Just don't apply to NASA or some such thing. Keep it rational."

"The first bipolar astronaut; do you think they'd go for it?"

"I'm just not trying to ramp you up and then have you get hurt."

"You just don't want everyone to get ramped up at the first job offer and make me feel uncomfortable."

"Wrong! I'm not that nice. I don't want your head to go swimming around with visions of Hercules or Zeus or any other famous Greek. You have to remember that you have mental illness."

"I oughta punch you in the mouth. How dare you say that? Do you know how hard it is for me some days."

"Aha! Now we're getting to it. What's the real scoop? Brother to brother."

"It's hard. You don't want people feeling sorry for you so you say it's okay. It's just hard. It scares you on a daily basis—sometimes two or three times a day but you have to live. You have to push forward. You can't give in. You fight it to the death sometimes."

"What does that mean?"

"Sometimes the thoughts tell me to kill myself."

"You never told me that before."

"I couldn't work it in the conversation."

"When does it happen?"

"When I'm really low."

"You could get really low hunting for jobs. It could take a while."

"I know."

"You're amazing!"

"Well, I get really low just doing the same job day after day. I hate that damn job. I know I can do better with my life."

"If you ever need anything at all, I don't care if on the night of the National Championship Game. You call me. I'm you're brother. You're my older brother and it's my job to take care of you."

Tears came to both their eyes and they finished breakfast quietly. Finally, Tony smiled and said.

"You're making up for the pain in the butt you were when you were a kid."

"I was not a pain in the butt. You wouldn't teach me about girls."

"It's best to learn on your own. Besides you did all right."

"Dammit!"

"Why are you so mad at me?" Tony asked.

"I don't know. I've been mad at you, me, mom, dad, and the doctors. It's not fair. Why did God make your brain that way? More importantly, why did it take so long to figure it out."

"Keep in mind that the official line is that nobody knows anything. It takes a long time to put all the pieces together. The mind is complex—even sane people have complex minds."

"Stop saying that. I'm not having breakfast with an insane person. I'm having breakfast with my brother."

"You and I both know I'm not anything without my meds. I am crazy as a loon without those things."

"Yeah, I guess you're right."

"It's not quite like a diabetic and his insulin. Is it?"

"Isn't it?"

"No a diabetic just dies. His mind doesn't torture the rest of his body."

"There's one thing I want you to promise me. I know what you just said about your meds and you may believe it this time because you've said it before…"

"Spit it out."

"If the side effects of your meds get in the way of your job, you'll promise me to stay on the meds."

"Yeah sure*** whatever."

"Never mind*** whatever."

"All right!"

"Look we go through this every time you have a change for the better in your life. In the euphoria you start playing with the meds and then you go off them. What's the deal? And I want the truth!"

"The truth is, every time I get an opportunity, it fuels the illusion that I'm healthy. I get a voice in my head saying wouldn't it be cool if I didn't need the meds and the drowsiness, weight gain, and tremors that went with them."

"Look, Tony, those drugs keep you sane and you aren't doing bad with your weight. You have to live with it. I hate to be the one that tells you this but that's the case. It's important that you win this battle because you have people believing in you. It's not all about you. It's about the family."

"I just want to be normal."

"What's normal?"

"I just want to be not mentally ill."

"Well, you are and somewhere you must understand you can live a life that's pretty damn good despite your limitations and do you know what? That's normal."

"Normal," Tony sputtered.

"Look, there are different versions of normal for everyone. You're just a little bit more constricted that's all."

"People say you can't even see mental illness in me," Tony smiled half proudly—half sadly.

"What do you want? Do you want people to know?"

"I'd like to have the freedom to gather myself when it bothers me and not have that look of fear at a job interview when I mention that my mental illness bothered me several years ago."

"Are you stupid? You don't tell people you don't know you have bipolar—especially in a job interview. What's the matter with you? The medicine and the therapy are there to help you fit into the world not make the world more accepting of behavior that is broken down from regular thought patterns. You're lucky. You want to hang yourself on a cross and be a martyr that's your business but I'm going to tell you something. You have Annie to think about now and you take care of your mental illness or no."

"All right. I deserved that."

"You're damned right you did."

"Let's say I pull this off and I get a new job that pays better. Wouldn't it be cool?"

"Yeah, it would and you don't have to be guilty."

"What?"

"You don't have to be guilty because you're doing better than some other people who are mentally ill."

"I do sometimes."

"So do I. I mean in my own life. I'm a press magnet and there are more articles about me have been written about me than most of the team. It's just the way it is."

"The way you play man. It's beautiful. You just are so smooth and you hit like a truck."

"I play for you. You have more courage than me. I don't know if it was me. I don't know if I'd be brave enough to make decisions like you."

"I don't have a choice. My doctors make it that way. They always ask: what do you think? They don't want me to get used to having other people make decisions for me."

"Even when you just got out of the hospital?"

"Especially then; you take baby steps. Of course, if I said something like, 'I want to own the world,' they would step in and give more a more realistic picture but all I said was I needed a job. They helped me make sure I went after a job that would challenge me. They didn't want me to underestimate myself. "

"Tony, if this doesn't work out, working with the mentally ill is a worthy profession."

"It is when it's going great. I just can't take it when I lose a client and the situation goes bad."

"Why haven't you told your therapist?"

"I did."

"And?"

"She told me there was no significant evidence that I should quit."

"You made me jump through all those hoops and that's what she said. Are you crazy?"

"Technically, yes."

"Don't you fool around with me. What happened?"

"I had a kid with bipolar who made the varsity soccer team at his high school and he committed suicide because he didn't start the first game of the season. He wasn't taking his medicine because he made the team and that convinced him he didn't need it. He was convinced he was quote unquote normal.

" I didn't even freakin' see it. I was just so happy for the kid. He had worked all summer working out. His parents thanked me for all my help. I felt ashamed. I felt dirty. That poor kid is dead because of me."

"I don't think he's dead because of you. Do you really want to leave it?"

"Yeah. I don't want to ever feel that again."

"What about your success? What about the clients you help? How will they feel?"

"I don't really know. I really don't," Tony shrugged his shoulders, "Maybe I'm not helping them as much as someone else would."

"Oh! Right! There's a possibility."

"You're not helping."

"I think you're making a mistake. Give it a month or two."

"I…"

"You're going out whipped and that ain't you."

"It's not a contest."

"It's not?"

"I lost."

"You say."

"People are just trying to spare my feelings."

"That's a hot one! His parents are just being nice to you."

"All right—maybe that was stupid."

"Maybe?"

"Screw you."

"Look, you know I'll support you no matter. We're in this together. Whatever you decide, I'll help as much as I can. It just seems that you were so happy there as a mentor."

"I was only happy because I was around other mentally ill people. The job was eating at me anyway. It's time to leave."

"Okay. I trust you."

Chapter 8

On Tuesday, Steve's schedule was open so he took the Green Line to the Heights alias for Boston College. He walked the campus and got several strange looks from students and professors who recognized him from the newspapers. He had to admit it was a beautiful campus that caused him to think about his own, unsettled views on religion. He was looking at the church when he heard a voice.

"What are you doing here?"

Steve turned around and looked to see Brian Gregory, the captain of the Crimson. The Harvard Crimson.

"Looking for talent."

"Do you know that's against NCAA rules?"

"Another kind of talent***"

"You want me to sing and dance for you."

"I might."

"I'll by you a coffee, if you tell me what this is all about."

"Let's go for a walk. Save your four bucks."

Steve told Brian of his plan and the volunteers he's had so far.

"Can I think about it?"

"Yeah. But keep the scuttlebutt confined to tour girlfriend. I'm only looking for ones and two's now. The team is pretty much set."

"I'll call you tomorrow."

"It's going to be a lot of work."

"Why do I get the feeling this is a prelude to something else?"

"One thing at a time***"

"I'd like to know as a matter of good faith."

"Get out your four bucks."

They found a coffee shop across the street.

"Double latte," Steve ordered.

"Decaf," Brian said.

They found a table.

"Lay it on me," Brian said.

"You know about the museum, which is a good start but what if we founded a sports photography company that provided pictures to the general public over the inter net like Michael Dell sells computers."

"You'd have to get sanctioned."

"Yeah, I would."

"What about the competition?"

"Brian, when you line up on the ice, do you worry about the competition or playing well?"

"Would you consider merging with anyone or becoming a subsidiary?"

"No. I am in it partially to give my kids an inheritance."

"Financing; Definitely through a good bank."

"Advertising?"

"Of course***"

"Running a business is a load. And you're going to play for the Bruins?"

"It's just like college—sort of. I demand a lot of myself."

"Why?"

"Because I can and a lot of people can't and the way I figure God will be upset at me for wasting my talent."

"You're an interesting guy."

"Do you have a girl?"

"As a matter of fact I do."

"We could go out for pizza tomorrow night to finalize things."

"Finalize things."

"What's going on Brian? You wouldn't be asking so many questions if you weren't interested."

"My dad has a marketing firm in the financial district and I'm expected sign on after graduation."

"I could talk to him."

"He's pretty important."

"Then we'll talk to him."

"You're going to get me in trouble man."

"And we're still going to win the Bean Pot."

"Oh-no!"

"Hey! You have to come home to win the Pot."

"One day we're going to win that thing."

"Not this year."

The next night, Brian brought his girl Colleen and Steve brought Susan. The girls talked for a while and the pizza provided the necessary nutrients for the guys to talk business.

"Is your dad really hard?" Steve asked.

"He's getting up there and wanting to spend more time on his boat at the Cape."

"He expected you to take it over?"

"Not really. I was supposed to be pre-law but changed majors at the beginning of freshman year. I didn't tell him because I thought he'd be upset. He wanted me to pursue every, little internship: Don't get me wrong, I've learned a lot. My dad's a good guy. Mostly though, I didn't expect Henney-Penney to come falling out of the sky yesterday."

"So, you're out."

"No. I'm in. But we're going to have to sweeten the deal for my old man."

"In what sense?"

"You have to do endorsements for his firm. They'll pay you fine but you have to do endorsements for his firm."

"I can't talk directly about that under NCAA rules. You know that."

"We'll talk later then."

"Sure."

"Then it's settled. On Saturday you meet us at Cappo's pizza at 10 am. They open the place special for me. Pizza and Cococa-Cola!."

"Pizza at ten o'clock in the morning?"

"Yeah."

"I'll be there."

"Bring a notebook and a couple of pens."

They chatted pleasantly the rest of the night but he sensed that Susan was uncomfortable.

"What's wrong?" He asked on the T ride home.

"Are we going to be spending all our free time on this damn business venture of yours?"

"Well, hello to you too."

"Look, I'm helping as much as I can but I'm not even your girlfriend."

"Well maybe we should stop seeing each other for a while."

"You're a jerk!"

"I'm a jerk! This is important to me."

"Why? You'll make a ton of money playing hockey. Why do you need more?"

"It's not about the money. It's about helping people. Playing hockey, almost everyone knows what it's like to be the star. In business, you have to win with a guy who might not believe in himself enough or a lady who is sure she can't do it because she's a lady. Personalities and heart affect people more in business because of their own mental limitations–what they have been told they are doesn't necessarily mean what they are."

"What about me?"

"It pays to have a Harvard man or two to teach.""

"Understood, sir."

"If I sleep with you, it's going to be a big thing and then I'll sign a contract and leave and you'll be babbling incoherently."

"You'd do that."

"Yeah, that's why I said keep it friendly."

"To spare my feelings, aren't you nice."

"To stop having to listen to you***""

"Well,"

"Look why don't we just go to bed and I'll see you for breakfast in the morning."

"Screw you. Go get your magnificent lay somewhere else."

"Hey!" He yelled as she jumped off the T a stop early.

In the end, he decided to let her go feeling liberated from the recently strained relationship. Now it left him in a quandary. What to do about a girl? Well, he thought, you gotta get back on the horse and the blonde in his management class was definitely appealing. His depression over, he walked back up Comm Ave to stop in the Student Union for a coffee. His mind fluctuated between the blonde, his homework, and his project in no particular order. Finally, he went home to do his homework.

The next guy he ran into was Mark Day, the BC senior goalie and Academic All-America candidate.

"What are you doing up here?" Day asked.

"I'm hunting you down."

"I can't transfer, I'll lose eligibility."

"Think big my friend."

"If you don't get to it, I'll think of something."

"You are a management major right?"

"Yeah, with a minor in, French."

"Doing pretty good?"

"Yes, fine? Didn't you tell me to go screw myself three weeks ago? What's the deal?"

"I meant that only in the sense that it knocked your concentration off."

"Well, that's inspiring."

"Yes, it is. You didn't lose your composure!"

"What are you talking about?"

"Do you like sports photography?"

"Yeah, of course. What are you driving at?"

"Buy you a coffee?"

"Give me the abridged version. I have to meet my girl."

"Do you know who the biggest imagery factory in the world is?"

"Un-hunh!"

"You go to BC. Manage something else, please."

"What are we talking about?"

"What if we convince them to use their photographers to establish art galleries in their own countries."

"Here's my phone number. Call me tonight. I'll be home at nine."

"Fair enough."

"Hey, are you crazy?"

"It depends on who you ask. Are you afraid?"

"I'm a goalie. I don't get afraid."

"Goalie's are psychotic. That doesn't mean they are aren't afraid."

"Call me tonight mother hen."

"What if we pull this off?"

"I don't know. How would they trust us?"

"What do you mean?"

"Think about it. We're young guns with lots of money and they are established in the business communityto say the least!"

"My mother raised a nice guy."

"Nice don't always cut it in business."

"From a BC man, I have to take this."

"You make people believe. Give me a call."

Chapter 9

The next day he took a leisurely stroll down Huntington Avenue to see what he could of Northeastern University. He wore his BU hockey, cap and jacket so he would be visible to the local gentry.

"What are you doing here?" A voice asked.

Steve turned around to see a guy about five feet nothing ask him.

"What's your name kid?"

"Peanut. What are you doing here?"

"What major are you Peanut?"

"Computer engineering and computer programming."

"Is that a fact?"

"True as I know."

"What do you know about sports photographs?"

"A lot I guess. I'm a sports junkie. What are you up to man?"

"You should've been a cop Peanut."

"Come on! You have me enthused now."

"Look, I'll buy you a coffee."

"Throw in a donut and you're in."

"Chocolate glazed."

"Boston Crème."

"Close enough."

So Steve sat down and explained the need for technicians and computer people for his operation.

"You're going to start a what?" Peanut asked.

"Skeptical?"

"A little."

"In Springfield. You're kidding? Is that what you're thinking?"

"Yeah."

"You ever been told by any of your professors to look farther than the usual."

"Where are you going to get the money for this?"

"My contract with the Bruins and corporate sponsorship***."

"You're not kidding."

"Not in the least."

"And I get paid for being your elec-tech. "

"Uh-huh. You get to stay close to Boston and you'll get some walking around money."

"Can I call you?"

"Better than that, We're having a meeting a Cappo's pizza on Comm Ave. tomorrow at 10 am. They open it special for me. Pizza and beer! Why not come? What's your real name by the way?"

"Paul 'Peanut' Done."

"You coming?"

"You have me intrigued. I'll give it a shot."

"How's the donut?"

"I can eat these things forever and not gain weight. I should've been a jockey."

Peanut extended his hand and Steve took it.

The next thing Steve did was head over to Harvard and he went into the Business School to pick up some brochures on the institution. He was waited on; by a clean-cut, blond, haired clerk.

"Aren't you Thompson? The hockey player?"

"Yeah."

The clerk lowered his voice.

"What are you doing here?" He whispered.

"I want to do some post grad work. I think anyway. I have to look it over."

"We're going to win the Beanpot this year," the clerk smiled.

"Oh! No! You have to come home to win the Bean Pot and that is straight down Broadway—Comm Ave."

"You guys are so confident it's sickening."

"That's our tournament man. By the way what's your name?"

"John Davis, class, of oh-five MBA program!"

"How are you doing?"

"Three-five. Not bad."

"Do you know where Cappo's pizza is on Comm. Ave?"

"If there's a pizza place, I'll find it."

"It used to be Burger King. Anyway, I'm founding a company. I think you'll find it more than a little interesting. In fact, you'll have a good time."

"You're still too vague. What's up?"

"What do you know about sports photography?"

"Well, I get *Sports Illustrated and ESPN the Magazine*. From a layman's point, I know some."

"What do you know about museums?"

"Where are you going to put it?"

"I'm trying to get it in Springfield mostly because that's where I was from."

"What do you say I come to the meeting and then we'll talk seriously?"

"Ten am sharp."

"I'll be there."

Chapter 10

The next meeting at Cappo's brought everyone, including, new editions Mike Gaines. The rugged, goal scoring right wing, African American from BU. Paco Alvarez, a slick second baseman for the Northeastern University Huskies, and of course, the goalie from the BC Eagles, Todd Day!

"Gentleman, we are here to discuss two ideas. One: the Museum Two: The magazine. As large as Massachusetts is, it ain't large enough to eliminate the competition. We have to do that by being better than the competition. Wider smiles when we do the job and with a realization that there is no other museum like this in the world and there are only two magazines pertaining to sport who are real magazines; *Sports Illustrated*, and, *ESPN the Magazine*. Both are totally interested in one thing; making money! They are backed by huge conglomerates and they hate to lose. Not making it different from us. Except we don't have the conglomerate backing yet***"

He raised his hand, "Who thinks this is impossible?"

"Why are you here?" John Davis asked.

"Excuse me?"

"You're going to sign an NHL contract. Why the aggravation?"

"John, there are probably a hundred levels where I could tell you a reason. The top three are. I can leave something for my kids—a family business. Two: It's going to be difficult. Three: My idea is different, a little broader scoped, and more of a gamble ergo therefore to make it more exciting. The name of the photography company will be *Americansportsview International*."

Hands shot up all over place.

Mike Gaines asked him.

"Where exactly are we going?"

"Europe and the Far East to start."

"Are you serious?"

"We're also going to cover Canada?"

"Besides pro hockey, what's in Canada?" Lynne Demarco asked.

"CFL and all the major Junior Hockey Leagues."

"You're not kidding," Shaun said.

"Look, anyone who has questions can ask them, anyone who wants to walk can walk."

"What about Spain?" Paco asked.

"The Tour of Spain, The Tour of Italy. Many great aspects of many great cultures; I expect this magazine to sell to college educated and youngsters who dream of seeing far away places. This is not going to sell to people who want every foreigner pushed out of the country. Except they can't decide who is the most foreign; the magazine will cover everything from doping to medals. It is an important tool for Americans in the Information Age to see how the world works through sport. I think very much that all of beginning Europe to share the national identities with each other as a positive sign that they can play together in peace on the playing fields and the ice rinks of the world.

"I hope you all understand that the world is more important to us than keeping prices low on our clothes. There are people out there and they have families and they like to win. Just like we do! So if you want to stay, I would appreciate it greatly. Anybody leaving?"

"No, sir," Mike Gaines.

"I'm, in," Paco said.

"Let's do it." Jay Billingsley said.

"I'm here." Chris Davidson said.

"We're all up Coach. Nobody's leaving." Tommy Vivenzio said.

"Yeah, I'll stay," Mark Day said. "You guys are going to need a lot of help."

"All right, one more thing. I know this is going to be a lot of hard work and we'll be doing project two projects at once and to do it right you will probably have to miss many social engagements between school and us. It's going to be grueling. I love you people already but I'm looking for that dedication. It's a test of my own volition. I demand this out of you, not because I'm a sadist but because it is necessary to win and everything we do from tonight on is representation of us. Your family will see you. You friends will see your work. Your parish priest, your congregational reverend, or whoever else you worship."

"I worship the Red Sox," Abie Shumor said.

"You're weird anyway," Gaines said.

"Fascist," Abe smiled.

"Gentleman and lady, if you please; I want to thank everyone for coming tonight especially the people from Umass-Amherst. Be careful on the way back. In the meantime just relax.

"Now, guys and Lynne, I just want you to mingle. Hang out. Relax. Eat some pizza. I have everyone's e-mail and phone number right here. I'll pass them around. Feel free to take notes."

The next practice, Steve was content to throw body checks at everyone he could. Coach Parlon had to remind him to play the puck constantly. Finally, the coach blew the whistle.

"Number seven, what is wrong with you?" The coach called.

"Nothing coach," Steve answered sheepishly.

"Do you realize we're all on the same team?"

Well, I didn't realize we had so many candy britches on this team."

"Twenty base blues. Everyone else hit the showers."

Steve skated his hardest during the punitive drills. Afterward, the coach brought him to center ice.

"You better tell me what that was about," Coach said quietly.

"I was dealing with stress," Steve huffed.

"Don't be a wise guy."

"Maine's a physical team. I watched those tapes. They aren't just going to let us go North-South—maybe not even East-West."

"Do me a favor. Let me coach."

"I thought it was what we needed."

"Excuse me."

"Do you want me to be one of the leaders on this club or not?"

"Watch your tone son."

"Sorry, Coach but you have to admit it got the boys' dander up. You were able to sit on the foolish penalties. We won't have a rerun in the game."

"You'd risk life and limb to get a win," the coach observed.

"In a few months, I'll have a degree from a good school. That allows me to take chances I wouldn't otherwise have. At the same time, hockey is the end all be all for me and it isn't. I play to win but there are other things out there."

"Go take a shower."

After his shower, he ate dinner alone in the dining hall. Later, he went to his room.

At ten-thirty Nate fumbled in.

"Well, if isn't the Hurricane Kid," Nate grinned.

"You think Maine is going to be any easier?"

"You took a run a run at everyone of us," Nate said.

"You're making fun of me."

"Yes! I am."

"Well if you weren't such wimps, there would be no issue. I have to talk to you about the company."

"Don't worry about your grand lives plan. Prepare for it and it will happen. It'll wear on you if you don't and that's not good for the team."

"I hope my favorite Professor has some insight."

"Who's your favorite?"

"Ms. Dale Cochrane."

"The computer lady."

"Nate, she's a pretty good egg. She's honest and she'll tell me the truth."

Nate said little. Actually he said nothing.

"What's with you?" Steve asked.

"I've just been hit with an odd offer."

He continued.

"I have an offer to continue my studies in Gothenburg, Sweden while playing in the Swedish Elite League. They know about the NCAA and we'll talk the minute the season ends."

"You've got to be kidding."

"It's interesting. It seems that since the lock out, the Swedes have been attracted to high profile North Americans."

"It's lunacy. What about your hockey career?"

"Lots of guys have played in Sweden before playing in the N.H.L."

"You'll be breaking your top shelf value. You'll be paid less when you come back."

"I'll still have more money than I'll know what to do with and it will be a great life experience."

"What language did you take?"

"Spanish."

"That should be helpful."

"It's still something to think about."

"Do you have any idea how cold it is in Sweden?"

"I hear it's beautiful. Especially the girls."

"Good point but they will tax your brains out."

"It's something different. It's seems like a once in a lifetime chance."

"You're realizing you are going to give the Montreal Canadians the bird."

"You told the Bruins."

"I'm not playing for pay. Montreal may get nervous about that. When you're a tenth round pick you can take excursions but not when you're number one."

"Anyway, it's just something to think about," Nate smiled.

"It sure would cause a ruckus."

"It sure would," Nate agreed.

"You could go to Germany. They have a league."

"Are you trying to trot me out?"

"Hey, you're Mr. Cultural Exchange."

"I have to do a lot of research."

"Oh, brother! You're really considering it."

"You consider all of your options. There are just some you consider and some you consider."

"Well, you seem pretty hot on this one," Steve shrugged.

"I always like it when a new possibility crops up. And then I consider it."

"Well, ain't you got it down to a science."

"All I'm saying is that it's nice to feel out your options. Now we are going to talk about something else."

"Maine."

"Maine is full of big, tough, fast country boys. They hunt as good as they play hockey and they don't care who knows it. Any questions?"

"Who do you think is the baddest Bear in the bunch?" Steve asked.

"That's easy*** Junior Ninno. Mean, fast, aggressive and he's got a thorn in his side about us."

"May I ask why?"

""Remember when Dan Willis broke his ankle with a slap shot during the Hockey East playoffs two years ago and we eliminated them. He was the Black Bears best player on the number one team in the nation back then. Well, to make a long story short, they have been hanging around number ten ever since. He doesn't like us very much."

"Wait until he sees me. I'll knock him on his butt a couple of times."

"Wait 'till he sees you. Well, did we take our confidence pills today."

"Screw him. I'm not playing second fiddle to some bow hunting prima donna with a stick up his but."

"Good you can play second fiddle to me instead. You have a lot to learn junior."

"Well, it seems you have a personal stake in this."

"I've earned it junior on the rink and in the class and I'm going to keep earning it one more year. That's what you have to learn. Even though you're a senior, you have to constantly earn it here. You then can worry about skewering the Black Bears."

"Well what do I do?"

"You back up your statements."

"I can do that."

"I know. You have potential but your too mousy."

"What does that mean?"

"You have confidence until someone questions it or how you deliver it. Take a stand man. Your opinion counts too—even in the big bad world of BU. In the land of great accomplishments and great egos—you count too. Hell, I was ready to shake your hand a minute ago."

"I thought you were going to yell at me."

"Only if you had said that to a member of the press, then, I would've freakin' killed you."

"I'm confident. I'm not stupid."

"Don't you have that early morning meeting with the Prof?"

"I'll be back by midnight."

"I'll tell the coach."

"Yes, sir. Midnight."

"Go ahead."

"That sounded like an order."

"You're still learning."

Steve was soon knocking on Susan's door.

"Hello," he smiled when she answered, "Let's go on the roof."

"We should talk here."

"About.'

"I'm sorry about yelling at you like a wild banshee the other night."

"It's all forgotten. I don't understand."

"I sat down after I had cooled off and thought about us and I don't think we can do it."

"Why? And please, I want the truth."

"Internship is nuts! I work a 100 hour work weeks and then you'd have the Bruins and your company. I don't think it would be a good match."

"Look, I wasn't looking for a match. I tried to tell you on the T. I like you as a friend. Why can't you accept that?"

"It's going to be a little awkward when I get a boyfriend."

"I don't have any problem telling my girl you're my friend and that's the way it goes. We can have normal people conversations. We can go out to dinner as a foursome. Stuff like that."

"Are you serious?"

"Girls are as screwed up as guys. They watch those damn shows about housewives screwing around and they wish they could themselves. That's why you don't have any lifelong friends and you deserve it."

"Is that your philosophy on life?"

"It's in microcosm."

"Why?"

"Because I see that in you!"

"Now I'm offended."

"I think you're looking for that rush all the time."

"I'm going to kill you if you keep talking."

"Maybe I'm naïve."

"You don't want to sleep with me."

"I didn't say that. I was worried about the fallout later."

"When the Bruins contract is going to change everything and you aren't going to be able to stay with me."

"Basically."

"Why?"

"I thought you had it all figured out."

"I was trying to draw you out. Why?"

"All right, let's take this in another direction. Let's say we do the boyfriend—girlfriend bit. And we sleep together. And I sign the contract. And I leave you. You've had fair warning."

She smiled and held her arms out.

"Come here."

"No. I want an answer."

"I'm going to kill you if you don't come over here."

He walked over to her and wrapped his arms around her.

"Fits like a glove," she said.

"This is probably the strangest position I've ever been in."

"Excuse me."

"Up till now all my best friends have been guys. I never wanted to make love to any of them. You better be right about this."

They climbed onto her bed and made love.

Afterward, she smiled, "Well," she said.

"I warned you and I warned you."

"Did you have a good time?"

"Technically*** everything functioned normally."

"Boy, aren't you one of the last of the red hot lovers."

"I'm telling you. This is a bad idea."

She started to cry.

"I told you."

"This was my first time idiot and all you can say is that this is a 'bad idea.'"

"Susan you could have a million other guys and you're leaching on to me because I'm from WMASS."

"Maybe that line would've worked when I was a freshman but not now."

"Really."

"Don't be smug."

He kissed her on the cheek and said.

"We're either going to end really good friends or we're going to screw up and not talk to each other for years."

"Oh! Really! How was I?"

"Don't act like a whore."

She blushed.

"I think you like me.'

"I'm sorry."

"Maybe you should go downstairs before I kill you."

"You're a nice girl."

"But not yours."

"I'm sorry again."

"You go be sorry. I'll go be heart broken."

"Over me? Are you kidding me? You could have a million guys."

"You're my present disaster though. You could at least be a fink and inspire me to throw something heavy at you."

"You will find someone and he will knock your socks off. I promise. What we both want in life would drive us apart. I know it."

"All I ever wanted to be was a doctor."

"I know. And I wanted to do what I'm doing."

"What do we do? Wish each other good luck?"

"A hug good-bye?"

"I can't believe I'm saying this but I wish you all the luck in the world."

"You too."

Steve's cell phone rang and he picked it up.

"Hello," he said as he was coming out of repose.

"Hey, it's Day. Goalie, extraordinare; I have a question. When is this great unveiling of the homework assignments going to come?"

"Saturday morning brother."

"Can you give me a hint? Because I have to arrange my schedule; It's kind of tight as it is. I teach Junior achievement to a group of kids on Wednesday nights. It's kind of what we're doing except we're much more professional and daring."

"I'll hold up about that. The first one is going to be cake. It's about you. You write a ten page biography from the time you were a child to the point where you are now and where you hope to be in ten years. Married, kids, living on the East Coast, living in Colorado because you can ski. I don't care where: it's your life. We'll stick you in somewhere."

"This isn't some little kids hobby: is it?"

"No. It's not some little kids hobby. I've been thinking about this since I was sixteen in various forms. I very much have an interest in this."

"You rich?"

"My parents have a little bit of money. Yeah. But mostly I'm swing this one on my own."

"Well, at least Cappo's makes good pizza."

"Definitely."

"Hey, what's the story with that kid Billingsley? He barely talks."

"I think he has 'overwhelmed disease.' I interviewed him myself. He's a Northeastern grad punch holes in the sky for Fidelity Investments as a stock broker. He knows how to articulate himself but he has this totem pole thing going on in his head. Northeastern is supposedly the lowest on the totem pole in Boston of the four majors. He'll come around."

"Baby him."

"Sort of unless he needs a real kick in the but."

"Just because we're different people, we're doing something different."

"You still have to go to work."

"Okay on that. I'll see you Saturday."

"We are going to keep whipping you guys this year."

"You know. If you weren't my boss***"

Chapter 11

Nate walked in smiling.

"I'm a genius," he said.

"You found a girl that would go out with you."

"Unfortunately no but I solved this wicked hard problem in Boolean Algebra."

"Why would one take Boolean Algebra?"

"In case he wanted to design stuff for NASA. Don't ask for me as a reference."

"What are you so pissed off at?"

"I'm thinking about Professor Cochrane. I'm as a nervous as a kid on Christmas Eve."

"She's a person genius. Relax."

The next morning at eight a.m. Steve presented himself at the office of Professor Cochrane. His palms were sweating bullets. When he knocked on the door, part of him hoped she wouldn't answer. She opened the door anyway.

"Come in," she said pleasantly.

Steve took a deep breath and went in.

"Well, Mr. Thompson, what are we doing here?"

"I was thinking about my life."

"Why?" She smiled.

"Do you know how people grow in college?"

"That's the rumor," she smiled.

"Well, I think it grew out of my dream to own a restaurant and I have this dream that I had in high school."

"What kind of dream?"

"Well, I'm starting to realize I can do things besides what people expect me to do. You know how it goes or I can do what I want. You've heard the joke. All ex-jocks open up bars or become color commentators. I want something different for me.

"I want to play hockey and win the Stanley Cup but I have an idea. I would like to found a sports photography museum."

"Well, that's really cool. Where?"

"Well, I was thinking of putting it next to the Basketball Hall of Fame back in Springfield but I don't know if that'll fly."

"I think that's a great idea. Why wouldn't it fly?"

"I don't know there's always last minute screw up on big projects—baseball teams and such. This would be a big project so who knows. I just don't want it to be a mess. I'll put it somewhere else."

"Well, maybe this will be different, you being a local boy and all."

"Once certain people smell money even being a local yokel won't help."

"You're being a pessimist."

"Maybe, it's important to me and I don't want little so and so's spray painting the walls of the building."

"I'm sure it will be important to other people too."

"Well, anyway, that's what I want to do. It's kind of like commerce and giving back to the community at the same time."

"Well, if you're going off to the NHL, I'm going to say one thing."

"And that is?"

"I want you to know you're hands are shaking. "

"I get nervous around important people."

"Thanks for the compliment. And that being said; do you know what helped me when I was your age? I had someone I respected say they respected me. I respect you Steve. You have to make hard decisions when you lead and you may have to tell important people that they are wrong. That can be sort of dicey because their egos can be quite vast. You still have to press on. Your opinions are right for you and they may be right for other people if you pick the right team. Just do me a favor."

"What's that mamm?"

"Make it a real museum."

"Mamm?"

"You know what I mean. The phony sneaker ads posing as photographs."

"Gotcha."

"I respect you a lot and for a student you're all right."

"I respect you too."

'Thank you."

"Well, I best be going," Steve said.

"One more thing, you're not just a hockey player. I've had those. They disappear into the woodwork. You won't."

"Do you know I'm rooming with a Rhodes Scholar candidate?"

"I've heard of him but never met him."

"He is what he is. I ask for advice all the time. He just knows stuff. It's spooky."

"Come to the business school and use their computers to see what you can dig up to see what you can dig up. Let me know."

"Okay. Thanks for your time."

"Go."

"Yes, mamm."

Steve walked home straight past the international houses on Baystate Road. He waited for the fall leaves to fall every once in a while. He thought about the museum and wondered if it would work. He would have to speak to some of the professors and dig around himself to find out who the best shooters in the world were. There were so many out there it was going to be difficult to pick the absolute best ones. He felt excited by the project but he knew he needed a team behind him to get the project done right.

When he was sitting on the roof later that evening, counting his lucky chair about eleven thirty, his phone rang.

"Hi! It's me."

"It's John Davis."

"I have a question for you. Why not put this in Harvard?"

"The museum? No. It must be BU."

"Why?"

"What do have against BU."

"BU isn't Harvard. Harvard is more culturally oriented."

"Are you saying we have lack for culture?"

"Sort of."

"How much do you know about BU really?"

"I'm just afraid people won't come."

"What evidence do you have of this?"

"Come on. You grew up there. The hockey team draws enough to get by and that's it. Do you really think they'll be interested in a museum?"

"Look. It's going in to BU. Now whether or not you or and your rich, kid friends will cross the Charles to come see it is their business."

"We'd be the only ones in there. Are you kidding?"

"And as a graduate of East Longmeadow High, you don't think I have an obligation to try it."

"You aren't going to have an obligation to anything if you don't make money and that's a fact."

"Anyway, I'm going to assign Hector Rodriguez the task of drafting a letter for insurance companies so we can get benefits going for our employees six months after date of hire. Fair?"

"Yeah, I forgot about that."

"I'm going to call Brian after this and speak to him about corporate sponsorship."

"Who do you have warming up in the bullpen?"

"Canon, Burger King, Mass Mutual! Kodak, and GE."

"Wow!"

"Yeah, I know. Isn't this unreal?"

Chapter 12

On Saturday morning the magnificent sixteen showed up at Cappo's. All sixteen! Everybody; was happy that their teams had won the previous night. Everybody was seated and breaking out the forks and knives for the four pizzas.

"Okay ladies and gentleman we are all here. Thank you very much from driving up from Umass. Basically, I have sheets here with contact numbers and e-mails. Start out talking about your background. Where you stand for in life and on the job; get used to every single person in this room. We will be a team. That's the most important aspect to success. You have plenty of chances to work into a challenge. That's why we have sixteen people sitting in this room."

"Who do we answer to?" John Davis asked.

"Me. When we talk a little more and see what each of us sees in the company future. There will be differentiation. You have the opportunity to move up the ladder right into project two. It is so top secret. It's unbelievable.

"Now, I have a couple of assignments. Don't get jealous, you all will get yours in time. John Davis, if you please, I want you to look up the two major stock photograph companies in the world and I want a draft of an introductory letter to each.

"Peanut, Start looking for spy ware and ways to protect photos from theft on the internet. Need a letter, dude."

"Wendy, You get *Sports Illustrated*."

"I can't do that. It's *Sports Illustrated*."

"Look, if I thought you were a houseplant, I wouldn't have hired you. I'm not going to let you out of this because you're better than that."

"Okay Boss."

"Now. We're doing something nobody has ever done before if you listen to certain people. We have a lot of different kinds of people. That means squat to me either way. I hired you because I thought we would have the best chance of success together as a team and as a family. Take a good look at the person next to you. He/she may save your professional life one day. Any questions?"

"Do you have a marketing strategy yet? Is it going to be in house or farmed out?" Brian asked.

"Right now. I'm looking at both options. If I perchance had a buddy of mine whose father owned one, I would probably look at his first."

"Thank you."

"What are you going to be doing?" Peter asked.

"I'm going to be writing letters to the Mayor of Boston, the Congressman, the State Senator, and the State Rep. Just to see if it can be done with the minimum amount of wear and tear."

"The Canadians, if you could please write magazines and the best papers in your city or the city nearest you."

"I left some assignments open. This is your opportunity to surprise the boss. Think of something and go after it. After that, all I have to say today is enjoy some pizza and get to know each other. We're all going to be working together and it would be nice if we liked each other. I'll give you and e-mail by Wednesday to schedule another meeting."

"I'm sorry about the ride from Western Mass but it's the only way we can do it with hockey season upon us and since we're in first place."

"Boo!" Bryan hissed.

"Anyway, I'm not one to gloat," Steve said.

"Far be it from us to notice," Peanut said.

"Seriously folks, we have to decide who we're going to tell about this project and why?" Johnny Daws said.

"What do you mean?" Steve asked.

"Well, we have to make connections for distributorship all the way across the Lakes. We have to understand who to talk to and why about marketing, printing presses, unions, and other entities a business deals with," Rico Barrini said.

"What exactly do you propose to do about it?" Steve asked.

"Sign a bunch of linguists up. It'll make the Europeans comfortable with us and the Chinese and the Japanese. They won't see another American monolith come in and take over."

"What about us? Will we be comfortable with that?" Steve asked.

"We can either go in there on good ground or we can slug it out every step of the way. Acting like we damned well own the place is going to get us laughed out of the building, sir."

"You make good points. Let me think about it. And if I think you're right, guess who's in charge."

"Yes, sir."

"Anybody else?" Steve asked.

"I figure we market to young people, high school through thirty-five—many of them physically active. But we have about five to seven years to get this off the ground. We're going to need sponsorship for the museum. Cannondale bikes come to mind and their association with Saeco coffee in Italy will help us great if we start looking for sponsor like BMW and Mercedes. We have to listen to their ideas about their own countries and what sells there because even though we are a journalistic entity: it's turning a profit that makes it all go. We have the perfect opportunity for success if we adapt our magazine to their country and it is customs. I agree with Rico, we should seriously consider talking to them and not at them."

"Who likes Japanese food?" Steve asked.

"Never had it," Day said.

"Do you like baseball?"

"I am absolutely totally nuts about it. It is the second greatest game next to hockey. You're sending me to Japan. Aren't you?"

"Would you terribly mind taking Japanese?"

"Why are you doing this to me?"

"You opened your mouth."

"Oh, good!"

"I need you to help me understand the mentality of the Japanese baseball player—especially ones that come to America. Is the game as incompliant as it may seem to the American audience? Is it really dying as the rumors say? Do they want us there?

"There obviously has to be some sort of interplay between us and them—if they want us there. That's where you come in. What kind of computer do you have?"

"Think differently..."

"Then it will perfectly happy to push through on this assignment."

"What if we run a picture on the cover of the magazine with some guy from the Hanshin Tigers? Is that going to attract the American reader?"

"That my friend is your task to find out."

"Okay."

"Guys, and gals, I'm going to tell you, whichever assignment I send you on. You do it one hundred per cent because even if the American public hasn't been exposed to the idea and their interest hasn't piqued: if my judgement is that it is an important story, guess what? We're running the story."

"A risk taker," Paco said.

"Not necessarily. It must be good journalism. Not the 'yellow stuff' like the twenties. Mike what do you think?"

"Well, I'm concerned about access, we may have to bring in some ringers—familiar faces to the players."

"And what else?"

"If I may speak freely?"

"Sure, shoot."

"I'd love to cover hockey but am concerned with me being a distraction."

"What does that mean in English."

"You ever know what it's like to be the only black guy in Hockey East. They don't want to hit you: they want to kill you. I don't know if they want to talk to me."

"Try it."

"Okay, I said my peace."

"What about me?" Lynn asked.

"You come from a small town right in Arizona."

"Not exactly, I come from Scottsdale. It's a city. How come you people in the Northeast think there's only Phoenix in Arizona."

"Sorry. Anyway, I was thinking you poked around the inter-net to find out just how much fun you can have selling our magazine in the Southwest."

"Well, I would need a format of our magazine first. We can have it printed at PIP in the Financial District. If anybody notices, we can say it's a class project."

"Call me a second on that one," Shaun said.

"Well, to the rest of you folks, split it down seven on a side and help. We're going to be ambidextrous on this one guys. Everyone is going to have a turn at speaking in front of the class. You're going to be breaking down a lot of demographics. You may get sick of it but I promise if you stick with it, you'll actually get paid."

Chapter 13

The next couple of games were against the Maine Black Bears and they were bruisers. The games were also close. BU took them both 2-1 and 3-1. Steve picked up an assist in each game. Steve also picked up a bruised shoulder when he went down to block a shot.

On Sunday afternoon, he was alone in his dorm room with an ice bag on his shoulder when his cell phone rang.

"Hello," he said.

"Hey! It's me!" It was Tony's voice.

"Tony! How are you?"

"Hey, I have a secret that you can't tell mom about."

"Should I need to know this?"

"Annie and I are trying to have a baby."

"You aren't kidding."

"No. Not at all."

"Did all the doctors concur that it was a good idea?"

"Yeah, they were happy for us. Go figure."

"How's it going?" Steve asked.

"I am psyched for it"

"Are you going to be able to handle this job?"

"I'm planning that I am. You can't plan to fail. I'm just worried. That's all."

"Well, we'll go easy at first to see what you can handle and then we'll tailor your work schedule around it. One thing at a time—easy as pie," Steve said quietly.

"What will the other people think?"

"You'll have to tell them you have mental illness and you go at your own speed."

"Please don't tell them that until I prove that I can't handle it. How's your shoulder?"

"How do you know about my shoulder?"

"I watched the game moron."

"It's sore. Thanks for asking."

"You're one hell of a hockey player."

"Remember when we were kids and went to play on that pond at the golf course?"

"You were gold then."

"How are you doing Tony? For real."

"It depends on the day. Some days I'm really good—like now. Sometimes it's not so good."

"This new job."

"Retail was worse. Mentoring I may go back to some day. Right now I need time away to get rid of the pain."

"You call me."

"I will. Don't worry about me."

"I just don't want you to go back in the hospital again."

"You know what's really funny?"

"What?"

"They helped me there. It's not a bad, evil place. It's just scary because the mental illness is so raw, so out of control. It's scary."

"It scared the heck out of me," Steve said, "I have to know. What's it like. Really. I won't tell mom or nothing."

"Mood swings are easy. I tend to cycle faster than most. One minute your sky high and the next you're way down in the dumps. See the usual way lasts hours or days but I cycle in like forty-five minutes. It's too soon for the medicine to take effect so I ride it out. Let them shoot all their bullets until they are empty.

"The voices are different. They say things to you like you can't achieve your goals because you are a loser. They tell me that nobody likes me."

"Well, that's ridiculous."

"Don't tell mom but there's more. Some of the voices want me dead."

"What does that mean?"

"They tell me to kill myself. Like I said before."

"Don't listen to those voices!" Steve thundered into his cell.

"Thanks for the advice."

"Did I sound like an idiot?"

"A well concerned idiot."

"What do you do when that happens?"

"Well I used to get mad but that created a lot of tension. So, like I said, I ride it out. I make it an I'm tougher than you test."

"Lord."

"I'm glad I have the doctors that I have."

"I'm glad you know how to win."

"Sometimes it's embarrassing. I'll lose my train of thought when people are speaking directly at me."

"Tony, you're not a freak."

"It's hard not to feel that way going to doctors all the time. It brings me down sometimes."

"When their advice isn't what they're looking for."

"Yeah, I guess."

"A lot of people who go to counseling don't have MI."

"Still! It's just the whole thing talking about it. Can't we talk about something else?"

"Tony, my job is to have fun with you but it's also to monitor you. I'm sorry I have to play cop but the doctors have trained me to find little places where you may be off."

"That's what makes me feel like a freak. I feel like I'm the only one who has to have it like that. It's like every person you know who knows you have mental illness is monitoring you instead of talking to you."

"Look, maybe I said the wrong thing."

"No. You said exactly the right thing and that's the problem."

"Tony, most people forget you have mental illness in the first place. They just talk to you. It's in your head."

"Maybe it is. I know why too. Because I talk to someone who likes me the voices scream out in protest."

"Geeze, Tony even now."

"Yeah, even now. You put it in a little box but every once in a while the tiger gets out."

"Do you know how the priests and nuns in Catholic school taught us not to hate?" Steve asked.

"I hate this too," Tony said," I hate this disease. I hate God sometimes when I ask him why I have this disease. I hate when I don't know what to do."

"Me too," Steve answered, "Is there anything I can do for you when it gets really bad?"

"Pray."

"Do you laugh at those voices? Everybody likes you!"

"Well, sometimes I can because I know how ridiculous it is. It feels really good too."

"I bet it does."

They both laughed.

"Voices change in mental illness. These new ones aren't the same ones as I was hearing six months ago. Now it's a new battle. I'll tell you what I wouldn't like to be my doctors because they have to react they can't anticipate. It's hard for them."

"You care about your therapists. Don't you?"

"They're sort of like really smart friends. They feel really bad when they don't have an answer to a problem."

"How often does that happen?"

"Rarely! Some things are beyond medical science right now and they help me accept it."

"I don't know. You know when you go to a doctor and you expect to get healed. You have a sore throat or some allergies. The doctor tells you what to do and you do it to get healed. That's been my experience with doctors."

"It's not quite as simple with mental illness," Tony laughed," Just when things are good. They can all go away if you think you don't need the medicine and/or the therapists any more."

"I heard some people can just take medicine and be one their merry way."

"I don't know but I wouldn't try it. You're in a sad state of affairs if you think a handful of pills make you cured for life. You must stay in contact with your doctors and tell them truthfully what's going on. They may change the medicine. It's not right in my mind to think some guy can just give out pills. They have to know you as a person."

"Yeah, I agree with you. It's too much for one person."

"The truth is," Tony said," It's kind of a balance between one eye on mental illness and one eye on life. I tried pretending that I didn't have it and I could just live and I paid for it. This disease is a killer if treated the wrong way. You have to be cautious."

"All right but if you ever need to talk about normal stuff once in a while. You can call me to take the pressure off."

"You're playing UMASS next weekend?"

"Are you coming to Amherst?"

"No. I'm not coming. What are they teaching you at that school? It sure has change since I graduated?"

"It's going to be a slick series. UMASS is slick with the puck. They're nifty and if you skate with your head down, they'll crack you."

"They're young. Do you really think they're in your league?"

"They're in Hockey East aren't they. If they get their act together they can win."

"You could've played for them."

"No, I had my heart set on the big city."

"You just wanted to party and get away from home," Tony teased.

"Who me?"

"Mr. Innocent."

"That's right. I want to enrich myself as I grew and matured on my own."

"We'll see how mature you are when Fenway Park opens."

"That's below the belt."

"Have you told anybody you're a Yankee fan yet?"

"It hasn't come up in conversation yet."

"Hah! I bet it hasn't!"

"I'm going to change the subject now. Coach Parlon really knows what he's doing. We're going to win the National Championship. "

"Do you really think so?"

"Yes. We have the horse and the prize jockey to ride him."

"What did you just say?"

"Why?"

"Mental illness interrupted."

Steve repeated what he said.

"Are you getting tired?" Steve asked

"No! Let's keep talking."

"We're going to cream them."

"Dad and I are ready. We have the BU stuff we brought from last homecoming. We'll show red and white. You guys better win."

"We'll win."

"You guys can beat Colorado College, North Dakota, or University of Denver?"

"You want to bet on it?"

"I'll bet tickets to a Bruins game."

"Deal."

"Well, my last weekend of fun for three and a half weeks."

"Good luck at school."

"Everybody needs insurance. Right?"

"Yeah, right. I bet school is hard."

"Thanks a lot."

"You know what I mean."

"Yes, I know what you mean. Thanks for your encouragement."

"Don't be afraid Tony. You're a smart guy and a BU man to boot. Just take it easy. One day at a time."

"What if I fail?"

"I don't think you will."

"Okay, wrong question."

"Damn right it is. I ought to kick you out of the family for being a pessimist. You'll do fine. Keep that in your head."

"Right."

"So what do you think?" Steve asked.

"About what?"

"About life in general moron."

"We have a good group of people in your excursion thing."

"My excursion thing?"

"The museum thing."

"If you just relax you'll do your job fine."

"You know those signs that you see at football games. 'Ya gotta believe!' That's me right now."

"It'll be okay Tony. You'll do great."

"Call Annie for me."

"Yeah. I will congratulate on the news."

"Sorry, I forgot."

"Tony are you getting tired?"

"Yeah. But go ahead. It beats TV."

"I think I'm going to break up with Susan."

"Got another one in the bullpen."

"I'm thinking about asking this blonde girl from my management class out."

"And three would be awkward."

"Two is awkward. It was fun for a while but we just are splitting ways. She keeps making remarks about the business taking so much time. I'm supposed to meet her father at UMASS. He's an ex-Marine. She adores him and talks about him ad nauseum. Mostly, I think as I spent more time working because I don't have to technically, she'll resent me.

"And I think the blonde is stunning."

"Well, do what you think is right. I am not getting in the middle of your love life. Talk to the girl first."

"Yes, sir. Come up with a good idea for the business."

"I'll try my hardest."

"One more thing, I'll be working on a thesis paper on the impact of sports in American society since the integration of baseball. I thought you'd might like to take a look at it. It will include Jackie Robinson of course and the influx of Latin American players like Roberto Clemente. It will also include other kinds of heroes throughout the years. It'll be about twenty-five pages. I'm good at writing so it's no big deal. "

"Just take your time with the mental illness."

"Honestly, if I work at more difficult projects, my mind feels sharper. I like difficult problems more than easy ones. The mental illness is still there on pretty much an everyday basis but it really bothers me when I'm just hanging out."

"Dude, I wish I could advise you but I don't get it."

"Me neither but sitting around is driving me crazy."

"Then go for it then."

"I figure if I'm going to go nuts, then I'm going to do it actively."

"You know from our point of view with the company, you may want to take a look at the paper through the kind of angle where the new breed had guys that were team guys first. Hell, I can beat anybody with six team guys."

"Okay, I'll concentrate on that."

Chapter 14

About a half-hour into Steve's studying, Nate showed up with several photocopies of articles about Sweden.

"Look what I found," the captain said.

"Don't bother me. I'm studying."

"Sweden. A lovely Scandinavian country."

"Yeah. It's so lovely. The hockey players are taught to use their sticks like scalpels."

"That's racist."

"I'm still recovering from the welts I got at the World Jr. tournament."

"That's because you're a wimp."

"I really have to study. Make your point man."

"I'm considering further."

"Consider this. You're a nut!"

"Look! The Swedish Elite League is a good league. It's produced some good hockey players. Plus I want to play on the big ice."

"You're being seduced by the Dark Side of the Force."

"I am not. It's a good league."

"It's not the best league."

"I'll learn a lot more about a part of the world that I wouldn't know before. That's enough for me. Hockey's not going to last forever."

"Now, UMASS. They'll come out flying on the first ten minutes but if we hold them we have them. They can't match us skate for skate."

"If we score in the first ten minutes, they'll drop. "

The Friday night game was in the Agganis center and UMASS did come out flying. Nate showed his leadership by stepping into UMASS players with thunderous checks. The other defensemen followed suit and soon the aggressive Minutemen forwards became timid and watched instead of attacked.

With eight minutes gone in the first period, the puck squirted right to Steve, who raced up through center ice. He took the puck all the way to the slot, where he was met by the lone defenseman.

Steve faked a backhand shot to the left and the defensemen dropped to his knees. Carving a big chunk out of the ice, Steve cut to the right. He heard the goalie yell.

"Screen."

And then he fired the puck backward to the left and into the netting.

Steve raised his stick in the air and basked in the attention of his teammates. It was 1-0 BU. BU received energy from that first goal and poured on the pressure. At the end of the first period, the Terriers led 3-0. In the locker room between periods, Coach Parlon tried to keep his team excited and wary.

"You guys are doing great but remember UMASS has plenty left. They're a tough club. Keep pouring it on. Now get some rest and have something to drink."

"Gentlemen, UMASS is a good, young team with lots of legs left. You be careful or we'll lose. I'm going to repeat this again. They have a ton left. I can feel it.

"You guys are doing great. Watch them. They'll come out hitting. Use your heads. Don't take stupid penalties. They're a tough club. Keep pouring it on. Now get some rest and have something to drink."

Soon the buzzer sounded for the second period.

UMASS was definitely more physical this period. They rushed to make loud, thunderous checks that jarred BU players. BU started to lose their cool and started taking stupid penalties. UMASS crawled back into the game with two power play goals. And the whistle blew at the end of the period with BU clinging to a 3-2 lead.

Coach Benson explained to the players another way to approach the physical play.

"Look guys. They are leaving wide patches of open ice. Go to the short pass. Don't hold onto the puck so long."

About a minute into the period, UMASS scored on a breakaway to tie the score at three.

"We've got a hockey game now," Steve yelled as he climbed on the ice.

The score held all period and then the teams played overtime. Neither team changed their style of play. With one minute left in the overtime Steve had the puck behind his net. He made the decision to take it out himself. He churned up the right side of goal cage. An angry UMASS player took a run at him but Steve was too strong on his skates and he ran the Minuteman player down.

Steve picked up speed through the neutral zone and passed one Minuteman after another. Soon, he was in the slot, fifteen feet in front of the goalie. He faked to his backhand and then fired a puck between the five hole and heard it clang in the back of the net.

The Terriers played pile on with Steve. UMASS players were seen hanging their heads on the bench and on the ice. Agganis Arena went wild. It was just plain loud.

Finally the pile on was over and the teams lined up to shake hands.

"Well, we'll see you tomorrow night," Steve said to a UMASS player.

"I have to say. You're one hell of a player," the Minuteman said.

"You guys have a good team. Hang in there—just not against us."

The next night, BU visited the Mullins center at Umass-Amherst. Umass was embarrassed in Boston and wanted if not revenge, then the ability to lay several, if not all of the BU players against the boards. They came out hitting and they forced BU to skate with their heads up lest they want to get buried in the ice.

About ten minutes into the game, Steve lined up a Umass player who was skating with his head down and he leveled him. At first he felt elation as he headed back into the play but then he realized the hushed quiet to come over the arena and as the referee's whistle blew, he turned around to see the player lie motionless on the ice.

The Umass player stayed on the ice for about thirty minutes as the trainers and paramedics worked on him. Steve stood mesmerized by the whole scene. Steve knew he had hit him hard and was pleased but now he saw results of the collision and he had become afraid for the Umass player's well being. It seemed like hours before they carried him off the ice and the players rattled their sticks on the ice with the obligatory salute.

After the game, a 3-1 BU win, Steve headed off to the hospital to see the Umass player. He was nervous, as he had ever been. He knocked on the door and heard the John Trombley say, "Come in."

"Oh, it's you!" Trombley said sourly.

"How are you feeling?"

"My butt hurts."

"Sorry. What happened?"

"I fractured my coccyx. I'm out four to six weeks."

"Geeze."

"You're a stiff. Do you know that?"

"Hey, I didn't mean it."

"That's why you're a stiff. If you were a dirty player, I just call you an idiot and be done with it. Besides, I wouldn't like to be you the next few games anyway. When the refs aren't going to be calling you for penalties, the frat boys are going to be running you all over the place."

"And you'll be gleefully watching from your bed."

"Popcorn in hand," Trombley smiled, "Much as it kills me to admit this. You didn't do anything wrong. It's just part of the game. Go in peace my brother."

"That means 'I'll see you on the ice,'" Steve smiled.

"Then all bets are off."

Chapter 15

The next day, Steve slept late and when he finally pulled himself into the shower, it was 11:30 am. He had lots of serious studying to do that afternoon so, after his shower he went to GSU on the corner and picked up a meatball grinder and hustled back upstairs. He studied all afternoon and quit for dinner around 7 p.m. was bug eyed.

He went back down to the same GSU and picked up a chicken salad sandwich brought them up to his room. Nate was there.

"What's new with you?" Nate asked.

"I am going to break up with Susan."

"I thought you were sleeping with her."

"It just doesn't feel right."

"She seems nice enough."

"I never comfortable speaking about important stuff. I had to force it out of me. And I hid a lot of stuff."

"Well, you'll find her."

"There's this amazingly pretty blonde in my management class. I'm going to try for her."

"It didn't take long to get over her you know."

"I've been analyzing this girl all semester. She's totally smart, which intimidated me to death."

"Until now?"

"To paraphrase Thomas Jefferson, 'Desperation is the necessity of invention.'"

"You got the hots for her."

"I'm a red blooded American male and damned right I do."

"I've got to hit the library. Tell me about your little trip to Fantasy Island."

Steve bit his lip Nate and called John Davis.

"What do you think?"

"You have a pretty mixed bag. How did you end up recruiting? Throwing darts on a board?"

"I take it you are not happy."

"We need some more experienced people—even if that means well meaning yet, hard ass college professors. You said you wanted to go to Harvard right. If you want to do this thing right, you get your Master's.

“I heard things about you. You’re a whiz in the classroom and kind of reticent. You better lose that ‘I’m too shy’ routine or you’ll be out the door. Marketing means meeting people constantly. And one other thing, you are in charge. Got it.”

“Yeah, sure.”

“I’m older than you and I have more experience. I say go to grad school first and just because you have chosen my fine school, that proves you have taste.”

“Anything else?”

“I think you have good potential. You aren’t going to like everything I say but see it as point—counterpoint until we bring the problems down to a minimum.”

“I think we need a winning attitude. I saw more different color sweatshirts than in a kaleidoscope today. We have to get some uniformity going. I’ll send out an e-mail saying shirts, ties, dress pants for men and business suits for women.

“And we have a confidence problem with some of our troops. They are looking like they shouldn’t be there because the plan is too grand. Wendy touched on it before,” Steve said.

“Yeah, I don’t know about you but some of the troops are looking through their glazed eyes with a look of, ‘I can’t believe this.’”

“At the next meeting, we ask them politely if they really believe in this project and give them until Wednesday of the following week to decide if they want to be there and then we find some replacements and move on.”

“I can peg two of them for slackers now. What are you going to do with them?”

“Let’s see if they get their first assignment done well and if they don’t then we’ll worry about nuking them.”

“You have one heck of an idea. You should legally protect it. I got a buddy just fresh from law school in a great firm. He could advise you.”

“For pizza and beer.”

“Just the three of us.”

“Are you serious?”

“Why did you ask for me?”

“Besides your mother thinking it I thought you were impressive.”

“Part of all this business is personal relationships. People get really close to each other.”

“You got a girlfriend?”

“Yeah. She’s a history major working on her PHD. You?”

“Recently, single.”

“Well, hell man I feel for you.”

“Nice?”

“Especially in the summer.”

"She made it all the way to Harvard?"

"Stranger things have happened but not much."

"Yeah, me too. I'm thinking about a million ideas for this project but I have put them through a filter of a centrifuge to get all the sediment on the bottom."

"That was polite."

"I think this is going to fly but I am concerned about location. Willard J. Marriott drove it home in his book. 'The most important thing is location, location, location!' You may be right but I want to have some feedback from sponsor candidates and so forth. It's still where I grew up."

"You have to think on business terms. Will the turnstiles keep turning. It's a black and white issue."

"Well, you know it's going to rely on most of its revenue from two sources; the young and the retired. The retired will be taking their grand kids and college kids will be coming for themselves. We have to attract the 25-49 year old range because earned money is better than disposable income because once it is disposed of it's gone. Earned money has the next paycheck to look forward too. What do we do?"

"We think about it."

"All right. Fair enough."

Just as Steve hung up, Nate, the Rhodes Scholar candidate, threw his books on his bed and sighed.

"I'm brain dead. I've been studying in the library since the time it opened this morning."

"Did you get lunch and dinner?"

"Yeah, sure."

"Then what are you complaining about. That's what college is for to build your brain."

"Screw you."

"Look, pal, you're day ain't over. I got a problem."

"What?"

"My brother is pretty close to freaking out because he's away at that school."

"Did he forget his night light?"

"Don't be a jerk. This is important. Use your Rhodes Scholar head to help me help him."

"What did the doctors say?"

"Relax. It's just tension."

"Then that's what I say."

"Tony is really intelligent—more intelligent than most—but he gets shook really easily by the disease. If it even flares up a little, he gets shook. The disease has given him a pretty bad time in the past and he has reason to be shaken. I am afraid that he's going to worry himself into failure instead of actually failing."

"Dude, he's going to have it for the rest of his life and if he gets shook and calls the doctors right away, then an once of prevention is worth a pound of cure."

"I think I drive him crazy sometimes because when I ask him how he's doing, it's always about the mental illness. It's not about if he read *Sports Illustrated* this week. I forget normal stuff with him. I treat him like a damaged case and he won't say anything but I think he resents it."

"Well, Junior, as long as you've identified the problem, you can change your approach."

"Do you think it's just stress?"

"Do you? You talked to him?"

"I don't know."

"I say go by what the doctors say."

"You don't know Tony. He puts a lot of pressure on himself besides the illness. I'm worried."

"Call him tomorrow and don't ask him how his mental illness is. Ask him what's happening to the Bruins. Normal stuff."

"He's a major Bruins fan."

"Do I have to draw you a picture?"

"Yes, sir."

"You're lucky you have a brother. Even though he has bipolar***"

"I don't wish he didn't have mental illness for me but for himself. There are times when Tony can really say brilliant thoughts."

"Working simple jobs must've frustrated him. I'm glad you had the guts to hire him."

"I did but when he has trouble with his disease, he can't function enough to even do simple tasks and that scares him. He's said to me many times. 'How can I graduate from BU and not do this?' The worse part about it is that mental illness has this stigma of crime and violence attached to it. People simply don't know that people diagnosed with mental illness can function pretty normally when placed in a situation that is comfortable for them."

"Tell you the truth, I didn't know a damn thing about it until I met your family. I had the same feelings I guess. Thank God for the inter net. I looked it up and found some information. It calmed me down a lot."

"I just wish he'd find a place that was comfortable for him. He works very hard at beating the disease and it would be very nice if he could enjoy life."

"He's married. He's not enjoying life?"

"I think he would, if he had a job that fit him. He's just kind of reaching around in the dark right now. He wrote a movie script once but nothing came of it and he got discouraged. I see him as a writer trying to be everything else. I wish I could get him writing again but he won't do it."

"He really wrote a movie script?"

"I thought it was pretty good. It was about a guy with some doubts about his ability to pitch until he met a coach that helped him a long. I liked it anyway."

"I'd like to read it sometime."

"You'd like it."

"Don't worry about your brother. He'll find out where he's going. It may not even be this job. But he'll do it. Maybe he'll actually be writer."

"Thanks. We used to talk about that when we were kids and Tony was always writing but never talking about it. He was embarrassed. He thought he was no good at it but he thought he could get better. It took me a whole semester, every night on the phone badgering him to let me read his story until he finally relented. He is stubborn. It's a great story. It's too bad it's collecting dust on the shelf of his room. Are you still going to Sweden?"

"Got my bags packed."

"Once this hits the papers, you'll have to swim across the lake. "

"How so?"

"Nobody will freakin touch you. They'll treat you like a terrorist."

"I'm flying out of Boston. Bruins fans hate Montreal. They'll love it."

"You're nuts man."

"If you want to know the truth, I'm trying to wangle a trade so I don't have to pay Canadian taxes."

"One question. Do you know that Sweden's tax bracket is around fifty per cent?"

"It's only for one year and maybe sooner if we can arrange a buyout of the contract. Montreal fans will be screaming bloody murder if the Canadiens don't sign their number one pick. They'll demand a trade. My mother would love that."

"What if they send you someplace colder?"

"Than Sweden?"

"Yeah, well they ain't trading you to Boston—not with all the bad blood they have with the Bruins."

"I was hoping somewhere in California. Nice and warm. God help me if they trade me to Buffalo."

"I hear Buffalo has good Italian restaurants."

"Yeah but they are always buried under snow. It's like Minnesota or Wisconsin."

"How the hell can you be a hockey player and not like snow?"

"All, I'm saying is I need a more temperature friendly environment."

"Hell, it's the NHL. I'll play anywhere."

"You're a sap junior. Let me tell you. It's a business. There's balance sheets and counter offers and everything. Unless you're really lucky and you're able to make a significant impact on a community, chances are you'll get traded to Timbuktu faster than you can lace up your skates."

"You having doubts."

"Well, hell, it is the NHL."

"You'll do fine. Just don't take the world by its feet in the first month of the season."

"I'm used to doing that."

"Well, aren't you the modest one."

"Who do we play next anyway?"

"The Providence Friars. Good, solid club. Nothing fancy but they know the fundamentals. If we go to the short pass with them we'll beat them because they run around once the heat of the action gets revved up and leave big patches of ice open."

"For all of it, I want to win the tournament huge."

"What do you mean for all of it?"

"For all the stuff that goes with it. Instead of just playing, we're students, and we're press subjects. I just want to win to prove to myself that for one last time, you made the right decision."

"I've watched you grow up and I commend you highly on your progress."

"I want to grow up faster. Some days I just want college to be done. I want to lace 'em up in the NHL and see if all the press clippings are worth the powder to blow them to hell."

"You'll get there soon enough junior."

"I get impatient you know. I have senioritis since my freshman year. I wonder if I missed all that money. And maybe Montreal would suck eggs so much if I was there."

"Look at reality, you're up to 215, you've shaved off three second in your forty, which makes you a fast white guy. A rarity for sure. And you're the captain and need I mention Rhodes Scholar Candidate from this here school. Deal with that."

"I want to get to the next level badly but I don't want to play in some hyper-intensive wacko, nut case racist world like I hear our mon ami in Quebec are?"

"Do you want to get a beer?"

"Nope?"

"What the hell are you talking about?"

"I've heard things, Quebecours talk to each other and that's it. If you're English speaking, it's a little bit more of a challenge."

"Shut up! You're going to be playing for the Montreal Canadiens. As many Grey Cups as anyone will win in the CFL, nobody cares except for what Montreal does. They could be in last place for decade and they'd still rule. No whether that's good or not. I don't know. Don't give me, 'The hockey team don't like me.' You're just damned scared. You want to get there and you don't."

"You were an annoying little dweeb when you were a freshman and you still have that damned crew cut."

"Thank you very much. Can I do my homework now?"

"Piss ant."

"I'm right."

"Yes, you are. Hate being trumped especially by my roommate of four years."

Chapter 16

On the way to practice the next day, Steve came sailing around the corner at the George Sherman Union and knocked the blonde haired girl from his management class right on her backside.

"Oh, Lord, I'm sorry," he said.

Steve scrambled to help pick up her books.

"Aren't you the hockey player?"

She asked him in accent that was unfamiliar to him.

"Yeah, my reputation helps when I do something stupid. I'm sorry."

"I'm tough. Don't worry about it."

Again she spoke in the unfamiliar accent.

"Where are you from?"

"Midland, Texas."

"You came from Texas to go to school here."

"I never saw snow before."

"Well, now that you've seen snow what do you think of the rest of it?"

"It's kind of like puff balls."

"What brings you out here?'

"I don't know. It seemed fun. I was the only one of my high school friends that went to a different part of the country. They all stayed home. Two went to UT. One went to Rice and three went to A & M. It was a good experience. I'm hoping to get a job that keeps me here for a while."

"What's your major?"

"Music with a minor in management."

"No kidding! Playing before a crowd?"

"Yes."

"Look, I have to eat with the team after practice but could we do something afterwards?"

"Are you asking me out on a date?"

"Sort of a friendship trial and error thing."

"I heard you have a girlfriend."

Steve swallowed hard.

"We went separate ways."

"You better not be messing with me. I'm from Texas. I'm tough."

"Let's just go out tonight. You can yell at me later."

"Kinda glad you ran me over. Aren't you?"

"The question is. Are you kind of glad?"

"Seven o'clock. Warren Towers lobby."

"Okay."

"Who was that girl you were making eyes at this afternoon?"

Nate asked in the locker room after practice.

"I don't know. I didn't get her name."

"That's twice."

"We have a friendship date later."

"Back in the saddle."

"Let's hope this one works out."

"Well good luck pal."

Steve, showered, dressed, and shaved again before heading out to Warren Towers. The blonde haired girl from Midland, Texas was sitting quietly in the lobby.

"Hey," Steve smiled, "How are you?"

"Fine," she got up and smiled at him.

"What do you want to do?"

"Do you want to hop the T to Fanueil Hall?"

"Yeah, sure."

"You look uncomfortable as hell."

"I forgot to ask you your name."

"Laurie. Laurie Jones of the Midland, Texas Joneses."

"Damn fine to meet you."

They took the Green Line all the way into Government Center and began touring the world famous marketplace.

"This is my favorite spot in Boston," Laurie told him, "I go broke at the Disney store. What's your favorite spot?"

"Don't tell anyone. I like Harvard Sq."

"How'd you come to Boston?" She asked.

"It was the only major city my parents would let me go to. It's an hour and a half a way from Springfield. Plus, it's really the only town with Division I Hockey that is in a city."

"Do you like it?"

"I like the guys on the team but that's pretty much all I see. I live a really cloistered life."

"Do you ever get sick of hockey?"

"I don't know. It's hard to get sick of something that has made better than most of your peers since you were four years old. I haven't thought about it. There's always another game to play."

"I played softball in high school. I wanted to go to UT on s scholarship."

"What stood in your way?"

"Talent."

"I don't mean to laugh."

"Yes, you do."

"So, what's your story."

"What do you mean?"

"I mean everyone has a story. What's yours?"

"I don't have one. I don't think it's much. I started playing the clarinet in the fourth grade and I was pretty good at it. I kept playing it all through high school. I made all-state by the way."

"Damn, good for you."

"I wanted to see the world or at least a different part of the country and I had never seen snow before so, I gave this a whirl."

"And now you want to go stay."

"I want to perform. It's different there. Everything is 'Yes, mamm' or 'No, sir. Boston has its pluses."

"I think Texas is a heck of a place. They even have hockey now. The Cowboys and everything. They seem to do it big in Texas. They sure as hell know how to throw a party."

"You're a typical guy."

"Thank you."

"So, what about this girlfriend of yours?"

"The flame is doused."

"So you're a free agent."

"Got any ideas?"

"Well, I like talking with you—so far."

"What do you mean so far?"

"I'm just teasing. So what do we do now?"

"We go to the Disney store and if you play your cards right, I'll get something for you."

She held out her arm and he took it.

"Brothers or sisters?" He asked as they went into the shop.

"One brother. He plays baseball at University of Southern Cal. He's a second baseman. He made all Pac Ten last year."

"What about you?"

"One brother. His name is Tony."

"You're an odd one Mr. Grinch," she said.

"Excuse me. You live like a monk to play hockey."

"I live like a monk because I want to keep my head down to get my degree. Plus I have plans. I'm trying to cram as much information into my head as possible before they boot me out of here at graduation."

"You want to explain that one."

"I'm worried it won't sell. At BU, I mean."

"Why?"

"For a college kid to spend $12 with a college ID may be a little steep and frankly. It may be a big draw for segments of the school's population, the general population of Boston may see it as a BU thing only and I have to ask them to beef up security and that's going to cost money. If the cost money wasn't there, I'd think we'd be all right but that would push the average person's ticket price anywhere from $16-$20. Between you and I you want it to be just high enough to keep the riff raff out but not bad enough to break a family of four."

"Boston ain't poor?"

"No. But Charlestown and Sommerville may have a problem with it. I don't want to lose money just to take the chance that those young people would take the plunge and then sad to say, you have to worry about vandalism more and so forth. Hell, I wish everybody could afford it. But the fact is, you have to run a business."

"Mr. nose to the grindstone. Wow!"

"Yeah, I guess but it will pay off. Unless I find some wayward girl from Midland, Texas who will lead me astray."

She just laughed. There was something easy about her that Steve liked.

"There's no college hockey in Texas," he said.

"There's football in Texas and you better believe that. It's fun though, every Friday night or Saturday the field is packed. Everybody's wearing their team colors. It's a riot."

"Have you been to many hockey games?"

"Some. I have a job at Burger King in the Union and I work either Friday so I get to about half the games."

"There's got to be a better job you can get."

"I'm working on it but for right now, it is what it is."

"Come on, there's something I want to show you," he said.

There was a little figurine of Mickey Mouse dressed up in his Fantasia outfit.

"It's yours if you want it," he smiled.

"You're a class act Thompson."

She picked it up and turned it around.

"I like the Mouse," she smiled," Thank you."

"We better be getting back," he said.

"Yeah, I guess so."

"It was nice tonight."

"Yes, it was."

"Come on, the Green line beckons."

"I've got an extra token. Here, take it," Laurie smiled.

She pressed her hand into his and he dropped the token. Clumsily, he bent to pick it up.

"Sorry," he blushed.

"You're cute."

"I'm a klutz."

"Yes but you're cute."

The train rode back to Commonwealth Ave. They sat next to each other and Steve reached for Laurie's hand. She took it and he felt an electric energy when he touched her skin.

"You'd like Texas—especially the football. Heck, the high school teams are better than some colleges."

"I heard it's hot as hell."

"I don't know. I grew up in it so I don't really feel different. I guess it's hot like New England is cold. I'm dying to get through this winter. I hate this cold."

"Laurie, I don't want to break your heart but that's what snow is. It's cold."

"I thought it was pretty and fluffy but too cold."

The train came to stop in front of her dorm and he walked to the lobby.

"I'll see you when?" He asked.

"Well, tomorrow night I have to hit the library. We could study together."

"Seven o'clock. I'll pick you up in the lobby."

On the way home, he used his cell to call Brian.

"How's the Heights?" Steve asked.

"Steve I have to tell you. I don't think it will work."

"Are you serious?"

"Yeah, I just don't see it happening."

"So you want to quit?"

"Basically, I just prefer the safety of my father's office."

"Well, I respect that and I wish you well. Good luck."

"How was the date?"

"She's nice but she seems like a lost soul. She wants to go home away from this inclement weather. I guess she's pretty hot with the clarinet. We had a good time. We went to Fanueil Hall. She's a good conversationalist."

"Are you talking to you or me?"

"I was thinking."

"What's her name?"

"Laurie Jones. She's from Midland, Texas."

"Texas?"

"That's right. The Longhorn state."

"And she likes you."

"As far as I know. I'm taking her to the library tomorrow night."

"Can't you take her out somewhere?"

"She has to study and I do too. There's always the walk home."

The next night the walk home lasted forty-five minutes and they talked about everything. Steve asked her if she would make it to the game Friday night.

"I'm working. Come pick me up afterwards."

"Deal."

"Kiss me."

He leaned over gently and brushed his lips to hers. He held her for a long time and he finally let her pull away.

"Too much?" He asked.

"A little."

"I'll work on it."

"You need me to practice on."

"Well, when you're available."

Chapter 17

Friday night came and Agganis Arena was packed per usual. Umass-Lowell came zipping in with their red, white, and blue uniforms.

"Remember," Nate said, "Use the short game and keep your head up."

"Right. Bet we win by three."

"Bet we win by five."

They won by one. Nate hit Rico Barrini with a pass in the slot with thirty seconds left and Rico buried it in the top corner.

"Guess, we were wrong," Steve said.

"Guess we were and the coach is going to tell us how wrong we were."

The coach did too. Once they got into the locker room, Coach Parlon hollered, screamed and kicked over garbage cans telling them what a no account no hustle team they were that night and that the national championship would go away in a minute if they played like that all season.

Steve didn't waste anytime in the shower. He knew he played a bad game tonight and he wanted to slide out of there without being scene by the coach.

"Thompson. Front and center!" Roared the coach.

"Yes, sir." Steve finished tying his tie and then jumped in front of the coach.

"You do know you were awful tonight. Don't you?"

The coach asked.

"I..."

"Never mind you. It's we. We played lousy because you played lousy. You and Nate set the pace. When you guys suck, we all suck. You better be ready tomorrow night or you'll be skating like demons on Monday."

"Yes, sir."

"Get lost. Go be a college student."

"Yes, sir."

Steve showed up at the Sherman Union as promised. Laurie was just finishing cleaning up.

"Can I take my tie off?" He asked.

"Leave it on. You look good."

"Fascist."

"In Texas, the football players have to wear ties and sports jackets just like you. I feel for those guys. It's so hot it is murder."

"What do you want to do?"

"I want to go home and shower and then we can grab a coffee at the all night place."

"I really feel bad that you're working in Burger King. Would you let me ask around for you?"

"You're a class act. What do I take in trade?"

"Nothing. Friendship."

"You are a class act."

"Come on. Let's get you back to the dorm."

"Kiss first. Uh-huh on the cheek!"

He waited impatiently down in the lobby while she showered and dressed. They stopped at the coffee shop and picked up two medium, regulars. They went for a walk on Comm Ave and talked a little before she asked what was on both their minds.

"Why are we doing this?"

"Why not?"

"I was just wondering how you operate."

He put his arm around her and she squirmed out of the way.

"Answer the question please."

"Because we like each other and it's good to have someone you can honestly talk to."

"We do that."

"It feels good when we're together. Doesn't it?"

"Yes. I guess it does."

"I'll work on that job for you."

"You don't have to do that you know. We haven't known each other that long."

"Well, if we're going to be friends then, I think we should cut the crap with all this false modesty and just accept the fact we can do things for each other."

"What can I do for you?"

"You can play me your clarinet."

"That's it?"

"Yes. I've been interested since you told me you played."

She blushed and said.

"I'm pretty good but I need work."

"Who isn't and who doesn't?"

She looked down at her feet and he put his arms around her.

"Are you cold?" He asked.

"As a matter of fact—yes!"

"Come on, we'll walk back to the dorm."

"You can come upstairs if you want," she said.

"I'd like that. Do you have a roommate?"

"No. I live alone."

The reached Warren Towers and went upstairs to her dorm room.

"Do you like living alone?" He asked.

"Sometimes it's good. I can play my own music, turn on the TV, just stuff. But other times it's not so good. You want to shoot the breeze with someone and they ain't there."

"Well, I could stay over!"

She ignored him. Steve sat on the bed and padded down next to him.

"Sit," he smiled.

"Why are you trying to get so close to me?" She asked as she sat down.

"Because I'm like you. And I think you're gorgeous."

"I appreciate your candor."

"Well, if you aren't the appreciative one. I appreciate you appreciating me."

"Well you sounded serious."

"That was part of my cover."

Quite on impulse, Steve tickled her ribs and she started to roar with laughter. He finally stopped when she almost passed out.

"You're a rat fink," she laughed.

"You deserved it."

"I'm just an innocent little girl. You thug."

"Thug? Tomorrow night we go to Lowell so I won't be back until really late. He could have brunch on Sunday."

"Sounds good hockey player. How's your roommate, the Rhodes Scholar?"

"He's going to turn the academic world on it's ear someday when he buys a hockey team. Other than that he's fine."

"So is he smart?"

"Sort of. He sort of corrects all my mistakes—like a big teacher."

"So it's me."

"I guess so. It's kind of late. I should go."

"Please stay awhile."

"I can't. Coach does bed checks."

"Ten o'clock Sunday morning."

"Eleven o'clock and we'll go to Harvard Square later."

"You'd go to Harvard? You big hockey player. What about the Beanpot?"

"It's a nice place to go to."

"Ten-thirty."

"Why?"

"I just have to have the last word."

"Ten-thirty it is," he laughed.

"Hey, before you go, can I ask you ask you a question?"

"Sure. What is it?"

"I'm wondering what you get out of this museum/magazine deal besides money."

"Well, that's hard to explain in one sentence. On a day to day basis, it's just the enormous task of trying to get all those different kind of people to work together. You have Mike Gaines who is an African American from Buffalo. You have the Stork from Boston College."

"Who's the Stork?"

"Day—he's six, six. Anyway, when we do get into disagreements, it's about the best way to run the company. It's not about heritage or religion or anything. Just general stuff on a day by day basis, working as a team, juggling people's schedules so they can make it to meetings. It's kind of like, you have to get them excited about being there even though they are worried about exam they have to take back at school.

"And for the second part, I'll repeat this a thousand times in my lifetime, I'll have the ability, if they so choose to join the team when they come of age, my children can help. I can't imagine anything greater than photographing the Olympics with my son or daughter or both."

"Is everything so personal with you?"

"I have my shot, it's been what I worked for when I was a kid. All I have to do is graduate and sign the contract and begin."

"What's your next phase?"

"Word of mouth, except you feed very large mouths. We're going to start drafting letters to companies all over the world, including America to ask them what they would like to see in the magazine."

"That's kind of amateurish. Don't you think?"

"No. Because 'the business of America, is still business.' I love sports, I love teaching people but this needs a bottom line and businesses, if you direct market them through their Human Resource Department, especially the factories, where it's predominately male, you can discover a market base. It's going to take five to seven years to get this thing off the ground and in the meantime, we're going to have to sell the heck out of it."

"I need to ask you a question."

"Why?"

"Yes."

"I hardly watch TV. I like to be learning on my own instead of just not trying. There's so much opportunity in America, if you work for it."

He jogged back to Shelton Hall in street shoes—just beating the coach.

"Where the hell were you?" Nate asked.

"Never mind where I was."

"You were with the blonde. Are all those blonde jokes true?"

"You're so immature. Really."

"So?"

"So? What?"

"Never mind. You're in a mood. You know that?"

"I just kind of like her. I definitely think so."

"At what point in time should I consider you considered."

"I'll let you know."

"You're going to get all emotionally screwed up over this chick and then she's going to go to Texas and fall for a Longhorn football player."

"I don't think so. She said she wants to stay."

"I don't want to hear it. You're setting yourself up for a fall."

"Sometimes you think too much. You're too smart for your own good."

"Look at logistics. Texas—down by the Gulf of Mexico—Boston has the Harbor. The only problem is they're about 2,300 miles apart."

"I'm working on that one."

"What the hell's in that screwy, little, pea brained, head of yours."

"I'm just thinking."

"Spill it."

"I'm still thinking."

"With you, that could take a hundred years. The presses are running. Come on."

"I just like her."

"That's it."

"I really like her."

"You're nuts. If you ask me, you blew it with Susan—not her!"

"What's past is past with Susan."

"Whatever. Look! Just think about this. It's Texas. It's not the East Coast."

"I will diligently study it on the inter net."

"I still think you're crazy."

"I like her."

"I'm going to bed. You're pissing me off."

"Go soak your head."

They went to bed angry with each other and woke up preparing for Umass-Lowell each set on their job. BU played scared all night and it led to a 9-0 rout of the opposition. If they had one more bad outing, Coach would skate them until they dropped all week at practice.

Steve got home relatively early and decided to give Laurie a call. He called and she wasn't home, which started his mind whirring that she may see another guy. He called her again an hour later.

"Hi!"

""It's me." He said.

"Did you win?"

"Yes, much better than last night."

"What was the score?"

"Nine to nothing. Hey! Where were you?"

"I went for a walk."

"Alone at night. In Boston. What do you think this is? Midland?"

"I stayed on Comm Ave under the lights. Oh! You worry over me, kind, sir."

"Oh, please."

"You could've said 'yes, I do.'"

"I wanted to but you wouldn't let me. You were just way to spazzy."

"Huh!"

"We'll have brunch and then we'll go to the Coop," he said.

"That sounds good. Remember ten-thirty."

He forced himself to go to sleep and when the alarm clock rang in the morning, he groggily swayed into the shower. He showered, shaved, dressed and put on his overcoat and stepped out into the cold, November day.

"Hi! It's me!" He buzzed up and she came down the stairs.

"How's the food here?" He asked.

"It's pretty uneven. One day good—one day not so good! It's hard to figure out," Laurie said.

"Yeah, it's something like that at ours. They make good nachos though."

"Come on I want to get to Cambridge."

They ate quickly. She ate sparingly and then they were off to Cambridge. They took the Green Line to Park St. to make the change over to the Red Line heading to Alewife. Harvard's stop was on that line. The T was packed on both lines—like usual.

They arrived and ran out the door to keep from being trampled.

"Whew! That was crazy," Laurie giggled.

"What do you want to do first?" He asked.

"The Coop definitely."

"Okay, lead on."

When they arrived at the door she said.

"I want to go upstairs to the poster and print department. I want to get a Monet print framed for my mom's birthday. I'll give it to her over Thanksgiving next weekend."

"I'll get it for you."

"I don't want you buying everything for me."

"Hey, honey take it as it comes."

"Please, for me."

"Yeah, sure. Is this an independence thing."

"It's an I-don't-want to-be-a-sponge-thing."

"Do they make all cow girls this tough?"

"I'm not a cow girl. I'm a belle."

"Excuse me."

"Come on."

She happily bought the framed print off lily pads.

"I've been saving for it in an around my expenditures."

He laughed and then asked.

"What were your expenditures?"

"Make up, clothes, and stuff."

"Could you define stuff please?"

"Well, I buy books in the bookstore. I read them for leisure."

"Romance novels."

"You got it."

"God help us all. How can you read that stuff?"

"Oh, it's just frivolous pap but I love it."

"Come on. Let's go downstairs. There are books all over the place."

"I don't have any money left."

"Do you know what a gift is?"

She rolled her eyes.

"Yes. I know what a gift is."

"Well, then take it and be happy."

After buying the book, they stepped out into the cold.

"Where do I get your money from?" She teased.

"Well, I worked for it over the summer. I was a counselor at a hockey camp and I worked in the YMCA."

"You do have to buy me things every time we see each other. I like talking to you. That's enough."

"Laurie, I feel this tremendous pressure to try and impress you all the time."

"You don't have to. I like guys that I can talk too. You don't have to keep buying me things."

He smiled.

"It's cold out here."

"Let's get a coffee."

"Hey, for a second there I thought we were boyfriend and girlfriend. What do you think?" He asked.

"I think after I go home for Thanksgiving and tell mom and dad what a wonderful guy I met then I think it can be official—right now it's just kind of rehearsal."

"It felt pretty real to me. Could we hurry up the process?"

"It's a few days. Boy, you're impatient. What are you doing for Thanksgiving?"

"We are going to Alaska for a tournament against some Canadian colleges."

"Alaska?"

"That's what I said. I can't freakin' believe it. This the first time since we've moved into this house and that's about five years ago that I'll miss Thanksgiving. We better win those freakin' games."

"Something's different about you."

"I like you. A lot."

"How much?" She teased.

"More than a little."

"I thought you said a lot."

"You were being smart so I figured it was my turn. What does this trip home have to do with us?"

"My parents just may call you."

"Just to say hello."

"Yes, just that."

"Is there anything I should know about?" He asked.

"Well, my dad and mom are pretty much regular people. They go to church on Sunday and then they root for the Cowboys later on. My dad's an English teacher at Sam Houston High School and my mom is secretary at a local law firm. I like 'em. When I was younger, I crossed swords them a couple of times but it's long forgotten."

"How do they feel about boy friends?"

"Well, they treat it as an inevitability but I'm still daddy's little girl. Get it?"

"Right."

"Why do you say it like that?"

"Nothing."

She punched him playfully on the arm.

"Chicken," she smiled.

"I'm not chicken. I'm cautious. I'd rather see them in person."

"I can arrange that."

"I should wait and do it in person."

"Look at it this way. You have time to sit and think between games in Alaska."

"You're a lot of help. What do they like."

"I'll tell you what they don't like some slick kid trying to buy their affections. They aren't really ostentatious. They're kind of set in their ways."

"How set?"

"They just take to knowing certain things are true and they live by them."

"Like what?"

"I don't think they've ever voted Democrat in their lives. I don't think they've ever considered it."

"Yeah, I know the story the other way around. Different strokes for different folks I guess."

"Yeah. I guess. I hate to say this but you must take me home. I have studying to do."

"Yeah, me too. We could study together."

"We could."

"Let's go home."

Steve went back to his dorm after dropping Laurie off so that he could get his books. Nate had written him a message telling him to call home immediately. He immediately thought of Tony.

"Dad," Steve spoke into his cell phone.

"Steven, where were you?"

"I was on a date. What's going on?"

"Tony, wants to talk with you."

"What happened?" Steve asked his brother when the phone was answered.

"Holyoke has baseball."

"What kind of baseball?"

"The New England College Baseball League; Wood bats like Cape Cod."

"Cool. How much are tickets?"

"Five bucks. Get this ten dollars for a family of four."

"That's not what you called to tell me about."

"I got a new job."

"Doing what?"

"It's an entry level job but it's in Smith and Carlson, the Ad Agency. I'm on the creative side, I get to sell golf balls for Top Flite and board games for Hasbro."

"Hey, I'm super happy for you. But can you handle it with your head?"

"Do you have a hole in yours? It's very important that I do this."

"Just don't put too much pressure on yourself. You do that."

"I do not."

"Mother always did like you best."

"Thank God for the Smothers Brothers or you won't have any material."

"It's my job to keep you safe and happy."

"You have no idea how royally unhappy I am not working for a job that I'm qualified for. I can't separate paperclips for the rest of my life."

"I just don't want you in the hospital."

"Me neither. But if I go at least I do it while living instead plopped down watching TV every night."

"Dude, that's so great! But I've got to do homework or they're going to boot me out of this place."

"Ah! College days! I remember them. Keep going slugger, you've got to finish the year."

"Yes! I do. If you don't mind."

"One more thing. I start Monday, what should Annie and I do to celebrate?"

"Will, you please go away?"

"That's what I'm asking. Where should we go?"

"Take her shopping in Keene."

"I'll think about it."

"You're cheap."

"Yes I am."

"There's no sales tax in New Hampshire miser."

"Hey, that's right."

Chapter 18

About midnight, his cell rang so he answered it.

"Steve?"

"Brian?"

"Yeah, it's me."

"How can I help you?"

"I want to play the game again."

"And how did you come to this decision?"

"I was sitting around with my nice safe life with my fancy sports car and realized I didn't have the guts to make it on the outside. It's not a good feeling."

"Look meet me here tomorrow night at seven o'clock. We'll go to Cornwall's and have a sandwich and we can talk."

"Fair enough."

So at seven o'clock the next night Brian jumped off the T in front of the School of Management.

"Well, are you pissed?" Brian asked as they sat down.

"Not technically. I'm a little confused but not angry. I'm thinking it was a little more than having happy feet. I need to know I can depend on you Brian but I need to know the real reason why you left."

"You're going to make me say it. Aren't you?"

"Well, what did you do? Commit human sacrifice."

"My father put the hammer down about me working in the firm until I came up with the bright idea to go on strike."

"Who the hell do you think you are the Teamsters?"

"I was a one man sit down strike."

"What about your old man?"

"He ain't happy. We talked and I told him this was a tremendous opportunity and he said that I would have to struggle when I could grandfather in all his clients. He thought I was nuts."

"So how nuts are you?"

"My dad's pretty pissed."

"Look, I hate to sound cold but I need your full and undivided attention. If your conflict with your dad is too much then, maybe we'll have to call it off."

They ordered their meals and Steve waited for Brian's answer.

"All right. I'm in. What can I do?"

"I need a human resource person. Somebody's got to be on the ball. We're looking at Blue Cross & Blue Shield and Harvard Health Plan to name a couple of insurance companies. We also need to have an ombudsman their as a buffer between myself and the employees."

"Human resources?"

"It pays $165,000 a year after the season is over."

"Will I have to fire people?"

"Sometimes. On Saturday, we have a meeting at Cappo's. Let's go and start fresh and relax."

"Fair enough. Are you doing anything?"

"No."

"Let's go up to the Heights."

"Can I bring my girl?"

"That was quick."

"She's in my management class. I was sweating it out all semester to ask her out."

"And?"

"I sort of knocked her over at GSU."

"I don't even want to know about it."

"You aren't bringing me up there to get lynched are you?"

"Look at this way. If it happens, we'll get a priest to give you the Last Rites."

"That's comforting."

Laurie was kind of quiet during the trip up as the guys talked business until she finally said.

"You know what we really need from what I see?" she asked.

"What?"

"We need more organization. It's kind of funny to turn one of the rooms into an office but when it looks like a bomb hit it, it's no good. It's hard finding stuff a whole bunch of people can get trampled on in there."

"Are you volunteering to clean it up?" Steve teased.

"No. We are volunteering to clean it up."

"I am a provider of photographs. I don't have time for that. Besides there's a pile for everything and everything has a place in the pile."

Steve looked at Brian who shrugged as if to say what's the difference?"

"If you guys ask me, you should close the shades so the Fire Department doesn't come and declare it a fire hazard."

"Remember the paperless society. Nobody was going to make a paper copy. Yeah, right?" Laurie giggled.

"You really worry about stuff like that?" Steve asked.

"Oh, yes."

"I don't want to get into it. You're my PA."

"Very good."

Brian took him to his room he was renting off campus.

"Do you want to see my car?"

"What is it?"

"A midnight blue Mustang coupe."

"Really?"

"My parents bought it for me when I signed scholarship papers."

"Nice," Steve said.

"When you sign your contract what are you going to get?" Rico asked.

"A Jag."

"Excuse me."

"A Jaguar."

"I think he knows what Jag stands for," Laurie laughed.

"It could be Judge Advocate General," Steve laughed.

"What do you think about law school?"

"I think I'm going to take my degree and make this work. I'm five feet two and weigh one hundred fifty-five pounds. I've been breaking my back in these classrooms learning stuff and I'm at peace with myself professional hockey wasn't in the cards but I got a damned fine education out of it. The first couple of years, it was rough," Brian said.

"I didn't have much confidence in myself in the classroom when I got here but now I know I can comprehend the work. I learned a lot about myself here. Let me call Angela and see what she's doing."

He pulled out his cell phone and called Angela and when he did he discovered that the forces of evil had given her enough homework to last her until two in the morning.

"Come on. You told me that you came to this place to test yourself."

"I know," she replied, "but it's interfering with my social life. Tell the kids I said Hi!"

"Good-bye dearest."

"Good-bye."

"A ton of homework." Brian explained.

"Well, what do you want to do?" Steve asked.

"Get in the car. I'll show you where my parents live."

"Shot gun!" Steve yelled.

"Hey! That's not fair," Laurie huffed.

"I get passenger seat. I yelled first," Steve teased her.

"Fink!" She replied.

Brian took them up towards BC weaving in between the streets and finally stopping near a two family apartment building.

"Yours?" Steve asked.

"That's where I grew up."

"Have plenty of toys when you were a kid?"

"Had to share 'em with four brothers and a sister."

"It's a beautiful home. It really is," Laurie said.

"Thank you. I'd invite you in but it's late."

"When can I assess our talent?" Brian asked Steve.

"Saturday at the meeting. Everyone will tell their stories and we'll see who worked and who didn't then we'll make some decisions. I'll tell you what. John Davis is good. He's very precise about his statements."

"Harvard man."

"Yeah, well, with any luck I'll be one too. Do you think that school really changes you after a certain age? I mean BU did because I was here as an immature eighteen year-old."

"BC did for me for the same reason. Maybe it does. I don't know. Don't get out that way much."

"Why's that?" Laurie asked.

"Because Disney Land here keeps me holed up with my books."

"You don't have to be conscientious man, you can just skate through it. Your old man has a business you've been working at since you were sixteen," Steve said.

"Is this a test of the emergency broadcast system?"

"Sorry, I telegraphed that."

"Yeah, I guess you did."

"What about you, Brian?" Laurie asked.

"I think about it once in a while but I don't think about it that much. I think if I'm out in the work force for a year or two; maybe I'll change my mind. I'm thinking about pulling a double major. Work for my dad to keep the peace at Sunday dinner and you?"

"It's up to you but that's an 80-90 hour week."

"You ever notice how we're always talking career all the time. We should just relax and calm down so we can enjoy ourselves."

"Brian, this is a real business—with business cards and everything. As Human Resources guy, you'll go around with the sales people, that means all of us and make the presentations. There will be sign up sheets where people can sign up and leave their e-mail address and resume so you can sift through the best of it in your opinion and make phone calls for interviews. Sad to say we may have to reshuffle the deck we have now.

The next day after practice, Steve's cell phone rang while he was studying. It was Laurie.

"Hey, kid," he smiled.

"How did your phone call go?"

"It was good. The family's fine."

"What did Tony say?"

"He just said the voices bothered him once in a while but the mood swings were pretty much under control. He thanked me profusely for giving him the burger and the job. Also, he got his own job. He didn't rely on dad or me. He just got hired by one of the biggest marketing firms in Western Mass."

"That's great! But geeze, why is he so susceptible to the voices? He must know they aren't real."

"He says it's like a real thought coming out of his head. That's the problem."

"Do you think that we can do something for him?"

"He told me he has to go it alone for a while just to beat the voices himself."

"Do you agree?"

"No. Tony's always been independent. If he had a problem in algebra or another subject in school, he'd just about die than ask a question. He's my brother and I love him so I respect him but that don't mean I have to like it."

"I think it's a man thing. Meet you for breakfast."

"Sure. Seven o'clock."

He met her for breakfast and ate sparingly. He was in a rotten mood. He had been up to four in the morning studying and field phone calls for his business.

"Boy, I feel horrible," he grinned awkwardly.

"Meet me in my room after practice," she said.

"Sure, what's going on?"

"It's my birthday," she grinned.

"You didn't tell me it was your birthday!" He exclaimed.

"I just did."

She kissed him on the cheek and pinched his cheek.

"Geeze," he jumped.

"See you later," she said.

"Happy Birthday!"

"One thing. What are you?"

"I told you I major in Music and minor in Business Mgt."

"Geeze, you define yourself by your major."

"For the amount of work I put in."

"Oh! Poor baby!"

"Well!"

"Would you rather be back in Midland with your magnificent body working at a cash register."

"Well, I liked half of the statement."

"I liked part of the statement."

"The being back in Midland part?"

"No, the body part. You really think I have a magnificent body?"

"In photographic terms. You have great lines."

"Well, why didn't you ever photograph my lines?"

"I didn't know you wanted me to."

"We could skip the photography. I'm more interested in your curves."

"And how are you going to find my curves?"

"Guess."

"I'm getting warm. What does life mean to you? How do you define yourself?"

"Well, if someone says, 'Hey, man I see the Italian in you.' It's a compliment. It means: I am accepted by them; same thing with the other people's. I'm kind of in a bind with the whole ethnic thing. Because according to grandfather who didn't even high school but had enough sense to tell to always be a gentleman. You do that to people. You be nice. I'm not really into the ethnic situation on a daily basis. I don't get up and shave and think, 'I'm going to stick it to whomever I think is looking at me funny because I perceive that they think I'm mixed, because it's never happened to me before.

"The ethnic deal is for Christmas, Easter and Thanksgiving. We enjoy our nationalities ways of celebrating the Holidays. Except for a couple of guys on the schoolyard growing up, I never had a problem with it wherever I went. I was able to take vacations. Heck, went to the Carolinas and I was expecting red neck city and they liked us so I figured what the heck? As long as you were a moral person, you has a shot."

"Is that why you speak English so well?"

"I speak English so well because when I was four years old my grandfather told me to learn to speak English well, because it is the language of America and that's your country. And he was full blood Italian."

"But it didn't catch you wrong?"

"I've been all over this country flying around here there and everywhere to tournaments—even the World Juniors and they call you some things on the ice something terrible. They talk about your mother, your heritage, just about everything. It's the nature of the beast. Hockey players are animals. Do you see those bumper stickers?

"I don't know. I was always one of those straight arrow, shake on the deal types. I never had many problems. It was just who I was and that was it. They had much more fun with the fact that I was going to make more money than them."

"I was lucky too. So I was able to see America on vacation. People didn't have a problem with it. I certainly didn't have a problem with it. You are who you are. You either can play with these guys at that level or you can't and you have to be honest with yourself then, again you may be the slowest guy freshman year and by sophomore you catch up and by junior and senior year. You're the man that separates the boys. You get the 'C'.

"It would be very embarrassing for me considering where we live and the lifestyle we live to say America wronged me because I was mixed. America's too good for that and I'd never say that even if I had a rotten life, I wouldn't turn my back on my country."

"I like who you are."

"Thank you. On off even days I like you."

"It's kind of really dumb to mix race with your job because instead of you concentrating on being the best hockey player you can be. Well, the coach doesn't like me and my left wing won't pass me the puck because he knows

I'm mixed, or Irish, or German, or Italian etc. etc. etc."

Steve practiced hard that day. He felt he had another level to explore but he knew he needed Laurie to explore it with him. He wanted to talk to coach but he didn't know how yet. In the locker room he was bent over breathing hard after the final skate.

On the way to study hall, he received two phone calls from Stan Johnson saying everything was AOK with their assignments and they were looking for something more on Saturday. Steve promised he'd get them on the side. Clarence was more concerned with the architecture of the place. He had drawn up a couple of plans from the photograph of the old Basketball Hall of Fame. Steve told them, "to relax gentlemen. Saturday's coming. We'll have a good time."

And then he went to Laurie's room. Beforehand, he picked up a sweater for her in one of the shops on Comm Ave.

"The sweater's nice. I like the shade of blue," she turned as she turned red.

"Well, Happy Birthday! I think."

"It's not easy to admit that I like you," she giggled.

"Excuse me."

Something inside him split and he giggled with. He held his arms out wide and she dove into him.

"God, you smell good," he said.

"Stay here awhile."

"I could stay here all night."

"In your dreams pal."

"Shoot! I was hoping I could slip that in."

"We need to know each other longer."

"How much longer?"

"You getting antsy?"

"Maybe," he smiled.

She looked at him with fear in her eyes.

"Would you leave?" She asked.

"No."

"You damn well better not."

"See, we are making progress. We have come a point in our relationship where we need each other mentally."

"And you would like to try physically."

"Particularly tonight."

"Wait a minute cowboy!" She giggled.

"Not yet."

"You do move fast," she smiled.

"I really like you. I'm not just in it for an easy lay."

She laughed.

"That wasn't supposed to be funny."

"How serious are you about me?"

"Like serious. Really deep and serious conversations."

"You're a jerk."

"I can see what you're getting at and one sweater isn't going to do it."

"Seriously is that what you think?"

"No, I just wanted to see that 'I'm going to kill him' look on your face."

She laughed and kissed him on the cheek.

"I've changed so much since I've been here. Getting my degree was the end all be all of everything in September. Now it's almost Christmas and I'm ready to leave," Steve said.

"You can still get your degree," she said.

"Yeah, I'm going to but I have so much of real life running around inside me. It's just a tremendous challenge."

"You know I hate to say it but I think we're growing up. Now I have a job and everything. A real job—not slipping on the grease in Burger King."

"You don't like that."

"Shut up."

"What do you want for Christmas?" He asked.

"I'm pushing Santa Claus for a lap top. I'm going to have to come armed if I'm working for you. I hear you're a tough boss."

"Nose to the grindstone lady. You don't mess with me."

"Ooh! I'm scared."

"Look, it's real work even for fire and brimstone seniors at Boston University. It's a lot of fun; people well, mostly guys and Lynn Demarco from UMASS via Flagstaff, AZ. She's nice you'll like her."

"So what's so special about work?"

"Serious up for a minute. I need your opinion."

"All right. Shoot!"

"Well, we have these guys mostly and so far we've all got the whole thing clicking but sometimes it gets a little tense around the dining table at Cappo's. Partially it's because I'm getting exactly what I want out of these guys because they are all hyper-competitive and are used to succeeding. The problem is they play it like the game they play and they don't know when to shut up when another guy has a better idea."

"Are there grudge holders?"

"Yeah, a couple. They get snotty like women."

She just looked at him.

"Sorry," he said.

"I bet."

"Anyway, if you were possibly going to put a lid on this before it ever got out of control."

"Be a combination of nice guy Richie Cunningham and Vince Lombardi. At the beginning, be nice say, 'Hey guys, we have to do this together as a family. Please respect each other.' If that doesn't work, ask them if they want a job."

Chapter 19

On Saturday, Steve introduced Laurie and reintroduced Brian. It turned out to be a spirited meeting with lots of discussion and exchange of ideas. Steve was really impressed at the chemistry of the group. People from WMASS spoke to people from Eastern Mass and vice-versa. It seemed that they left their college sports rivalries at the door and enjoyed the look at life from another campus. Steve met what he had begun to think of as his team in the pizza shop. Maybe the hyper-competitiveness flu went away.

Steve had to guide the letters to *Sports Illustrated*, *ESPN,* and *Getty Images International* but otherwise there was good solid work. He was especially proud of Tony's marketing to the 18-49 year-olds.

"What do we do now Chief?" Paco asked.

"Well, on one of your days off; I want you to Hit the bricks to Springfield and see what we can learn from the new Basketball Hall of Fame. Then I want you to walk Main Street to see if you see any obstacles in doing this thing and then you come tell me."

"What about sales records from the Hall of Fame?" Lynn asked.

"Mike, you watch over miss lightening here. Work with her," Steve said.

"What if Springfield cans us?" Shaun asked.

"I don't think they will. I really don't. I've run every disaster scheme over in my head and I honestly think it will come to pass."

"How far did you get on the letters to corporate sponsors?" John Davis asked.

"I think they're pretty good. Right now I'm going after IBM, Canon, Xerox, General Electric, McDonald's, and Kodak. I'll give us a couple of more weeks to shine them up and then I'll send them up."

"I don't think it will work here." John Davis said.

"Why? It seems like a nice enough place?" Abie asked.

"Because I came here last summer with my father on a Saturday and there was nobody here. We were the only two people in the building. The NBA can float this thing all to midnight but we can't. I say put in Boston somewhere. There's just more traffic," Davis argued.

Steve looked at him hard.

"Look, everyone give it a hundred per cent shot. We'll gather the information and then we'll make a decision together. It's very close to my hometown and I want to give a look. Good? Very good! Rico, my friend, you've been awfully quiet. How is the political end going?"

"Good enough Boss! I had an idea. We should be making phone calls to area restaurants finding out who are the presidents to the local service groups in the area."

"That would be good but what about the pols?"

"The election for mayor in the city just happened and the incumbent won by a good margin and he's in the middle of a fight with the teacher's union. Maybe we should wait."

"Maybe he needs some good news," Steve said, "work on it."

"Yes, sir."

Chapter 20

The next night BU hosted Northeastern and it was an atrocious college hockey game. There was spearing and cross checking in abundance. Steve took a full swing at a guy that refs missed so he got away with it. The game was brutal. Steve scored twice and assisted on one as the Terriers won five to three.

On Monday, Steve talked to Laurie about seeing the Sports Information Director about the job for her and he said he could give her twenty hours a week. Steve kissed her on the top of the head. And then came the hard part. He knocked on Coach Parlon's office door. He went in when hailed.

"Coach, I have something to tell you."

"Is it bad?"

"You ain't going to be happy."

"Did you burn the dorm down?"

"I'm working on something that is becoming more important than hockey."

"Hopefully, it's your school work," The Coach smiled.

"Well, not exactly. You know about the museum project. Don't you?"

"Yes, I've heard of it in some sort of a tertiary way."

"Yes, sir. Well, it seems that the action of business makes my brain accelerate and my heart beat faster."

"You're a damned fine hockey player."

"Thank you, sir."

"Well, I don't think we have a huge problem here. Look at problem logically. You came here thinking you were just a hockey player. You did your due diligence in the classroom and you discovered you could do what you were trained for. It's not a question of whether you like more than one activity, which you can by the way. It's no sin. Right now you're on a high—everything is clicking with the business and hockey is going well.

"When you end up with a new experience in your life, it kind of takes over for a while. It evens out and things look good all around."

"So, all I've worked for on the ice isn't lost."

The Coach through his head back and laughed.

"Yes, sir. I understand."

Steve left happy that his coach could joke about the situation.

Steve called his parents on his cell phone on the way home from the arena.

"Hey, dad. It's me."

"What's going on, son?"

"I had a heart to heart with the coach. And he set me straight again."

"You aren't thinking about dropping out of school. Are you?"

"No. You can relax. I actually found something that is more fun than hockey."

"What would that be?"

"The museum project."

"We're just clicking along. People are doing their assignments and we're really working together as a team. I'm glad I went to different schools because it gives you a cross section of people across the Commonwealth and their ideas and life experiences. We are working well despite the fact that everyone knows BU is the best team in the country."

"Well, God forbid they don't know that," His father chuckled.

"Damned straight."

"There's probably ten of the sixteen we really need at this point but I keep the others around for flexibility and because they work hard."

"I can't believe you're really doing this."

"Tony helps a lot too."

"You are going to play hockey?"

"Absolutely. It's still fun but I think I'm so happy because I have a reason for my degree. I was wondering what I was going to do with it for a while."

"Well, you run with it. You have as much fun as you can."

"I'm thinking more and more that I can accomplish what I want to in life.'

"Well, that's what college is for. You can learn all the facts and figures you want but if you don't come out with determination and confidence, you are done."

"I'm good with my path in life right now."

"You sound like you're asking my approval."

"I guess."

"Son, you're a respectable young man. You don't do crime, and you work hard. I'm very happy with your goals in life but you can't live your life worrying what the old man thinks. It'll be a terrible monkey on your back."

"Yes, sir."

"Any other news?"

"I got a new girlfriend."

"That was quick."

"She's gorgeous."

"I know. Tony said."

"Anyway. She thinks I'm cute."

"Hey, you can't beat that."

"Not with a stick. Dad, the best thing about the project and the company is that they keep me from having the thousand-yard stare. They keep me focused in the classroom. I'm so busy running around, just sitting at the desk and making me study is a relief."

They chatted for a little while longer and then Steve said good-bye.

Steve went over to Laurie's place and he sat next to her on the bed then he asked her.

"I keep thinking about the Bruins."

"Good for you. But I'm thinking about something else."

"Let me guess. Playing for the Boston Symphony Orchestra."

"Not quite but an admirable goal."

"You would like to stay in Boston with this great new job you have."

"Partially, but to do what?"

"Does this devotion begin with an M."

"I would like you to spell it."

"M-A-R-R-Y."

"Congratulations. You got it on the third try."

"We've only been seeing each other a couple of weeks."

She blushed.

"We'd have fun," she said.

"Praise the Lord and pass the peas. You said it. All you had to do was say that at the beginning."

"Do you love me?" He asked.

"Yes. I do."

"Can't I at least kiss you?"

"Absolutely."

They ended up making love all night and then he sat next to her and held her hand.

"Give me a subject to talk about," he smiled.

"Now?"

"Preferably."

She took a deep breath and said.

"Parents."

"My parents will ask me a million times if I'm sure," He said.

"Are you sure?"

"You have my undying devotion."

"Good. What about my parents?"

"No."

"What do you mean no?"

"Hey," he whispered as he gently shook her.

"That's what they'll say. They dated for a whole year before he proposed."

"We'll double team him."

"Oh."

She blushed.

"This is embarrassing," She said.

"Yes, that would be how I described it. When did you start speaking with a drawl?"

"When I'm really excited. I can't hide it."

"Why would you hide it?"

"Because I'm up east and don't want to hear the Minnie Pearl and Hee Haw jokes especially from guys that I turn down."

"What about guys that you turned down?"

"Don't worry about it. I didn't turn you down."

"Yeah, well, obviously not."

"Don't you have to go to class?"

"At one o'clock. What about you?"

"Nine o'clock."

He groaned and rolled out of bed.

"We should eat breakfast," he said.

"Yes, but I don't know."

"Pardon me?"

"Now you're getting better."

On his way to class later that afternoon, Steve grabbed a paper at the newsstand and like usual read the sports first. On the front page above the fold the headline read Bruins trade defenseman Steve Thompson for three draft picks in the next two years. One in this year's draft; a two and a three in next year. He closed the paper and called home on his cell phone.

'Well, we are going to be young and enthusiastic,' Steve thought. He called his father.

"Dad, did you read the sports page yet?"

"No, I haven't. Why?"

"Do me a favor. Read it."

"Holy smokes!" His father shouted over the line.

"Can you believe that? I'm shocked."

"The Bruins are getting me some big time help. You can't beat that."

"You guys are going to be too young to go out and have a drink at the bar together."

"Yeah, but we'll be a team. We'll take our lumps early on but we'll be a team. We'll sweat together and we'll perform together."

Steve cheerfully went to class and his head was whirling all day including practice. The guys all asked him what it meant. Steve didn't exactly know what it meant until he met them personally but his gut feeling was that it was good for the Bruins and good for Boston.

He finally was able to meet with Laurie outside the Sports Information Director's Office and asked her how her first day on the job was.

"It went okay. What happened to you today?"

Steve explained what happened as the papers reported about the Bruins that morning.

"Are you kidding me?"

"I guess they're playing to win."

"You're serious."

"It's in *The Boston Globe*."

"What are you going to do?"

"You have to believe in me"

"Why?"

"Because I love you!"

"All right let's figure out this rationally. You're about to join a young exciting organization in a vibrant, exciting city and you're still going to want me."

"And what?"

"Why would you want me?"

"I think your clarinet is sexy."

"Come on."

"You're beginning to drawl."

"You know. You can be such a jerk sometimes."

"All I'm saying is I know you want me to stay so, don't get that soap opera stuff in your head. It'll make you crazy. Let's just get married okay."

She slipped up close to him and he put his arms around her.

"It's going to be okay," he said.

"Do you really want to cart me around out here or are just doing the right thing?"

"I'll tell you something, in the past six months I've grown up tremendously. The company, the hockey team, and school have all influenced me beyond words. I'll tell you, if you ever want to teach a guy with a big head some humility, let him lead a group of people! And then there' is me! I'll try to be as nice as I can see things running together but they ain't running fast enough."

"You have no tact but I'll take you," she smiled.

"I'm serious. The people here I have are too nervous about stuff. I'm the one who's supposed to relax them and I'm nervous."

"I'm getting sick of you."

"Why don't we develop a plan. To find a place and begin to enjoy ourselves."

"I'd go anywhere with you most of the time," she said.

He held her even closer and kissed her passionately.

She pulled away quietly and held out her hand. They walked for a while in silence and then went to her room to study.

"How's Boston doing?" Laurie asked.

"They are in third place playing about five hundred. Not bad. We should go higher with me next year."

"Aren't you confident?"

"Aren't you?"
"You're enthusiasm challenges my pessimism."
"You're still worrying about some girl."
"Am not."
"Oh, okay. Come here."

Chapter 21

That afternoon Mark Wilson showed up at his front door.

"Hi, boss."

"Hey, Mark."

"I have a question for you."

"Shoot. But first come in. Do you want a Coke?"

"Sure."

Steve popped a couple of tops and gave one to Mark keeping the other for himself.

"What's going on."

"Why did you pick me, sir?"

"For this job. I thought you were qualified."

"That's it. Not because I was black."

"I could've hired another one. Yes, partly is because you are African American. Hiring many African American ball players who were growing up. I thought you earned it and you played fair. I thought you deserved it. How's the Coke?"

"Very good, sir. Out of respect for you. How did you get this crazy idea?"

"High school."

"No kidding."

"You've been around America?"

"Some. Not much!"

"What the hell are you doing playing hockey?"

"I wanted to be different."

"I'll see you boss. I have to study. Thanks man."

"Don't forget your Coke."

"Yes, sir."

Just as left, Lynne Demarco called.

"I'm having trouble finishing this assignment."

"So am I; what is your assignment again?"

"I'm supposed to make something up."

"Look we're having really big conundrums trying to market to the 18-49 crowd. Tony is working on the same subject. Call him and collaborate."

"Good. Thank you. Can I ask you a question?"

"Shoot!"

"Do you think John Davis is right?"

"My big concern with Springfield is vandalism and disposal of waste. If people dump stuff on the ground or spray paint the walls, it would not be a good thing. You know how it is: if it's nicer, it's easier to trash."

"The Basketball Hall of Fame held up pretty well. Why don't you do your paper on security? Discreetly ask the Hall of Fame who does theirs'?"

"Yes, I could do that. I just don't want this thing to get wrecked."

"Me neither. Sad that we have to think about it, huh?"

"Yeah, it stinks."

"Look, I have to call my fiancee about breakfast plans tomorrow morning."

"By all means."

"Good-bye."

"Ciao."

The next thing he knew his cell phone was ringing. It was Peter Blute.

"Hey, it's me. I have a question for you. When are you going to the Basketball Hall of Fame?"

"On Thursday, Brian, John and I are going."

"We'll pile in if you let us—The Euro-Scandi connection."

"John will have to take his car. Anyway, if we do that, we'll ask Paco too—just to see what his schedule is like."

"Well, I've got an eight o'clock and after that I'm free. Everybody else has squared it with professors. That will be a good experience. I've never been that far West before."

"Well, unfortunately a lot of people haven't."

"Why?"

"Because Springfield thinks Boston a town full of rich jerks and Boston thinks Springfield is a hole in the ground. I'm pretty sure this generation wants to make us one Commonwealth."

"Well, is it true? Is Springfield a hole?"

"It needs some paint and shingles but it'll be all right. I'll show you the best hamburger/hot dog place in Massachusetts for dinner."

"Does Coach know?"

"He squared it with me. You guys have to suck up."

"All right, we at least have an out. It's an educational experience."

"Yeah, that's what I said."

"I'm poking around *Der Spiegel's* web site learning about sports photography. Lots of hockey now a days and soccer will be starting soon."

"Don't try and do it all yourself Sprickenzie Duetsche to the photo editor."

"Okay, boss."

"See, you Thursday nine fifteen."

"What about practice tomorrow?"

"Oh, I forgot."

"Boy, you better have Laurie arrange your schedule for you."

"Danke."

"Don't mention it."

On Thursday, they had a good crew lined up for the trip to the Hall and the Hall didn't disappoint at all. The members of the team spent about an hour and a half—just observing and scribbling notes.

"What do you think?" Steve asked Laurie.

"It's pretty impressive," she said, "—many ways to amuse yourself but it seems to manage to hold the interest of children and adults."

"What did you learn?"

"Well we need that special kind of lighting. What is it? Kelvar?"

"Kelvin. What do you think?" He nodded his head at Brian.

"Well somebody knew what they were doing when they designed this place. I say we find out who it is and get going."

"That's the number one because without a price tag to show the sponsors; we're not going anywhere." Steve said.

"That's what I think," Brian said.

"What did you like about this place Brian?"

"I liked going along clockwise. It kept the flow easy. But again we can't appear to copy the Hall. I say we go to the professionals."

"I'll call Clarence and have him draw up his final plan and then we'll send in a proposal to architectural firms. They are an architectural firm right in West Springfield," Steve said, "Next week ties about the assignments. Brian, John, and I will review them and give you an evaluation."

"I like the way they used the boxes to put memorialbellia in. We could put an 8x10 shot by the photographer and a small bio using the Kelvin balanced light," Kim said.

"Good idea. John you've been awfully quiet."

"Well, Chief, I was thinking of the twenty by thirty lighted pictures. Obviously our place is going to be more, well lit. I was thinking we use the regular photo-paper and we cover it with polyethylene so when people try to touch it, it will keep the acid from their hands off the prints," John answered.

"Right. I'll take that under advisement."

"Paco, you've been quieter than John."

"Well, coming from an accountant with not much of a flair for the artistic, I'll stick with the interactive stuff. We definitely get different examples of digital cameras from pretty basic to grande large and we charge a small fell to get the print from a printer. We can get college interns to do the grunt work."

"Everybody like?" Steve asked.

"Good," John said and the others followed.

"Good it's time for dinner so that everyone can go study."

"I didn't hear anything from you Nemo," Steve said.

"Hey, I'm a good worker. You tell me what to do and I'll do it," the Finn said.

"Fine. I'm telling you to answer the question."

"Well, we should have a Scandinavian/European room because most Americans aren't familiar with what we play. I'll work you just tell me the job."

"Explain that in more detail. Lars?"

"I agreed with Nemo. My policy is the same. I'll work if you give me the project."

"Fine. Work on it together."

The pizza came and Peter whistled.

"We don't have any of this in Germany."

Steve looked over at Tony who excused himself and went outside. Steve followed him.

"Hey. Are you okay?" He asked.

"It's just the mental illness. When I'm around more than one person it gets like this. I just have to come out and get some air."

"Well, I'll stick around."

"You'll miss the food. Go inside."

"Come on back in. Everybody likes you. Come on in."

"Okay! Okay!" He laughed.

"If you feel weird, start talking."

"Where'd you get that theory?"

"Not to everybody—just one person; It'll keep you focused."

"Maybe that'll work."

When they got inside, Tony asked Peter what Hamburg, Germany was like for him.

"Well, without BU, I'd be playing in the German Elite League and working the docks for the cargo ships that traversed the Elbe just like my father. I enjoyed growing up on 33 Strasse. Hamburg is a fun city to grow up in. A kid can get a lot of notice if he works hard. But I'm glad I came to America. It opened my mind to different people. I'll be cosmopolitan by the time I graduate. I'll be an engineer by then."

"What's your story Lars?" Kim asked.

"Nothing really out of the ordinary; I started skating when I was four years-old in the Gulf of Bothina off the coast of my home city and the capital, Stockholm. Loved hockey from the second my brother cut down one of his sticks for me. Love it more that it got me an education in the States. Have two years left and am hoping to get drafted by the NHL. I'm an ordinary guy off the ice. I don't wear ties except for this project and that's only because it is important."

"Your turn," Steve turned to Nemo.

"I live in a town called Vassa also on the Gulf of Bothina although north of Stockholm, which theoretically makes it colder but who cares after -5. I started falling all over the ice when I was two. I haven't stopped since. Just like the sport. Most of my countrymen are cross-country skiers. Tried it but never really liked it. I am a History major going into my junior year. If I don't hook on with the NHL, would like to play in Sweden or Germany just for the experience."

"My turn, I guess," Rico said, "I'm from Syracuse, NY, which is known for it's college hoops, Italian food, and snow—in no particular order. I didn't want to play hockey. I wanted to play the trumpet but all my friends played hockey so I stuck with it. I'm a poly-sci major and hope to be an attorney in four years. My goal is to intern on Beacon Hill. I can still play the trumpet but it's more of a fun thing. I have had a tremendous time working for pizza and beer. It's starting to get real now though and that makes me even more excited."

"Mark open your mouth son," Steve said.

"Well, I'm from Brockton Massachusetts and am proud to say I was a member of the Brockton Bombers football team that won the state championship."

"What position did you play?" Brian asked.

"Safety. I was interested in drawing and I got pretty good at it. So I went to the computer in school freshman year and asked it what people who could draw could do to make a living and it spit architecture. So I got my grades and waited for BU. There's not much too tell after that. I graduate in May pleasing my parents all to death. I've done a couple of internships at really good firms in Boston. It's time to see if I can do it for real."

"Lynnie, your turn," Steve said.

"I'm from Umass-Amherst. I'm a Marketing Major with a minor in Italian Languages. I heard about this opportunity in the school paper and thought about it before replying. I'm from Flagstaff, AZ and am looking forward to this because I think it would be really good for people to see sports photos from all over the world."

"Brian?"

"Nothing I haven't said before. Looking to push this organization to a new level; Applying what I learned at school and I'll be damned if it doesn't work. I'll graduate in May and then the serious work will begin. I know that you guys are in a sticky position but I loved BC."

A chorus of boos came up from the group. "And lastly, my PA Laurie Jones."

"I'm from Midland, TX. I've been around sports all my life—especially football. I'm a music major and management minor. Like both courses of study. I play the clarinet and am very happy to be here. Will graduate in May; I have had many dreams since I came to BU about what I wanted to do with my degree but I'm happy with where I'm at."

"Hey! What about me?" John Davis asked.

"Well you were sitting over there munching on pizza and plotting the overthrow of the free world. I know how you Harvard guys are," Steve laughed.

"I will ignore the last remark. Gentleman and ladies! I will keep it short. I did my undergrad work at Ohio State and headed East because it seemed like a cool thing to do. I am this close to graduating and am just so waiting for it. We are actually using the MBA material at Harvard, which justifies the sinking ship that is my trust fund to pay for this little adventure. It's tough to balance this job from homework because this is so much fun. What about you Paco?"

"It's like Brian and you said, my classes actually mean something. They are making me better. I graduate from Northeastern in May. And I've been drafted in the seventh round by the Los Angeles Dodgers to catch."

"No kidding," Steve said.

"Yeah, my parents through a big party for me; All my relatives and friends were here. It's not really a big thing. It's only the seventh round."

"How many kids play baseball in this country?"

"A lot."

"You got it. So judging by that standard it is kind of something."

"Yes, I guess."

"Why did you stay in school?"

"I just thought my parents would be so mad if I dropped out. I was afraid of my father," Rico said.

They finished eating and Steve paid for the tab, keeping the receipt for tax purposes and then they piled into the two cars. Lynne drove herself back to UMASS in her own car.

"Chief, our drawings are finished. We can go over them tomorrow if you want," Clarence and Mark spoke up before they left.

"All right, we'll do it after the game and then on Saturday, we'll display it for the team.

"Good. I'm up for that."

The weekend was filled with hockey as UVM (the University of Vermont) came from Burlington for Friday night. UVM was a good team but Steve seemed to be the best player on the ice without scoring a point. Boston University won 5-0. Steve was still voted second star for his suffocating defensive play.

The next night the Terriers went to Burlington and froze. It was cold. Steve scored twice in this one as the Terriers won 4-2.

Chapter 22

The season raced by as BU won game after game, by the beginning of February they were ranked first in the country. Steve was leading all defensemen in scoring and plus/minus. His play improved now that Laurie could make it to all the games. In the first week of February, the Bean Pot tournament came around and the four major schools in Boston were invited to play at the Bruins home ice, the TD Banknorth Garden, to play each other for bragging rights to Boston's major college hockey teams. It was the most prestigious college hockey tournament in the land. The Bean Pot.

The first night BU played Harvard who was ranked tenth in the country. The play was spirited with much physical play. Steve produced a tremendous hit on Harvard's star player in the second period drawing the cat calls from the Eagle fans not to mention making himself a target from the gentlemen from Harvard.

"Knock that stuff off?" The captain at Harvard said as he whistled by Steve.

"You guys from Harvard are nothing. Nothing at all but origami."

"What is origami?"

"It's Japanese paper art."

"Aren't you the clever one?"

"Stork taught it to me."

"You're listening to BC. For what? Tonight just shut up. Will, you please."

It turned out to be approximately the most thrilling Beanpot first round game ever. Harvard scored with forty-five seconds left in the game to take a one nothing lead. Coach Benson pulled his goalie and BU went on the attack. Steve got lucky when Harvard's goalie got his skate caught in the ice and he tripped and fell. Steve slipped the puck past him into the net. There were twenty-seven seconds left.

In twenty more seconds Steve passed a pass inside Harvard's blue line to Nate who blasted a slap shot into the upper corner giving BU a 2-1 win. They would play in the finals against BC the next week.

Steve found himself in the midst of a gaggle of reporters. They kept asking him one question after another about the thrilling victory. Steve answered them one by one until he looked at his watch and realized Laurie would be missing him and then he hung it up.

"Sorry, guys my girl's waiting."

He picked Laurie up by the bus and gave her a kiss.

"You get on your bus. I'll get on mine and we'll meet at the athletic center. Deal?" She asked.

"One more kiss first."

"Okay."

The bus home was raucous. Steve smiled contentedly in his seat until Nate caught up with him.

"Not in the mood to celebrate?" Nate asked.

"We haven't won anything yet. We have to go through BC and they're ranked sixth in the country."

"You have to learn to blow off steam brother."

"I just want to win this thing. It's my last."

"Relax, we'll win."

"You're pretty presumptuous."

"I don't know but we've been on fire all year. We're destined for good things."

"We got by with the skin of our teeth tonight."

"Yeah but we were victorious. No matter how desperate the situation, the better of a chance we have."

"I like those one's that aren't so desperate—nice, easy wins."

"What are you going to do tonight to help us win next Monday night?"

"Nothing. I guess."

"Look, we're going to Cap's Pizza when we get back. Why don't you bring Laurie?"

"Well, let me put it this way. If you could spend the night with her—not that you can—but if you could, what would you rather do get roaring drunk and eat pizza?"

"Okay! Okay! But I'm telling you, it's important that you lighten up. Have a little fun."

"All right, do you know I'm going to the NHL?"

"Yeah, it's been mentioned once or twice. So what a bunch of us are."

"Never in my life did I think I could see another city like that. I'm very lucky."

"You're a lucky man. Now will you have some fun?"

"Absolutely!"

The guys were in the back of the bus shooting the breeze and the subject gravitated toward beating BC.

Howard Franklin, a reserve winger asked Steve how he thought they could beat BC "Well, first we have to get through Maine this weekend and then we just have be faster than BC. We have to get to the puck quicker and hit the holes faster," Steve said.

"Man, you were great tonight," Rico Barrini said.

"If the goalie didn't trip we'd still be playing," Steve said.

"Are you going out with us?"

"Beers?""

"Cold wet ones."

"Yeah, that sounds good."

"Don't bring your lap top. Just come out with us."

"I can't bring my lap top.'

"Look, Linus please do it all at once if you like. Drink and be typing."

"I think you were right the first time."

The bus rolled into the parking lot by Agganis Arena and Steve unloaded his equipment bag so he could bring it to his locker.

"Hey, let's see if P.F. Chang's is relatively slow tonight," Steve said.

"What about T's?" Nate asked.

"T's is bombed. I have something important to say to the team about the team."

"All right! Everybody who has a car pile in."

So they went to the Chinese restaurant and ordered about ten kinds of food and drinks with little parasols in them to beers like Tsing-tao from China.

"Man, if it ain't a good feeling," Rico said.

"They are not as tough as they think they are, those Crimson aren't tough at all," Joe Barnum said, "I had those guys all night."

"What's the big announcement?" Mike Gaines asked.

"Guys," Steve stood up, "I hope you are enjoying so far. For the most part we are winning with effort. It's just we have to be careful, with what we have and that's talent. If we start coasting during a big win that other team is going to be upset and they may take liberties here and there. That leads to injuries, fights and suspensions. We don't need these. So I'll stop preaching and tell you guys played great tonight. We had an excellent time.

"How many beers have you had?" She asked when he got home.

"Four pina coladas!"

"Aren't those girls drinks?"

"I like coconut."

"Yes, actually I can too," she pushed closer toward him.

"You're my kind of girl."

"We'll have a Superbowl Party."

"Hopefully the Pats will be in it, right?

"What kind of question is that?"

"Oh, I forgot. My apologies, sir. The Cowboys and The Patriots."

"Whoever loses cooks and cleans supper for the week."

"Ooh! That's a nasty bet but I can take it. On second thought, that's kind of a big risk isn't it?"

"You're such a jerk. Besides my dad is coming to visit that weekend."

"But here from Texas!" He exclaimed.

"Don't worry! Dad won't bring his gun."

"Bring his gun?"

"They are both flying up next week to meet you. But they expect it to go well and they figure the Superbowl will be a cool way to get together."

"That's great they'll make the Beanpot. But we better start looking around for a house or we'll be renting a fishing boat."

"I was just teasing. Besides I wanted to find out if you really believed it. That'll be so cool playing at the football games."

"Is everything you think about related to sports?" She asked.

"Yes! And I'm mighty proud of it."

"A terminal adolescent," she smiled.

"Can I ask you a question?" She asked.

"Sure."

"What do you think it's going to be like with millions of dollars at our disposal?" She asked.

"I don't know. I really don't."

"What are you trying to do? Snow me?"

"What do you mean?"

"You haven't thought about it."

"Well, I'd get my parents a house at Cape Cod—the same as Annie and Tony."

"Are you going to get us a house?"

"We'll sleep on the North Shore."

She laughed.

"It'll be nice having money," he said, "The college kid bit is beginning to wear thin."

"Any charities in mind?"

"*The National Alliance of Mentally Ill*, *The United Way*, and .I'd like to do something special that I'm still thinking about. One for my brother and two for the children; that'll be enough! I don't want to get too spread out because if they want me to donate my time I want to have the time to give."

"I knew there was something about you I liked."

"What about you?"

"Well, I've begun to have more confidence in my playing. I'd really like to play in the Symphony."

"What brought you to music?"

"I don't know. Mom asked if I would like to try an instrument when I was about nine and I thought it would be fun so I tried the clarinet. It was neat. We hit it off right away and I had some talent for it."

"You still do."

"I know I was just going through some freshman self-doubts. I'm more confident now. I feel much more confident."

"We could go back to you room."

"Yes, that would be good."

"I need to talk to you first."

"I'm good at talking."

"Fair enough!"

They went back to her room and she lay down on the bed holding her favorite teddy bear.

"Okay? What's the scoop?" She asked.

"You look troubled."

"What kind of car do you have?" She asked.

"It's a four cylinder Mustang that can't get out of its own way if you shot it. What about you?"

"I have an old VW Beetle. I stress old."

"What do you want to drive?" He asked.

"I don't want something big, like a Cadillac. I kind of like Mercedes. You want a Jag right."

"Oh, you're right there miss."

"This is kind of neat."

"You little materialist you."

"Excuse me. But aren't you the one who wants the Jag?"

"Yes. But you looked troubled and you're making up stupid conversation."

"I saw a girl looking at you from the stands and she was looking, if you know what I mean."

"That's what's bothering you?"

"Sort of, "She answered sheepishly.

"Do I have to say anything else?"

"If I say anything, I'll incriminate myself."

"One of these days, I'm going to tickle you to your sides split. However, tonight I will let it fly because you were nervous because of the game. Let's change gears here. Did you come from means?"

"I came from some. Not terribly wealthy but we could afford vacations and stuff. We did all right. What about you?"

"The same; we had fun. I told my father he could retire. He said he wouldn't know what to do with himself. I told him to travel. He said maybe."

"Me too!"

"I'll get him tickets to Long Horn football."

"Her too! She's a bigger fan than him."

"What's their names?"

"Gregory and Alice."

"Are they tough on boyfriends and girlfriends?"

"Believe it or not they are pretty steady people."

"You've had experience with this."

"Just once. He was a real jerk."

"So you like me better."

"By yards."

"Oh! Don't I feel good."

"I always thought I had to go for my Masters but I don't feel I have to now. If I get to perform and have a baby, I'll be happy and that's the name of the game. What about you?"

"I'm going to finish my coursework early here and then I'm going to pursue my MBA."

"Why?"

"I just want to learn at this point."

"Learn about what."

"If I tell you my secret, secret plan will you believe me and not tell anyone about it."

"Tell me kind sir."

"I'm serious. You have to shut up about this."

"Okay, I will keep my mouth shut."

"A company based on the fans where they could read about and see action photos of their favorite athletes."

"I just want to let you know from a girlfriend's standpoint—it sounds like *Sports Illustrated*."

"That's why it will be easier to work in conjunction with *Time Corp.* I definitely need more schooling and hockey isn't going to be there all in forever. I know some guys from BU and I'll meet some people from where I continue my education. God willing. I'll learn there. He stopped and she looked at his feet. He ran his finger under her cap and brushed her blonde hair away. She looked up into his eyes and bent down slowly to kiss her. His lips reached hers and they held tight until they couldn't breathe anymore.

She opened her top draw in her bureau. She reached in and pulled out a picture of Bobby Orr scoring "the goal."

"It's yours," she said.

"Are you serious? With the frame it must've cost a mint. You didn't have to do that."

"I love you," she smiled.

He put the picture down on the desk and carried her to bed. They love and she cried a little.

"Hey! It's okay!"

He held her and rocked her gently.

"What are you crying for?" He asked.

"Hold me."

"I am."

"Tighter."

He held her tighter and said.

"Hey, what is wrong? You're scaring me."

"I've never been so in love."

She trembled in his arms and he held her close.

"Do you want to get married?" He asked.

"Yes."

"Good! Then I'll announce the engagement when your parents arrive."

"What about your parents?"

"The following week."

"Oh boy."

"Nothing like churning 'em out on a regular timetable."

"I guess so."

"We're really friends. Aren't we?"

"Yes, we are. We going to be married knucklehead. We better be."

"What I meant to say it isn't just hormones."

"Well, it is a little bit hormones."

"Well, at least you're honest."

"Absolutely not."

"Hell no!"

"Very good answer."

He held her close and pushed herself close to him and closed her eyes. He ran his fingers through her blonde hair. A few minutes later he asked.

"Do you want to make love?"

She kissed him passionately.

"So that's a 'yes?'"

"You are so anticipatory."

Afterwards he asked if she was okay.

"I'm just thinking."

"About what?"

"My wedding dress."

"Nice and white."

"Very funny."

"We'll have it designed."

"Uh-huh. I'll wear my mothers."

"Okay then. I'll guess I'll have to wear a tux."

"I guess you will."

"Everybody says playing in Boston has a lot of distractions."

"Yeah, I know."

"What does that mean?"

"Could it possibly mean women?" She smiled.

"No, it could not."

"We've already been over this."

"I just wanted to hear it again."

"You're driving me crazy."

"I just wanted you to know I'm in the game."

"You are the game."

"Give me a kiss."

He kissed her deeply and then said.

"I have to go. I'm sorry. I have work to do."

"Goodnight my love," she stuck her tongue out at him.

"Oh! That hurts!"

She blushed and then giggled.

"I'll see you tomorrow," he winked.

"One more thing?" She demanded—asked.

"What?"

"I need advice."

"About?"

"My mother and father have the chance of a lifetime to move to California for the summers and my mother doesn't want to. Something about she grew up in that house and she isn't leaving it—even for three months. My father is trying to explain to her in the most polite way he can that she may like it.

"And she said, 'I'll know I'll like it. That's the problem. Everyone likes it out there. Pretty soon I'll be giving up all the memories of my youth. And I need those as much as I can get.' What would you do?"

"Start her off on one month vacations. She can't OD on Hollywood that quickly. Besides they have real good baseball out there—even the minors."

"Did you ever study anything besides sport?"

"I don't really know. It's been so long since I read a book. I'm good at life."

"Right."

"I wish I could just read the book but I have to worry about what the professor is looking for and what I'm supposed out of it and then what it really is according to the professor. I do read miss and I'm offended by my own remark."

"You better go home."

"You think?"

"Yeah."

When he arrived back in the dorm, Nate was there hopping up and down.

"What is wrong with you?" Steve asked.

"*USA TODAY* wants to interview us."

"Really, that's kind of cool. When?"

"Next Wednesday at eleven o'clock…"

"Hey! That fits into my schedule."

"I know I looked at it. Ain't this cool."

"Did they give a hint about what we were going to talk about?"

"No. He just said he wanted to talk about our experience as college hockey players."

"Okay. I'll give it a whirl. What else is new?"

"I met someone."

"Female?"

"Yes, wise guy."

"Well, what's she like?"

"Well, she's from Colorado. She's an English major. She wants to be a writer."

"Is she good looking?"

"Yeah, she is but you have yours."

"Are you kidding?"

"Okay, okay. How is Laurie?"

"We're engaged. We just have to tell her parents this weekend and then mine the following weekend. We'll see."

"Think it will be like last time?"

"Nothing will be like last time; we were destined to fail."

"Okay. Don't get me involved."

"Buddy, I really have to study but there's one thing I have to ask you."

"Sure?"

"What it is it?"

"What's like being mixed race?"

"Nothing out of the ordinary; it depends on who you meet. Some people think their whole life went wrong because of it. Some people, like me don't bring it up because they want to be known as a hockey player, or a journalist or a businessman. I have other things to worry about. I'm worried sick about being a good father and she's not even pregnant yet.

"Mostly, though, I know I wouldn't trade the country I'm in to do it any other place in the world. You know how it is. You run into jerks and you run into nice people. I like my heritage. I'm comfortable, different and the same but they are always people. To make it a short answer; I'm not going to go out stealing cars or doing other nefarious stuff. Now, I don't know which part gives me the moral standing to do this…"

"All right, I got it. Thank you very much."

"You're a glutton for punishment."

"Yes, I am."

Chapter 23

The Friday night game against the Maine Black Bears in Orono, Maine was pretty much a circus. Instead of a grinding game like the last two, there was plenty open ice, free skating, and quick passing activity. Steve couldn't believe Maine wanted to try and Match BU to its strength. He especially liked the wide-open play. He scored two assists with two long passes over the centerline from the defensive zone. He also scored twice BU won 7-4.

After the game, Steve met Laurie's parents briefly but successfully in front of the fan's bus just before boarding the team bus. He thought they were nice people but anticipated a grilling tomorrow night after the game in Boston at the coffee shop.

The second game, in Boston, produced another lop-sided victory for BU. Maine just couldn't keep up with the speed of BU. The final score was 8-3 with Steve piling up four assists. Steve hurried out of the locker room afterwards.

"Mr. and Mrs. Jones. I hope you enjoyed the games."

"You were spectacular," Mrs. Jones said.

"Come on. Let's go to the coffee shop," Laurie said.

Steve could feel Mr. Jones eyes on him like he was sizing him up. They arrived at the coffee shop and found a table.

"So, what's the big announcement?" The father finally smiled.

"We're engaged," Steve said.

"And how long have you known each other?" His father asked.

"Long enough," Steve said more confrontational than he wanted.

"You're going to take her out to Boston?" Mrs. Jones asked.

"Mom, don't worry. We can talk to each other. I hate to admit it but he's a very nice guy," Laurie said.

"Oh, are you?" His father asked and sipped his latte.

"Dad!" Laurie exclaimed but her voice broke and she started to cry.

"When are the nuptials supposed to take place?" His father asked.

"This summer some time," Steve said.

"You are talking about my only daughter."

"I know, sir."

"She's your friend."

"Yes, sir."

"Well, the Lord bless you both then."

"Mamm?" Steve looked at Mrs. Jones.

"It's okay," she smiled as her voice cracked.

"Are you staying for the Beanpot tomorrow night?"

"We were planning to go to a nice restaurant and watch the game from the bar," Mr. Jones said.

"You're kidding," Laurie laughed.

"You can't do that. I have comp tickets. My parents can't come and they're just burning a whole in my pocket. It's live!"

"Wouldn't that be fine?" Mrs. Jones asked.

"Are you kidding me? That would be fabulous," his father said.

"Can I speak to you for a minute?" Mr. Jones directed his question at Steve.

"Sure. Let's go outside."

'Oh, Lord,' Steve thought, 'I'm dead.'

"Have you and my daughter been together?"

"Romantically?"

"If that's what you want to call it."

"Sir, I love her and for the record we have—twice."

"It's awfully hard talking about this but she's been bombing us with e-mails about this great new guy she met. You said twice—right?"

"That would be me. Yes, sir."

"Yes, that would be you."

"You don't want details. Do you?"

"Well, my daughter has picked an honest man."

Mr. Jones extended his hand.

"Welcome to the family."

They went back inside and talked a little while longer and then Steve excused himself so that he could get back for bed check.

"I'll be right back," Laurie said to her parents.

"Tagging along are you?" Steve teased.

"Don't be a jerk. Slow down. Will you?"

"Yes, mamm."

"Do you want a kiss goodnight or not?"

"Do you realize that you're parents are sitting thirty feet away?"

"Will you kiss me please? Geeze you're such a spaz."

So Steve kissed her very quickly.

"How was that?"

"It was lacking."

"You're parents are over there!" He exclaimed.

"Well, look at it this way. They'll definitely know you love me."

"That's a point. So? You want to do this again."

"Hmm. Hmm."

Steve kissed her deeply and then he tilted her back. After a minute, he pulled her back up.

"They're mighty curious," he smiled.

"Well they've got to grow up sometime."

"How about I just start walking to my dorm?"

"Why don't you do that?"

"Bye-bye sweetheart."

"You're such a chicken."

"Hey, give me a break. He shook my hand."

"You better back me next week when you're parents get here."

"Yes, dear."

The next night BU lined up against BC, who was now ranked third in the country. Steve skated quickly during warm ups and adjusted his helmet until he put it on comfortably. Nate skated over to him.

"What do you think?" Nate asked.

"That's why I'm here."

Nate tapped him on the shins.

"Good luck," the captain said.

Steve found Cameron O'Hilery during warm ups. The Maroon and Gold C on his uniform shown brightly on his left shoulder.

"We're going whip your butt tonight," Steve said.

"I don't talk to people like you."

"That's because you have to respect your betters and it pisses you off."

"In your ear."

"Look, man you come from a peaceful school. I come from a peaceful school. Why can't we just be friends?"

"Because this is a hockey game. I hear Stork is your buddy. Go talk to him."

"I'll do that."

Steve zipped past the goaltender's net.

"Your Captain is an idiot."

"Oh, you've met Cam. Actually, he's a great guy—helps the other guys study with their homework. You're just wearing the wrong color jersey."

"He's cruising for a bruising Stork."

"I'll tell him that."

"You do that."

The puck dropped at center ice from then on it was up and down action the whole first period. Both teams relied heavily on their goal tending. Steve picked up an assist and, a goal late in the period; as BU took a two to nothing win, as the points stood up. BU was able to pose at center ice with the Bean Pot trophy. Steve was relieved. He definitely didn't want to play poorly in front of Laurie's parents.

"Free dinner. That's going taste so good," Steve smiled.

"I can't believe you guys," Cameron said as he fought to control his anger.

"Look Cameron, don't get upset. All you have to do is think how much exercise you got. If you just look at it like a good skate, you'll be fine. The Bean Pot is ours."

"You, know in the World Juniors, you were the same cocky little so and so."

"Why don't you like BU?"

"You're a professional hockey team with a minor league school."

"How about we're better?"

"No. We are."

"Not tonight, Jack."

"Look at all the stuff we have. All you've got is a stinking hockey arena."

"Look I'm not going to fence with you. Shut up and go to the locker room because if I get tossed for fighting, I'm going to beat your brains out."

"I'll see you around."

"Heck, I hired half your team. You think they're going to come after me?"

"Why didn't you ask me?"

"Is that what you're mad at?"

"Yes!"

"Tomorrow, I will call you in the morning. We will have lunch at Corrnwall's on me in case your busted and we will figure this out. Okay?"

"I'm from Canada?"

"Get your 'green card?'"

"You can be really sickening. Do you know that?"

"Yes, I am. I practice it at home in front of the mirror."

"No earlier than ten o'clock."

"I think you'll find the Little Red Schoolhouse quite a busy place."

"You guys still didn't have Doug Flutie."

"Nobody had Doug Flutie. He was God's quarterback."

It was kind of hectic after the game with reporters wanting to talk to Steve and him trying to rush out the door to get to see the Joneses.

"Ladies and gentlemen, I really have to go," he finally said.

"Have a hot date."

"Yes, as a matter of fact I do."

"You going to let us in on it."

"Look you people can ask me whatever your heart desires but my friends and family are private."

They grumbled a little but Steve finally got to take a shower and get dressed.

Steve went over to the Jones' family for a brief moment and then hopped on the team bus back to the Agganis Center. Laurie took the bus full of fans and her parents drove back to the hotel. Steve sat back in the seat on the bus and closed his eyes.

Nate popped up and jostled him.

"Wake up! We just won the Beanpot and you're tournament MVP."

"Ungh. You're worse than the press."

"You look like you've had a rough weekend. What happened?"

"I asked for Laurie's hand in marriage to her parents."

"And."

"You ever been successful at something that scared you to death; it's like your heart stops and you can't hear anything. And the only thing you do is say 'Yes, mamm,' or 'No, sir.' Then you actually pull it off. Now that's amazing."

"You were really shook up—weren't you?"

"Absolutely! Yes. It was her parents for crying out loud."

"Did you tap dance?"

"No. I'm not very good at that. He asked me if I was her friend. I thought that was a classy thing to do. They have an eight o'clock out of Logan tomorrow morning. I have a late class so I'll be up early to accompany them."

"Is Laurie happy?"

"She didn't try and pull the daddy's little girl deal. I hope she's happy. Geeze***"

Nate laughed.

"Well you probably don't want to hit the town."

"I have to go to bed unfortunately. Boy, I'm so relieved I feel like a bowl of Jell-O."

"You have a hand in one point and a goal in the other four points and you're this spazzed out."

"A hockey game is a hockey game but meeting your in-laws for the first time scares you."

"It won't scare me," Nate smiled.

"Right."

"It won't!"

"Go away."

Nate laughed.

They rode the rest of the way together with Steve wondering if he could spend some time alone with Laurie before he went to bed. When it seemed they finally hit campus, Steve was wondering if he could articulate what this weekend would do for their relationship because he was so happy that Mr. and Mrs. Jones liked him however, he didn't want to sound like a blithering idiot.

"Hi!" She smiled as he got off the bus.

"I'll walk you home. I want to hear the way you normally speak."

"Are you sure?"

"I like it."

"You were spectacular tonight," she said in her normal voice.

"I was so nervous. I wanted to play well for your parents. I actually can't believe they liked me."

"That's cause you're a jerk. Of course they were going to like you. I've been bombing them with e-mail since we met."

"You should go into politics. You can be a speech writer."

"I don't know about that. I think I like my music too much."

"Where are your parents?"

"I told them to go to the hotel and get some rest."

"You told them?"

"I was feeling invincible. What a great night!"

"Come on. I'll walk you home."

"Let's get a coffee."

He looped his arm around her shoulders and gingerly walked down Comm. Ave.

"Are you going to miss this place?" She asked.

"I don't know. I'm just trying to win the rest of our games. I haven't had time to get nostalgic yet. I'm going to miss the camaraderie with the guys and there are a couple of Profs I'd like to stay in touch with. I guess yes but life is moving so fast. It stinks. When you first get here, you don't want to leave and then by the time you're a senior things seem so familiar that anything out there seems better. You have to be careful I guess or which 'road is less traveled by.'"

"You're too serious about what you do. You should lighten up."

"It's the only way I know to be successful. I'm successful because I prepare not because I'm especially fast or big. If I look too far ahead, I'll lose."

"When do you relax?"

"At the end of every season, I take two weeks to go see some movies that I haven't seen. Maybe take some time to relax but then I get itchy and I get back in the gym and on the ice."

"What are we going to do after the year is over?"

"Well, I have to find an agent. You go back to Texas and we burn up our cell phone minutes talking to each other until I sign a contract. I hope it's not messy. I just wanted a good, fair contract."

"How much do you think?"

"I don't know—seventy million-seventy-five million over four years. Maybe more but how fast can you spend seventy or seventy-five million. If they came to me and said, 'Hey we can get that guy, if we restructure your contract.' And the guy's an all-star? Well, heck, I just want to win. I'll be taken care of. They'll be endorsements and so forth. I'll do all right."

"Just don't get short changed."

"Yes, mamm***"

"Hockey's a hard game. Were you good at any other sports?"

"I was a good field—no hit shortstop for my high school team. I think I could've made the basketball team but I would've just been a role player—not scholarship material."

"I like you a lot. I like talking to you," she smiled.

"Come on, let's get you home. Morning will come soon."

"I've just started my coffee," she smiled.

"I want to call Tony," Steve said.

"Aw, man I was hoping you'd call. You guys were awesome. How's Stork taking it?"

"He ain't happy. He's a competitor. He wants to win. He just can't beat us. And that for 'the love of Mike' gets him in a wild, Irish rage. He's getting over it over a beer. It's all in good fun, if something ever happened to either one of us on the ice, we'd probably get flowers sent to each us just to know they cared. They'd go out the window in about two seconds but that's beside the point. He went to the wrong school. What do you want from me?"

"How are you feeling?"

"Better. I got a little nervous at the pizza place but it worked out. I calmed down."

"Well, good news. I'm sending e-mail to everyone saying the real thing is Sunday. They submit their final projects and then Brian, myself, and John Davis will pour over them and then send them out to whomever they concern. I got the business permit. We're listed as LLP a limited partnership."

"Geeze, this is for real."

"Can you believe it?"

"Tony, I just want you to know you're doing an exceptional job. You really are looking good. You're a valuable member of the team."

"You aren't saying that because I have mental illness. Are you?"

"A little."

"You moron."

"Well, I didn't know how you would react when this started. We're a little informal. I thought you weren't cognizant of the fact that this is a real job."

"Me and everybody else."

"I'm just proud of you man. That's all."

"I can't wait for Sunday."

"Me too."

"Look, I have to go to bed. I have afternoon classes so I can get some shut eye."

"Call me tomorrow."

Steve went home and studied for about an hour and a half and then fell asleep. He woke up at 7:30 and he called John Davis on his cell phone.

"Hey, it's your boss. Good morning."

"Ungh!"

"Ungh! What?"

"Come on man it's seven am."

"It's 7:30. Wake up! Start the day refreshed and ready to go."

"All right. What's going on?"

"Well, we're into this whole magazine concept but what we have to do is come up with why the Tour of Italy is worth more than the Italian readership to the United States and since you're kind of swinging between projects, I want demographics. I want you to take five people and start looking. People that are good at analysis and have them take five events around the world besides the Olympics because we draw then and I want you to analyze them. Don't spend too much time on one country or too many events. Have Stork and Japanese baseball be the first look."

"Geeze, if we ain't doing this."

"I think I found a Chief Financial Officer. You'll never guess in a million years."

"Who?"

"The one, the only, Cameron O'Hilery."

"You are joking."

"Not at all. Actually, it's not a bad buy. If he played for BU, I would've been chasing him down in a minute."

"We have Stork and Cam. Two BC guys."

"And?"

"Look, I hate to tell you something. Between you and me it's little joke—sometimes they get littler as the night goes on. However, there are some guys that want either side all dead. It's nothing personal but that's the way it is."

"That's when the art of conversation comes in. You ask them is if their game 100 per cent or could it be better. They ask you the same thing. Say for instance, 'Number three likes to slash so watch it;' and so forth and so on. It's called fraterenarazation with the enemy but it keeps the injuries down and gives the fans some excitement when he's chased into the boards by three guys. It's fair and it's legal and the only punk who has a chance of getting hurt is the guy out there to deliberately hurt other guys. It works for about eighty-five per cent of the league and it works for me."

"I never knew that's how it was played."

"There are guys that don't belong playing college in my opinion. So you may have tell the Captain, "Hey, that number 12 of yours cross checked too much last night. My guys are mad at him. You tell him to knock it tonight. There are good Captains and there are bad captains.

"I'm putting you in a position of leadership role. Sometimes people don't play fair. If there's people doing the 'I want to impress the boss hokey-pokey. You're going to get some of that. You have to have to get them back to 'team thinking.' I don't expect anyone cross checking anything. However, you have strong personalities that want to succeed; more than that their presentation in their mind has to be the best.

"I like or formation so far but as we grow there's going to be a need for more management positions. I think you have the right tools for it. "

"So this is trial and error."

"More trial than error. John, just play it the way you feel it."

"Look, I can do what I do. I'm great at Marketing. I've been trained for it at Harvard no less. Why? How sure of your success ratio on this one?"

"Moving you to management? Fairly high! The group likes you. And you're the first person to raise your hand in the meetings. However, you have something else."

"Which is?"

"You're unselfish and you give credit to the other people. Yet, on the other hand you take the lead when necessary. Somehow, you make the people feel that. They don't get screwed by your own manager for working hard to develop your own ideas. You'll do a fine job. You just have to have confidence in yourself."

"I hate to bring this up. Mistakes?"

"We'll deal with them as they come. Don't get all freaked out. I have got make a phone call at ten o'clock to the Crown Prince himself. "

"Why did you hire him? You haven't said anything nice about him yet?"

"He's all everything and sometimes guys like that have to be taken down a peg."

"And when they don't?"

"Let them go and do their thing."

"I have no experience with real leadership, you know?"

"You had to lead something."

"I always positioned myself as a good worker. And I worked like heck but I don't know if I can do it at this level."

"Dude, you're good at seeing walls but not the ladders to get over them. For absolutely once, please, could you think of yourself as a success? You made it through Ohio State and Harvard with honors. At this point in your life, I don't know what to say. Just take the next step and you begin to enjoy yourself. The team likes you and they'll work for you. Who do you like for the team?"

"Demarco, Gaines, Vivenzio, Davidson, Stavros Vargas and the Stork."

"That's six."

"I need them."

"You got them. Why not any Euros or Scandis?"

"I'm afraid they won't be here if they don't make the NHL and NHL teams demand more of them as acclimating to the league and culture. I'm scrambling that they can help out back home. What I'm concerned with is that when the guys turn pro—how big is there commitment going to stay. I am giving them heavy assignments now in hopes that they like what we're doing so much they'll continue once they get the dollar or the Euro depending on where they're playing next year. "

"Are you sure that's the reason?"

"To be perfectly frank, this American Company founded on American ideals. I think we should sway towards them a little. The Euros and so forth can be considered as welcome guests for sure but our company is our company."

"That's why I can count on you John because you're so diplomatic. You watched Rush Limbaugh when you were a kid. Didn't you? Look, in the interest of this project, we have to have people over there. In order for you to make an informed decision instead of assuming; talk to each one of them. Air your concerns because I don't want it to look like 'British are coming;' in reverse. Okay? Do me a favor on this one will you?"

"Yes, sir. I am learning on the job. "

"Meet you for dinner at the Greenhouse at five to discuss things further."

"Good, enough. I'll bring Rawlings. He owes me a dinner. Free food."

"Fine by me."

Steve dressed warmly because the weather was well below freezing. He started off for the dorm and when he arrived she was waiting in the lobby.

"Geeze, you look terrible," she said.

"I think I slept last night."

"That's not good for you."

"Yes, mother. I couldn't help it. I was on an adrenaline high. I was so fired up about the project's progress."

"Who are you playing?"

"The University of New Hampshire, Can you do me a favor and play something?"

"Sure. Sit down on the bed."

She played delicately and he closed his eyes and lie down on the bed.

"This may be an odd subject to bring up but did you ever think of making love?" He asked.

"With you?"

"Very funny."

"Yes. I have but this morning? Right this second? Absolutely not!"

"And that's your final decision."

"I have to go to class genius."

"Can I hold you at least?"

"Yeah, I think you can."

For fifteen minutes they held each other and then she said.

"Let's go."

"Oh, okay. I should shut my mouth."

"No. You can keep it flapping. I know you make no sense anyway."

"We'll marry and I promise I'll keep teasing you for the rest of my life."

"Well, thank you."

She turned her head back and laughed and he squeezed her hand.

"Good. I would say the same for me but I never get stressed," she smiled devilishly.

"You have changed. That girl I met before wasn't as confident."

"My music is getting better and I have you."

"I love you Laurie."

"I know. I love you too."

He held her close for a while and didn't speak. She pressed herself against him and brushed her hair in the mirror while touching up her make up. He smiled and called good luck.

"Make sure you lock the door on the way out!"

She kissed him.

"Yes, dear."

His cell rang as he was walking back to his room.

"Hello?"

"It's Jack Rawlings."

"Jack, my brother. How are you?"

"I'm cutting film for my project. The architect included a movie theatre, right?"

"Yes, definitely."

"Look, I know cut down is Sunday but can I have it extended until Tuesday?"

"Can't do it brother; Gotta be done by Sunday."

"Oh, well sleep is overrated. Do me a favor: meet me here at 4 p.m. on Saturday. I can show you what I've been working on. I can't take the equipment from the school."

"All right. You got it. Tell me it's something hot Jack."

"Smoking!"

"Harvard men."

"Hey, you're going to be a Harvard man. Don't eat too much pizza. I'll take you out to dinner. The concept I have is stupendous."

"Well, I'm glad you have some excitement for the project."

"It's huge, dude."

"Okay."

Steve showed up the next night with a navy sports jacket, white dress shirt, blue tie, tan chinos and black wing tips. He also brought the roses.

"Hi! Boy, do you look good," she smiled.

"Do you like the roses?"

"They're beautiful. Is it you're birthday or something?"

"You have fifteen minutes to get dressed. We're going to the Twenty-one for dinner."

"Why?"

"I'm taking you out to dinner. Hurry up! The clock's running."

"Call a cab. You don't have to tell me twice."

She whipped into her closet and then into the bathroom.

"Call a cab," she said on the way by.

"Okay."

They jumped into the back of the cab and he held her hand as the yellow cab drove off from the curb.

"I'm impressed," she said.

"Have a nice time tonight. That's what it was meant for."

"Why was it meant for tonight?"

"Because I'm practicing."

"For what?"

"For our real engagement; when I get you the ring."

She laughed richly.

"Are you laughing at me?" He blushed.

"Yes! I didn't know you were so worried."

"I just want it to come off right."

"You're hysterical. You really are. All this fuss and bother for a little, Texas girl like me."

"You're running with this aren't you."

"Yes, I am. This is great! I'm being treated like a queen."

"Well, I'm glad you're enjoying it."

The cab ride was adventurous, skipping though the Boston traffic, and eventually landing at the famous steakhouse twenty-one.

"Can I ask you a question?" She looked up at him from the menu.

"Sure. Tonight's your night."

"How are you paying for this?"

"I had jobs over the summer? I saved money. Look if I could only afford your night at McDonald's then I probably wouldn't be with you because you deserve more than that."

"Are you sure?" Her voice trembled.

He held up his water glass.

"Cheers," he said.

"Look at this way," he continued," I could blow it on CD's or something, "I'd much rather give you a night."

"Fair enough but I get the tip."

"Are you crazy? This is your night. I better change the subject. Do you think being in the pros will be different? We went to college in Boston? How different can it be?"

"It will be too much."

"Too much of what?"

"It's going to be a blast."

"Honestly. I just want you to be sure."

"I'm going to step on your foot if you keep this up."

"Really."

"Will you please stop?"

"Laurie, I just wanted this practice night to happen so I knew I wasn't forcing you into anything."

"Honey, a steak isn't going to force me into anything no matter how good it is."

"Okay. Just checking!"

They ate their dinner quietly; Steve kept looking at her in the half-light. She was beautiful.

"Sweetheart, there's one other thing we haven't discussed."

"This better be good."

"Children?"

"Eventually?"

"That's not what I meant. Mental illness runs in my family and there's a chance however small that I could pass it on."

She looked up with tears in eyes.

"So this has been what's eating you," she said.

"Sort of."

"I have this dream sometimes. We're married and everything's going fine and then my son is diagnosed with mental illness and he kills himself because the disease wins. I don't know. "

"We'll put it in the Lord's hands,"

"I guess so. It feels terrible that it could come from you. You know? It's not like they break their leg playing hockey. It's part of your genetic makeup that's wrong."

"I think you're worrying way beyond what you should be worried about. I'd bet anything on you. We'd be able to handle it."

"I love you so much."

"Just tell me next time what's bothering you."

They each had a coffee and then took the cab back to her dorm.

"Can you stay a while?" she asked.

"I can't believe I'm saying this but I have to study. I'm sorry."

She kissed and hung onto him.

"It'll be okay Steven. Whatever happens we face it together."

The next day, in class, Steve was day dreaming big time and his professor caught him. Steve looked like an idiot. He finally stumbled out the correct answer to the calculus equation.

"Sorry," Steve said.

"You don't have a game until Friday night. Keep your head in the books. Do you understand?"

"Yes, Mr. Cooper."

The rest of the class snickered and Steve was guilty about thinking about Providence College. He was also thinking about Tony and his parents. He also wanted to call Tony and his parents. He found Laurie studying in the Sherman Union on the way back from his embarrassing moment in Calculus class.

"Hi," he said.

"Hello," she smiled.

"Good news. My brother is doing better. He's been really energized by this job."

"That's fantastic."

"They are going to the game Saturday. Your turn."

"Oh!"

"What do you mean? Oh?"

"Well, I can be nervous."

"Don't worry kid. They'll love you. What are you studying?"

"Music Theory and Composition."

"Sounds interesting?"

"It's pretty interesting. I'd much rather be playing though."

"Will you be free tonight?"

"Yeah, sure. Not another 21."

"No, just a quick sandwich somewhere."

"Deal."

Chapter 24

They met later that night at her dorm.

"Let's go for a walk," she smiled.

On the way, they met a couple of Steve's teammates Bob Wilson and Dick Hermon.

"What brings you out on such a frigid night?" Bob asked.

"My fiancee wanted to go for a walk," Steve answered.

"Not cold enough for you in Texas. You had to come here," Dick smiled.

"You guys are hockey players and you're afraid of the cold," she giggled.

"We're dainty," Wilson grinned.

"You're wimps!" She laughed.

They all laughed too.

"See you at practice tomorrow," Dick said.

"Bye, Laurie," Bob said.

They walked for a little while and ended up down by Emerson College.

"Let's keep going to Newbury Street," She tugged at his arm.

"You sure! It's cold!"

Two youngsters noticed Steve and Laurie crossing the street and they waited for the couple. When they made it across, the two boys pounced.

"Mr. Thompson, my name is Matt Stanley and this is my brother Chris. Can we have your autograph?"

The little boy jammed his pen and pad in Steve's face.

"Whoa! Big Man. Take it easy. Let me see here. 'To Matt and Chris from BU number seven Steve Thompson. Best wishes to you both and hopes of a fine hockey career," Steve then signed it.

"All right, where do you want to go?" Steve asked after he patted the boys on the head and sent them on their way after "Thank-you's" were exchanged.

"There's an art gallery," she said.

"Paintings or photography?" Steve asked.

"Paintings."

"Let's go see it."

There was some really beautiful stuff in there which Steve took some time to admire seriously for when he signed his contract.

"There's a used bookstore down the street I want to go see," Laurie said.

"Aren't these beautiful?" He asked her.

"I especially like the one of the cottage by the lake. Now that's beautiful."

"Well, when my contract gets signed." He asked.

"Well, we'll come back another day. Let's go to the bookshop."

"Okay. What's with you and old books?"

"It's like going to a cemetery and checking out the old headstones. It's a piece of your past."

"Honey, that's weird."

"It is not."

"Well, you lost me on the gravestone thing."

"You go to the cemetery and look at the old stones. For instance, a woman dies in her early fifties and she has twelve kids."

"Busy."

"Well, the times were different then. You wonder did she have a happy life or a sad life. Was she ill or well? It's the same thing with books. They let you in for a glimpse at the moors of the times."

"I'll get you one," he offered.

"Come on I like these little pocket books. They're mysteries. They're kind of pap but it's fun."

"Pick one you like."

She picked one with a blue cover and the title *Witches' Brew*."

"Take lessons?" He asked with a devilish smile on his face.

"I can handle it on my own."

"I've never seen it."

"You'll know. Trust me."

"Could you give me some advance warning so I can head it off at the pass?"

"For instance, never say anything bad about the Dallas Cowboys."

"How 'bout dem boys? Huh?"

"Exactly."

"And?"

"Don't mess with my man."

"God bless Texas," and then he thought a moment, "Hey, how come I came in second to the Cowboys?"

"The most important one was second."

"Oh!"

"Anywhere else you want to go?"

"There's a couple of more art galleries and a Persian rug dealer," she said.

"Well, we better hurry. It's getting late."

"Right!"

They walked for another five miles it seemed, stopping at several shops along the way.

"Are you up for some quiet time in my bed room?"

"Sure but what's going on?"

"I'll tell you inside. It's kind of private."

"Is this like life and death? You aren't trying to break up with me. Are you?"

"Don't be stupid."

"Well, we better get back then. We should stop for dinner first."

"Why?"

"Because I'm hungry; We'll get take out at Burger King."

"All that fat and cholesterol; that's gross!"

"I'll take you to Sherman and you can get a salad. Fair?"

"Deal."

"What's wrong?"

"Nothing's wrong exactly."

"However?"

"We aren't home yet."

"There's nobody here on the street. It's just us. Talk to me!"

"All right. I was thinking ahead. You see I need a plan. I just can't wing it."

"A little faster because I don't know what you're talking about."

"Well, I was laying in bed this morning."

"I wish I could've seen that."

"Thanks! Anyway, I was thinking about babies."

"Well, at this point it's impossible."

"True but summer is coming, and you know what that means."

"It'll be hot."

"In more ways than one***"

"And you were asking me?"

"I want to finish my Masters before we start a family."

'That's what you were so nervous about telling me. I got you a coincidence—me too!"

"Oh! Good! I thought I was going to end up a drop out."

"Well, you're not. So take it easy. Geeze, I thought you were breaking up with me."

"You always think I'm breaking up with you."

"That's only because you're so gorgeous. In many ways, you're out of my league."

"Oh! Am I?"

She was blushing deeply and he put his arm around her.

"I'd just like having you around because you're a nice guy. When I really to talk to a nice person, I talk to you."

He gave her a little squeeze and she pressed against him.

"I mean it," she said.

"I know. You're my friend. No matter if you are in Texas, California, or Boston you're my friend and I love you."

They stopped for a moment and he kissed her for a long time. When they finally broke apart, he looked at her. She was crying.

"We'll be married," he said.

"I know. Damn you. You got me all riled up."

"Sorry, I think."

"Drop me off at the dorm."

"I can't come inside."

"Please."

"Why?"

"Because it's my place and not yours***"

"Come on."

"Look, Smiley, if I go in there with you things will happen that I don't want to happen until I'm good and ready."

"That's all you had to say. Geeze!"

"Well, I thought you used your powers of perception to figure it out."

"Well, to be honest with you. I figured the same thing for a different reason."

She burst out laughing.

"You're such a jerk."

"I love you."

"You're my saving grace."

They pulled up in front of the door.

"So what are you going to do for the rest of the night?" He asked.

"I'm going to read my used book. And you?"

"I'm going to go sit in a bucket of ice."

"You're nuts," she giggled.

"Have a nice night, miss."

When he arrived back at the dorm, Nate was studying furiously for a test he had in International Marketing.

"Nice night?"

"Yeah, kind of a cool ending though."

"No-chance-no-way!"

"Yep! Did my dad call?"

"Oh. I forgot! He did! He said everything's AOK! Tony does better every day."

"That's a relief. I'll call him tomorrow in between classes. Study hard. I'm going upstairs.

He brought his cell phone and called Brian.

"Hello," Steve said.

"Hey," Brian answered.

"You ready for Sunday?" Steve asked.

"Yeah, I am. Have you decided on the linguist?"

"I say thumbs down. He should have a job working for the government.

Brian I just can't hire indiscriminately. He may be a nice guy and I wish him well but it would be difficult to fit him in to the corporate structure."

"We have a corporate structure?"

"Yes, we do. Things are moving fast. After we do the markups we're sending the letters out and then the fun begins. If you act big league from the beginning and follow through on what you say, you will be big league."

"You know some think that you would work eighty hours a week on this company if you didn't have school and hockey? Can't you talk like normal stuff?"

"Brian, I've measured that against myself by myself and have discovered that I have to do it this way. You make sacrifices, if you can call them that. Sure, I'd like to be more personable and talk about your girl but I don't have the time. It's not that I don't have the inclination. It's just that everything's put into this story."

"And I'm telling you that's not healthy. You're my friend man. You're going to burn yourself out and your heads going to be in the middle of next week."

"Okay, how's Boston College."

"Did you ever notice there's a grave yard by one of the dorms?"

"I know. I know BC's a competitive school but what's the deal?"

"Alumni like to get buried there."

"That's gross Brian."

"We should go to one of the basketball games this year."

"I can't do that. I don't have enough time."

"Shut up and come."

"Okay. Just forgot for a second. No problems here."

"Good we'll set a date tomorrow. I lost the damned school. If you bring one notebook or set of pens, I will kill you."

"Okay. I get it."

"Now, I have a problem with the company."

"Brian!"

"Listen. Here me out. That guy Chuck Witherspoon is a stiff. All he does is bring negative energy to the meetings. The guy doesn't know how to win. It's we, 'We can't do this.' 'This project isn't meant for people like us.' I feel bad for him because his parents are paying big dollars for him to go to school and the guy just sees walls not possibilities. He's only nineteen years old. How can he be so negative? I took him out for beers one night to find out and the guy was a nice guy but he was afraid of the possibility of success at this level."

"So do we teach him or do we kill him?"

"Give him two more weeks. I'll call on him exorbitantly to shake his cage and see if he can develop some self-confidence in himself. If he doesn't, we may have to talk."

'"Just don't cut him indiscriminately. He's good people. He just has not succeeded on this level before. I understand we have a game to win but don't give up on him yet."

"Why?"

"Specifically; he's a good guy. A good guy will break his back for you while a weasel with more perceived talent will jerk you around. Nice people think they are indebted to you and they will work harder. Nobody's perfect but if you work up and around their deficiencies and they will even work harder for you."

Chapter 25

The weekend series with Providence came. The Friars came out in their black and white uniforms and they played a trapping defense all game. It gave BU trouble but on the other hand didn't produce much offense for the Friars.

In the third period, The Terriers caught a break. His mark fell down at center ice and Steve raced into the offensive zone the friar defense collapsed on him. He saw Al Johnson out of the corner of his eye and flipped him a pass. Al fired a slap shot right through the five hole and the puck landed with a clang in the back of the net. BU won the game 1-0.

"Well, tomorrow's the day," he teased Laurie after the game.

"What should I wear?"

"Oh! No! Don't get me into that!"

"Why?"

"What if I purposely told you the wrong thing?"

"Why would you do that?"

She pinched his nose.

"Because they'll love you if you wear a corn sack."

"I need a coffee."

"Why don't we go for a walk?"

"Why?"

"Because you're strung out enough as it is."

"Thanks a lot."

"They're nice people. You're nice people. Stop worrying."

"So what are we going to do? It's cold out here."

"I could take you up to the roof."

"That's promising."

"Sold."

Steve took her up to the roof and they looked out over Cambridge.

"Nice," she pushed up against him.

"Yeah, it is."

"Do you come up here a lot?"

"When I need to think: you're worried about tomorrow aren't you?"

She blushed and that gave her answer away.

"Listen. Just relax with them. My parents are pretty progressive. They don't expect you to be a baby factory and neither do I. When the time comes, it'll be right. Okay?"

She put her arms around him and squeezed.

"You know, we could get married," she smiled.

"Do you think so?"

"I think it's possible."

"Okay."

"You're easy,"

"Well, that's only because I have the most beautiful girl in the world."

"You're sicky sweet honey."

"I know. It was the only way I could express it."

She laughed and his ears burned.

"I didn't mean to laugh," she giggled.

"Give me a break. I'm a hockey player for crying out loud."

His phone rang and it was Day.

"Hey, I was wondering if I had to take Japanese since I've written several teams for information and they sent me stuff in English and Japanese."

"I'd say if you ever went over there, for hand to hand combat in restaurants and stuff, you might want to learn some."

"Some or a little?"

"Two semesters***"

"Great. Do you know how weird a six- six Irish white guy is going to look on the streets of Tokyo. You'll have to come with me."

"Yes, Linus you like blue right."

"Hey, Steve if you weren't my boss."

"What's Japan like?'

"What?"

"What's it like?"

"It's an island off the coast of China. Their stock market is called the Nikkei, it's high point was in the eighties and has wallowed around a bit since a huge loss in the nineties. They are a sports driven nation most particularly sumo wrestling, gymnastics, baseball, running, swimming, diving… Basically you name it. Very disciplined orderly people, it is accustomed to take your shoes off and to wipe your feet when entering a Japanese household. From the ones I talked to they are nice people."

"Well, aren't you the student?"

"It started at baseball and I was late in the dorm poking around online and I figured what the heck? So I started looking around Japan and there it was. Different from me but they seemed nice."

"Right now let's count on gaining their trust so you take all the Jesuit credibility and take it to the max. Get it?"

"Yes, sir. I'll call when you have more information to hear."

"Japanese baseball," Laurie said, "Making progress?"

"Absolutely, The Wonder Twins are scouring Italy… basketball, skiing, soccer…anything they can dig up basically."

"What can I do?"

"How much work do you have with school?"

"A lot. But that's BU. Is there anything out there?"

"Do you know how to speak German?"

"Yes."

"Good you can work with me. We can go to Germany after the season is over for our honeymoon. In the meantime, we have online."

"Better yet, we have the German house at school."

"Oh, I forgot. That's exactly cool."

"Look maybe; this is a little different from the way the American public views the way the American public goes to work."

"What do you mean?"

"Well, they see farmers in Nebraska, the UAW in Detroit, and the Teamsters all over the interstates. If they actually knew how much conversation went on between countries representatives of the Companies, they may not buy anything ever again."

"I hate to be a snob. But not college educated people."

"This thing is a tremendous risk; trying to market it to Middle America and Europe. Europeans don't want Americans getting involved: America doesn't give a hoot about the Tour of Italy. What gives?"

"Well, if you give, the whole thing will fall. I believe in you."

"I like this project. We may reach people all over the world, if you do it right and professionally. I'm not as concerned professionally."

"Why?"

"Personally is what I'm worried about. I have put my blood, sweat, and tears into this. I know I can come off as some kind of a flip wise guy sometimes but that's just to keep people loose. I don't want them seizing up with fear."

"You can do that."

"Exactly! I'm the boss."

"So? We'll go to the German House and stick a note on the tack board to see if there is interest. What about the Greeks? We have to them. They started the Olympics."

"The whole thing about this is that I'm going to sign people to three to five year contracts and I can't really send a bunch of economists running around the globe asking questions and poking their noses around because everyone will notice. You have to do part of it blind—on instinct.

"I'm just worried a little bit about it dying and me not having enough to pay severance pay to the employees. People have to support their families."

"Anything else?"

He laughed.

"We'll figure out a way to get it done. Let's talk about something else."

"How many do you want?"

"Babies? I think four."

"Is there a scientific methodology for this or are you guessing."

"It's good because they have each other to rely on besides us. They're not alone. I was a only child and it was tough sometimes."

"Geeze, I was thinking ten or twelve."

"Keep dreaming pal."

"All right but they have to be boys."

"Why do they have to be boys?"

"Because if a boy does something, you can set him down let him know it. If a girl does something wrong she'll start crying and then I'll start crying. Get it?"

She just laughed.

"Girls…"

"Girls know how to press daddy's buttons—just like their mom does."

"Why thank you."

"I thought you'd appreciate that."

"I'm glad I struck out into the world."

"Yes. I hear it has its rewards."

"It made me appreciate Texas more too. Far away is exciting but it's good to e-mail friends back home."

"Boston is different than back home. It's bigger, more, grand. You have to understand. Boston and Springfield hardly get along just because Boston is bigger and more, grand. People from Springfield like UMASS-Amherst and Boston is busy with their own colleges. The fringes are like the fringes in a political party. Nobody likes them but everybody needs them just in case, you see. It's a hard row sometimes because innocent people get messed up."

"I'm sort of a quasi-big shot back home. People look at you walking down the street like you're some kind of God. In Boston, it's easier, you can be private because there's about a lot of other famous people. I'm really private. I don't like the attention. It's weird."

"Do you know what I'm really excited about?"

"The way the people we have on the team are acting and becoming the whole positive energy by helping each other out. There's kind of a divide between WMASS and Eastern MA but this group is working together and that makes me feel really good."

"Why didn't you go to UMASS?"

"Because I have too much of you in me; I wanted to see the world. I can't believe I have a shot at Boston—with money. It's beyond my wildest imagination."

"You're a good guy Steven."

"At the same time, I don't want to end up a 'big shot' to everybody back home."

"Relax. You won't."

Steve went back to his dorm and barely made bed check but he made it. He fell asleep quickly and before he knew it was morning. Nate was snoring loudly in the bed next to him. Finally, Steve tossed his pillow at his roommate.

"Will you shut up?" Steve asked.

"What the heck's a matter with you?"

"You're snoring beats the planes at Logan. Wake up! Give the world a break!"

"I was asleep and you woke me up."

"Yes! I did! It helps out the noise pollution!"

"Fascist!"

"Come on. Wake up! I need to have your genius brain help me solve a problem."

"What is it?"

"Well, did you ever hear that statement that says we shouldn't get too attached to our wives because it would get in the way of boozing it up with the guys."

"And chasing skirts?"

"Oh! Of course!"

"It's pretty stupid. Isn't it?"

"All I know is that I'm nuts of over Laurie. It is pretty stupid. Besides I don't like to drink to get drunk anyway."

"Look, kid there's lots of ways to go through life. You can be a moron if you want or you can be a good guy. You're a good guy. Stay that way."

"All right. I can do that."

Steve showered and dressed to meet Laurie. She looked beautiful in navy blue slacks, and the light blue sweater Steve gave her.

"Are your parents here yet?"

"They're back at my room sharpening their cleavers."

"Very funny."

"Promise me one thing. You won't be embarrassed when you see them. They're average folks. My dad likes sports. My mom likes jazz music. Come on. My parents are nice people."

"I bought them a gift."

"You didn't have to do that. They're the ones grilling you. What is it?"

"A bud vase!"

"You're out of my league on that one."

"You put cut flowers in it you knucklehead."

"Oh! I knew that! Come on let's go."

They arrived at the dorm saw Mr. and Mrs. Thompson. The interview as Laurie called it went well. Mrs. Thompson loved the bud vase and Mr. Thompson asked for Steve's attention for a minute outside.

"What's up dad?"

"Where'd you find her?"

"I bumped into her in GSU. I knocked her over."

"Did you pick her up?"

"Of course!"

"She's a nice girl and she's a long way from home. Are you sure about this?"

"Yes."

"Do you know the responsibilities that it will bear?"

"Dad, I love her. She's my friend."

"She's your responsibility."

"I know."

"You two are awfully comfortable with each other."

"Dad, I'm not the run around and chase skirts type. She's different. She's a musician but she's so grounded and she keeps me grounded. A lot people have said a lot of stuff since I was traded and two per cent is even true but when I get mad all I have to do is see her. It's easy after that."

"One more thing; here's the deal breaker. You both get your degrees before having children. You stay in school. A college education lasts a lifetime."

"Okay. That's fair. Dad, we'll both graduate with our class this May."

"Oh, well within God's good grace you'll actually learn something. Look it's not a vacation just because you'll have that large contract. Take it seriously."

"Yes, sir."

"Now come on, we'll go to Fanueil Hall for a couple of hours before team dinner. Let's have some fun but don't forget what I said."

"Dad, the NHL is a one and a million shot. I'll work hard. I promise."

"Hey! I'm proud of you."

Steve looked at his father and shrugged his head in embarrassment.

"Thanks dad."

They went back into the room and Laurie was talking with his mother.

"How about a trip to Fanueil Hall, everyone?" His father said.

"Sure," Steve said and then winked at Laurie.

He held her hand all afternoon and was mildly surprised that Laurie carried most of the conversation with his parents. He knew she would be a hit but he didn't realize she would enjoy it so much.

"I love you," he whispered when they had a free moment.

"Please don't kiss me here. I'm so nervous. I can't stop talking."

He laughed.

"How am I doing?"

"Well, I think you have won them over."

"What does your dad think of me?"

"You aren't the problem. I am. He gave me the junior high school speech that school is important and not to be lackadaisical in the pros."

She smiled.

"Yeah, like I would. The Dallas Stars—incredible."

"Anything else?"

"No children until after we graduate."

"Well, that was going to happen anyway."

"I think he was talking to me. Just in case I got happy feet with the pros!"

The day was a success and the night was a success. Steve picked up two assists in a 5-1 win over Providence.

Chapter 26

"I hate to break your heart," Nate said.

"About what?"

"The Bruins."

"Oh, Lord, I knew it was coming. Here comes Dallas"

"The Bruins haven't won the Cup since 1972."

"And?"

"Where are you planning to live?'

"Who cares, I'll be in the NHL."

"You're mindless and I'm going to be freezing my butt off in Sweden next year."

"You could be freezing it off in Montreal."

"Aren't you the funny one?"

"Is something wrong that I don't know about?"

"She broke up with me. She said I was self-centered."

"Curses."

"Shut up."

"Look at it this way you're going to the land of blondes. Wait until then."

"Maybe you're right."

"You're not even self-centered."

"I know that."

"See. She was wrong."

"We're going to the NHL, and I can't quite believe it. That's the grandest adventure of a lifetime. Think about that. We'll get to play each other and everything."

"I see you're taking to the idea of playing for profit."

"Well, first I thought was weird—hockey with professionals—like whether they'd be motivated without their contracts but now I now I just want to get there. I'd like to get an apartment for the season and then in the off-season buy a house for us where we can be happy."

"You're going to be working your tail off, you know."

"Hey! You're only young once. Besides; when I get the chance, I'll be able to photograph the sporting events. It'll be cool."

"Why didn't you get into all that stuff here?"

"Aw, it's not important. I'm going to Dallas and am happy. That's what counts. This place got me to the pros and is going to get my degree."

"You will have to learn to do interviews."

"Yeah, I know. Maybe that'll help."

"Well, you'll have to learn the Stars way."

"I can do that now."

"Yeah but no bum performances."

"I'll ship you a bottle in Sweden if I have one."

"Two."

"I still don't think what you're doing is right."

"You've mentioned it. And if I don't like it well, it's only a year."

"Well, it's up to you. I'm taking a shower."

"I think it would be cool to see another country."

"And you snore so loud the walls were shaking."

"Rhodes Scholar candidates don't snore. It's a law."

"Un-hunh!"

Steve called Tony on his cell on the way to class and he reached his brother.

"Hey!" He said.

"Brother, what's going on," Tony answered.

"How are you doing?"

"I've been writing a lot too. The new medication they put me on has allowed me more energy. But I'm sort of angry actually."

"At the company."

"Why?"

"I didn't get picked for Davis' thing."

"I told him not to. You're an independent manager on your own. I wanted you to sit in and observe. He didn't tell you that?"

"Actually no!"

"Well, that's what you do. Call him and find out the particulars and by the way: Tony you're a good writer. You hang in there. It's not easy to get established sometimes but don't lose faith."

"Yes, I know."

"I am very happy with what you did for me. This job has boosted my confidence a lot. I thought I was stuck in retail the rest of my life. I feel like I'm justifying all those student loans."

"Tony, I knew if you just stuck it out, you'd get your feet wet and be swimming fast in no time."

"How does your mind feel now?"

"Good. A little weird but good overall; It's not even mental illness now. It's what to do about my story. I know the story was about a guy with mental illness who was occasionally great but wondered if he could be great consistently. I feel that same way about myself since we started the company. I am getting over my fear, of myself. And what I think about my performance on the job. The character mirrors me very well. I also viscerally feel better. I get up at four am and take thyroid pill; then I get the cobwebs out of my head from the medicine from the night before. I eat breakfast, take a shower, shave and start writing. Usually I'm so psyched to write, I jump into write away, showering and shaving just in time to get to work."

"Geeze, man!"

"I just get more energy every day. Somebody once said, 'Winning breeds winning.' I guess that's true."

"Well, look at it this way, you're not supposed to have a good time in a hospital, you're supposed to heal. Now you can actually live and that's the best feeling you can have. Just take your medicine every day and talk to your therapist. Tony, you have one of the best minds on the staff. You're creative, aggressive, you know the target audience you want to reach. You are going to great things for us."

"Call me later."

"Sure."

Chapter 27

Sunday the group gathered at the usual place and a gentleman by the name of Chris Davidson raised his hand tentatively. Chris was from Umass.

"Shoot, Chris."

"I don't think this is going to work."

"Why is that?"

"I think we have a turkey of an idea."

"Then why did you finish the paper?"

"I don't know if I'm the man for the job."

"Look, Chris, this a private conversation we're about to tread into. I'll drive down Thursday and meet you for lunch and we'll discuss things."

"I don't know chief."

"Look, people that down think they can cut it don't finish their assignments. I'll meet you Thursday at noon and we'll talk."

"You better leave early because guest parking is nearly always filled."

"There you go."

Steve jumped on the T to make his four o'clock appointment at Harvard with Jack Rawlings.

"What's going on Chief?" Jack smiled.

"This better be good Jack."

"Watch and enjoy."

It was a documentary of photography in the Olympic Games and the technological advances that came along with it. Steve was very impressed.

"I tried to get some moving picture stuff in here and that meant Bud Greenspan. He's the King of Olympic Documentaries."

"Throw some more stuff in there. It's only fifteen minutes. We need a half hour."

"You mean I broke my back to edit that down and you want more."

"You did a good job but I need fifteen minutes."

"Okay, Boss."

"Look we'll get a sandwich and you can tell me what brought you to Harvard?"

"That's easy. I'm a legacy. I'm going into the family business. My dad owns his own studio in LA."

"Really?"

"That's two years off. I'm only a sophomore."

"So, I can't buy you a beer?"

"Not unless you want to get arrested."

So, they found a café and grabbed a quick supper. They had a good talk about their various experiences in college and the challenges each school offered.

"It's going to be a good place, if we can pull it off," Jack smiled quietly.

"And you look like you have something to say?"

"Well, you're from that area and you may be offended."

"Lay it on me."

"Well, I went to the Hall on a Saturday and it was dead. Will we draw?"

"I don't know. I'm trying to put together letters to the Symphony, the Hall, and the Springfield Falcons hockey team to have rotating promotional activity between all of us to get the word out. Just to be safe, we're working on Harvard. People in Springfield can be funny sometimes. It's an odd balance. I hope we draw. We're hoping that putting it on the waterfront helps because in the city it's a tough place sometimes. I hope we draw."

"Wait a minute. You made a decision on 'I hope we draw.'"

"The power of positive thinking!"

"I hope you're right about this Boss."

"Well, they've been clamoring to get the water front done for years. This is getting the waterfront done."

"You know what? I'm spoiled. I live in California on the Island and everything was done. I get here and everything's done. I've never been part of the ground up before."

"It is kind of exciting, huh?"

"You know what's cool—if this thing flies—and I'm beginning to think it will, someone will see my stuff and judge it. And that's cool!"

"What's it like growing up on Catalina Island?"

"Oh, the girls man! And tourists at that! You guys should see 'em."

"Geeze, I thought you were going to talk about the flowers."

"I was. You'll have to come out one week."

"Gee, thanks!"

"Do you think we have a shot at this?"

"Yeah, we can do it."

"Well, I hate to eat and run but I have to meet my girl at the library. This is after all Harvard."

"BU ain't far behind. I'll see you Chief."

They split the bill and split up.

The next Monday Steve went to class. School was challenging but not impossible and he found his business classes interesting. Steve liked the idea of going into management because he liked the leadership opportunities. Writing the term papers was probably the toughest. The oral work in class treated him better but at the end of the day, he still looked forward to hockey practice to get his energy level up.

After class Steve went down to the frozen over bike paths by the Charles River. The river itself was frozen too. He looked out across the Charles and visualized what it looked like in the spring with the sailboats and the crew teams practicing. He wondered if crew was as difficult as hockey. It didn't seem so the way they just cut through the water. He smiled and hoped spring came soon.

He thought hard about how his life would change come May. He would need to pick an agent and he would have to wait and see through the contract negotiations. After which he would get married. The next second he felt a snowball smack on the back of his head. He turned around and there was Laurie smiling broadly.

"You think that's funny. Do you?"

"Yes!"

He chased her down and tickled her until she couldn't laugh anymore. Finally, she gasped and sat up.

"All for one snowball," she gasped.

"Yeah, but it is fun tickling you."

"For you maybe; to me it hurts."

"Yeah, right?"

"Okay maybe it doesn't hurt but I feel foolish."

"Hey, I didn't throw the snowball."

"You're such a baby."

"What do you mean?"

"You are."

"Do you want to go to dinner or not?"

"Do I have to sit next to you?"

"No, you can sit across from me."

"Why?"

"I want to see your face."

"I'll buy that."

So, he took her to GSU where she ordered a chicken salad sandwich and he did the same. They found a table in the corner and began to converse.

"How was your day, dear?" She asked him.

"Aren't you the funny one?"

"No. I'm serious."

"It was okay. Coach kicked my butt because I pass too much. He wants me to shoot more."

"What about the real reason you're here?"

"What would that be?"

"School dummy!"

"It was okay. It took work in my management class to get a concept. The professor is really touchy-feely and I crossed swords with him."

"Over what?"

"Well we were talking about motivational theory and I said sometimes you as the boss just have to tell the employee what to do. He rambled on about the delicate psychology make up of today's employee's. I understood what he said to a point but I didn't buy all of it. Overall, a successful day, you?"

"Today wasn't a fun day. It was all theory and composition—no playing. You need theory and comp but a musician is born to play and sitting around with six hours of class work can get a little taxing. Tomorrow will be better. I'll get to play. I didn't figure you to cross swords with a professor."

"Me neither. I just asked a question then I made a statement and we were off. I think he kind of liked it because it was the first question in twenty minutes from anybody. I don't think he's mad at me anymore. To tell you the truth, if pressed, I think he'll even admit I made some sense."

"Just don't get thrown out of this place before May."

"You would've been very proud of me. I didn't even raise my voice."

"Oh, Lord!"

"So! Are you going to play your clarinet for me tonight?"

"One better; I'm going to play you one of my own pieces."

"Great! I'm come by about nine o'clock."

"Why so late?"

"Homework and I've got to call Tony."

"I hope you like it," she blushed.

"I bet it's great."

They talked a while longer and he held her hand.

"Does your brother know about what we're going to do?" He asked her.

"He's quite flabbergasted," she giggled, "I was the mature, responsible one. He doesn't know what to make of it."

"I'll talk to him anytime he wants," Steve offered.

"Give him a little more time. "

He laughed.

"Come on. I'll walk you back to the dorm."

"I think that's a good idea. I'm just going to play my clarinet for a while to get myself psyched up for the books."

They got up and left GSU. He walked her home and then kissed her deeply.

"I'm glad you knocked me over that day. What a kisser you turned out to be!"

"Why thank you. I will be back later."

"See ya' later Batman."

He called John Davis and rather urgently told him to share the information with people that needed to know as fast as they can. It was a short, pleasant, frank conversation that lasted all off thirty seconds. Steve went home to study for a couple of hours and then called Tony.

"Hey, it's me," he said.

"Steve, you could be more of a gentleman on the phone."

"Hey, look pal, take it as it comes. How are you doing?"

"I'm hoping to bring Annie to Boston to see you play soon. I can't believe it's already February."

"That's great. The four of us will go out to dinner."

"They are adjusting my medicine and it feels better—much better. I'm not dragging around tired all the time. That was almost as bad as the voices."

"Do me a favor."

"Anything! You have it!"

"Make your letter extra special for Sunday. I want to read yours first."

"That's loading the deck."

"And putting pressure on you; do you think you can handle it?"

"Yes, I'll try. It shouldn't be a problem since you are reading it."

"What about your writing? Are you writing?"

"Yes I am!"

"Is it fun?"

"It's a little close to home. Technically it is fun. Now if you were mentally ill, I'd have a real story because you are a jock and jock itch sells well."

"Thank you very much. I appreciate that."

"I was just kidding. It's difficult with the hospital scenes and stuff. Some of the hospitals I've been in were not so good and some were great. What is the writer to do? Accentuate the positive or dwell on the negative? Plus, I don't want it to be a hospital book. You know, he keeps going off his medicine so he ends up in the hospital time after time. I know there are people like that but they aren't me."

"It damn well better not be you. You take your medicine."

"Yes, Chief."

"How are you besides?"

"Two jobs and a novel keep me busy."

"How's Annie?"

"She likes the work at the hospital. Like I said we're trying to get away for the weekend to see you play and hang out in Boston. I'm looking at graduate school."

"Well, I'll be damned. What for?"

"I'm just looking—nothing major."

"Why?"

"Because I feel that I missed BU the first time."

"Are you only looking at BU?"

"Pretty much now? Because I went through a million other schools and I just thought that BU was home and all it needed in our relationship was some paint and shingles."

"What are you looking at?"

"Some kind of MBA program; I have to talk to a counselor. They all look good. I'm hoping to narrow it down."

"People are going to want to talk with you. You'll be a walking interview."

"I don't know about that. I just want to do my job."

"With the book, and everything—and Annie? Are you going to be able to handle it?"

"That's the point. My other story was made up but this I have experience with—plus I think it's important for people to know that people can live normal lives if they get treatment."

"Did you also tell them that many people commit suicide without treatment? Get the picture?"

"Yes, sir. I'm putting up with this only because you are my brother."

"What does that mean?"

"Stop lecturing me!"

"All right! My fault! You have such a bright future. You're a good writer. Stick to that."

"No I have more in me than just being a writer."

Steve laughed.

"You're such a jerk."

"Do you really think I can write?"

"Do you?"

"I think this story has some legs."

"Good for you! Tony, look, I'm just scared. Remember that time we were playing on the ponds and I got sticked in the face? I wasn't even scared and then your attacks come and they scare me more than seeing Hell wide open."

"That has hasn't happened in a long time. You still see me as that guy in the hospital and that part of my life is dead. Gone and buried forever. That will never be me again. I'm doing well with the company. Aren't I?"

"You are doing great! Maybe even spectacular! I just wanted to throw that out at you because we're going to making presentations to clients and we're going to need good presenters."

"Maybe I should do it myself then?"

"You are aggressive. Good! It's settled. I knew I had a man for a brother. Well that's good. Stick to the writing. I want to read it when you get a little further into it.

"Well, as long as it's cleared up. That would've been a horrendous mistake—even for us."

"Do you remember that time we got caught switching the mail in the mail boxes at the duplex we used to live in?"

"Mom and dad were not happy."

"How long were we grounded for?"

"I think two weeks. No TV, no candy, and no music."
They both laughed.
"Brother, I want to get back to those times," Steve said.
"Me too."

Chapter 28

He hurried over Laurie's place and buzzed her room. She came down to pick him up. She was dressed in a ski jacket and jeans.

"Are we going somewhere?" He asked.

"I'm in the mood for a coffee and a lecture."

"Whoa! Wait a minute. I thought we were going to listen to your new piece."

"It's not ready yet," she sniffed.

"Gotta cold!"

"As a matter of fact yes?"

"So I can't kiss you?"

"I'm not dead but I'm not healthy. If you want to, go ahead. But I advise against it."

"I'll kiss you on the cheek. That's safe."

"Come on. I need a coffee."

They sat down in the all night coffee shop and he asked.

"So, what's up?"

"Nothing! I want to know what's up with you?'

"What do you want to know?"

"Well, you know, in my romance novels…"

"Oh, Lord!"

"Well, I'm worried about you."

"In what way?"

"Well, extremely driven people have this aura about them—a huge ability to do a lot of things like you but they do them because they have some deep, dark secret about them. The thing that confuses me and separates you from them is that you are nice."

"What the heck is that supposed to mean?"

"It means you must be unhappy somewhere along the line and I must be the cause of it."

"Stop with the coffee for a minute."

"I don't know whether to laugh or tell you to shut up."

"Then why do you do the things you do?"

"It's all good! It's fun. I like it. And I like the people I work with. Being driven isn't a bad thing. It's important to push yourself the entire time even when you're relaxing watching a ball game. You keep score, what the pitch count is, whether or not the Rangers will ever beat the Red Sox."

"You shut up!"

"Ooh!"

"Anyway, in all seriousness, you just play the game of life to win. Tony's my biggest inspiration. That guy is looking at grad school already, so soon out of the hospital—I'm proud and happy for him. Everything he does, he fights. My life is just studying but for him, he studies over and over. Plus he's doing great with the company."

"The team is coming together and we tacked up the notes on the German hostel and the Greek house."

"You're always about the business."

"Well, I can't kiss you? You'll give me the plague."

"Come on you've changed since this afternoon," he reached for her hand but she withdrew.

She looked down at her feet and blushed.

"Are you breaking up with me?"

"No," she answered quietly.

"Then what is it?"

"You're going to break up with me."

"On whose orders?"

"I just have a feeling you'll see all those girls and that'll be it."

"Are you nuts? Who put that stuff in your head?"

She blushed again.

"Can I have your hand?" He asked.

"Only if I get it back; anybody can make a mistake."

"You are a menace," he smiled and squeezed her hand.

"I have post nasal drip. And you're hassling me."

"Don't ever do that again! You scared the pants off me."

"I'm sorry. I was just flipping through the *Sports Illustrated* and saw a picture of the football cheerleaders and I got to thinking."

"Oh, is that what you were doing?"

"Well, if you weren't so charming and handsome!"

"That's kind of sickening you know."

"Why? You're not handsome or charming?"

"I'm an average looking guy. I may have some charm but I'm average looking."

"Maybe you should hear it from the girl's perspective."

"I like you more and more every day."

"You were ready to kill me five minutes ago."

"Well you scared me."

"I think you're still scared."

"Maybe I am."

"You think I'd leave you."

"Sometimes!"

"Stop shrinking in your seat."

"Yes, mamm."

"Listen to me very carefully. I'm not going anywhere. You're stuck with me. I love you to bits. Get it?"

"Well, look at us," Steve said.

"We're so silly we have to be together."

"You're going to go home and play me that tune?"

"I can't I have post nasal drip. I can't breathe right. It came on about three o'clock and I've had it ever since."

"Germ."

"Thank you. Now you can take me home."

He gently looped his arm around her on the way to her dorm. On the way there was a man in a black sweat suit lying on the cement sidewalk and he was talking to himself. Steve gave him a couple of dollars and then kept walking.

"That was nice," Laurie said.

"Life is harder for some people than it is for others. Maybe he can get a slice of pizza with it."

"Are you thinking of your brother?"

"Yeah, sometimes! For a while it was like; why did it happen to him? But now it's like, can anything stand in this kid's way?"

"Well, he's got a good family. He's lucky. And he's doing better than fine."

"So are we. Lucky to have him I mean. I wonder where that guy came from. He doesn't look like he's having too good of a night."

"Homeless people are alone."

"I've seen it in Tony. Self-isolation is part of the disease."

"Geeze!"

"You know, I've seen some weird stuff in my life but I've never quite got a handle on mental illness. It can take Tony who is an intelligent, well-liked, hard working, genial guy and turn him into that without his medication and treatment plan," he said.

"You're beating yourself up."

"Tony almost went to prison."

"Hey, past is past. You can't change that."

"Yeah, I guess. Come on, your dorm is right here."

"Don't kiss me. I'll get you sick!"

"On the cheek! Just one on the cheek!"

"Boy you're really hot and bothered. Aren't you?"

"It's because you're so gorgeous."

"You do flatter me."

"Well, I'm trying hard."

"Don't worry you're getting it."

He walked her upstairs to her room and kissed her good-bye on the cheek.

Steve finished his homework in study hall so he had nothing to do. He went home to look up a camera shop on the internet. Sports photography was his hobby and shopping for the equipment on the net really had him thinking again about his life will change when he was able to afford living like a grown up.

He was also thinking about Laurie and thanking the Lord he bumped into her at GSU. She was out of hand tonight though. He really was frightened. Steve had the same feelings. She just was quicker in expressing them.

The camera equipment zoomed by and he was incredibly excited about the 'long glass' that he saw but he kept thinking about Laurie and wondered if she'd be interested in learning sports photography. He just wanted to be with her. The phone rang.

"Hello?" He said.

"Hi! Handsome!"

"I'm already engaged."

"Very funny," Laurie giggled.

"Hey! I was just thinking about you."

"It better have been good."

"Do you want to learn sports photography?"

"Maybe! Can you teach me how to photograph flowers?"

"Flowers?" He said with offense, "Are you kidding me? That's what girls do."

"Well, I don't want to overstate the obvious."

"I'll try."

"Then I'll try sports photography."

"Deal."

"Hey!" His voice softened, "Besides your post-nasal drip. Are you okay?"

"I guess. It's just fear of the unknown I think."

"I know you're going to yell at me."

"Oh good. I have to hear this."

"Just hear me out. Everything is changing or will be changing in the next few months. And like it our not, when we get married it'll be my job to take care of you."

She laughed.

"I'm serious. You can't laugh at me."

"I think I'll be fine."

"Look, so do I but that is I'm responsible for you."

"Oh, my Lord, I'm marrying a caveman."

"Well, what am I supposed to do?"

"Just be my husband!"

"Yeah, but my dad told me you're my responsibility."

"Look, I can take care of myself. But I need you. You're my friend. I can handle myself. Relax."

"Okay. Now there only four thousand nine hundred ninety-nine things I have to worry about."

"You're worse than mom."

"I'm a planner. I can't help it."

"Look, I don't have time to go through the list. Let's start with the photography and then we'll be in business."

"Do they have flowers in Texas? I thought it was all cactus and brush weed and stuff."

"You're a jerk."

"Give me a break: I've hardly been out of Massachusetts."

"If you were here, I'd punch you in the nose."

"Is there a reason why you called me?"

"Oh, yes. I forgot. How would you like to go to dinner tomorrow night—my treat!"

"Sure! Where we going?"

"Harvard Square. Pick me up at seven."

"Sure."

"Good-bye Laurie."

"Good-bye Steven."

They hung up and Steve went back to the web. He was looking for a camera shop in Melrose, MA that carried professional equipment and was having trouble finding one amongst the seemingly millions of point and shoot shops. Finally, he quit around midnight when Nate came in.

"Do anything important?" Nate asked.

"Why?"

"She wants to go back out with me."

"Really? Why?"

"Thanks a lot."

"You're going to give up the 'land of blondes?'"

"Now you're in favor of Sweden."

"There are advantages to almost everything."

"You think I should let it lie."

"It might be wise. Don't be so cheap. Take her to a nice place. Find out where you're at but be honest with yourself. She ain't the only one left."

"I don't know."

"Tell her you just want a casual thing for a while."

"That's what got me in trouble the last time. She said I was too self-centered to have a real relationship."

"Well it seems like you've got to take the plunge boy."

"I keep thinking that there's something better out there."

"If you want my opinion, I'd heel—toe it. Tell her you haven't known her long enough and that you just want casual for a while. If she really likes you, she'll agree. Have you told her about Sweden yet?"

"No."

"Well, that may change things."

"Think she'll like forty below?"

"I think you should wait."

"Yeah but…"

"Hey, it's a free country. That's just my opinion."

"I think I'll explain to her about Sweden first and then we'll see."

"Can you trust her to keep her mouth shut."

"Yeah, I can."

"Well, that's one plus."

"I just want to get on with graduation."

"I thought you wanted to stay here forever."

"I'm getting itchy."

"Me too."

"Well use baby powder."

"Very funny;. Part of me thinks that this grand adventure you are about to embark on is pretty cool."

"It will be. I'm kind of curious about how people function in a fifty per cent takes bracket. I'll only do it for a year but I wonder how the average guy does."

"I'm kind of curious about Boston when you don't have to save your money or ask your parents for money. I wonder what it's like on your own. Now I'm connected to my parents financially and otherwise but I'm thinking what about making your own decisions—what's that like and am I going to lean on my father? Laurie thinks we'll do fine if we start slow."

"You wouldn't be scared. Would you?"

"For the record, no I wouldn't. Can I be dismissed now your honor?"

"Laurie's a nice girl that's all."

"That's why I'm marrying her."

"That's why you take care of her."

"Yes, sir."

John Davis called next.

"Marketing questions." John said shortly.

"In what regard," Steve answered.

"Well, we have an opportunity that we didn't think of."

"And?"

"Arena football."

"Hey!"

"Yeah, hey! Network television and all. Not to mention tons of little folk for fans."

"It is still too risky. I don't they are as financially well off as they'd like to be."

"I want New York! I want to meet Bon Jovi."

"Where do you get these ideas?"

"I was reading *Sports Illustrated* and do you know what else they might let us have a crack at X-treme sports, although that may be a bit tougher to land."

"Well, e-mail me the letters and I'll poke around with it later."

"How much later?"

"Not much. Shaun is really looking at this Japanese baseball league stuff seriously."

"Yeah, at least I'm in the same country as the rest of us."

"Cool. You made your point. Send it when it is finished, I'll start on it when I get it."

"Hey, do you know what?"

"What?"

"The most beautiful girl asked me out the other day."

"How the heck did that happen?"

"She said she saw me walking around campus. She said I was cute and she asked me out."

"What's her name?"

"Dana."

"Well?"

"Tomorrow night. We're going to go shopping and grab something to eat at the Cambridgeside Galleria."

"Nice."

"Should I buy her something?"

"Yeah, cheapskate."

"Well, with that piece of advice, I will hang up and leave you now to your activities."

Chapter 29

Sunday came and there was a meeting of the minds at Cappo's. The proceeding two nights had BU beating Vermont twice and that sent Steve into the meeting relieved. There was great discussion—sometimes heated over location.

"'Location, location, location!' Willard J. Marriott." John Davis argued.

"Where's Chris Davidson when you need him?" Steve asked.

"Sir?"

"You expressed the same concerns to me. What are they?"

"There's simply more traffic in Boston. More traffic means more turnstiles turning. I don't see how we can do it in Springfield. I went to the Basketball Hall of Fame on a Saturday during peak hours and there was hardly anyone there. It is hard for me to say this because I have friends from Longmeadow. I just don't see it."

"We need customers," Paco said, "Every business needs them and ours isn't a specialty business. It's about getting as many people through those turnstiles as possible."

"I'm split," Rico said, "On the one hand we'd be trying our best for Springfield but on the other hand, I agree with you guys. And if they really wanted to come, they could get out the horse and buggy and drive to Boston."

"Well, if we are going to do this, I propose that we put it near a school," Steve said.

"Why is that?" John Davis asked.

"Because, on the whole, educated people are more into visitation of those types of places. I think Harvard's the place because it's close enough to the Museum of Fine Arts but not too close."

"Back to letter writing?" Brian asked.

"Let's not overkill. Break up into groups of five and then come up with something by next Sunday. Meeting adjourned. Good luck and Godspeed."

The next night Steve picked Laurie up at seven and they took the T to Harvard Square. When the got off, Laurie asked.

"Did you ever think of playing here?"

"For the Crimson? Yes, I guess I did."

"Did you apply?"

"I didn't think I was smart enough so I didn't apply."

"I am not bitter that they traded me. I'm grown up now and will apply for that special two year program they have. It's a certificate program. I want to continue my language studies—Italian and German and I want to take some digital photography classes. I learned a lot in four years. I just never learned that about myself in high school. I was just a hockey player then. Late bloomer. It sure is nice here though."

"Regrets?"

"Not really. BU got me to the pros, which is what it is supposed to do. I have a good, solid, four: years of education behind me—almost—and we won the Beanpot!" He smiled. "I also met you by the way."

"Still?"

"Sort of. I don't come here much except with you. It's a case of 'if I knew then what I knew now.'"

"Well, let me buy you dinner like I said. It may cheer you up."

"I'd like to show you something later."

"Deal."

"What about you? Any regrets?"

"Well, it was rough in the beginning the musicians were all so good here. It took a while to get my feet wet but once I did it was okay. Also, I met you."

"Where are we going for dinner?"

"There's a German place kind of off the Square. Do you like German food?"

"I've had it in a German place back home. I like the raw herring."

"You're kidding?"

"No I'm not."

"Better you than me."

They were seated quickly and talked as they looked at the menu.

"Spatzel is good," she said.

"I'm going for the cholesterol shot—the bratwurst and kraut. And the herring for an appetizer."

"In one sitting. I'm hungry. I didn't eat lunch but that's a pretty hefty meal."

"I burn it off."

"What about your hometown?"

"I was kind of quiet growing up. I am still that way sometimes but I spent a lot of time on the rink and saw people running the gamut between nice parents and nice kids; to absolute spoiled brats with the worst kind of hockey parent you could see. The two things I regret were giving up the trumpet and Scouting. Mostly it was books and hockey."

"What bout you?"

"Midland is kind of quiet. Friday night football—hardly any music majors. It was still a nice place to grow up. Hot though. In the summer it was just incredible."

"Why'd you leave?"

"I wanted to see the world. When this adventure began, I was going to see one Commonwealth. I had like four really close friends in high school and they all stayed in Texas. Two went to Rice, one went to A&M, and one went to UT. I was the weird one for going out into the world."

"You ain't that weird."

"Neither are you."

"But we're both a little weird."

"I agree."

"Do you still want to stay?"

"Why yes? It's another adventure."

"What if we have a baby?"

"If?"

"Okay. That's good."

They ordered dinner and the waiter, young college kid like themselves asked Steve if he was the guy who beat Harvard in the Beanpot.

"A lot of guys beat Harvard in the Beanpot."

"Do you mind if I have your autograph?" He whispered.

"Do you go to Harvard?"

"Psych major. Minor in German."

"Well, here's your autograph."

"Wow! This is great! Thanks! Danke!"

The waiter quickly put their order in and they went back to talking.

"Brother, am I a long way from Texas."

"Tell me about it."

"Why?"

"It's kind of difficult to articulate."

"Try."

"What do people do for fun back in Springfield?"

"Well, they have the Big E."

"What would be the Big E?"

"The Big E is a fair hosted by Massachusetts for all the states in New England and for three weeks you can go and see as many things as you like—food, theme buildings—everything. Too bad it only lasts three weeks. I went twice last year myself."

"You're comfortable with the museum decision?"

"Yeah. I had reservations myself. See I think Hall of Fame can run in the red; because the NBA owns it—at least for awhile. They must make their money on presentations by groups and stuff because walk-in is kind of slow. Ours can't. We have to turn a profit. It's a numbers game. Sorry to say but I can do more for the museum in Cambridge than Springfield. What I'm hoping is that me being local will some kids to see Harvard or BU when they are young enough to plan their future to have a chance at attending there. It really wouldn't hurt them to go to Boston once in a while."

"They don't come to Boston. It's an hour and a half a way."

"What I'd really like to do for Springfield is recreate Main St. there are some old factories like a block to the back on the East Side that would make great artist lofts or condominiums. Whatever as it is not left to be whatever."

The waiter arrived with Steve's herring.

"Thank you," Steve said.

"It's very good," the waiter said.

"I'm sure it is, thanks again," Steve looked at Laurie who scrunched up her nose.

The waiter left and Steve began to try his herring.

"Very good," he said.

"I'll take your word for it."

"Chicken."

"Have you ever been anywhere else in the world besides Midland?" Steve asked.

"No. I had dreamed and read books but I'd never been."

"Why Boston?"

"I wanted to go to Fenway Park."

"That's it. What about your education?"

"I knew BU was a good school."

"But you wanted to go to Fenway Park."

"Yes. I didn't tell my parents that of course. I told them of the cultural opportunities and so forth. I guess part of that was true."

Steve finished up his herring and waited for dinner.

"You're quite the girl. Do you know that?"

She blushed.

"You should've heard my parents when I told them we were staying in Boston for the summer. They were nuts!" She whispered.

"Oh! Really!"

"They were convinced you were only after me in the biblical way."

"They didn't seem that way."

"I told them I wasn't stupid enough to fall for a guy like that. I think they were impressed by my debating skills."

"Do they really like me?"

"Oh, yes, they really like you but they panicked. To them the summer is permanently in Boston and all that."

"Why didn't you tell me?"

"You were nervous enough as it was."

"Yeah, I guess but it's square now. Right?"

"Absolutely geometrical."

He laughed.

The waiter brought their main course and Steve smiled at Laurie.

"Better than dorm food. Huh?"

"A little bit," she laughed.

"I like German food," he said.

"Yes, me too."

"I'd like to go to Europe one day. Go to England and work our way in land."

"I'm just like; well I moved seven times before high school and it wasn't detrimental to my health. In a way it was really cool. We met different kinds of people and learned to share and stuff. It was good. The problem is got happy feet. I just want to keep traveling. It's good for me but I've been thinking about going back to BU and getting my Masters. I don't want to have Tony swinging there alone."

She giggled.

"What?"

"My fiancé, the dreamer. You can't sit still for five minutes. Can you?"

"Is a ton of abuse coming on?"

"What about the NHL?"

"Look, as far as it goes I'm a loyal Bruins fan however, they lost a whole season of hockey and the fans may be upset. I was really upset last winter. It was kind of surreal. I couldn't go to UMASS games because then I would've had to answer all those questions about not going to UMASS and I couldn't turn on ESPN to watch a game. It was awful."

"I forgot your life is dominated by hockey."

"It's not forced fed. I just enjoy it. It's really weird because when you're all over the country when you're a kid, you have to adjust. You're are like a paratrooper. They drop you here there and everywhere and you better be able to read a map and a compass. Sometimes you feel left out but other times you can just settle in and enjoy people."

"All right. So what about a home?"

"Like shoveling snow and all that?"

"Well, I was thinking people coming over to view the Christmas tree…"

"And wondering how the heck we got it in the house."

"Exactly."

"In social settings, I can be pretty flexible—even relaxed but when I get in the board room as we call it at Cappos', I change. I become the leader of some very talented people. And, when the push is on, they want my answer as the final say. That gives me intrinsically what I want and that is to make sense. We have enough to do without getting into personality conflicts, which definitely helps. We have what I'd hoped for—a team. Young enough to be aggressive but not foolhardily to be reckless."

"Do you have pressure now in your life?"

"Of course."

"What's the number one thing?"

"You. I want to be perfect for you."

"You are."

"Wait a minute. That time I fell asleep on your concerto, you weren't mad."

"Okay, so you're not perfect."

"Look, the way I grew up is the way I grew up. My dad traveled a lot for business. I didn't fault him because he was doing good for us. You could either make a good situation out of a bad or you could stay in the house and not talk to anybody. We moved into our house in East Longmeadow in the eighth grade and have been there ever since."

"You jumped around quite a bit when you were young."

"Sometimes I got in fights. Won some lost some. Winning's better. I made a point of it to avoid fisticuffs in high school because you get a reputation as a punk. Overall, I made it to college, which I guess was never debatable—but a school like BU—that may have been a question mark. Still, I'm in and can't believe it."

"Well, you better, you're going to graduate in a couple of months."

"Yeah, I guess. I kind of like to keep this way though because if you expect to be successful every time, you kind of take the shine off it."

"Yeah! Definitely! My formative years were very formative. I learned a lot at BU but now that I have the confidence level where I want it; I want to work through Harvard to see what I can see."

"What does that mean?"

"I'd like to meet people from different parts of the world and I really would like to challenge myself with my photography. I took a couple of courses and really like it."

"First you have to sign the contract."

"Yes, I've been thinking about that."

"I bet you have."

"It's not just the money. It's the lifestyle. You hardly ever see a Bruin in the society pages unless he wants you to. You can still be a person and walk around this place."

"Boy! For a guy who likes cameras you sure don't like them pointed at you."

"That's because I honestly believe I can get more done if I am doing it instead of posing."

"You have to show up for the ribbon cutting for the museum."

"That's different. But if you keep involved in several charities, it looks like self-promotion. You look like a real jerk."

"Thanks for dinner."

"I owed you one."

"Kind of quiet tonight aren't you."

"I did it."

"Excuse me?"

"I went out into the world and staked my claim."

"Feels good. Doesn't it?"

"We'll have to go to Fenway before the semester is over. We'll get box seats," he said.

"On spring break, I'm staying in Boston; we can go then. I checked. They're playing Detroit."

"You have it all planned out. Don't you?"

"I've been looking forward to it all year long."

"Before it gets too late, we should pay the check and get out of here. I have something to show you."

"Is this real or are you teasing me?" She asked.

"It's real."

"We were having a nice dinner."

"We're going to be late. Please."

"You said please?"

" Yes. Now can we go?"

"Okay." She paid the bill and left a generous gratuity.

He helped dress her up and put his overcoat on and they walked into the chilly February night air.

"What's so important?" She asked.

"I'm going to show you the Yahd!"

"The what?"

"Harvard Yard complete with library and chapel."

"It's cold out here."

"We'll do it quick. You'll have to see it."

"Okay, but you'll have to hold me by my arm."

"Absolutely, that's a spectacular idea."

He walked her through the brick and iron gate and onto the asphalt sidewalks.

"It is impressive," she said.

"I thought you'd like it."

"What if we got photographed here?"

"Oh, I don't know the guys would never let me forget it."

"Are we going to the Coop?"

"Yes, I just wanted to show you this."

He was studying hard that evening and for once he thought he escaped the torrent of phone calls from anyone connected to the company—until two o'clock in the morning.

"Hello?" He said groggily.

"Hi! It's me!"

It was Lynn Demarco.

"What?"

"The funniest thing happened. My mother called me earlier tonight and said that I was wasting my time on this. I gave her the, "Yes, mom treatment." I came off that phone pretty confused. Why would she send to college anyway, if she and pops thought I couldn't do something great. It's that Old Italian freakin' guilt trip. She wants me to buy the house next door, get married, have eighty-five kids and basically give up all my education."

"You're not happy."

"Absolutely not. I like working for a dream. I have caught the fever as you say. She's driving me nuts. I got into a big fight almost every night this week. She lives in Springfield by Veterans Golf course. We've had a fight every night this week."

"You had to tell me this at two o'clock in the morning. Didn't you?"

"Sorry!"

"Do you want to quit?"

"I want to make this a success."

"Yeah, so do I. so what are you going to do?"

"Obviously, I'm going to keep working. But I'm just not going to take my mother's calls for a while. I don't know. By the way I've found the biggest source of dissatisfaction out at UMASS. It's cynicism. They are taught to be workers here. An extension of their working class routes. It's unfathomable that one guy can take twenty people and mold them into the beginnings of the team that will become a force in sports journalism around the world. It seems worse among the Italians though, which surprised me because have had a great heritage as Italian Americans. It's like they gave up."

"I don't know. I honestly think if you win at the level you're at now and keep winning you would get converts or even believers. Don't sweat it all too much. Just focus on doing your job. Please don't take this as anything against your mother however, do this, take home the thickest book you have. Put it on the kitchen table and say, 'I've learned all this; and I liked it. Get the picture." I know you. You bury yourself into a project. You take it personally. You may be taking this mother thing a little too personally. As a friend, I'm telling you to relax."

Chapter 30

The next morning Steve awoke in his own bed—alone. He briefly considered why she wanted to wait and then came to the conclusion that she may not trust him one hundred per cent. He took a deep breath and said to himself.

"Crud!"

After showering, dressing, and shaving he went to class and again he cross swords with the management professor.

"Sir, I just don't think a middle level manager should be so laizze faire regarding employees," Steve said.

"You'd micro manage then," the professor shot back.

"No sir, I'd give the employees autonomy but I'd keep an eye on them."

"Well, when you run your own company you can do it that way but this is the way we do it in class."

"Thank you, sir."

"I'd like to see you after class Mr. Thompson."

The bell rang and Steve went to the gallows.

"Yes, sir," he said.

"Do you have a rebellious streak to your personality, Mr. Thompson?"

"No, sir! Sir, if I could say something."

"By all means***"

"My questions aren't an affront to your authority. They are simply questions. I need to know the answers because I have plans beyond this place."

"You are very intelligent but your presentation is wrong. Knock that cocky smile of your face and we can do business."

"Sir, I was just trying to inject humor into the queries."

"Sometimes you fall flat."

"I'll be aware of that next time, sir."

Steve went to his other classes without incident and went through practice and study hall with his teammates. Finally, he was able to call Tony.

"Hey!" He said.

"Good evening," Tony said.

"Man! You sound good. How are you feeling?"

"Well, they stabilized the meds a bit and I'll know in a couple of days if it takes effect."

"I'm glad you're doing well. Are you going to watch the game Friday night?"

"Yeah. I'm hoping to be able to come to the Hockey East Playoffs."

"You think so?"

"I'm optimistic."

"Good. You're taking your medicine."

"Yes, sure, definitely."

"Tony, you keeping working hard at the Project because you really have a quick mind."

"I know."

"Good. I'm glad you know."

"I went through a period when I was really frustrated because I couldn't win or put myself in a position to win because of the mental illness. I kind of just imploded. I didn't talk to anybody. I was convinced people hated me. I feel ridiculous now because I know that's untrue."

"Tony you have to fight because people see you and what you stand for and they admire you. How's the clan?"

"They're all looking forward to the playoffs—even Annie."

"Good. We'll give them a show."

"How's Laurie?"

"Good. Gorgeous as ever."

"Mom and dad say she's really nice. You ran her over in GSU."

"I didn't mean to."

"Have you picked out an agent yet?"

"Yeah, that big conglomerate; they have an office in the Financial District. I can' talk to them until the end of the season though."

"That's so cool."

"Yeah, I guess it is."

"You guess?"

"It's kind of fun—like I'm growing up on my own for the first time and I can make these decisions myself."

"Well, you can always talk it over with us."

"I know but there's something about doing it yourself. Don't worry I researched it thoroughly. "

"My little brother's going to get a real job. I'm so proud of you."

"Hey, what do you think the Project is?"

"Hey, I was talking about a real night job."

"Look, we went through our tough times and if we have to go through them again we will. You're my brother and we stick together—no matter what. Besides you'd have nobody to wake up on Christmas morning."

"Well, let's see. You know what you're problem is, you were born a wise guy."

Steve laughed.

"Hey, it was good talking to you brother, I have to go take my meds and then hit the sack. Annie and I are going mall hopping tomorrow. We need a bed."

"Better you than me. I hate malls. They rob the charm away from shopping in little mom and pop stores."

"You know how picky Annie is, right?"

"Have fun brother."

"Oh Lord, I'll go to Heaven with a recommendation."

Steve just laughed.

"I'll see you my friend."

Steve did homework the rest of the night and at about eleven-thirty Laurie called.

"How are you doing?" She asked.

"I'm alive. Lot's of reading and arithmetic tonight. What about you?"

"I've been working like crazy on my piece. I can't quite get it the way I want it but I'm getting closer."

"Good luck kiddo."

She giggled.

"Maybe you can pick me up and we can go for a coffee?"

"Maybe I can. I'll be right over."

"Good-bye."

"For now***"

He hung up, put his coat on and jogged over to her dorm.

"Hello," he said when she came downstairs.

"My eyes are bugging out," she grinned.

"Mine too."

"I don't really want a coffee. Let's go for a walk."

"Sure. Do you have something to talk about? You look so serious."

"I got an e-mail from one of my friends at UT and they want to transfer to Tulane and her parents are giving her a lot of static."

"She didn't like Texas."

"Something didn't agree with her there and she won't tell me what it is. I think she broke up with her boyfriend."

"Why Tulane?"

"It's got a great Pre-Med program."

"She wants to be a doctor. Wow!"

"What do you think?"

"If I was a parent and because she's a girl."

"What's that supposed to mean?"

"Just what I said because she's a girl; The Big Easy gets a little wild around Mardi Gras the answer is: I don't know. I'd have to make a trip to the school and talk to a recruiter and ask all those the fatherly questions that embarrass the hell out of you and me."

"You're going to be a tough dad when we have kids."

"I'll ride herd on them."

"That's your job."

"Oh, yes, and I take it quite seriously."

"Geeze!"

"What? I'd give her a campus visit. We'd fly all the way out to Tulane and stay in a hotel. That's pretty sweet."

"Anyway, she's closed mouthed about wanting a transfer. I don't know if something bad happened or she really just wants to see a different part of the country. She said she followed the family tradition. She had two brothers and one sister and they all went to UT so when it came to college it was…"

"UT." Steve interjected.

"Right! Maybe she's just growing into her own person."

"Tulane is a tough school."

"I think they are the Big Green Wave or something like that."

"Yes, me too."

"What's her name?"

"Carol Layne. She's from Midland. Nice people. You'd like her. Kind of a zany sense of humor."

Steve laughed.

"All right. What else?"

"Nothing."

"I don't think so."

"Oh! I'm so worried about this piece I'm composing. I finally came to the point where my professor notices me and I have to get this down for my final. I'm nervous as heck."

"You'll do it."

"I feel like I'm climbing out of a big hole."

"You'll do fine."

"Promise."

"Oh, yes. Definitely."

He looped his arm around her shoulder and brought her closer to him.

"We could go to the Museum of Fine Arts on Sunday," he said.

"There's an Impressionist exhibit," she smiled.

"Would you like to see it?"

"Very much so."

"Good. We'll go."

They turned around and he took her home.

"Come on upstairs. I want to try something on you?"

"Excuse me?"

"I meant my music."

"Really," and then he thought a moment, "hey, I don't know anything about classical music."

"Just tell me how you feel when you listen to it."

"Okay. I can do that. Geeze I thought you referring to something else."

She laughed and shook her head.

"Boys will always be boys."

"Yeah, I kind of like it that way."

She played her clarinet for him and he was impressed.

"That's magnificent," he said at the end of the piece.

"You didn't think it was too allegro in the middle."

"I could if I knew what allegro meant."

"It means too fast knucklehead."

"I don't think so. I honestly really liked it."

"I still have to tinker with it I think."

"Don't drive yourself crazy."

"It's my job to drive myself crazy. That's when I produce my best stuff."

"Are you serious about driving yourself nuts?"

"No. I just know as a musician there's more work to be done."

"Well, you have a few more weeks."

"It's going to be odd. I have to play alone in front of the professor. At least you go out with teammates."

"Do me a favor, put the clarinet back in the case and come sit with me."

She did as she was asked.

"You put way too much pressure on yourself. You're a good musician. Amazing I think. Better than I could ever be. You have a gift. You'll do fine."

"Okay, I'll believe you but only because you're my fiancé."

He laughed.

"I hope you weren't laughing at me."

"Yeah, I was because I asked you to marry me and you accepted."

"Sometimes boys can be boys and sometimes boys can be stupid."

She laughed until tears came to her eyes.

"Tickle time!"

"Oh! No! Wait a minute!"

She laughed until her sides seem to split and then he kissed her deeply. She pulled away.

"Please," she said.

They made love.

"What religion are you anyway?"

"Protestant—Presbyterian. Why?" She asked.

"Is that why?"

"Partially. Why?"

"You sure have a strong faith lady."

"Well, what are you?"

"I guess I'm Christian. I believe in Christmas and Easter but I'm not much on church going. It drives my mom nuts. I guess technically I'm a heathen."

She smiled.

"How can you turn a simple question into something so foolish."

"Foolish?"

"Yes, you don't believe in the Lord."

"I didn't say that. I said I didn't go to church."

"Why is that?"

"Because, I always feel like I did something wrong when I go to church like I was terrible little fuzz ball."

"Do you have facts to verify this?"

"Yeah, well, actually, no. But I am working very hard to make that actuality come to a truism."

"That's it."

"I may think of other things later but I guess that's it in a nutshell."

"Why don't you come to eight o'clock service with me Sunday and see what you think?"

"Eight o'clock."

"There's a ten o'clock but I want to go to the museum and I have to work on my piece."

"Remember, we have the meeting at noon and then the museum."

"This is cool."

"Yes it is."

Chapter 31

That night, he checked his messages on his cell phone. One was marked; Urgent! Call Chris Davidson. "I hope nothing's wrong around the house."

"Hey, Chris! It's me."

""I have bad news. I can't do this," Chris said.

"Can't do what?"

"The company***"

"Which company would that be?"

"Ours**"

"Oh, ours! So you have included it as part of your life."

"Boss, you better hear me out."

"You've got two minutes to prove your point. Starting right now!"

"Fine*** I suck eggs."

"You what? Who said that?"

"I'm behind in all the meetings."

"No, you're not. That's why I call on you constantly because I know you have at least a workable fashion of the correct answer. Do you think I'm just busting your chops?"

"No. But you could tell a person these things. I get scared."

"Who the heck doesn't? Hey, pal if this doesn't work, I'm on the hook for millions of dollars."

"Look…"

"Shut up, please."

"But…"

"You're a lousy quitter Chris. You didn't come from the scrubs of freshman year to a solid senior one without some intestinal fortitude. You did the same thing at Umass. 'Oh, I don't belong in college. Boo! Freakin' Hoo! You get in the damned fight. We have a brunch of pizza and more pizza. Somebody's got to eat it. You be there. Don't even think about this quitting stuff. You want nice go to your Reverend. I'm telling you that you can excel at this job. You get wishy-washy on me now, I'm going to get really upset."

"I need this at one in the morning."

"You coward!"

"Yeah, that part of me has to go away: I guess."

"Look, Chris if I say it a nice way, then you may not take it seriously but

I'm telling you that you have talent and to throw it away because some stupid teacher in junior high school called you stupid because of your dyslexia is wrong. You've worked hard to get where you are today. Don't give up now. You keep pushing. You don't have to be perfect—just get in the game."

"This damned pizza better be good."

"Best ever***"

"Okay."

"What the heck set you off?"

"Nothing; bad day with the girl? She was a little upset that I've been so wrapped up in this company deal and I got scared thinking maybe she's and I don't belong here."

"Shut up."

The BU Terrier Men's Hockey ended the last two games of the regular season against The University of New Hampshire. Steve dominated both games scoring two goals along with assisting on three others in the first game, which ended in a 7-1 rout. In the second game, which was closer, he scored one goal and had two assists in a 5-4 win.

"Let's go celebrate!" Laurie exclaimed when he jumped off the bus.

"We have to be at service at eight, remember."

"You don't have to go," she said.

"No, I'll tag along."

"Let's go to your place."

"We can't. Nate's there."

"Nate and who else?" She grinned.

"I forgot her name—some girl he's temporarily giddy over. I have five bucks on it he'll drop her sometime this summer."

"So, what do you want to do?"

"We could go back to your place."

"As long as we talk***"

"Haven't I always?"

"Maybe it's me."

"It could be," he smiled as they walked to her dorm.

They arrived at the dorm and went in. He sat at one end of the bed and she the other.

"I'm perplexed," she said.

"Why?"

"Why would *Sports Illustrated* give a hoot about a young upstart with miles of pizza behind him?"

"We don't have a viable idea that can turn a profit if test marketed correctly. We have to do the first three hundred thousand in English for each country because frankly word of mouth or the trickle down effect works—particularly in European countries and especially the far East and Russia where the government rules and sets the pace of the nation's economy."

"Yes! But can you sell it?"

"Yes! We can but we have to do it as a team and we have to be able to stay focussed instead of splintering off into separate parts. Now the tricky part of that is to be open to new and fresh ideas. People get comfortable with a certain way of life and they like reading your magazine to reinforce their own beliefs. The hero is always squeaky clean and the villain is the LA Raiders."

"You talk more about this than hockey."

"In many ways it's more fun. I went to college for something and it worked."

"Do you think you could've made it without college?"

"Probably not; I would've played in the Canadian Juniors. Just for the experience. I would've played in the Ontario Hockey League, a speed league definitely."

"Ain't life grand?"

"Playing hockey doesn't seem like a big deal next to this but then I hit the ice and it's the most magical thing. Everything disappears for moment and then we get introduced as starters. Hockey kept me in school for awhile but lately school has kept me on the ice. You learn a lot. You ask tertiary questions in class because you're halfway between not wanting people to know and recruiting. It's fun but still chasing that National Championship has me focussed. The coach keeps asking me if the company is going all right. I think he's kind of proud."

"I like working for you. But you should lead more."

"In what way?"

"I don't know: leaders figure that out."

"Give me a for instance."

"Well, I know you like to keep everyone loose. Everything light and inspiring but sometimes it becomes like junior high school."

"You're saying I should crack the whip."

"Just remind them why they're here."

"You're right. My motto for the troops is, "If it ain't fun don't do it." But you're also correct that it can't degenerate into PMS or jock itch. By the way, you have a real live German who called back from the German house. Also we have a Greek guy who is a graduate student fellow who teaches Greek Mythology."

"Do you want to call them now?"

"What's the matter with you?"

"I've never been in this position before."

"Me neither but I am relishing it."

"You aren't nervous; I mean with what the papers are saying."

"It's kind of fun right now—like being on the Olympic team I guess. The team's winning. I'm doing well. If we don't finish this off, then I'll hcar it."

"What I was going to say before I was so rudely interrupted is that I can't believe my parents are letting go through with it!"

"Maybe they trust you."

"I don't know. I did bring you home."

"Thanks very much."

She placed her right foot against his left and smiled.

"I think my parents think that I landed a heck of a guy."

"Well you did."

"Aren't you the confident type. Evidence please."

"I was kidding."

"No, no, no. You started it. Why are you so convinced you're a heck of a guy?"

"I don't know. You like me. That must count for something."

"True. My opinion carries a lot of weight."

"Come here."

"Steve…"

She cuddled up next to him and they talked for awhile and then they both fell asleep. Steve awoke with the sun at 5 o'clock and he looked at Laurie in his arms.

"Hey!" He whispered, "Wake up."

"What?"

"We fell asleep."

"What do you mean we fell asleep? What time is it?"

"Five a.m."

"You're kidding."

"Well we're half way there."

"Go home and change. Be back here for seven."

"Yes, mamm1 Oh! Should I wear a tie?"

"It would be nice."

"I knew you were going to say that."

"Hurry, hurry, hurry!"

"Slave driver***"

"I'm doing the work of the Lord. I'm bringing a heathen to church."

"Do you really think I'm a heathen?"

"Will you go? Please?"

"Okay."

He closed the door and headed downstairs. When he arrived back at the dorm Nate was waiting for him.

"Where were you?"

"We fell asleep."

"We?"

"Yes, Laurie and I?"

"I want to hear the 'great romantic story.'"

"There is no story. We just fell asleep. I have to take a shower. She's taking me to service."

"No kidding."

"Well, don't say it like I have a disease."

"I'm just surprised. You never went to church before."

"We'll see. I'll give it a shot."

"Go shower or you'll be stinking the place up."

"Thank you."

Steve took a quick shower and the dressed in his Navy blue blazer and tan chinos. He wore a simple blue tie and striped, blue, shirt. He buzzed her door at seven and she came down.

"Where are we going?"

He asked when they headed for the T.

"Cambridge. There's a delightful little church in town."

"Every Sunday morning you go here?"

"Pretty much!"

"Does it keep your spirit pure?"

"No but I get to apologize."

He laughed.

"I didn't know you were such a Puritan."

"I'm not."

She turned bright red.

"Who started this conversation?" She asked.

"My hot little hands are in competition with the Almighty?"

"Pretty much***"

"Well once we get married and you bear me ten kids the Lord will love you for being fruit full."

"Do you realize we're going to service?"

"Yes, I do. I just want to let you know what I'll be praying for."

"Come on. It's Sunday."

"Look you wouldn't be offended if this little experiment didn't work."

"Why wouldn't it?"

"I haven't been to church in a long time. Maybe it won't work."

"Just go and listen to the sermon. Just enjoy it. He's a young reverend."

They sat through the service and at the end Steve felt better about things so he guessed the process was good.

"Well," she said on the way home.

"I feel a little odd. It wasn't quite familiar."

"But?"

"But I feel better."

"Good. Are you ready for the MFA?"

"What I'm ready for is the Hockey East playoffs. They start Friday at the TD Bank North Garden."

"All you have on your mind is hockey."

"I have more than that on my mind."

"Like what?"

"Like you, school, Tony, lots of things."

"I was teasing."

"I think I'm just worried about life changing. I see tremendous opportunity in the pros but I wonder if I'm up to the task or if I'll fit in. A hockey teams' chemistry is almost as important as its talent level. I will wonder how to play it next year. Should I be aggressive and take charge or try and fit in."

"I really think you'll know when you hit the ice."

"I've made a decision but am wondering if Harvard would be on the same page. It's kind of risky. I'm going to finish class early here so I leave right after the Frozen Four so I can get to the NHL as soon as possible. And then I'm going to ask Harvard to accept me as an individualized major some different languages, some business, and some photography."

"You're the most worrisome person I've ever met in my life."

"Maybe going to service every Sunday is worth the price of admission. Can you pray to stop worrying?"

"I guess so. Well, drop me off at my dorm and pick me up at 11:45. The meeting should be over by two and then we can go to MFA."

"Okay. Thanks for asking me this morning."

"Thanks for coming."

"Hey, I know I can be really sarcastic sometimes but this was nice. I can learn how to be a sky pilot."

She laughed in spite of herself.

"You're a jerk. It's going to be my full-time occupation keeping you out of mischief."

"Yes, but you'd be board stiff without me."

"I love you."

"Me too!"

They arrived at the dorm and Steve took her upstairs.

"Do you want me to come in?" he asked.

"Yes, but I have homework."

"But***"

"I'll see you at noon."

"Rats."

"Noon!"

"I'll see you then."

She closed the door in his face. He walked back to his dorm and the March wind whipped off the Charles. He stopped in the dining hall and grabbed an English muffin with orange juice and then went upstairs to study.

"How was it?" Nate asked.

"It was good overall but it was strange because I hadn't been in a house of worship for a while. It was different."

"Are you going next week?"

"Yeah, I think I will—just to see."

"Right!"

"Whatever happened to the little Miss?"

"I told her I was going to Sweden. She said, 'Are you nuts?' and that was pretty much it."

"You sound heart broken."

"I'm going to 'the land of blondes.' It'll work out. "

"I love an optimist."

"What are you doing this afternoon after the meeting. I'm glad we made the decision to move it to Harvard."

"Yeah, the area isn't ready yet but someday I want to do something down there. After the meeting we're going we're going to the MFA. There's an impressionist exhibit. Want to come?"

"And be the third wheel. No thanks."

"What were you going to suggest?"

"A movie?"

"Maybe next time***"

"The tournament starts Friday," Nate said.

"We'll do all right."

"We'll win the thing."

"That's what I meant."

"Then the big one. The National Championship Tournament! They put the Frozen Four in Albany, NY my senior year. It couldn't have been in Boston."

"I'll call up the NCAA and see if I can get it changed."

"I already did. They didn't go for it."

"You know if we weren't going to be hockey players when we grew up that would be a pretty good gig."

"What do you mean?"

"Working for the NCAA?"

"Yeah, I guess. I kind of had my heart set on owning my own team."

"I guess I kind of have my heart set on winning a Stanley Cup for the Stars. Hopefully more than one!"

The next morning, Steve was pleasantly surprised by sunshine on the way out the door. He was met by a man in a dark trench coat.

"Hello, Mr. Thompson."

"Who are you, sir?"

"Clarkson Walters, President and CEO of Hasbro Corp?"

"Yes, sir."

"Well, son you can relax. I was just wondering if we could drive you to class. My wife, Mary, is in the car driving."

"Sir, I can't accept anything until after the play-offs."

"We understand that son. We just would like to talk to you about something we think is pretty good."

"Okay."

They jumped into a vintage blue Jaguar and headed up Baystate Rd.

"Well, sir, I'm in. Would you please tell me the plan?"

"What if you win the National Championship?"

"We'll win it. We have the best team. The best family; we'll win."

"Say you do. What are you going to do after that?"

"Graduate early and turn pro."

"I was thinking about the party."

"I don't know. That's run by the athletic department. Those are the people you contact, sir. But I can see what you're driving at. I think."

"Ever heard of Chez Josef?"

"Had my prom there!"

"Let's say some corporation wanted to show that WMASS was as interested in BU athletics as say UMASS. Because those who go out there bring us back rewards ten fold and if it were free for a guest and four relations to come and celebrate your victory would it be worth the time of day?"

"It would be worth it to me. Heck, I'd go."

"Who do I talk to?"

"Jack Bemson my assistant coach and the head of team parties. He makes the sure the children don't get out of hand."

"Well, I will then son. Thank you."

"Okay. Now I have to get to my management class. You know how it is. It was nice meeting you both.

""'Mamm."

Chapter 32

They arrived at Cappo's right on time and everybody was there.

"Ladies and gentlemen; We've been together a few weeks now and I want to say you've all worked very, very hard. It will get harder from this point on. Now! Here is the drop off point. Whomever, wants to leave can do so. I wish you wouldn't to be honest with you. I consider you my friends who took a chance on a different idea. I think we have a winner of an idea here. If anyone wants to go, please do so now," Steve said.

Nobody moved.

"We are talking museum issues for us. What is the most obvious question out there for us?" Steve asked.

"What if Harvard says no?" Laurie answered.

"That's right. Gold Star! But are we crippled? Do we quit?"

"I think you'd have to get traded to another state to do it," Brian said.

"Brian. I don't think so. But since we're all going to be in the area except Mark who's going to play ball and keep track of us with his brand new laptop that he's going to buy with his bonus. Right, Mark?"

"Right, Chief!"

"Anyway, we hold our ground and begin negotiations with them. This is a good idea and they just may need clarification. And do you know what? We may need some too."

"Have you taken the GMAT's yet?" John Davis asked.

"In June***"

"I can help you if you want."

"All right, Thanks."

"You'll owe me one."

"Ah! Capitalism! What am I giving in trade?"

"A Red Sox Warm up jacket."

"You're from Ohio. Shouldn't it be the Indians?"

"In the last two years, I've been to more Red Sox games than Cleveland games and since I'm living here I'll support the Sox."

"All right it's yours. Just get me through that damned test."

"Let's say we have a winner out of the box. What do we do?"

"We invite the guys and gals from Harvard to Cornwall's for a blast," John Davis said.

"And after?"

"We work with Harvard to find a construction outfit to build the place," Clarence said.

"We work with Harvard to promoting it," Chris Davidson said.

"No matter what we stay positive and believe that all challenges can be solved," Steve said.

"One more thing; we all came here with different backgrounds and different similarities and we worked through our differences to come up with a great idea. We're going to do this thing and I'm hoping you all go home and pray that we do this thing in Boston."

On the way to the museum, Steve asked Laurie if she thought he looked confident and self-assured in front of the class.

"Yes, very much so why?"

"I was sweating bullets up there. I didn't want to appear fatalistic that their hard work had gone to waste."

"Have a little faith. Will you?"

"Yes, mamm."

"I love you."

"This is incredible," he whispered to her.

She laughed and slapped him gently on the side of the head.

"Let's get inside. I want to see the exhibit before it closes," she said.

"I heard somewhere that painters look at the picture from the side to see the layers of paint the original artist used to get the coloring and reflection. Can you tell the difference?"

"Actually no; I can't."

"Me neither. It surely is beautiful though."

"Monet is my mom's favorite. I don't know enough about the technical aspects of impressionist paintings but I do think they're beautiful."

"Well you can just enjoy the work. You don't have to be an expert."

"That's why I'm here."

"I wish I could pass a painting class. I'd take one then."

"Are you sure you can't?"

"Trust me. I have a coordination problem with writing, painting, and drawing."

"Me to***"

"It sure is beautiful."

"I wonder what it took to paint these."

"What do you mean?"

"The patience I guess. They must've been incredibly patient."

"They must've been laughed at in the beginning."

"How do you figure?"

"Well, it's different and anything that's different gets laughed at. Unfortunately those are still the rules today. I bet they went through some aggravation at the beginning."

"Yes, I can see your point."

"I had it easy at BU. I was on the hockey team. I didn't tank my grades or anything but it's like your automatically accepted on some level. It kind of works against you too sometimes but over all you notice, a difference and it can kill you if you aren't smart."

"For instance***"

"You get to think the world owes you a living because you are a hockey player and you start not doing the right things in the classroom and pretty soon that good life you're living evaporates and goes away. Your reward is driving a truck plowing snow for the Department of Public Works. You have to be careful listening to people telling you that you're great."

"Everybody goes through something I guess."

"Still, I'm not weird though. Am I?"

"Can I claim the Fifth?"

"You think I'm weird."

She giggled and he looped his arm around her and pulled her close.

"What am I going to do with you?" He asked.

"Marry me."

"I'll have to. You tell me the truth. I need that. I am kind of weird. "

"All right*** Fine! You're kind of weird."

"You're supposed to say, 'No honey. That's not true.'"

"You can't argue with a block of cement."

"Can we talk about something else?"

"Sure. It's five o'clock. What do you want to do?"

"I want to take you to the North End and show you Paul Revere's house. Then I'll take you out to dinner."

"Where?"

"Oh, there are a million Italian restaurants in the North End."

"Italian section?"

"Uh-huh! They have feasts like every weekend in the summer for one saint or another. It's starting to break up a little. Non-Italians are starting to move in but it's still mostly Italian."

"Any gangsters?"

"I'm sure there are but I don't want to meet them."

"We could go to Copley Square. There's a Legal Seafood."

"I was kind of looking forward to taking you to the North End."

"All right, I'm buying."

"We'll go Dutch."

"You're such a man. Can't you accept a gift?"

"No. I'm supposed to be paying for it."

"Hey, by all mcans."

"Good. Hey, are we fighting?"

"We are having a strong discussion."
"Is it over yet because?"
"I think so."
"Can I kiss you?"
"By all means ***"
He dipped her back and kissed deeply and they heard a little boys laugh. Steve broke off the kiss and turned around. There was a little boy who was pointing at them and giggling.
"What are you doing Mister?" the little boy asked.
"I'm getting out of the doghouse," Steve smiled as he stood Laurie up.
"I think you're pretty funny," the boy smiled.
"Well, we'll be seeing you."
"Bye Bye," the boy waved and then disappeared around the corner.
"Do you feel humiliated?" Laurie asked.
"I was trying to make amends."
"And you did very well."
"Really?"
"Very well***"
"Well, let's get to the North End."
"We'll take the T instead of a cab. I like the T. There nothing like that in Midland."
"There's nothing like that back in Springfield either."
They took the T and she sat quietly as they past through the lighted tunnels. He held her hand and she smiled.
When they arrived at Government Center, he walked her through Fanueil Hall and underneath the over pass onto Hancock Street. Eventually they found Paul Revere's house.
"It's small," she said.
"I think people were smaller then. It's too bad it's closed. It's really cool inside."
"You like history."
"Yes, very much***"
"Do you think you'll fail in the NHL?"
"Where did that come from?"
"Well, you seem to worry a lot. I'd like to get it out in the open."
"Definitely not; I just think about possible disaster scenarios so I can minimize the chances that they may occur."
"Just like that?"
"What are you asking me?"
"I was going to pump you up and give the greatest motivational speech ever but you're ruining it. I didn't expect you to be so confident."
"It's the opportunity of a lifetime. I don't know I guess. You play as hard as you can for as long as you can. Geeze, miss, we haven't even had dinner yet

and you're hitting me with all these deep questions."

"Sorry, but is the NHL?"

"Trying the back door; are you? Look, these days the scouting is so intense. They measure you for everything shoe size, how long your tongue is—everything. You have to trust them a little bit. They must know what they're doing. Besides I was drafted at eighteen. I'm a much better hockey player now"

"I want to stay despite the cold."

"Yes, Boston has something. I don't know what it is but it is something that attracts you to it."

"I agree."

"I second my own motion."

"I have a subject about work that needs to be addressed."

"What is it?'

"We need five laptops for the troops. All they have are PC's."

"Okay, that is good. What do you recommend?"

"We could get them refurbished."

"No. I like the way Dell does things with the three-year 24/7 maintenance policy on their new models. I'd rather pay now than pay later. I can just imagine being at Coca-Cola or somebody and have the laptop die in the middle of a presentation. And even is it does, there's a good chance you can fix it over the phone."

"We also have a little problem with Rico and Mark."

"What would that be?"

"An over abundance of healthy competition; they're more interested in beating each other up than getting the right answer."

"Sometimes I see that by it's like that on the ice."

"We can't drop our gloves in the board room and go," she smiled.

"That was good. I liked that. Look, I'll be aware of it and I'll tell them to knock it off it gets too bad. The truth is; they're both doing good work for us."

"I just don't want them to kill each other."

"Well on next Sunday, we three wise men get to look over the letters—type them up and send them out. Then we wait."

"What are you going to do? You spent all this time on it."

"Just relax—maybe go to the MFA a couple of times. Head home on a Thursday. I don't know. I figure it will be a month before they reply."

"Well, no matter you've done a great thing."

"How so?"

"You had all these kids working together without them killing each other."

"It's only a great thing if you succeed on a great level."

" You put a lot of pressure on yourself."

"Cultural differences between states."

"Massachusetts is a Commonwealth,"

"After almost four years here, you think I'd remember that."

"I should probably call Hekyl and Jekyl tonight."

She smirked.

"Well, I don't want things to get out of control. Plus they may have a real issue that's bugging them."

"Do you play hockey because you're the best or because you love the game."

"It's a lot more fun when you're winning. But sometimes I wonder what it be like if I stuck with the trumpet or Scouting. I have some regrets but hockey has been and will be very good to me."

She blushed.

"You're a special person."

"Come on."

"I'm serious."

"So are you."

"Life sure is fun isn't it?"

She giggled and then she laughed.

"I love you," she said.

"I'll love you always."

"We could go for a walk."

"Yeah, I guess we could. Let me call Rico first."

"Hey it's me," Steve said.

"What's up Boss?"

"Rico I have to tell you seriously about the company."

"I'm not out. Am I?"

"No. It may not even be a major deal but I wanted to touch base with you. You seem to have a bit of tension with Paco and it's going nowhere. He's going to get the same speech so don't worry. What's bothering you?"

"He has a title and I don't. I work hard. I deserve one."

"A title?"

"Yes, sir. He's Director of Accounting and I'm head flunky!"

"Look, the reason you don't have a title is because we're going to hire an attorney to fill the position. Maybe you could get the lay of the land before you start that internship this summer and find out who would be interested contingent on the fact that he or she takes you on as assistant legal counsel."

"You'd do that for me."

"The only thing wrong with you is you're young. When you pass the bar, you're a lawyer. Then you can act like an adult."

"Geeze, I thought you were going to can me."

"You work too hard. We'll find something for you to do. Square things with Mark; go out and have a beer."

"Yes, sir."

He called Mark next.

"Mark, it's your long lost Boss."

"Hey, Chief, what's going on?"

"Well, I'm kind of concerned. It seems some tension has developed between you and Rico."

"It's just fooling around. Schoolyard stuff***"

"You can't do that in the office. Mark, I'm going to say it simply. You have to grow up. You have an important position in the company and you weren't correct in evaluating Rico's worth to the team. You're both important and I talked to him. He'll square it with you over a beer. I don't want any punches thrown. Nice easy conversation! Get it?"

"Yeah, Boss. I was just kidding. I didn't know that he was that upset. It's kind of nice having a title thought."

"Be good with it and it will stay. We're a team. A family! Get it?"

"Yes, sir! Can I say something, sir?"

"Yeah, sure!"

"I ain't never worked for a company like this before. In my other jobs, they were high school even in college—everybody cutting each other up—stuff like that. It was how you proved yourself."

"Which job do you like better?"

"I understand, sir."

"Good enough, I'll be in touch."

"Anyway," he said after they hung up, "I'm contemplating a lifestyle change."

"What does that mean?"

"Well you see I was a Yankee fan. Or I am a Yankee fan. And now that I'm living in Boston full time, I don't believe that it would be right not to support the Red Sox. However, it would seem terribly opportunistic now that they have won a World Series."

"Just wait for them to be terrible again."

"That's not practical. They actually seem to have it together. They trade for big name players and sign them. It's kind of like a real baseball club."

"Well, what's the problem?"

"I only became a Yankee fan after my grandfather died; because he was a Yankee fan. I was a Red Sox fan before that and I suffered Bucky Dent, and Bill Buckner. I can't even say Bill Buckner's name because he is a gentleman and he shouldn't be tagged with that moniker."

"Which is?"

"Choke artist."

"They went for a walk up and down the streets of the North End. Steve had still not solved his problem but he put it away in the back in the back of his mind. It was quite amazing. People were everywhere as Boston was waking up from a cold winter.

"Do you want to get a cannoli?"Steve asked.

"Uh-huh! I ate too much at dinner."

"You ever have an espresso?"
"Yes. It's rocket fuel."
"Nix on that too huh."
"Let's just walk."
"Come on, I'll show you the harbor."
"I've been there. It's nice. Walk me home before it gets too late."
"From here?"
"Sure."
"Why not?"

He walked her over Beacon Hill and up Newbury Street. He held her hand close to his body like one would a small child and brought her to her dorm. It was about nine o'clock when they arrived.

"Good enough?" He asked.
"Perfect."
"May I?"
"You better."

He leaned his head down and kissed her on her cheek. She started to laugh.

"I was getting around to it," he smiled.
"All right, be serious. Try again."
"Okay."

He bent down and kissed her right on the lips and she still started to laugh.

"I'm trying my best here," he said.
"That one was my fault," she grinned.
"All right again!"

He kissed her deeply and she clung to him.

"You're beautiful," he said.
"I'm in love."
"Me too."
"Come on upstairs?"
"Homework."
"What do you think you're in school or something?"
"I don't know. That's the rumor."
"I'll call you later."
"Everybody here thinks you're a hero," Tony said as the phone rang.
"I'll be back for the party—when we win the National Championship!"
"Do you ever feel like people are just being condescending to you?"
"What do you mean?"

"They suck but you have to deal with them at work because they are good at adding one hundred dollars to the price. They're the most money grubbing weasels I've ever seen."

"Is this your mental illness or are you just pissed?"

"The team lost an account today over $150 that we tried to slide in at the end. We were so discouraged. The boss sees no Forest for the Trees. He wants to nickel and dime right now. Right here!"

"Calm down. Calm down."

"We worked our butts off for three weeks."

"What was the program for."

"Oh, a coffee company; He made Juan Valdez look like he was riding a donkey. It was beautiful."

"Tony, slow down, you're talking about coffee."

"It was good coffee though."

"Will you stop? Things will change. I guarantee it."

"I have some ideas that will make the magazine marketable. Some range from the cheap like insertion cards for subscriptions to the ultra expensive—using live athletes in ad space. The problem is our image. What do we want to project?

"Are we hip and fresh and crap like that or are we conservative or do we move with conventional values."

"You got anything for all three?"

"I knew you were going to say that. No, not yet. Early next week the latest. We're really starting to work together."

"In Springfield, they passed up Red Rose."

"They are working together. I'll give them that. They ended up at the East Longmeadow Public Library. Is that dedication or what?"

"Lay it on me."

"My agency is kind of out of the loop as far as Boston is concerned—others aren't. Could you be doing better business for that area?"

"No. They don't seem to mind me scoring goals and I'm from East Longmeadow."

"I finally have something good to tell you about."

"Definitely lay it on me."

"Well, it's not really official yet but I am thinking heavily about grad school."

"Where?"

"Well, that's what I wanted to talk to you about."

"Money?"

"I hate it man. You either have too much or not enough."

"Tony, you're my brother. Do you need the money for grad school?"

"We'll sit down and make a budget of what you need and then we will divvy it up by months. You would really like to go to BU. Wouldn't you?"

"Yeah. I had a lot of anger when I graduated because my grades weren't where they should be. And anger piled on top of anger when I was diagnosed. It took me a long time to get over it. I'm ready to go back and finish what I started."

"MBA?"

"Would you be offended if it was Entrepreneurship?."

"Well, isn't that cool."

"Are you telling me the truth?"

"Why wouldn't I be, it is my money.'

"Well, what if I want to do something else?"

"Like?"

"Well, it is more like I want to launch my own business, well ***"

"Could you spit it out please?"

"I'd like to own a bookstore or two or three. I don't want to go globe hopping like you. I want a nice job so that I can come home to my wife."

"Yes but does that make you a good man."

Tony laughed.

"You don't think I am a chicken or anything, are you?"

"You are my brother. What am I supposed to think? Listen, it is no fun if you don't want to be here. On the other hand, I don't want to think you are a failure because you want to go to your kid's little league games. Personally, I am going to miss you."

"I can do this job you know. It's not too much for my mental illness."

"Tony it is not too much for you as a human being. You are a good man. Stop measuring yourself against a disease. It is liking breaking your arm or having diabetes. That's it!"

"Annie says I should just give it up and just teach. Get the Masters and teach but I like my idea."

"Don't worry about negative people. That's how my idea started. You work hard because you have talent."

"Do you have negative thoughts. I figured you'd be wring your hands and the whole bit."

"If you train people to be happy then, it comes back to you. This is the United States of America. If you treat good people well, what goes around comes around. You need to go back to your parents place, watch your favorite DVD and hang out with a couple of buds."

"Yeah, that sounds good! Maybe a vacation!"

"I hear Arizona is nice. You can golf."

"No. I can't actually."

"Why?"

"I have about a 10,000 handicap."

"Yeah, but if you were really smart, it's only dry heat out there. Straightens the ball and makes it go farther."

"Shut up. I'm making a life's decision here."

"Don't be rude."

"Honey, I'm going to call my brother."

"Hey, it's me! What's up?"

"Absolutely nothing; I got hornswaggled by my own wife."

"We were going to buy a nice little condo. Perfect starter home. Nothing too fancy—just the basics. She took me to Wilbraham and bought a 2,700 square foot colonial. She must've put something in my orange juice. I don't know what came over me. I said, 'Yes!'"

"Look, dude. I don't want to break your heart but that shows signs of more children."

"Well, I don't mind that. I have two acres of lawn to mow."

"Well, that's why we have children."

"I can't believe I signed the papers. I must've been out of my head."

"Is it a nice house for crying out loud?"

"Brand new, right from the carpenter's tool shed. We move in six weeks from now."

"Hah! Hah! Hah!"

"Look, smart guy. I'm working like hell, to pay for it between your job and working for Mr. Maggoo, I'm pulling eighty."

"Look Tony, I've said this a lot to people lately, in order for us to get off the ground salaries and bonuses remain fixed. I'll make it up as soon as I can."

"I know but still a real house. It is very, mind numbing. I thought, I was going to get dad and mom's but as it happens I'm have just a combination of pride and abject fear."

"Dude, it's a house, you're not going to the moon."

"I hope you are right. Annie's running around the mapping the whole deal. This is the baby's room. This is the master bedroom, etc… All I want to know is where we can we put the TV. I don't think I'm going to have much say in the matter. Once she gets a head of steam up brother, that's it."

"Well, look at it this way you could've spent six months with Annie buying a house. She takes six months to buy shoes."

"We will; e mail shots of the house and the terror a split pea land later."

"Explain the second part please."

"It's the baby. All he eats is pea soup."

"Good-bye."

"What?"

"Good-bye."

"You're a Fascist. You know that."

"Call me tomorrow."

"All right! Hey, you know that crack about eighty hours. I don't really care. From a personal standpoint it's more than I could ever imagine me doing. Just between you and I it gives mortgage payments, vacation money, and investment opportunities. You really shouldn't hang up though because I want to ask you about those personal trading opportunities."

"Well, as near as I can figure, they're open for the rank amateur or the seasoned pro. You have a business degree so that helps. You know about location, sales, inventory etc. You have to balance all those demographics in your head and decide if it's a viable investment. Apparently you can talk it over with the counselors they have there. I really should get involved in that because you have to grow up sometime."

"I'll dig around al little more on the net and see what I can come up with."

"Good-bye."

Chapter 33

"Are you guys ready?" Laurie asked him the night before the Hockey East Playoffs.

"Yes, without a doubt we'll win "

"Good!"

"Yeah it is. We'll be celebrating, I anticipate."

"I have to learn how to cook."

"Any other pressing needs?"

"Well, it's just something that I thought of."

"Take out sweetheart."

"I love you."

"I still have to cook for Christmas and Thanksgiving at least."

"Don't worry. We'll figure it out."

"Do you know how to cook a turkey?"

"Baste it and wait until the little white thing pops up."

"Well, that's one up on me."

"You make your own luck."

"Can you imagine our first Christmas?"

"It'll be great."

He scrunched his nose.

"Excuse me?"

"Well, I'm going to be expected to do interviews and that really is weird for me because I'm not used to talking about myself. You just want to go through life trying to build instead of tear down and there are a lot of people who think you don't have the guts if you don't stick a guy. I want to build a reputation as a hard hitter but fair guy. I don't want to goon it up. That's not what I'd teach the kids at the hockey school. I don't want my contribution to the sport to be one that's not detrimental to the values of the game."

"Do you really think about this stuff?"

"It'll be my profession."

"You're an idealist."

"I just don't want my kids to read in the paper a headline that reads *Thompson Most Hated Player in NHL*. There's hockey and there's hockey."

"Do you think they'll be a big adjustment?"

"Yeah, I'll have to learn the ins and outs of the big leagues. I'm hoping to find a guy that will take me under his wing and teach me about the pro game."

"You have to find an agent."

"Got that one covered. They contacted me before I signed my letter of intent."

"Are you ready for tomorrow night?"

"We'll win."

"Confident."

"Our team is playing desperate like they haven't won all season. They're hungry."

"What if you don't win?"

"Look! Let me tell you, you always think you're going to win and if you have the talent, which we do, it usually turns out that way. It means we'll win."

"What drives you?"

"Nothing really! It's more the *Curious George* affect. I wonder if I can do it, and then if I can inspire other people to get into the same dream. It's the challenge of getting really talented people to work as a team. I do it for the enjoyment. It is the teaching and the ability to learn."

The first round game was between UMASS and BU. BU went out guns a blazing in the first period and scored three times. Steve picked up three assists. UMASS got two back in the beginning of the second but Nate scored once an assisted on Jeff Philips goal to bring the score up to 5-2. The third period saw the teams trade goals with Steve picking up another assist. BU had gotten beyond the first round.

Afterwards Steve was deluged by the press corps.

"How many assists were you going to rack up?" One scribe asked.

"It just happened to be one of those nights, fellas. Somebody had to put them in the net."

"Didn't you want a goal?" Another one asked.

"An assist is a goal. It doesn't matter to me who finishes it as long as it is finished. We won as a team tonight. I made the pass but somebody finished it off."

"Some people say the great ones look for the goal first. What is your response to that?"

"Well, we won tonight and that's what matters. We'll suit up to win the next game and winning will be what matters—points or no. I'm comfortable with my role on this team."

"Are you thinking about the Stars?"

"All I want to do is get through this tournament alive for right now. The day after we win the Frozen Four, I'll call the agent that I want and start negotiations for a contract."

"Could you tell us who the agent is?"

"Guys I can't do that. The NCAA has rules."

"Yet. You have contact with an agent."

"He contacted me before I signed my letter of intent. I remembered him. Guys I really have to go. My parents and my brother are here."

"One more question."

"This is absolutely the last question so make it good."

"Is it because of the money that you'll be leaving before graduation?"

"I'm prepared for the jump to the NHL. Now guys I really have to go. I'll see you in the next round. I'm just graduating early—not leaving school."

The press reluctantly dispersed and Steve reluctantly put his tie back on. He checked his hair in the mirror and walked out of the locker room. The clan was milling around the entrance including Laurie.

"Four points," Tony smiled.

"We won. I just got into that conversation with the press corps," Steve smiled.

"Yeah, but you were great!" Tony smiled.

"Thanks Tony," Steve smiled embarrassed.

"What are we going to do?"

"Well I don't have a bed check so I can go back pretty late or pretty early as the case may be. But first I'd like to talk to Tony and Dad—men's business."

The male Thompsons followed him.

"Well, what are we here for?" Dad smiled.

"I'm thinking about becoming a Red Sox fan," Steve whispered.

"You've got to be kidding," Tony laughed.

"You. Mr. Yankee. To buying into the Sox?" His father asked.

"Well, I only became a Yankee fan when Grandpa died and that was because he was a Yankee fan. This is a major life decision here. It could affect how my kids grow up."

"It's baseball," his father said.

"Not in this town. It's religion. I just have one problem with my decision. It seems like because I'll be getting a rather large paycheck from the Bruins, it will be an example of buying into the Sox."

"Weren't you a Red Sox fan before?" Tony asked.

"Yeah, they win now however and that's the problem. If they stunk, nobody would notice."

"I say go with your heart," Tony said.

"Me too," his dad said.

"I'm still thinking."

"Here comes mom," Tony said.

"We could go down to the Theatre District," Mrs. Jones suggested.

"Do I hear an ulterior motive, dear" Her husband smiled.

"Well I thought it would be neat to see what's playing. Maybe we could catch a play sometime."

"I think that's a wonderful idea. We should drive though. It can be a tough section sometimes," Laurie said.

"How many cars do we have?" Steve asked.

"We're good. We have two. Annie took hers because we left later."

"Why don't you kids ride together. There's late night parking right out front," their father said.

When they sat in the car, Steve was quiet. He was thinking about another couple of possible points he could've had.

Laurie kicked him not so gently on the ankle. He winced and looked at her. She whispered.

"I've never met these people. Say something."

"Laurie's feeling a bit out of place because she doesn't know you. Please talk and make her feel at home."

He stuck his tongue out at her as he rubbed his ankle.

"We tried to civilize my little brother but it didn't work. Don't mind him," Tony said.

"Don't feel shy around us. You can say whatever you want," Annie said.

They talked along the way and the girls got along especially well. When they arrived at the parking lot in front of the Wang Theatre, they waited for their parents.

"I can smell it. Spring is coming," Tony said.

"It means flowers," Annie said.

"It means baseball. Thank God for that."

The girls met their parents but the boys hung around by the car and talked.

"Can I ask you a question? Straight up?" Tony asked.

"Fire away."

"I don't want to put this in an awkward way but are you prepared for the change in lifestyle you're going to be exposed to?"

"You mean the money?"

"That's part of it."

"Yeah. I know. It's the big leagues. I plan on going to the rookie tutorials. The do's and don'ts of being a professional athlete are written on the wall for the guys. The whole trick to it is picking honest and trustworthy people to work for you. Dad used to say, 'Untrustworthy people can't find a trusting person because they don't know what qualities to look for.'"

"You just make sure they're good, Sonny Boy."

"Feeling better aren't you?"

"Come on I'm serious. Don't fall for slick bum. Use your head."

"All right! I understand."

"You can always call me."

"I used to hate it when my big brother said stuff like that. Now it's not so bad."

"We've been through some bad stuff but it's coming around," Tony said.

"Do you want to come to Albany?"

"Sure, I've never been there."

"It's the capitol of New York State I heard."

"Must be impressive***"

"I looked it up on the internet. Mostly, rural area around the city!"

"You looked it up on the internet."

"I was curious."

"Come on the girls are getting fidgety."

The men caught up with the rest of the family and went to the box office of the Wang Theatre and although it was closed, they were able to pick up a copy of the schedule and the web site where they could order tickets on line.

"*The Sound of Music*, *The Lion King*, *The King and I.* Wow! They're all coming!" Their mother said.

"I say *The Sound of Music*," Steve said.

"I say *The Lion King*," Tony said.

"That's a kids show," Steve teased.

"I've never seen the movie," Tony said.

"You haven't seen *The Lion King*?" Annie asked.

"No. I never have," he answered seriously.

The girls giggled.

"I've seen the other ones though," he said defensively.

The others were roaring now.

"I'm licked," Tony smiled.

"Anybody have a quarter?" Steve asked.

"I have one," his father said.

"Call it," Steve tossed it in the air.

"Heads! " Tony yelled.

The quarter hit the pavement and rolled on edge in a circle and it laid down. Tony scurried over to it.

"Ah! Hah! Heads!" Tony said, "*The Lion King*!"

"Okay! We'll go see *The Lion King*." Steve grinned.

"Let's go to that nice, seafood place. They have a bar," His father suggested.

"All right that's fine."

They ordered a couple of appetizers and drinks. They talked until almost closing—mostly about what awaited the almost newlyweds out there. Steve looked at Laurie who he thought looked uncomfortable a couple of times but he kept quiet because he thought she pulled out of it. Steve was busy himself trying to think of anything that could go wrong with the plan. He found one. He worried about minutiae and he knew it and it was driving him crazy but he figured it would be worth it in some way. Laurie nudged his elbow and whispered.

"Are you okay? You haven't said a word in a half an hour."

"I'm just thinking that's all."

She looked at him strangely but didn't say anything.

The evening broke up and everybody kissed goodnight or shook hands before the two couples headed to their hotel. They made plans for breakfast in the hotel at nine a.m.

"This just leaves us two," Steve said.

"What were you so quiet about tonight?"

"Let's go upstairs."

"Fine but you have to tell me."

They went upstairs to her room and they lay next to each other on the bed."

"Stop being a wise guy."

"I wasn't."

"You're awfully preoccupied."

"The Bruins are old. There are lots of thirty-something guys that didn't even get them to the conference finals. It is ripe picking for a team needing one more piece to the puzzle but too old to function with the elite teams in the league. Hence, trades for picks to rebuild around you."

"That means me and more than a few others."

"The Stars have to get some young legs or they'll just be five hundred forever."

"You took the wrong major. You realize this. You should be a coach."

"You could kiss me."

"Yeah, I could."

"It'd be kind of neat to have snow at Christmas. I never planned on that before."

"Will you kiss me just so I can shut you up?"

"Sure. I'll buy that?"

It took awhile to shut him up but it was well worth it for both sides. He held her in his arms afterwards and didn't say anything. The next day, he picked up a paper and read that the Boston Bruins had traded for a second round and a third round pick in next year's draft.

"I told you I'm a genius," she smiled on her way to breakfast the next morning.

"Do you know how much GM's agonize over those decisions?"

"I don't think they agonized too much over you."

"Why thank you?"

"Now; it's just a normal breakfast: don't scare your mother. Talk to your family."

"Yes, mamm."

"And don't talk to me like I'm an old maid."

"I was trying to be polite, Miss."

"Now you're getting it."

"But***"

"Hey, I could've been really sticky and said Ms."

"You know just because you had a hunch doesn't mean you own me on hockey knowledge."

"Embarrassed you got beat by a girl?"

"Yes."

His phone rang and he answered it.

"I can't believe you did that! What's the matter with you? We had a deal. You'd take it easy."

"Excuse me. Who is this?"

"You damn well know who it is."

"Oh, Chris Davidson, is this you?"

"You killed us."

"We did not. Do you have something on your mind?"

"In my spare time, since baseball is my favorite sport, I want to cover some UMASS baseball games just for fun."

"Get them published in *The Collegian.* Go for the hard stuff. Chris you have good ideas but you only meet them halfway. Believe in yourself. Once! Please!"

"Yes, sensei."

"I'm serious. Now what's on your mind?"

"I may want to write for the magazine. I'll do my marketing stuff. That's not a problem. It's actually kind of fun but I'm just going to try this writing thing."

"Fine, get a pencil and paper."

"Okay, wait a minute."

"Got one?"

"Yeah! Go ahead."

"They way you write an article is. The lead sentence at the top must include this information: Who? What? When? How? Why? And it is written in the inverted pyramid style. All the important information is at the top and it drains into a funnel at the bottom."

"I don't want to sound stupid but why?"

"Because when your nasty editor comes by with his sickle—he starts hacking off the bottom first. Your masterpiece can stay untouched on top."

"It took you one semester to learn that."

"Shut up!"

"I'm trying to save enough wealth to buy a note book. I want one of those new space age ones that you can do computer graphics on. We have to have one of those."

"Do you sleep?"

"Three hours a night."

"Really?"

"It is Zoo Mass man, nobody sleeps."

"Well, I'm sorry but we will be winning again tomorrow night."

"You're lucky I write a column."

"I bet you guys just had an off night."

"You're sickening."

"Yes. I am. Don't forget to memorize that stuff. I'll get you out fitted to be a professional journalist later. Get a tape recorder."

"Yes, sir."

Chapter 34

On the way back to his dorm, he saw Nate coming down Comm Ave.

"Hey, your mother's going to get worried," Steve smiled.

"I don't have a mother."

"Are you serious?"

"Don't be a jerk."

"Could you please tell me something?"

"Yeah!"

"How come you don't say anything at the meetings?"

"I guess I'm rolling around the possibilities for this project and the launching point for the second stage."

"And?"

"We're doing well! But still it's formidable. Basically we're waiting for sponsorship right now. The letters will go out and things will progress."

"I'm going to need somebody in Canada for stage two."

"Your already proving and abiding by the success of stage one?"

"I'm cautiously optimistic."

"All right! Then until we hear different it will be a success."

"I have a personal problem."

"Laurie?"

"Baseball!"

"What?"

"Well, since I'm going to be living in Boston, I thought I'd come back to my youth."

"What are you talking about?"

"Well, I became a Yankee fan because my grandfather was sick and eventually passed away. I figured someone in the family had to carry on the tradition. And then the Red Sox got new owners who were able to play the game at another level. Also, somehow the grief of my grandfather wore off."

"Well, you have a decision to make."

"This is serious business you know. I'm talking life-altering stuff. This baseball is in Boston."

"I truly do think you're twelve years old sometimes.'

"A life isn't anything without the Yankee—Red Sox rivalry."

"Which side are you on?"

"I don't know."

"Well sleep on it for crying out loud. Let me ask you a question. If you stayed a Yankee fan and I a Red Sox fan, would it affect our friendship?"

"No. There are other things that could affect our friendship."

"So?"

"I'm trying to look at this logically. Fenway Park is the better park but the Yankees have better uniforms. On the other hand, Boston seems to have caught winner's fever signing guys to make them better even though they are really good anyway."

"Keep thinking you'll screw yourself into the ground."

"Steve Thompson—A loyal member of Red Sox Nation!"

"You could be worse."

"I don't know. Even though they were my grandfather's team, I kind of like them myself. I think my grandfather was kind of a complex guy. On the one hand he always told me to be a gentleman. He probably gambled sixty per cent of his take home pay away. Maybe I just like the Yankees."

"Geeze, that's rough. You're neurotic—absolutely and totally."

"Hey! If you had children, what would you teach them?"

"To experience as much of the world as they could. Why?"

"I'm talking about baseball—you idiot!"

"Look, there's one eternal team in the major leagues. No matter what success or what dereliction of duty to the baseball Gods they have: it will always be the Boston Red Sox. If I were you, I'd join history. It can't hurt."

"The Yankees have something like twenty-seven World Championships. That is a lot; even for New York."

"It seems you have an edge."

"Do you realize, we've had less complicated conversations about politics?"

"Baseball transcends practically any other activity in the world. Hockey's good, but if I could hit a curve, I'd be playing ball."

"Go to church you heathen and pray for your lost, immortal soul. How can you be a Yankee fan?"

"It's not that bad. I think."

"The Red Sox have better uniforms too."

"What if I change? Everyone will laugh."

"Look, as important as baseball is to you and I'm not making fun of you, however, there is thing inside of you that has to be appeased and that is your soul so I'm suggesting that you go to church and stop bugging me."

"So should we talk about something else?"

"I'll never forget this damned school. I love this freakin' place. I learned how to win here—especially in the classroom. When I get my sheepskin, I'll know I finished and I'll be prepared to move on. I sound like a recruiting ad but it's true."

"You all play some hockey."

"The best part of it all is that if I blew out both knees tomorrow, I wouldn't be another dumb jock looking for a job."

"Well, we're almost there. Graduation***"

"Do you remember when we were freshman and we got lost walking up Comm Ave. to go to GSU?"

"Yeah, did I feel like an idiot!"

"That's the spirit."

"Now, can we talk about something important?"

"Like?"

"Tomorrow we hit the letters."

"You need a hand?"

"You have too much homework?"

"Hey, for my degree, I'll work harder."

"Okay. We meet at ten."

"What the hell? This place must be teaching us something."

"Yeah. I've been thinking that lately too."

"As long as you play the way you play, you can call yourself what you want."

"Look, I play to win and there are times that a punch in the mouth is the way to win. Sometimes you don't like doing it. Sometimes, you catch that little so and so who's been sticking you guys all night and by divine Providence that fool comes over the line with his head down, there ain't nothing sweeter."

The next morning, Nate asked.

"Did we have an intelligent conversation last night?"

"God help me. I think I'm a Red Sox fan."

"Again!"

"Well I went to church? And I saw Jesus."

"Oh, Lord."

"Exactly."

"You're hopeless."

"'Be nice to nerds they may be your boss someday,' Bill Gates."

"You ain't a nerd. You're just really smart. And you have finally come to a positive conclusion in your life."

"I need a hat."

"It's called a cap genius.' Anyway, the merits of playing in Sweden, and playing in Montreal culturally of course are very much good for a young guy."

"Since, I have been trained for one soul thought about hockey and that is Montreal sucks. I don't know if I can help you that much. I know that Sweden gets three hours of light a day. Good luck on your tan pal."

"Come on, you're a college educated guy. You must know something."

"Dude it's the same thing in Montreal. They have the ice festival there and it lasts until May."

"Nothing against Sweden***"

"Ah, you're toast with them anyway?"

"I think you're making a mistake."

"Hockey was like a tool for me. It got me a college education and I was able to partly see the United States. "

"And now you want to see more of the world. The NHL is the only league in the world where you can be in Phoenix one night and Montreal the next. You want to see the world; make the Olympic team."

"Maybe. It just seems I've played hockey because it was a thoroughfare to an education and know I find out that I'm looking for that education again."

"So take French Canadian."

"Oui."

"See? You're only about nine million characters short."

"I'll think about it."

The phone rang.

"Hey, it's Boston College calling. Where the heck have you been?"

"Did you get the league offices for Japanese baseball?"

"Absolutely, and totally," Shaun said.

"I've had a life altering experience this weekend. I'm a Red Sox fan."

"Why?"

"What do you mean why?"

"What's in it for you?"

"Nobody paid me."

"I'm sure, you being of high moral conviction would never take the money anyway. What's in it for you?"

"I'm getting sick of you."

"Please answer the question."

"Well, I look at it this way. If they keep winning, I will no joke be the happiest man on the face of the earth. However, if they tank*** I'll just photograph the images as an artist and not think about anything. It'll be like three to four hours of novocaine."

"You know every conversation I have with gets weirder and weirder."

"Yes but…"

"Do you mind? We have business to attend to."

"What business would that be?"

"Well, we're getting good reception from most of the league but we still have a few hold outs. I'm learning Japanese one word at a time it seems gai jin means something more impolite than foreigner. And I am learning polite Japanese one word at a time. Hai means Hello, Domo means thank you informally, and Domo Arigato means thank you formally. They want me out there the first week I can get free."

"Well, well, well if we ain't making progress. Mr. Vivenzio is hot on the trail of the tour of Italy and Lynne is fast talking the Italians into access for soccer teams. We'd like to do all the sports right away but budget constraints.... Well, we have to be careful."

"I don't want to be rude. But why did you send me to Japan?"

"Do you like it?"

"The people seem nice; it's just a little different."

"Do you want me to take you off?"

"No. I think I'll follow through. It's just I can say things to anybody else in the group here and it's not considered offensive. It could even be funny on an odd day. But the cultural differences just are a little different. And I fall flat."

"Do yourself a favor. Stick to the job. "

"Anyway, that's all the news I have. We'll see you in the tournament."

"When I score the winning goal in overtime; no hard feelings okay."

"You narcissistic, over bearing...Never mind."

"Have a Nice Day."

"Drop dead."

Chapter 35

After practice the next day, Steve dropped in over Laurie's.

"Hello!" Steve said as she opened the door to her room.

"What?" She smiled.

"Well, I have a game tomorrow night and I need someone to talk to so they can keep me loose."

"I'm not a they. I'm a she."

"Are you in? She?"

"I don't know I have a lot of homework. Where are we going?"

"I was going to ask you. Where do you want to go?"

"Let's just start walking and we'll get there."

"Okay."

"Do you need me to psych you up?" She asked.

"No. I need you to keep me level. I'm jacked up to the roof."

"How does one do this?"

"We talk about anything besides hockey."

"You're nervous."

"Maine scares me. They're bruisers. They only time they were beaten badly all year was when they tried to get into a speed game with us. But they hit like heck. Trust me."

She squeezed his arm.

"We could have dinner in one of those cute little places on Beacon Hill."

"You think?"

"Come on. It will be fun!" She smiled.

"I'm not wearing a tie."

"You're wearing a collar shirt. That's fine."

"I don't get up in that neck of the woods much."

"Every once in a while I like to go up there."

"I hate to ask. Why?"

"I think since this is one the original colonies. Democracy started here."

"Yeah. I guess. Hey, are we going to take the T?"

"No, we're walking."

"Oh, okay!"

They found a nice little café up on Beacon Hill. Tony had a salad and Laurie had a bowl of soup.

"Well, we're here," he smiled.

"Are you any more relaxed."

"I guess. The company is nice."

She blushed.

"Do you think we could possibly do something really cool the weekend after the Frozen Four?"

"What do you mean? Go somewhere?"

"Because of his job, he has enough travel points at his hotel to stay there for like a year. He said, anytime you'd like to borrow them—to go ahead. What do you think?"

"Where?"

"I was thinking here; that hotel by the waterfront."

"You're kidding?"

"That bad an idea?"

"Yes. What is going on with you?"

"I was thinking about home."

"Which one? You have three of them?"

"That's the point. Where is it?"

"What do you remember about Springfield?"

"More and more hockey—Also some bad stuff. What some of his so called friends did to Tony after he had mental illness. He cracked up. He lost it. He was cool and then he was a loser. It hurt Tony badly. On the other hand, there were people that hung out and waited for the end. Mostly, though it was hockey. We played ice hockey, roller hockey, street hockey in between paper routes, home work, cub scouts—even the trumpet. We had the most fun."

"What do you think Dallas will be like?"

"I've never been to state with no college hockey. I don't know."

"I can't believe I'm marrying you."

"Hockey was a big part of my life."

"What does Boston mean to you?"

"More hockey but something else. Something inside me changed fter about two months on this campus. It was sort like an epiphany."

"Should I hear this?"

"Why not?"

"Bring it on?"

"The professors here expect you to win. There are no vagaries to get lost in. Just go out there and do your job every day. Be consistent and don't lose confidence. And if that doesn't work, they will kick your butt."

"Fair enough but do you really know what I'd like to do and skip the hotel for now?"

"What?"

"I'd like to go to Symphony Hall."

"We could do that instead, if you'd like but…"

"But what?"

"Nothing, I was just going to shoot my mouth off."

"I can't believe I'm asking but what were you going to say?"

He blushed.

"Just let it go. It was in poor taste. Please, for me. My mind is on that damn game. Speaking of poor taste; my mind is still on Massachusetts."

"Lay it on me."

"I have to think about this time I beat up Tony."

"You did what?"

"He was eating and eating because a new drug just kept him spiraling up in weight. He became depressed and he gave up for a while and just ate. I smacked him around pretty good. We had some time because my parents were out and I cursed him out. I wanted to humiliate him in front of his younger brother. I think I did."

"And?"

"He requested a new medicine two days later at his appointment. He lost eighty-five pounds. We never spoke of it between the two of us again,' he smiled, "It wasn't the usual formula describe by dieticians and shrinks. For good measure my dad whacked me good but it was worth it.

"Well, I had a conversation with Nate the other night and well, I'm afraid if I told you, you'd be mad that I didn't tell you earlier."

"You didn't find anybody else. Did you?"

"No. No. No. Nothing like that!"

"And?"

"Well, you see I don't want you to be offended if I tell you this because it's kind of stupid and irrelevant at this point."

"Will you please tell me what it is?"

"I have this yearning for an Olympic Gold medal."

"Yes. But where's the news? What did you think I would think?"

"It's not you. It's the guys in the locker room. In the NHL, the game is played for the Stanley Cup. It is tradition bound and glorified since the league's Original Six."

"What's the Original Six?"

"The Original Six Teams—Toronto, Montreal, Boston, Chicago, the New York Rangers, and Detroit."

"It's important to me to win the Gold Medal. We haven't done it in a while. They think hockey is dying in the NHL. I don't think so. A Gold Medal would get a lot of interest back. No pressure on anybody or anything."

"Well, if I were you, I'd do double duty and go for broke to get both."

"I'm trying. I really am. I start thinking and I'm so incredibly filled with a combination of patriotism and practical thought that I really don't even feel like I'll be a rookie when I get to the NHL. Just let me get through this month and I promise I'll be my normal, silly self. I promise."

"Honey, you're going to have to relax. What are you going to do next year when you're playing in the NHL?"

"I know. You're right. We could go to bed and not worry about anything."

"Are you really not serious about this?"

"Yeah what do you think?"

"I think it was the same game you played as a kid."

"That's not what I was asking."

"All right, let's go."

"All right. One question?"

"You're asking me a question before we go to bed?"

"What about you, miss? Midland and all…"

"It's the weirdest thing. You know that song, 'God Bless Texas.' That's what it's really like. I wanted to come to Boston. I never had seen Fenway Park or Symphony Hall, or many of the historical sights.

"My friends were all aghast. 'What happened? Did you get in a fight with your parents? They are really letting you go that far away. What's the deal?" She laughed.

"Well, how did you find it?"

"Well, from a friend point of view, really good, from an academic point it's view pretty hard. And from a hockey point of view, pretty damned great."

"Oh, yeah, what about a boyfriend point of view?"

"Do I have a boyfriend?"

"What do you think I am?"

"You are a little too hot and bothered lately."

"So we aren't going to bed."

"You get hot chocolate in my room. That's it."

"Fine, I'll sit on the other side of the room—in the corner!"

"Disappointed?"

"Are you flirting with me?"

"Yeah, did you really think I was going to cook you hot chocolate?"

"I was going to have to fend for myself."

"It's easier to take my clothes off."

"How about I help?"

After they slept together, Steve smiled.

"We have to win this championship or everyone will forget the year we had."

"Any other reasons?"

"Because I want my ring; I sweated for four years, risked injury, and wealth. On top of that I worked my butt off in class. I want my ring. "

"What about the guys?"

"Do you know what it's like to score a goal and have your teammates jump all over you? It's the greatest feeling in the world. We all worked hard and we kept our grades up. It's our time. I can feel it."

"Then stop worrying. You're driving me crazy," she laughed.

"Oh, I wasn't really nervous. I just roll possibilities over in my head. I play Devil's Advocate so I can eliminate the mistakes of the previous game."

"Couldn't you just have said that in the beginning?"

"I had to work up to it."

"Why?"

"I'm thick headed."

She giggled and then she laughed.

"You're a nut!" She smiled.

"Yes! That's my job. I'm here to tease and get you all riled up. Are you laughing yet?"

"No, you jerk. I was really concerned."

"I got you!"

"Jerk!"

"Come on, I have to walk you home before it gets too late."

"I'm paying for dinner," she said.

"Why?"

"Because Caveman I want to."

"But…"

She just looked at him.

"Are you really mad at me?"

"Ah! Hah! I got you!"

She laughed at they walked down the hill. She kissed him on the cheek.

"See, I can tease too," she grinned.

"When you take your clarinet to the game tomorrow, you play for me. I'll be listening."

"Always***"

"How beautiful are you?'

"How beautiful can I get away with?"

"Just enough—far and away—enough!"

"You say the nicest things sometimes."

"It takes me a while to get it rolling but every once in a while I can hit the curve."

"Baseball."

"Right."

"You're a strange man sometimes," she smiled.

"All I've wanted all my life is to play in the NHL and then something happened. I went to college and something changed."

"You don't want to play in the play in the NHL?"

"Yeah, fat chance. No I meant education. I'm thinking about coming back here for another tour. That's something that put me on another plane. I remember reading a story in the Freep my freshman year about a former Terrier. His name escapes me now but he played in Germany and he was all over hockey for letting him see a different country. It's sort of the same thing with my educational opportunities."

"Well, BU is us."

"You think?" He was only half kidding.

"Look. You're almost through this place and you have a 3.5 GPA. Maybe you'll even do better at chasing your masters."

"Maybe," Steve said.

"Thinking about the game?"

"Yeah."

She pushed herself against him and they walked the rest of the way to the dorm.

"Hey, I'll see you. I've homework," Laurie said.

"Me too miss. Breakfast tomorrow?"

"Seven o'clock. One more thing; who do you feel closer to?"

"You! Why?"

"I meant of your bloodlines."

"I guess I rely on all three of them but I learned the English language and grew up in America so, there were a lot of different guys I looked up to."

"Whom being the most?"

"Wayne Gretzsky, Bobby Orr, Ted Williams, and Carl Yaztremski."

"You weren't old enough to see Orr and Mantle play."

"Yes. But I saw tapes."

"Maybe you'll get to meet them someday."

"I'd love to. That would be huge. You know what's funny. It isn't my ethnicity that people are in awe of. It's the fact that I'm the number one pick of the Bruins. You see it. When we walk into a place, kids eyes get big as saucers. I'm in it for the fun, miss."

"I'll see you tomorrow."

He went home and studied until a little after midnight. Then he called John Davis.

"We're sending out letters to everyone and their uncle," John said.

"Something will hit," Steve said.

"This is really something to put on your resume."

"Well, I'm glad you came aboard."

"Do me a favor. Call Jack. He's all fired up about some steak restaurant. "

"Do you think it's worth pursuing?"

"I don't know. He's fired up about it though. Hey! I heard you were buying lap tops for some of F-Troop."

"Yeah, we have too."

"Do you think it will fly with those who have older and slower models."

"How many would that be?"

"I figure four more but—you know."

"What are you getting at?"

"My Uncle could help."

"Did you ask?"

"Not yet. But he's ecstatic about this project ever since we met and I joined this little operation."

"What does your Uncle do?"

"He's a financier."

"Well, we aren't going to run over and get them tomorrow. We may be able to get sponsorship from Dell and get comp ones."

"Good enough. But the offer's still there."

"Thanks. I'm going to call Food Connosieur Rawlings and see what he's babbling about. We'll meet at high noon at the steak place"

He called Jack Rawling's.

"Hey! It's your boss."

"What's going on?"

"You master life or it masters you."

"All right! I propose a wager. If this Steak place is so hot, whomever wins it buys the dinner for the four of us—girls included."

"You're on."

The meeting lasted three hours. They ate a lot and drank a ton of Diet Coke. The service was good and the food was excellent. The waiter came over and looked at Steve.

"Sir, you have a phone call."

"Excuse me gentlemen."

"Where's the phone?"

"Follow me, sir."

"My name is Bob Linne. I think I can help you."

"How?"

"You guys have a web site?"

"Not yet."

"Look I go to Mass Art and I'm pretty good. I could show you some of my stuff."

"Do you have any internships?"

"No. I work here to buy my equipment—lap tops and so forth. Internships don't pay. I have a 3.5 though."

"How many hours do you put in here?"

"Thirty to forty."

"You have me curious."

"Me too."

"Let's get together tomorrow for lunch."

"Okay."

By the time everything got squared away, the museum project had a web designer.

BU had earned home ice throughout the Hockey East Tournament and they went out and blew the doors off. Umass-Lowell came out in the speed game and BU raced right past them. The final score was 8-3. Steve picked up four points on a goal and three assists. After the game was out of reach, it became really snippety. The Lowell players lost their composure first and the jaws started going and then the sticks started slashing and then the pushing and shoving started. They didn't run out of fights, they ran out of time.

Laurie was waiting for him outside.

"Hey gorgeous!" He smiled.

"They used the speed game," she smiled.

"They must've decided to recruit differently for next year. That's all I can think off. They sure are taking their lumps though. That can't be any fun when it's getting broadcast back to Orono."

"What do you want to do?"

"I want to sit down and talk with you. I need your opinion?"

"Uh—oh! What kind of trouble are you in?"

"This is a whole new kind of troubles. You'll love it."

They ducked into a salad bar and they ate quickly.

"Excuse me, Mr. Glutton, could you tell me why we're here?"

"I'm here because I need a favor from you tomorrow that borders on having you make coffee."

"What is it?" She giggled.

"Could you please go to the student bookstore and get two black ink cartridges for my printer and one hundred fifty-sheets of white, cotton weave paper, if I give you the money?"

"Sure. Are you stacked tomorrow?"

"I've got mounds of studying and I have to go to SMG tomorrow to get the material to apply for the school."

"Can't you just do it on line?"

"I just may want to look it over. I may not do it. I'm getting a lot done without a Masters. I don't know. I'd like to have some time with you."

"But if it's too enticing?"

"I'm there."

The cell rang and Steve answered it.

"Hey!"

"Boss! It's me," Mark said.

"What's up?"

"I have to leave."

"Why?"

"I'm taking off to play ball. I was signed by the Orioles today."

"Are you still working for us?"

"No. I'm sorry."

"Why so glum?"

"I want to go play ball that's all and I feel like a louse pulling out."

"If I could play ball, I would. Don't worry about it."
"I'll drop my files off tomorrow."
"Fine."
He turned to Laurie and said.
"I lost Mark. He's playing ball."
"That's too bad. We have to pick another one."

Chapter 36

About eight o'clock, Mark showed up with his bag of records.

"Hello," Paco said quietly.

"Hi," Steve said back.

"I'm sorry about this. I just have the opportunity to play ball."

"You are going to finish school. Aren't you?"

"Yeah, I will. Going to buy me that brand new lap top too***"

"You have my e-mail address. Can I help you in the minors?"

"Keep in touch and I want an autographed ball."

"Yeah, sure!"

"Aren't you mad?"

"Look, it's your childhood dream to play in the big leagues. I knew you were going to go sometime. Good luck and Godspeed. However, for an accountant, you have a gift for talking to people. Don't go in high pressure if it comes across as to what you did in college, just talk a little bit about your senior project."

"I'll make it."

"Good. We should have a Coke to toast."

"Boy I thought you were going to tear my head off."

"Son, it always comes back to you in America. If they're good people, and they have a different dream, you work with them and try and help them up. Quality meets quality and they share the knowledge of winning. You could be hanging out in center field for the Baltimore Orioles in a couple of years. Who knows where the future will bring?"

"I'm getting my degree."

"See, quality breeds quality."

"Thanks for the Coke. I have to pack. I'll get you the ball. Nice and white!"

"That's what we're looking for."

"I can help in other ways. I'm not just an accountant."

"Famous last words; what are you?"

""I'm good and people want to be around good people."

"What did you have in mind hot shot?"

"I could sell."

"I'm listening."

"You're not going to tell me what to sell?"

"I just want to hear what you have in mind."

"Well, I know that Latino's buy from Latino's and they would sacrifice all the freedom they risked coming here—not to mention their lives just so they can see a guy like me make a major league roster."

"Keep thinking."

"Well, I'm thinking that maybe we could have a guy work the Spanish satellite networks. We'd need money for some of these guys. "

"I can do some of these guys but not all of these guys. Start with your three top role models and see happens. Call me in a week."

Not wasting anytime, Steve headed to SMG and stuck an ad on the corkboard looking for a senior accounting major.

Chapter 37

About three days passed and Steve came out of practice drop—dead—tired. Rico came up to him in the locker room and sat down.

"Hey Boss!"

"You look good."

"Was it me or was coach upset?"

"Well, if you didn't screw up the mood. What's up?"

"I've been thinking. I want to stay with your company and not go to law school."

"You're crazy. Passing the bar has been your lifetime dream."

"You don't want me then."

"That's not what I said. I want you in a different capacity."

"And what does that mean?"

"I'm going to need a good corporate lawyer."

"But we'll get separated. Maybe I'll get a job in New York or somewhere else."

"We won't get separated. As for now, you're a good worker and you're creative. I just don't want you to give up everything you've worked for your whole life."

"You think so?"

"Yes."

"But?"

"Look, I'm not going to get killed with some Italian lady chasing me down with a rolling pin. 'Momma I'm going to be a lawyer. 'You better be a lawyer.'"

"She'd chase you down with one of my sticks. You made your point. I do love the law. At least the theoretical part of it; it's so neat in the books, you know. You listen to opening and closing arguments and it seems clear. Yet, if you actually observe in a court room, it's much different."

"Why didn't you want to be a prosecutor? You're an idealist and you have guts. I've seen you dive headlong into the corner with three guys there?"

"I'd be charging half my relatives—especially if I went back to Syracuse. I wanted to become a lawyer because it's an honest profession. I never liked the jokes how harmless they were about Italians in the Mafia. In the old days when they protected the neighborhood my views may have changed and I'd be a little less of a prig but now with the drugs and so forth—it's bad business.

"The way I figure it is that I do the best I can at the profession I'm in to be the best Italian-American I can be."

"You do realize that that system of government has lasted since the fall of Rome."

"And there upsides and downslides ever since. Drugs are a downslide. The old glory days of Brando and the Corleone's are gone. 'Why hurt your own?' has been replaced by, 'Show me the money.' I take pride a lot of being Italian but there are some things I have questions about within my own people."

"Can I give you a piece of advice?"

"Sure!"

"You're good. Your values are solid but understand that there are people who can go where you can't and they maybe don't want what they are doing on anyone else.

"You're right. The drugs are awful. But to a man, the soldati are Italian Americans. You grew up with good parents' right. 'Eat your vegetables, play hockey as hard as you can, go to church on Sunday etc."

"Yeah, of course."

"What if your father was a wise guy? And his father?"

"Understood, sir."

"Maybe by running a business the correct, we can show those guys different?"

"You still need a lawyer."

"Hell, yes!"

Finally, he was able to see Laurie.

"Hi! Honey!" She smiled brightly.

"You're very chipper," he smiled.

"You look like you've been hit by a truck."

"Tough practice."

"I've made up my mind."

"The wedding isn't until June. That's four months. Can't you pick the dress later?"

"That's not what I meant. You got a brand new letter from *Sports Illustrated*, Kodak, Dell, GE, McDonald's and Coca-Cola."

"So, did you open them?"

"I wanted you too."

"Ooh! Boy! Here it goes."

He gently opened each letter and read them through—sometimes twice in disbelief.

"Geeze, they want to sit down and have discussions about what we have in mind."

"You're kidding?"

In the next days, many other companies sent similar overtures but they were still waiting on Harvard's response.

He and Laurie walked to GSU where they ran into Clarence.

"Grab a seat my boy," Steve grinned, "We're in a celebrating mood."

"I see," The tall, architect (almost) smiled, "What's in your fist."

"This, my friend, is a stack of letters confirming interest in our idea."

"From who?"

"IBM, Coca-Cola, McDonalds, Kodak, to name a few," Laurie said.

"We did it."

"We almost did it," Steve said.

"What does that mean?"

"Harvard hasn't approved yet," Laurie said.

"So it could be dead in the water."

"I'm debating whether to call. Do you think that would be presumptuous?" Steve asked.

"Wait a week, I think. Maybe."

"Geeze, thanks for a definitive answer," Steve answered.

"I'm an architect, which brings us to a little problem I have."

"Which is?" Laurie asked.

"Well, I have this thing about standing up in front of the CEO of IBM and presenting my drawings."

"Well, you better get unstuck because you have work to do," Steve said.

"What do you do when you speak in front of class?" Clarence asked.

"I psych myself up saying the team needs me."

"I don't know about it."

"Then you'll spend four years in college for nothing. That's the truth. Do you think this school trained you well?"

"Yeah, of course!"

"What's the problem?

"All right, all right; who did you send the letter to?'

"Endowments."

"What? You're going to give it as a gift. You're not an alum."

"Not yet."

"Wow."

"Go home and practice your presentation and I'll practice mine."

"Yes, sir."

He walked Laurie home and she asked.

"Why?"

"I don't know. Maybe, it's for a good reason."

"But you can't say that?"

"People sometimes want good things to come from terrible things. I just had fun playing sports—even the ones I stunk at. I'm going to get up on the podium on door opening day and say to the crowd. This is a gift to Massachusetts and to people in general world wide who like great sports photography. Imagine getting a letter from a ten year -old from Italy, France, Germany, China, or England after he visited the museum. Heck, I'd be hoping for some from my hometown. It doesn't get any better than that."

"Texas is like you in some ways."

"How so?"

"It always does things big. I'm not even talking about sky-scrapers. I'm talking about cook-outs in Midland. Word gets around the neighborhood and it's more the merrier. Who's bringing what? Oh, you're bringing chicken, don't worry I'll bring brownies."

"Sounds like a home a bit. But the Patriots are better than the Cowboys."

"The Cowboys have better uniforms."

"I'm going to have to get a credit card with frequent flyer miles on it. Fly my friends from back home out there. I'd really like to go to Houston and see LBJ…Outer space. I told my mother I wanted to be an astronaut. She smiled and said no way. I said why not? She said there are big green men from Mars who eat little boys. Hockey became number one after that."

"Midland is kind of different."

"How so?"

"The first thing out of your mouth is that you can't say you wanted to be part of the big city. City folk are considered—especially Easterners."

"Wouldn't it matter that I'd be playing for the Stars?"

"Nope."

"Well, what do I tell them?"

"You're the Journalism major communicate."

"What if I brought a bunch of BU caps and t-shirts and spread them around the picnic?"

"You'd be a hero among heroes. Just tell them that Boston is in New Hampshire."

"I can't believe I'm marrying you. Do you think maybe I'm abandoning home?"

"It depends. What are your friends like?"

"They all stayed in Texas. They worked hard for four years and then came back to small town suburban life."

"And you don't want to do that?"

"Well, it's weird. I want to be small town in a big city. I've never even been to Dallas."

"What about Boston?"

"I hated the Bruins when they dumped you."

"Hey!"

"You know what I mean."

"You know what I mean."

"I don't know what happened there and, I'll probably will not know everything…. Life goes on. At least it wasn't a third of the way through the season when we were becoming a team."

"You say it so matter-of-factly—like it doesn't have any affect on you."

"Oh, it has an affect. I'm going to drill them when I play them."

"Besides that."

"Boston's my adult home. Greater Springfield is my youth's home. I was planning on enjoying them both."

"You'll love Dallas."

"I'll have plenty as I see it."

"That's not encouraging."

"I'm a little discombobulated by the whole thing. It is after all Texas."

"Which means?"

"They don't pump up a football without having a celebration. I'm kind of…"

"You're not reserved so don't even go there."

"I wasn't born in Texas. You know Texas."

"Well, what do you think we are?"

"You're all Cowboy fans."

"We have a team in Houston now."

"The baseball team has a better offense."

"They throw punches in Texas you know."

"They carry guns."

"Big ones***"

"I'll watch myself."

"You do that."

"What's going on with you?"

"What do you mean?"

"The snappy one-liners are coming fast and furiously. What's going on?"

"I think you should have articulated your feelings better in the press. At least I'm going to a place I'm wanted doesn't cut it."

"It's too late now."

"It's too bad because it rubbed some of them the wrong way."

"I was too stunned to talk right."

"Do you know a lot of the Wright Brothers? They have airplanes now you can visit in the off-season."

I know. That will be fun. It's just that; I was turned down by the Boston Bruins. They were sucking eggs but they were still the Bruins.

"Besides I hate flying into Logan. You fly over their water. What if the wing fell off?"

"Are you some kind of a nut?"

"Right! It would be great to actually visit like a normal person and then head West to the rest of Massachusetts.

"My buddy from hockey school wants me to do a hockey clinic with him already."

"So what has you so upset?"

"I got traded by the Boston Bruins!"

"Calm down."

"At this point we should go out for a beer."

"You will have a keg of beers at this point. I'll settle for a cherry coke at Al's."

"I would've asked for less money or restructured my contract or something. What's wrong with them?"

"They haven't made good trades or found good talent in the draft in ten years."

"Well, they could've started with me."

"That's arrogant."

"Hey! They buck stops here. I'm going to get an offer from Dallas, those hearty souls enough to kick me over the Hollywood sign."

"What does that mean though?"

"It means that I learned to lead from the time I get there. By the end of training camp, the guys have to know that the pocket jokes have to go and they will follow you anywhere."

"What about me?"

"You'll be my wife. You'll be happy."

"What are you some kind of caveman?"

"What?"

"I meant about Midland."

"I don't know what the problem is smarty. They have cars. Just drive there."

"All right touché. But we still have the problem. You can't small towns and small cities unless they want to themselves."

"You better explain that one."

"Nobody wants anything to change. Someone with a new idea is a threat to them. It's egomaniac city."

"Are you saying Midland is like that?"

"It's a very tight community. I gave you the example of the barbecues. That's the good—especially Mr. and Mrs. Larsen's Christmas party. Huge the whole town shows. The adults get pretty lit.

"But there are other times it's not so good. Everything is perfect in Whooville so that we're perfect. It's like that in Boston too in some areas. People get drunk on their own accomplishments."

"You're trying to solve too many problems at once. Slow down. What's most important to you?"

"I'm the one that left. Get it. I went twenty-eight hundred miles away. It's not even the Prodigal Daughter. It's more like the anti-Christ. In the Information Age with almost every house having at least one computer, we still have to deal with that mentality. I don't understand it.

"I can't even help the benefit with my information because I left."

"You have a soft heart. You need a harder head."

"What does that mean?"

"You have to take your four friends and figure something out—like a charity and make the community—get involved in it."

"How am I going to do that?"

"Embarrass them."

"Oh! Great? Hello, Mr. Congressman, my name is Laurie Stevenson, do you know where Midland is? Great. Could you help us organize a collection of not used musical instruments for the high school?"

"See you have it already."

"I'm not as devious as you."

"It's called barter and trade. Now you owe the Congressman. See how that works."

"Some people are plain ignorant. They couldn't tell the truth if you hit them over the head with a baseball bat. And they'll say anything about anything because they are that ignorant. And the only recourse they have in life is, 'What are you going to do with us? What are you Nazis?'"

"So what are you going to do them?"

"Price them out of the market for my photos. If that's all they bring to the table, they aren't me. They can be them but they can't stand for what I represent. You have to move everyday to be better than you were the day before."

"I like you. I really like you."

"Is there a possibility you could play something for me?"

"I might manage but you have to do something for me."

"Could you please do me a favor and take me to a movie later?"

"You can use the barter system so well."

"You are so cool!"

"What do you want to see?"

"Miracle***"

"I have seen it eight times but I missed a couple of spots when I went to get popcorn. Absolutely."

Chapter 38

University of New Hampshire came into Agganis Arena full of fire and played an exceptional fifty-five minutes. Unfortunately for them, the game lasted sixty minutes. Steve and Nate took turns rushing up ice and scoring goals during the last five minutes. They were behind 4-2 at the fifty-five minute mark and by the end of the game, which they won 5-4. Steve got the game winner on a blistering slap shop and Nate got the other two.

“Coach is going to have our heads,” Nate said.

“Yours maybe; We won,” Steve said.

“I don’t think he’s going to like the way we won.”

“What? We didn’t play dirty. They just didn’t hustle the last five minutes. It’s not our fault.”

“I’m the captain. Will you shut up for a minute.”

“Let’s go shake hands Captain.”

UNH looked terribly shocked that they had lost that game. Most of the Terriers looked terribly shocked that they had won the game so it was about even. Coach Parlon said one thing in the locker room.

“Don’t ever do that again!”

“Coach, we won!” Steve exclaimed.

“Shut up Thompson,” the Coach said calmly.

Steve couldn’t tell if the coach was serious so, he erred on the side of caution and kept his mouth shut.

The press came in and it was pretty much a free for all because the boys and girls from the Fourth Estate had it seemed like a million questions. Some of them were even intelligent. One in particular caught Steve’s attention.

“With each loss in the Hockey East tournament, it could possibly ruin a perfect season and end your season for good, how are you preparing for the final game against BC?”

“Just like every other game.”

“Are you still as confident after having to pull a rabbit out of the hat tonight to win?”

“More so*** We know how to come from behind.”

“But…”

“Sir, to be honest with you—We aren’t going to lose. We have been working too hard in practice all year long. This is our time.”

Nate winced in his locker next to him.

"Okay, boys and girls that's the end of that," Nate smiled graciously but firmly.

After they left, Steve smiled.

"And we were just getting going," he said.

"You have the biggest mouth I've ever seen," Nate said.

"Yes! But I spoke the truth. I'm not going to say we're afraid of BC because we're not."

"Yeah, but you still have a big mouth."

"Thank you very much."

"You say, quite diplomatically. We both have a chance at it blah, blah, blah…"

"You've got to be kidding me."

"That's how it's done in the real world."

"That's how it's done by someone afraid to stand up for his teammates."

"Hey!"

"Hey! Nothing man. You have to lead from the front—not from the rear."

"Never mind; who's going to look after you next year? You'll be a calamity waiting to happen."

"Do you realize I'm going to graduate from this school and I can dress myself, eat, shave, and brush my teeth all by myself?"

"You're a pain the butt," Nate said.

"I'd love to stay and chat but Laurie is waiting."

Laurie was waiting and she smiled at him—a big, wide smile.

"Hey," he smiled as she ran up to him and gave him a huge kiss.

"Thank you," he grinned afterward.

"What's wrong?" She asked.

"Let's go for a walk."

"Is it us?"

"No."

"Tony?"

"Nope; it's just how sorry we played for most of the game. The guys weren't even interested it seemed. It was the first time I had ever experienced that here."

"What are you going to do?"

"I'm going to talk to them before practice tomorrow. Do you know what?"

She snuggled close to him.

"What?" She asked.

"You make it all right. You make everything okay."

"That's my job."

"Do I do it too?"

"You'd get an 'A' in that department."

"Oh, brother, I feel good now. I have to call Tony."

"Uh, now?"

"I sort of promised."

"Hey, it's me," Steve said.

"You guys were so lucky."

"Yes! We were. Hey! I've got some news for you."

"About the museum?"

"We have people all over the world wanting to talk to us about this little venture."

"Why didn't you tell me earlier?"

"There's one little glitch. Harvard hasn't confirmed yet."

"Damn."

"I'm going to go there tomorrow and poke around then I'll call them the day after."

"Call Chris Davidson. He's a good kid. He is gaining more and more confidence every day. He's like me, another Denis the Menace. This should give him a shot in the arm."

"Now, don't be rude when you talk to them."

"Like I would."

"I'm serious. Do you know how many pieces of paper float across an endowment officer's desk in a week?"

"I will ask very politely if they had come across our piece of paper."

"That's the spirit."

"Well you hit your knees for the next couple of days and I'll spend some time in Marsh Chapel and we'll wait."

"Fair enough; I'll see you later."

"Night!"

He turned his attention to Laurie.

"Sorry," he said sheepishly.

"What if Harvard doesn't go for it?" She asked.

"I'm not even thinking like that. Until they say no, which hopefully they won't, then they haven't. But it is nerve wracking. "

"Give them a week and then call."

"So we can both teach each other to cool our heels. I don't know if, that's the relationship we want. Maybe, I'll call them tomorrow morning before class."

"I say wait. You'll just force them into a position they aren't ready to take yet. You're more likely to get pushed aside. Besides, it won't hurt you to call back some of the more promising corporations and have firm talks with them before you talk to Harvard. That way Harvard knows where you stand."

"You think so."

"Ya' all have a winner on your hands here."

"Yes, mamm. We do."

"Coach Benson will be ecstatic."

"I don't know. We picked Harvard."

"It is one true fact in this word is that you can't hate Harvard. They're like your cousins."

"Geeze you really think like a New Englander."

His cell phone rang.

"Hey, it's me Brian."

"Clarence called me. That's news, man. Why didn't you tell me?"

"Dude, I thought it was a good idea to wait—only because Harvard is thinking about it."

"Still we did good. Geeze, I'll have to buy a suit for the presentations."

"I'll have to get some dress shoes."

"Don't forget the wing tips."

"Very funny***"

"So what's the next step?"

"Are you doing anything tomorrow?"

"Semi-sort of but I can cancel it."

"What were you going to do?"

"Becky and I were supposed to go shopping but she'll live without it."

"I need you hear about eleven o'clock if possible."

"That's fine. What are we going to do?"

"Answer some of these letters. Bring your cell."

"Yes, sir."

"You uphold the brethren in green and I'll do the rest."

"Fair enough***"

"Listen I have to call Chris Davidson. I haven't heard a peep out of him in a couple of days. I need to see what's up."

"See, ya later."

Steve hit the out dial.

"Hey, it's me," he said into the microphone.

"Steve," Chris answered, "how are we doing?"

"We've got more letters than Santa Claus and most are positive. Brian and I are calling tomorrow to see what more we can facilitate."

"Geeze, man I'm from UMASS. I'm not used to this."

"Well, son, you can be great or lousy from anywhere. Now the big kicker is that Harvard still has to say yes."

"Okay. What do we do till then."

"Are you religious?"

"Not especially."

"Well, I'd advise you to start."

"We're really going to do it."

"Yes, we really are."

"And I almost quit."

"Well, it's water under the bridge. Don't worry about it."

"You know, when I came to school four years ago, I really wasn't sure I belonged there. But I got good grades and then I only figured it was only UMASS. It wasn't like it was Harvard or anything. Yet, I'm involved in a project that when it goes through will become a part of the oldest academic institution in America. It's quite humbling."

"I'm glad you stayed. You just need more confidence in yourself."

"How do I get more confidence in myself?"

"It sounds really weird but you stand in front of the more and you say to yourself. 'Nothing can stop me! I'm going to have a great day!'"

"Yeah***"

"Uh-huh!"

"That sounds pretty hokey."

"Hey, you should see what happens in the locker room when we psych ourselves for games."

"Human sacrifice?"

"Close***"

"Can I help?"

"I can e-mail you some letters and you can print them out but go to the bookstore and get white cotton bound paper. I'll reimburse you later."

"No. Forget it. It's on me."

"How about twenty-five?"

"Good enough."

"Do you think we can invite the head of Harvard's endowment committee to one of our bull sessions?"

"Those are board meetings."

"Well, then it makes sense. I was just clearing it up."

"UMASS is a good school."

"Thanks. But you guys are different."

"How so?"

"You don't have as many doubts as I do."

"But UMASS fine tuned the capacity to learn so you could notice that and apply it to your own life."

"Yeah, I guess it has. Well, I have lots of studying to do."

"Good luck."

"Now the hard part," Steve said to Laurie.

"I'll offer you my body, if you don't make another phone call."

"One more and that's it."

"Brian, it is Steve."

"Didn't we just talk?"

"Brian, do you like Human resources?"

"I like the interview part but I'm kind of lousy at firing people."

"Yeah, I could tell. I know Chinese food is your favorite food so if you would please change over to the sales and marketing manager, I would take you to P.F. Chang's and give you your new crown."

"Well, if I don't like that! Yahoo! I don't have to fire anybody anymore."

"Could you be a little excited about the food? It's going to cost me a mint."

"Yes, sahib, I will be very grateful for your dinner. When?"

"Tonight."

"Good. Six o'clock. At Chang's."

Brian showed up the next night.

"I didn't eat lunch. I want an appetizer, meal and desert."

"Anything else?"

"I was very much afraid that you were going to can me."

"No. You're too valuable to the team. The boys and girls like you. By the way, the way you'll be working closely with the new kids on the block, the German, the Pole and the Greek. The Greek can help us with research a lot. The German is a photojournalist so she should know where to find other great ones. The Pole is a writer, we need at the very least free-lancers but we need recognizable faces for every month. We need to drive sales with some familiarity to the product."

"All right we can do that."

He called Tony a few minutes later.

"Hey, it's me."

"This is not a good time to call."

"Dude, it's after midnight. It's the perfect time to call."

"I am so mad at my boss. The team elected me to speak for them because this guy's son has been running this business into the ground. He thinks people will pay an extra $100-$150 just because he's the corner on the market for advertising and he's going to breed competition. Everybody knows we're the best but word of mouth is going around and I bet our sales are off 15-20 per cent because we're trying to stick it to people. It's not good business. And it makes for lousy morale. We're used to nailing our orders. Now, everybody is like well, "Maybe."

"He's a cocky little weasel—about twenty-eight—thinks he knows everything about everything because he did a stint on Madison Avenue. Arrogant to no avail***"

"You are thorough."

"Oh, don't get me started."

"So anyway, Stork is having a great time for himself discovering the wonderful and wacky world of Japanese baseball."

"You know what I'd like to do? Take French and make some phone calls to the Quebec Major Junior Hockey League. There's at the very least a photo shoot waiting to happen. I'm making good money even though the boss is a jerk maybe I'll take French."

"Are you going to fly in?"

"I don't know. Gas is like a zillion dollars a gallon in Canada. But I'd like the privacy of my own car. On the other hand, flying is cool."

"Don't go by cool genius. Go by comfort and when you are writing all this off on my expense account save the big meals for the clients. You can eat bird seed for all I care."

"I should introduce you to Attila the Price Increases, you'd get along great."

"Do you know I'm the boss?"

"Aw, come on, show some imagination, it's a different country, different customs. Forty below weather? Nice."

"Try and pick out one team and see if you can tag along for a season. Write a novel about it. And photograph until your heart is content. We need shots for presentations to service clubs etc. We'll have to be our own photo editors until we get some. We'll make sixteen by twenties up and place them on easels with background paper from Michael's."

"What is wrong with you?"

"What?"

"Every time somebody suggests something to you, you turn it into a envisage."

"Just do it please."

"Hey, if you okay it then, I'll go. I don't need to know anything else. I even have a medication company who will ship my meds to me."

"Doctors?"

"Working on it."

"I can't tell you how to write: That's your ball game. Just make the pictures crisp and blow out the backgrounds. Shoot as wide open as you can."

"I'd like to shoot Laval because Raymond Bourque played there. I'll have to go on their web site to see what they're up to."

"Do you want to put that much pressure on yourself?"

"Yes."

"Why?"

"Because I bought this new lap top and it's been sitting around on the kitchen table not knowing what to do. All I do as use it at home."

"You want to take your lap top on a vacation? What about your health?"

"It is just too much fun to listen to you panic."

"This is serious business. You could end up in the hospital."

"You know you got me all pumped up and now you're chicken?"

"I am not chicken. I just wanted to see if you'd panic."

"Who the heck are you a behavioral psychologist?"

"I'm your brother and I've seen you go through some serious stuff."

"Look, it's very important to me to go away for awhile—do my job...

"With Annie?"

"Yes, with Annie. And put some pride back in myself. I have a score to settle with this mental illness. It took away what I wanted to do for a long time. And I get to play Roger Clemens and throw a fastball at its head. It's my turn to live my life. Besides; Annie will shop to death in old Quebec. "

"What about graduate school?"

"I may go back someday, I thought that was the thing I got cheated out of but after some soul searching I just wanted to try Canada. It's closer than Ontario so it's really there for me."

"I want to go to grad school. Some of this stuff that we're doing could be a lot easier if we weren't winging it."

"Well, you're the boss. Are we on schedule for five years to publication?"

"Yeah, were doing all right. I never thought sports would be broken down into so many demographics. I had one that said, 'Amount of Gatorade used.'"

"You know what we what have to do? I'll come up from Springfield and we'll have a couple of work nights where we'll hang out and see what it will cost for our employees to live in home offices and we will buy them computers, printers, faxes etc to make them uniform and on the same team."

"You always got me spending money. We have to play the tax game too. The people have to know cell phone costs, which will also be uniform. Now, I don't care where their home office is but occasionally we'll have to act like grownups and rent a room in a hotel like the Marriott for monthly meetings. What else can you think of that people need to do their jobs besides cars?"

"Access to media events around here; we've been so enraptured with Europe—not that it's a bad place. Very, very beautiful but we have got to go after sports here."

"I'm afraid if we do that, we'll end up a circular in *The Boston Globe*."

"Dude, it's cheaper. That's what you need to know right now. You can't spend money like wild fire. Win where you're at and move on."

"All right, Lynne and Chris can handle UMASS and the rest of the area."

"Nobody has a really decrepit car except you and you should take care of that."

"Cameras?"

"Don't mess with anything but the best for us, they're more diverse, Canons, the one with most pixels and most durability; Along with business lenses."

"Tape recorders, note pads, pens, etc."

"We must understand also that we are opening up as a public corp. LLP. That means we will have money coming in at the beginning at about $20 per share with a $.50 dividend."

Steve laughed. Tony did too.

"Can you believe we're making these decisions?" He asked Tony.

"I let Annie balance the check book."

"Laurie is pretty good about it. She has one of those printable ones. Man, this is more fun than hockey and I'd never thought I'd say that."

"We actually have to open for business for it to be real."

"I have a printer."

"You going to let me in on it?"

"Sullivan paper in East Longmeadow supplies the paper and F.A. Bassett in Indian Orchard does the printing."

"They can do what we ask them to."

"I told them it would be nothing but full bleed pictures, straight forward action stuff and typesetting, their graphic design department is quite the operation."

"You have got to be kidding. They did it. They laughed us out of the building before."

"That was before the old man got wind of it. He remembered those days when nobody believed. He thought it over and believed it was good business so he took the job—500,000 printing world wide—English only at the beginning. Get a good suit for the opening on NYSE."

"Yeah, sure, of course!"

"If you go to Canada, please explain that we are an American company sensitive to Quebec's needs but we are also Journalists and if we perchance see a seventeen year-old shooting up with steroids or using smelling creams we will report it.

"Tell them by no means are we there to turn junior hockey upside down."

"It's going to look like we are telling then to hide the stuff."

"Well, I'm trying to be a businessman, a journalist, and ambassador all in one shot and its starting to make me angry."

"I say you have a beer ands go to bed."

"If I have a beer, I'll think of something else I've got to work on."

"Mike Gaines called me and voiced his concern about focussing on hiring some seasoned vets for the scribes. He thinks we have good quality shooters but we need to beef up the print part."

"Well, we do those, maybe next summer. We'll get out a roster of both shooters and writers later. We can't ask them to wait five years. Mike's a good guy but he gets too excited."

"He would like more access to you."

"All he's got to do is pick up the phone."

"He's got the black, soul brother, fraternity crap in his head. You're the boss. You take him."

"What the heck does he think I am? I have three blacks working for me."

"Oh, you're going to love it."

"Let me give him a call."

"Good-bye!'

"Hmm***"

The phone rang once before Gaines answered it.

"Do you have a problem working for us?" Steve asked.

"Sometimes***"

"When?"

"I think I'm under represented at meetings."

"That's because you never raise your hand like everyone else. Sometimes the hare wins."

"You can't call on me."

"Who are you? You know how we run things. It's informal. We get people involved and if you don't want to be involved well, we'll just get another black guy from this fine school. That's the cool thing about having so many of you guys. We can just pick another one. You want to play the black on white thing that's your business. It's not mine and it never has been."

"We play together on the ice and you say that."

"Well, that's what it was about, right?"

"My brothers say you're just using me as a front. Me being black folk and all!"

"I am so close to firing your black folk it's unreal."

"Yes, sir?"

"Look, if you don't raise your hand in class, you class, you flunk. Simple. Now, you've got something like a 3.4 so I don't get it. You're a smart guy. And if you want to play the dumb, black guy from the hood because you're working your butt off six ways from the middle then I don't know what to tell you."

"Wait a minute. Hold up here. You said what?"

"Hey, if I came out of your neighborhood, I wouldn't want to go back for anything."

"Fair enough! I don't want to go back. I admit it. It's no place to have a wife and kids. But I look at it this way, if I can get another kid out then I've been successful in life."

"You, in your present state?"

"I want to contribute more to our team."

"So do it. What's stopping you?"

"I am sorry about the yelling. I just want to see if you'd crack."

"I've been accused of that before—being cracked I mean."

"We can really do this. It's taking shape."

"Yeah."

"I'll see you at practice tomorrow."

The phone rang just as he put it down.

'Well, so much for my minutes,' he thought.

"Hey, sunshine!"

"It's two o'clock in the moon beam."

"Like you've been doing anything all night."

"Look, miss. I've been putting fires out all night. Me and Gains went at it pretty good."

"And?"

"We sort of have an agreement. He gets more swings at the plate and we have the advantage of more of a black readership."

"Does that mean we have to do hip hop?"

"No it doesn't. It's my magazine."

"Don't you feel important?"

"Not really. It's just that everybody else seems to think I'm important. Do you know what's pretty weird? I've been getting more and more students asking for my autograph. Up and down Comm Ave. It is the first time I've ever been noticed by my peers like this. It's weird because they seem to think that I'm above them in some way. I just am who I am. The genuflecting can stop at any time. I just play hockey."

"Oh! Is that what you just do? Look, you have to realize that you want. You want to be captain of the Bruins and you want to be the point man for the museum. That makes you by definition better than some guy who doesn't want any responsibility. Some are your peers but you have to use your head about downplaying your role because frankly, like it or not someone will definitely volunteer to take your place."

"Message understood. You're a pretty good personal assistant."

"I like you because you don't want to make people feel inferior but sometimes you have to lead and that doesn't mean pleasing everyone all the time."

"I find this quite embarrassing."

"What?"

"Well, getting lectured by you."

"It has to be done because some has to tell you these things. I'd rather have it be me."

"Me too! You're right. So is the decaf good?"

"Sort of, how's the latte?"

"Better than average; I've been thinking about the museum."

"Lay it on me."

"I've been thinking about Harvard, specifically if we missed anything in that letter."

"I think we'd have a really good idea of why Cambridge would be a good location. My advice to you if you're really stressed about it, is to go to Marsh Chapel and ask for guidance. There are so many plusses to this."

"Well, that'll help I'm sure. I hope anyway."

"I think maybe we have a shot but I don't have any leeway for mistakes."

"This is kind of fun. Isn't it?"

"Yeah*** In a nerve wracking sort of way, it's a lot tougher than hockey."

"Yes, I guess."

"Well, that's my little assignment," he said.

"Let me look it over when you're finished," she smiled.

"Boy, you give a lady a title and she's all over you."

She laughed.

"We are going to make a great team," she smiled.

"You know! You look great in a business suit."

"Thank you very much."

"If get picked up early by a corporation, we may be spending time in their offices. We have to get it done somehow."

"Do you want your name on it?"

"No. I wouldn't even care if they called the IBM Computers National Museum of Sports Photography as long as the advertising was tasteful and not gaudily run all over the building."

"You're conservative."

"What I'm afraid of is that people won't come because their assumptions will be that it's jock reminiscence and not a real museum. That's why I want some interactive exhibits and so forth to show people the art of sports photojournalism. I don't want them to think some hockey player got two of his brothers tweedle—dee and tweedle—dumb together to make a gallery."

"Corporate backing will be a plus."

"It sure will."

"How are you going to pay them?"

"They pay you for the privilege of using the project to advertise their products and services."

"How big is it going to be?"

"Well, I don't know. I would say about fifty thousand square feet."

"That's pretty big."

"There's a lot of history to record plus more in the years ahead. We'll have to make it work. If need be we'll ask for donations from private citizens."

"It sounds like a plan."

"We'll figure it out some way. You stick with your blueprint but at the same time you remain flexible."

"Would you happen to have a back up plan if this doesn't fly?"

"No. I'll worry about it later. I'm putting all my eggs into one basket."

"Psychologists tell you that is not smart."

"Maybe, I don't see a way around. That's the best option and you pour all your heart and soul into it. And you pray your guts out."

"I'm sure the Lord will appreciate that."

"Well, I hope he does."

Chapter 39

Steve was near sleep when his cell phone rang. It was Tony.

"Hey," Steve said.

"Just wanted to talk***"

"Serious talk or goof around talk."

"A little of both***"

"Serious talk first."

"I was typing on my new IBM notebook in a bar."

"You brought a brand new notebook into a bar? Are you nuts?"

"Well, technically yes. Will you shut up and let me finish?"

"Excuse me."

"Anyway, I was writing away and this guy comes up to me and asks what am I doing? I tell him I'm trying to be a writer and he seems impressed so, we get to talking and he's a newspaper reporter from down in Hartford. He says he wants to interview me for a piece on Sunday."

"That's wonderful," Steve said.

"Not so wonderful. I want to tell him about my mental illness but am afraid editors will run for cover if they hear about it."

"I was the one that told you not to tell anybody. Wasn't I?"

"Yeah*** However, writers are in the teaching business. Right?"

"I guess."

"I can help people understand that most people with MI can lead normal lives if treated correctly."

"Just be careful."

"About what?"

"People may think you're using you condition to sell your book. I know you don't have to. You're a good writer but if you lay it on too thick, people may presume that."

"There are some miserable freakin' people in the world. I guess there could be some of that but the thing that has me about the interview is that I'm a private person and some of the stuff is very personal and once you do it—you don't do it halfway."

"Tony you're a good writer. I know it and you know it. You have to stick to it. It's a tough business. Being mentally ill makes it tougher. If you ever get depressed about it or feel like giving up just think of the joy you feel when you write."

"I think I'll do the interview."

"You'll tell him about your mental illness?"

"Yeah, I think it will help more people than it will hurt me."

"You've got guts I'll give you that."

"Thanks."

"You'll have to tell them about the hospital stays."

"Yeah, I know. I finally got well in one but you know they were all pretty much the same. Criminals mixed with innocent people. Really good staff mixed with very disinterested staff, and the total humiliation of being in the ward anyway. It's like this very polar-opposite view of the world when you first get there because needless to say you're out of bounds and then the medicine kicks in and it slowly filters in light to your decisions. Maybe not light in a religious sense to some but you can think better. I think it's light in a religious sense. God's giving another chance to get out of places like this because let's face it nobody wants to be there including some of the staff."

"What makes it so humiliating? You're sick and you go to the doctor for some pills. They help you."

"The humiliation for me was—honest to God. I was a Cub Scout and Cub Scout's didn't end up here. I also had a lot of disbelief in my doctor's telling me I could be successful, get married, and have kids. I also worried about my children getting it and getting it worse than dad:" They talked for a little while longer and Steve was happy for his brother and wondered if he would have the courage to do what Tony was doing. "My rallying point became that I was a Cub Scout and I couldn't stay on the bottom."

After he hung up, Steve threw his pillow at Nate. Nate threw it back and the race was on. They finally stopped when they were thrown back with laughter.

"Foam pillows suck. Feathers are much better," Steve said.

"I agree," Nate grinned, "Don't sweat the engagement. It'll be fine."

"I was also thinking about the Frozen Four."

"Aren't we all?"

"Chief, we've got a lot of work to do. I kid you not."

"There are some talented hockey players coming to Albany. That's for sure."

"I have thought about that. It would justify why we play the game, huh?"

"Yeah, I guess it does. The better the competition then, there is more of a chance at being remembered."

"I never thought about it that way—about being remembered I mean. I always played for the moment. I didn't worry much about the past or the future. I just wanted to win that game on the night I was playing it. But now that you mention it, there does seem some attraction to the historical side of it."

"You may have a chance at it all. You know?"

"What does that mean?"

"The girl, the Cup, the contract—everything!"

"Well, the girl is something else. She keeps me on my toes. As far as they Cup is concerned, I'm going to need some help to get that. The contract is self-explanatory and you forgot one thing. I'm going to need work ethic coming out of my ears to get anything done."

The next night the Terriers played BC for the Hockey East championship. It was a rough game. Bodies flew everywhere. They banged and banged all night. Steve squirted through the carnage with five minutes left in the third period and lifted a wrist shot over the BC goalie's catching hand and into the net to give BU a one to nothing lead. The next five minutes BC forgot about defense and threw everything they had at BU.

Joe Barnum, the BU goalie worked overtime jumping into shot after shot. He made a dazzling glove save with a minute and a half left in the period. BC pulled their goalie and the offensive firepower intensified. Finally, the game ended with BU holding onto a 1-0 score.

"We'll see you guys in the tournament," the captain said to Steve.

"We'll be there," Steve answered.

He skated over to Stork and gave him a hug.

"Get away from me you moron. How could you do that?"

"Stork, besides Joe, you are the best goalie in Hockey East. But tonight you sucked on just one play. We'll see each other in the tournament."

"Were you trying to make me feel better?'

"Yeah, of course."

"Get away from me or I'm going to kill you."

"See you in the tournament."

"I'll call you tonight after I'm through being shall we say upset at you."

The two teams shook hands at the completion of a great college hockey game. Nate picked up the puck and gave it to Steve.

"This one's yours junior. Keep and remember it."

"Thanks brother."

The locker room was pretty crazy afterwards. Guys were dunking their buddies' heads with soda and spraying each other with the shaken soda.

"Three more games," Steve said, "and then we're the best college hockey team in the nation."

"You're always thinking business. Don't you ever relax? You want to play the next game tonight?" Nate asked.

"I was thinking it was more of a relief."

"Are you crazy? We're the only unbeaten, untied team in the country. We're marked men."

"And I'm serious."

"Well, you should be."

"But…"

"Oh, never mind."

"I'm going to take a shower now. There's enough crazy people running around here."

"Are you seeing Laurie tonight."

"Fair enough; I will be seeing you because my girl calls."

"Ain't you the lucky one?"

"She is cool."

"Go shower you bum."

On the way out of the locker room, Coach Parlon smiled broadly.

"Great game kid but it ain't over yet."

"What does that mean?"

"You get to entertain my friend and yours the press corps."

"Come on coach Laurie's waiting for me."

"No whining."

"I knew I should've passed of."

"Don't say that when you go out there."

Steve tried to reason with the press.

"Ladies and gentlemen, if you had your boyfriend or girlfriend out there, waiting for you. What would you do?"

That brought some chuckles from the press.

"Can we at least make it quick?" Steve asked.

"How did you feel about getting the goal?"

"It was amazing. The whole arena was shaking and the guys piled on top of me. I felt like a million bucks. Anything else?"

"Moving right a long; are you looking forward to the pros?"

"Very much so; I thought it was going to be with the Bruins but they traded me to the Stars. The Bruins thought they could get another player that would fit into their system well. They gave me the first exposure to the NHL and I'll always be grateful for that. I hope to get a long term deal by training camp."

"What's it like rooming with Nate Williams."

"It's like having a really smart Reverend Jim from Taxi."

The press corps tittered on that one.

"Seriously, he's probably the smartest guy I know."

"What about BC? Everybody assumes they'll get the at—large bid."

"Oh, they'll be there and they ain't happy about tonight. They're a dangerous team with a lot of guys who can skate very fast."

"Are you afraid of them?"

"Not exactly, however they are a well put together club but I think we have their number this year. I think the trophy is ours for the taking and that should about wrap it up. Thanks for your time."

Steve skirted down the hallway and out into the street.

"Hi!" She smiled.

"I was detained by the Fourth Estate."

"I bet you had a great old time," she smiled.

"Actually I'm like the fish out of water. It's pretty much people asking for your opinion and then hundreds of thousands of people will read it and form their own opinion. I already know what BC's opinion will be."

"Give me a hint."

"We want to beat them."

"Well, they're going to love you."

"Yeah, well somebody had to get the goal. It might as well be me."

"That was a spectacular goal. You zipped right up the middle of the ice and then cut to the right to shoot back to the left. That goalie didn't have a chance."

"Stork was killing us all night. I just got lucky."

"Everything you ever did on the ice was lucky."

"Look, miss. There are two kinds of hockey players out there. There's guys that help win Stanley Cups and there is everyone else. Most of the game is fractions of inches. Ergo…most of it is luck."

"Fine, but from a girl from Midland, Texas' point of view, it looks like you have an awful lot of talent."

"Well, thank you but take it from a guy who has been on the ice. It's luck."

"Okay. Whatever you say?"

"What are we doing tonight?"

"Do you want to go to Corrnwall's and get a drink?"""

"Sure. Why not?"

"I'm going to bust one of the days and say to the whole world we're going to champions," he smiled.

"Think about something else just as taxing."

"The company?"

"I know it's on your mind."

"Writing letters and such is just the introductory phase. The big deal if we get it is the presentation. We'll have to nail that just like in class except not."

"You called on Friday and Harvard said?"

"Call me on Monday."

"Then what did they say?"

"We talked about hockey and how I had the nerve to help beat Harvard. It was a very neutral kind of feeling each other out conversation—quite bland."

"Yet, they said call Monday."

"Yes, they did."

"And now you're worried about Monday."

"Yes, I am."

"I forgive you."

"I can't wait to start playing for the Bruins. I also can't wait to see if people would be interested in the museum."

"Wait until you get to home. There will be tons of volunteers."

"My job is to weed out the flakes from the talent."

"How many do you think you'll need to start."

"Seven."

"Are you nervous?"

"About the Elite Eight or the Frozen Four?"

"Yes, about that," she laughed.

"Honey, the way I sweated over my grades for four years, I can just feel success coming through me. "

"You're really serious about this. Aren't you?"

"Yes, I am."

Chapter 40

On Monday, Steve called between classes and Mr. John Ashford III answered the phone.

"Son, we need more information. We're interested but we need to know specifics. It's like applying to BU. How about the week before graduation we sit down with your people and have a presentation?"

"Are you serious?"

"Absolutely serious***"

"Well, we can do it. That's for sure we can do it."

"We will give you the most time to prepare. So how about Friday at nine in the Dean's chambers?"

"Yes, sir. Best opportunity I've had all day."

Steve called everybody starting with Laurie, working his way to his family, and the team. At practice he told Hans, Pemo, Lars, Rico, and Nate.

"Gentlemen, I give you the opportunity to back out now because the rest of us will be working over time to get this done. Anybody want out."

"Not me man," Pemo said.

"Me neither, " Nate said.

"Ha, so close to glory!" Hans said.

"You have got to be kidding. We're making it and you want us to drop?" Rico said.

"Yeah, that's unfair boss," Lars said.

"We have to be very damned good gentlemen. Nobody getting busted for too much booze: after we win. Get it?"

"Yes, sir." They answered.

"Seven o'clock meeting at Cappo's tomorrow night. I mean it. It's as much about being good as it is about being smart. You guys have had it easy up till this point. You're going to work harder. We're going to practice each part of the presentation with a partner and then you are going to be on the hot seat in front of all of us. We have a chance at something nobody's ever done before so I think you should go back to your rooms and do what you normally do and think about tomorrow."

"Boss, we'll be ready. Don't worry about it," Rico said.

He called Tony on the way to Laurie's and Tony asked.

"Why don't you come home on Thursday and have some dinner with

Annie and I?"

"Spaghetti and meatballs?"

"Homemade. You're too fired up too think right now."

"And Annie's food will send me down?"

"Don't tell her I said that. I meant it in a nice way."

"We are making progress."

"You think you're giving the establishment too much respect?"

"Maybe and maybe not but I tell you one thing. We're going to nail that presentation right down the Pike."

So on Thursday, he hoped a Peter Pan bus lines motor coach straight down the Mass Pike into Springfield. They made it in an hour and forty-five minutes.

Tony picked him up in a bear hug and rubbed Steve's brush cut.

"We had a good meeting on Tuesday. I am going to make some phone calls tonight to make sure everyone is at next Thursday's meeting. "

"Do me a favor. I want you to shut up about the damned meeting and enjoy tonight. You going to drive yourself crazy."

"I can't help it. Just to be considered is quite the honor."

"You know, somehow you'll find a way to get it done. I know you can do it. You just have a way of not losing. Now come on. Annie has some news for you."

Steve gave Annie a hug when she answered the door. They exchanged greetings and then they sat down in the kitchen.

"Well, I'm in the mood for news. Anybody got any?" Steve clapped his hands and rubbed them together.

"I have some for you, Mr. Hockey Player. I am real close," Annie said.

"To what?" Steve asked.

"You know," Annie smiled.

"How long have you known?"

"A week***"

He looked at Tony.

"You kept me out of the picture for a week? Am I keeping you to damned busy?"

"You were worried about the company"

"Man, this is great."

"This new job helps a lot," Tony said.

"Hey, you earned it."

"Wow, we're going to have a baby in the family," Steve said.

"Would you be his Godfather?"

"Oh, yes, of course. This beats the meatballs."

"Hey, I made the meatballs." Tony kidded.

"Is it healthy?"

"So far," she smiled.

"Well aren't you two the happy tripled up."

"The what?" Tony asked.

"Well, you know—the three of you!"

"Hell of a metaphor, man." Tony said.

"Well, you have any other news."

"No. That's it." Annie smiled.

"Let me just do one thing."

Steve dialed up Laurie on his cell.

"Hey, it's me. Guess what happened to me today?"

"What?"

"Annie and Tony confirmed that Annie was almost there, again."

"Are you serious? Are you with them? Can I talk to Annie?"

"Sure."

Steve handed the phone to Annie. They jabbered for a good half-hour. Tony looked at his brother and Steve shrugged.

"Can I talk to you a minute please?" Steve asked his brother.

"Yeah, sure*** Let's go in the den."

They got in the den and Steve threw a bear hug around his brother—rubbing his knuckles into Tony's close-cropped hair.

"Will you knock it off you idiot?" Tony picked him up and threw him on the sofa.

"Hey, are you okay with all this?" Steve asked.

"Yeah."

"I mean about passing it on."

"I know what you meant. You know there's two things in this world you never leave—God and your family. God will protect Annie and I like he has before and besides we may be planning for the worst and nothing may happen."

"Do you know what sex it is?"

"We didn't want to know; just as long as the baby was healthy and so far so good."

"Man, I can't believe it. I'm going to be an uncle. You know you're a stud."

"Yes, it comes naturally. You on the other hand are a Shetland pony. You can't believe it. We had been trying and bought one of those EPT things and then she went to the doctor and guess what? Boom!"

"Do mom and dad know?"

"Huh, huh, huh, dad passed out. He had to find a chair. Mom's propping him up in a chair and talking on a phone with Annie."

"Geeze, you could've floored me too. You do all that baby names stuff?"

"Yeah, already! She likes Anthony Jr. I could go for that but we'll see. God, there's a million things going through my head—why I got sick—why I got well. Geeze, I'm going to be a father."

"I never thought I'd see you like this."

"You know in the hospital the last time. I thought I had to be there for a reason. There must've been a reason I wasn't dead or wishing I was. This is it. Now I know why."

"Why don't you drive me home and stay over. I'm just going to get home and call you anyway."

"I'll have Annie sleep with her parents."

"Don't worry."

"I'm not worrying. I'm just cautious. Man you can't beat this. Our first baby; and the job came along at the right time—even though we have yet been paid. I slip up once in a while but I can get in the fight. The whole reason we tried is that I was doing so well at this job. I have no luck finding the words that will thank-you for hiring me."

"Tony, you're my brother."

"Was that the only reason?"

"I was kind of curious. I wondered if you could do it. I had no expectations because I never hired a guy with mental illness before. To be honest with you, when it gets bad and I can see it in you, I get worried. A lot of the times though, you find some way to beat it with a joke or you just read from prepared notes. I can see you dig in and that's what makes you valuable to the team. You should however, talk more. If I wanted someone just to do work, I would've hired a mute. Do the world a favor. Enjoy yourself during this time. Go nuts! Paint the spare room blue. Just have a great time with it."

"We're going to make history," Tony said, "We're going to do something nobody has ever done before."

"Between the company and the baby; I guess you're right. He's going to BU."

"Yes. I think so. Enough of this freedom to make up your own mind stuff; he'll go where we say and he'll like it."

"I was kidding."

"Me too! I'll make myself ready for both the job and the baby."

"That's what I don't understand about you. You're always planning something. Can't you just let it ride?"

"No."

"Oh, well. I'm glad you thought that over for a nice rational answer."

"It had one letter and one vowel."

"BU grad right there folks. Yet, your idea of the market segmentation idea is worth pursuing—tie it in to certain sponsors moving their companies into particular areas of the world."

"Right."

"I'm going to get Mark Linne to have me view the progress he has made on the web site."

"How is that kid?"

"He's an artist—sort of flaky but almost maniacally driven to produce his own best work. He's a hard worker I'll give him that—plus he has that waiter job. You have to watch him every second."

"Why?"

"He's kind of adventurous with his attitude."

"Which means?"

"He knows he's damned good. Chris Davidson has been coming along, huh?"

"Yeah, for some reason he had the 'I didn't go to the right school so I can only go so easy stuff.'"

"Yeah, how do you suppose he got that?"

"I think since he took this position he's gone over a turnover in friends and he's dropped a couple of professors off his wish list for talking about 'people like us.'"

"Well, he's smart anyway. He should go far. I'm very happy overall with the quality of people we have."

"Yeah, they all seem to be doing their thing."

Steve's phone rang and he answered it.

"Brian Gregory. Long time—no hear."

"Look, I need a job. My dad and I ain't working out."

"Did you try anywhere else?"

"Not really. This is where I'd like to work."

"We have this conversation before. I just don't think it's right."

"You're wrong and you're losing a soon to be Harvard alumni too boot."

"Yeah, I guess but we're doing what we always do."

"Which is?"

"Arguing*** I just don't see it."

"Do you know what a Harvard alumn, can do for your business?"

"We wouldn't have a business if we argued all the time."

"I can't believe this."

"You're a good guy in the correct situation for you and this ain't it."

"Well, that's it. Do you really think I'm a bad guy? I mean incompetent?"

"I think you want to be the boss now and you are having the same situation with you're your dad. Face it, until you cut your teeth you're, a wet nose."

"What's the difference with you?"

"I've been working on this since I was sixteen. Give me a call in another month. I just want to check up on you."

"You're an idiot but you're my friend."

"Why don't you consider something away from Boston?"

"I have really. I think my dad would like me to go somewhere at this point."

"Stay in the hockey industry somewhere doing something."

"Well, to be honest with you. I was either going to get the job with you or ask a for a reference for Christian hockey sticks in Minnesota."

"Fine. You've got one. Brian you're not a bad guy but you're so stressed out about not working with your dad and staying in the same city… Right now you just need to find who you are professionally. You're very competitive and you like to win. I don't know all the reasons with your dad but I don't want them to get worse."

"Do you know how cold it is in Minnesota?"

"Yeah, but you can sell enough sticks in that state to sink a battleship."

"That's what I was thinking. Plus I'd get to meet the brothers and the son who won Gold. That's pretty cool."

"We should go out to Corrnwall's or something. Oh, by the way, Annie in her modest way said, 'I am almost there again.'"

"Wow! He did it. That's great! Wow!"

"Look, I have to go. Tony is driving me back."

"Yes, sir! Congratulate the pregnant couple."

"Later. A month!"

"Right!"

"Well?" Tony asked after Steve hung up.

"Brian is sort of different. He's all set up with his dad's business but he wants to strike out on his own and find his own place in the world and to be honest with you, I think he has to get rid of some of that anger he has in himself. I don't think he'd be a good risk right now."

"Yeah but will you hire him again?"

"I'd have to take him to a Red Sox game and shoot the breeze with him; get him relaxed as possible. He's a bit high strung."

They piled into the car after saying good-bye to Annie and then headed for the pike.

"What about Marty Hoon?" Tony asked.

"I figure him for sales. He knows how to learn the marketing skills and applying them to the particular audience he's seeing that day. He told me something the other day."

"Makes sense I guess. Ever say anything to you like that."

"Once or twice?"

"What do you have in store for me?"

"You stay exactly where you are—marketing manager. You get bumped up to $100,000 salary plus bonuses. "

"Where are we going to get the money for that now? We're all on scholarship."

"Some from me, Some from BU, some from corporate sponsors, and some from public and private donations! I'm going to force the issue and see if I can get the presentation sooner. I think our presentations will become stale if we wait."

"You're going to confirm a guy with mental illness in a management position with a permanent salary?"

"Yeah, now shut up and do your job."

"You know in a strange way I needed that."

They arrived back at Shelton Hall bout midnight.

"I have to check my e-mail. Make yourself comfortable. There is Coke in the fridge," Steve smiled.

"Here's something weird. It's from Rico. 'URGENT: Call as soon as you get this."

So Steve called him.

"What's going on?"

"I have a question for you."

"Oh, brother? I thought somebody died."

"Where should I go to law school? Harvard, Yale, or Columbia."

"You can get in to all those places."

"I ain't much of a hockey player but for some unknown reason God gave me a brain. I'm also noble, honest, and with a burning desire to find his wife."

"Why are you asking me this?"

"It will take me three years to finish Law and the Bar. I want to be around to help you out when you begin to start the company."

"Yeah but don't you want to go where you want to go."

"It's easier to make contacts in the city you're in. You know that."

"I'd say get into New York. Don't wear your Red Sox cap though. You'll get killed."

"Anything else?"

"The presentation*** I did this on my own. I wrote the mayors of Cambridge and Boston for their endorsement of the idea and I have two positive responses so when we go into that presentation ready to roll."

"You know I was sitting here enjoying a nice cold beer and I started thinking. I'm the third one to go to college. My two sisters are doctors. One is an orthopedic surgeon and one is a pediatrician. I was always fascinated by the law. I think that doing all that prep work in the pizza shop in high school made me mentally tough. Guys who got the easy internships are already falling by the wayside. Do you think that's true?"

"I think I can relate. One summer I worked in a factory tempering saw blades. Excruciatingly hot. It gave me an appreciation about why I was at BU. Maybe your theory is right. Would you do it all over again to come to college?"

"Absolutely! But after all is said and done, I want to be the youngest partner in the firm I'm hired by."

"Thanks Rico."

"Look, I've got about a million e-mails to check out. I'll see you tomorrow."

"Tony, Rico's a good guy. He hustles his kiester off, on the ice and a good guy in the locker room. He could play minor pro but he wants to study the law."

"He's one of those guys you just have to have around because he's like glue. He ties everybody together. I have never seen a kid like him—talk to anybody. Just enjoying it all. He saw Boston, now he'll see New York, especially the girls. He'll do all right."

"What about you?"

"For a week, I've been nervous, happy, nervous—all kinds of stuff. Just bouncing off the walls! Thank God I had to go to work. There I had to function."

"Well, we're on!"

"What do you mean?"

"The hockey season: school, the baby, and the company. We're all letting it rip!"

"Do you think we can do it? The company I mean?"

"Do you know, the publisher of *Der Spiegel* invited me personally to Berlin for talks with several art galleries in Germany—just in case! I think that's a positive step."

"I don't know what I'm doing wrong. I've done everything I know to attract Italy in some form or another and they aren't responding."

"Give them time. The Italians despite their reputation as hot heads are very meticulous about who they partner up with. If they like you, you're in. Don't press them too much. Give them a month and write another letter—don't e-mail. Use the company letterhead."

"Ooh, boy I feel like such a grown up."

"Remember when you were kids in school and the teacher had you write down a paragraph about what you wanted to be when you grew up?" Steve asked.

"I wanted to be myself. None of the teacher's got it. They were looking for a profession," Tony said.

"And what self did you want to be?"

"I am just a regular guy with his family and an Ace at work. Like mostly every guy."

"That was a better answer than mine."

"Hockey player?"

"I've grown up a lot at school; there are people out there somewhere. When you grow up in the same neighborhood for your whole life you hear things. Lots of things and most of them are so off based it is ridiculous."

"Like?"

"People who are really successful don't care about people. When I came here, I was afraid to talk to anyone who had really made it because I was really shy. I thought it was some terribly exclusive club that you had to be a mean, crusty stiff to get into.

"Most of the people I know or have met that are really successful are pretty cool. I had to relearn a lot. What about you?"

"I was to busy trying things out when I got here. I went to the Museum, Fenway more than a couple of times, the Symphony, I admit it, I did go to Conte Forum to catch a couple of Eagle games, when to Harvard Square…"

"Did you have a good time?"

"Boston looked MAHVOULUS!"

"How did you pass?"

"I was a good cram studier but I tell you, I learned a lot about life outside the classroom."

"It's too bad you were alone."

"I had God."

"You must have."

"I went to hockey games too."

"That's why you had God."

Chapter 41

Steve and the other Terries climbed onto the bus at noon to the Providence Bruins Arena for the elite eight.

"We better win tomorrow night," Nate said on the way over.

"No problem, we're a team of destiny," Steve answered.

During warm ups, the Alternate Captain of the Team of Destiny was tying his skates when a Colorado College Captain faked tying his next to him.

"Hey," the Colorado player said, "I have a question."

"No. We will not go easy on you today."

"Should I go out after freshman year and enter the draft?"

"Going out early sucks eggs. You want to drive a truck if you blow out a knee?"

"Yeah, yet, that's a lot of money."

"You'll end up a dumb hockey player."

"The NCAA bylaws say…"

"The NCAA bylaws have several flaws among them staying in school. That's a dumb move man."

"You could've just said go ahead."

"I would've lied."

"Who the heck are you George Washington?"

"You're telling me I'll end up a mutt."

"I'm telling you that. It's a stupid move all around. I've been there. They've been throwing money at me for three plus years. You do what you're best at, at the time you are best at it."

"I'm going to whip you personally tonight."

"We're the Team of Destiny. Move over pal."

Well, the team of destiny ran into a little problem against Colorado College. Colorado College didn't know they were supposed to lose to BU and they played a real hockey game. The game was tied 5-5 with two and a half minutes left. The teams were playing up and down hockey with a fair amount of hitting and Steve was looking to hit teammates with passes out of the zone. With forty-five seconds left, there was a whistle in BU's end.

"Take the puck out yourself. Lug it up the ice," Nate told him.

"Why don't you do it? You're the captain," Steve answered.

"Because you're better than me***"

Steve didn't say anything. He just nodded his head in agreement. The puck squirted out to Rick Barnes who passed it back to Steve. The senior defenseman curled behind the net and began his charge up ice.

He avoided three players before he was at center ice. With two, defenseman left, he faked a slap shot to get one to fall. The other defensemen came out to challenge him. Steve fired a quick wrist shot between the defenseman's legs. The goalie reacted a fraction too late and the puck zipped right past him into the net. Steve leaped high in the air. The clock showed three seconds on the clock as his teammates mobbed him.

"We have three seconds," Steve said.

The guys lined up at center ice. Colorado College pulled their goalie and won the face—off but they could do nothing with it and BU was able to officially celebrate when the horn sounded to end the game.

Steve met the press again but this was different. This was the national press. He even talked to a guy from ESPN magazine and a lady from *Sports Illustrated*. He found it rather embarrassing actually. Steve couldn't quite believe what fascinated people about athletes but there must have been something because they wanted to know everything—what kind of food you liked, what was your favorite class, what about your girlfriend. He kept the policy about keeping his mouth shut about Laurie intact.

It sure was strange to him that he garnered so much attention. He tried to be polite but it was tough through his fog of amazement. He stumbled over some questions—sometimes searching for answers but other than that he did all right.

"Boy, I'm glad that's over with," Steve said from his bus seat back to the hotel.

"You know Providence is nice."

"You ignored me."

"Yes, I did. You go through the same thing every time you talk to reporters."

"I was talking about the game. Hey, why'd you say what you said on the ice?"

"Because it's true. You have the wheels brother."

"Yeah but you're the captain."

"I made a decision that it was your turn to grow up. You did. That's what captain's do. Besides you're an Alternate."

"Is your ego bruised?"

"Actually my ego is flying a high flag. I made the decision that won the game."

"I knew you'd find something good out of it."

"That's my job."

"You want to hang out with me and Laurie?"

"Nope! I've got some thinking to do."

"Do you want to let me in on it?"

"It's not that I'm having second thoughts about Sweden but I'm going to have to listen to what a spoiled brat I am from the North American press. I don't know, maybe I should just play through until free agency and then sign south of the border."

"Your market value will be higher, quicker."

"I also thought it would be cool to go to Sweden. Meet different people—see how they live."

"You really do have happy feet—don't you?"

"I just think it's an opportunity—that's all. Something different***"

"What if you hate it there because of the weather or because of the way they treat foreigners."

"You're wildly optimistic. Do you know that?"

"I think it's a mistake. French Canada is different people too."

"Just give me tonight to go home have a beer and think it over."

"You're going into a bar alone."

"Cornwallis'; the owner knows me. He'll save me a quiet table in the back."

"Don't get soused. I ain't cleaning up after you in the morning."

"Me! Mr. Reserved."

"Look, Mr. Reserved you must put this to bed. Why don't you just go to Montreal? You have a chance to in the National Hockey League. It's the best league in the world with the best players. Even the referees aren't bad. I really think you're crazy. You're worrying about money too much. I got news for you. You aren't going to starve. So sign until free agency and go."

"Let's go have a beer. Why don't you and Laurie come with me."

"Sure but I'm not drinking tonight. I need a clear head tomorrow."

He picked Laurie up at Agganis Arena and asked her if she would mind if Nate took them to his favorite watering hole.

"You're drinking?"

"He assures me they have Diet Coke. You want to come?"

"Sure."

"What's the problem?" She asked as they sat down.

"Nate doesn't know whether he should sign a short term deal with Montreal or play in Sweden for a year to leverage a trade."

"Oh!"

"That's what I say," Nate said.

"Go to Montreal. It's got all the snow and cold a guy wants. You could make major enemies around the league. They'll trade you all right. They'll trade you to the worst freakin' team in the league. Use your head. They're one of the Original Six."

"Your cultural exploration deal is covered too. French Canada is different from us," Laurie reiterated what Steve said before.

"I'm going to pay through the nose in taxes."

"Yeah, it will be the NHL and when free agency comes, you'll have respect around the league."

"Yeah, I can see your point."

"Finally! Dear Lord!"

"So what are you going to do?" Laurie asked.

"Well, I'll sign with Montreal."

"Is it your final decision on *Jeopardy*."

"Yeah, I have too much on my plate right now. I have to put it behind me. God, this beer tastes good."

"I am not carrying you home."

"We'll, have Laurie do it," Nate smiled.

"Are you going to let him say that?" She looked at Steve.

"Honey, you'd be much better at it than me because you are much more kind than I am. I'd be bouncing his head of the walls."

"You guys."

"Seriously though, Montreal and Old Quebec are really nice. You should like it there."

"And all they talk is hockey," Laurie smiled.

"Good, I need something fun to talk about. My classes this semester suck eggs. All we talk about is the bad parts of history. I back loaded them to my last year and it finally came—now I'm stuck with them."

"How bad can it be?" Steve asked.

"Well, in one class, we attack Vietnam, in another the Kennedy assassination, and the other Pearl Harbor and the effect it had on the American people up to and including Manzanar."

"Big deal, you're taking one less class."

"If you let me finish, please, programming in Cobol."

"Why is that your academic life?"

"I don't know. It seemed like a good thing to do at the time."

"So basically your senior year sucked eggs," Steve said.

"I have to graduate. I promised mother."

"Then you're up to the Great White North."

"Let's talk about something else," Nate said.

"Speaking of winning. Three games left. The first is against Minnesota-Duluth. We can take those guys, huh?" Steve asked.

"They're good."

"Aw, come on, we're better. We're the best team in the tournament."

"You said that before Colorado College."

"Well, was I supposed to say we were going to lose. Come on now."

"I almost like you sometimes."

"I'm going to save that one for me scrapbook."

"You're right. We'll win."

Minnesota Duluth was a big, fast team that played a quasi-European style and was very proficient at it. They had only lost twice all year. They also had attitude with multiple players using their mouths to get under the skin of opposing players. Their fans did also.

"You suck Thompson!" Somebody from the stands yelled and then the rest of the Minnesota side began to yell.

"Thompson sucks!"

Steve laughed a little but gritted his teeth and went back to the bench.

"I didn't know you sucked," Nate said.

"Fine! Believe strange fans and not me."

"It's still not hard to believe."

The horn sounded and the game started. By college hockey standards it was a very boring game. Both teams played a collapsing, trap defense made to stifle the free wheeling offenses each team had. With, two minutes left in the last regulation periods, the score was tied one to one. Steve hopped around a bit because he blocked a shot off his ankle and it hurt.

"Flood them. They have to defend their zone. Overload to the slot and slam the net. Jack Franklin, can you win me that face-off?" Coach Parlon pleaded.

"Yes, sir."

The referee blew the whistle and the teams lined up. Franklin won the face-off and drew it back to Nate, who passed it to Steve who wound up and fired a low slap shot into the pile. Somebody got a stick on it for BU and the puck shot over the goalie's shoulder and into the net.

Left wing Ty Clark came out of the pile with his stick raised high and in the middle of dancing a clumsy dance. The guys mobbed him.

"We still have a minute and a half left," Steve warned.

BU clamped down with the trap even harder, slamming Bulldog players into the boards and back onto the ice. Finally, the horn sounded and the boys celebrated.

The locker room was kind of quiet. They left all their celebrating on the ice. Two more games in Albany and they would be National Champs.

Steve dressed quickly and waited for his family to meet him.

"Hey! Son!"

Steve turned around and saw his father.

"Hey! Dad!"

"Great game!" His dad said.

"Where is everyone?"

"We got reservations at the hotel restaurant. Come on."

"Dad, I have to be in bed for bed check."

"You're kidding."

"How's Tony?"

"Waiting to be a proud papa***"

"Is he taking his meds?"

"Yeah, he's going fine. He's writing some."

"Good. He was always happiest when he wrote."

"How's it going with the company?"

"A little here and a little there; Nothing really earth shattering, now it's time to do your day to day stuff—mostly, not screwing up."

"How are you holding up?"

"Okay, I'm too stupid to know I'm tired. I'm living a dream with my brother no less who at one time I didn't know if he would make it out of his room. You know something, the funny thing is, in these kinds of stories there is always a reason to tell someone to stick it. People spit on you or say you can't. I've never had that reaction. They look at me with awe and admiration—like I'm a King."

"Well you keep this in mind King. There are no Kings in America—only people. I haven't given up on you yet."

"Yeah, sure pop! What kind of chances do you think we have?"

"The hockey team is a great chance."

"And the company?"

"I've never had two sons involved in a company that has evolved from infancy into a possible worldwide operation."

"Tony's really pulling his weight. One thing that bothers me though, he mentions his 'old enemies' once in a while. I think that we can work together longer than he thinks."

"You guys work it out. You're men now."

"When things are going well, his voices tell him the doctors are crazy and that he doesn't need the medicine. He laughs at it now but it scares me to death."

"What does he do to combat them?"

"He thinks of the baby and Annie. They are his to take care of."

"Does she know that?"

"Not at supper time. She cooks and cleans. When he wants to feel noble, he'll run out to the convenience store for ice cream."

Chapter 42

The Terriers played the Michigan Wolverines in the preliminary game of the Frozen Four in Albany. The drilling and digging from both sides was omnipresent as the physical, play dominated on both sides. The only problem was that Michigan was bigger. The banging took it's toll on BU and going into the third period they were pretty banged up and behind on the score board 2-1.

Steve was frustrated. He fired the trash can up against the wall.

"You freakin' bunch of babies. Oh, number two hits from behind. Number six slashes. What's the matter with you guys? We are going to lose the chance to play for the National Championship. You suck it up. If I hear one more guy complaining, he'll deal with me personally. You get in the fight. I'm tired of you complaining like a bunch of miserable old ladies. You get in there."

BU Did. They sacrificed their bodies—diving to block shots and running hard into Wolverine players. Peter scored with thirteen minutes to play on a breakaway to tie the score. And then Steve took over piling up three assists. One to Rico and two to Nate; BU won 5-2.

"Nobody celebrate. We have tomorrow to think about," Steve shouted.

"We play BC tomorrow for the whole thing. Let's everybody be ready," Nate said.

"Well, we won," Steve said back in the hotel room.

"I never saw you so emotional," Nate said.

"I knew the guys had it in them. I just had to bring it out of them."

"One more game?"

"And then our college playing days together our over."

"Yeah, I'll stop carrying you."

"Drop dead."

"You and Laurie are really going to get married."

"Yeah! Finally! I've known her a few months and she's become everything to me."

"No offense, you have a lot of everything going on."

"It's true. To be honest with you, the making love is great but she can make you happy, or sad, or she makes you do homework when you don't want to."

"Well, there's a plus."

"She's my bud."

"You know, of all the hellions on this team, we're the only ones that want to get married and have kids as soon as possible."

"That's because we're more mature and after they break their backs in their chosen profession for a while, their figure out that whisky, vodka, and one night stands ain't enough. They'll grow up."

"You have such faith in people. I'm impressed."

"We're going to beat BC."

"I just have a feeling you're psyched out if you're them. We beat them every time they played us this season."

"Do you really think we will play each other next year?"

"Bound to happen!"

"That'll be weird."

"You're weird. It'll be complicated."

"I hate to tell you but we have to win tomorrow. The whole season will be marred by one stupid loss."

"You say that every game. You were spazzing on game one."

"I'll never stop."

"You're a nut."

"We have to win tomorrow because BC can't get the best of us."

"Stork plays for BC."

"If he wins, I'll send him to the Aleutian Islands. He can watch the pelican races."

Instead of sleeping that night, Steve looked out of his hotel window and thought to himself, 'What if you retire early? What if you play in the Olympics, take home your medal and run the company. Are you really wanting that?'

He looked out the window for a long time and poured himself a Coke Zero from the refrigerator. He thought a long while on the subject and he smiled ruefully, "All that money, up in smoke!" He grinned. Well, I can run a multi-national company but the kid's college tuition may cost more than my company by then. Maybe, I should just play hockey until I drop or my family and I decide to hang it up."

The thing that bothered him right off was that on the eve of a National Championship Game in college, during his senior year, he was more concerned with looking over a stack of resumes when he flew home to Boston. He never realized the amount of fun that this company had afforded him—especially working with Tony. His brother ended up with more confidence to enhance his life every day. He had his days but the tremendous drive and determination to just enjoy life after what the mental illness has done to him. He had the ability to thinks, the courage to step out of the crowd and be himself. That was very satisfying to Steve. Maybe he should just play until Vancouver and end it.

The phone rang, and he picked it up.

"Hello,"

"Hi!"

"What are you doing up?"

"Laurie, if you didn't want me up, why did you call me on the phone?"

"Honey, it's my job to make you feel comfortable. Why are you uncomfortable?"

"I'm not really uncomfortable. I have too many choices that I created for myself tonight. I'm thinking of playing until Vancouver and then hanging them up."

"Yeah, right! You're going to hang them up. Where will you put them?"

"Don't you think it's living like you're permanently sixteen? I want to grow up sometimes. I want children and church on Sunday."

"And you can't have that playing in the NHL?"

"I guess I can but the more I pour into this business, the more rewarding and challenging it is. I am confident we will make money."

"How much? Probably enough to set up three generations quite well***"

"For pictures?"

"Don't be a doubting Laurie."

"If perchance this crazy dream comes true and you quit hockey, what am I going to do? I like watching you play hockey?"

"Really?"

"Yes, I do. Stop worrying about Dallas. It will be there for you. You're nervous. That's all it is!"

"Do you think Dallas would like to meet me?"

"In what way?"

"Not the cameras and stuff but let's say I'm in a bookstore. Would they like me? Am I a Texas kind of guy?"

"I think so."

"You think so. That's it."

"Well, you never put it to me in those terms to me before."

"But..."

"Go to sleep and enjoy your last college game tomorrow. College is hockey is a sports spectacle—enjoy it. It's your last game and you're wearing the whites. Your lucky color! Don't worry about Dallas, you are just too much of a spastic case. You've played this game since you were four—go out there and hustle young man and for crying out loud have fun!"

"I just don't want to play for the money—like I can't do anything else. I hated those bumper stickers that said, 'Be kind to animals! Kiss a hockey player!' I never wanted that for me."

"Excuse me, but could you please slow down. You are there. You are walking the walk. Just go out and play tomorrow."

"If we lose…"

"You're not going to lose."

"What?"

"You'd mope around that campus for month. And I'd kill you."

"Thank you for the talk. I really, very much appreciate it. I will see yo tomorrow after we win."

"Okay!"

The National Championship Game was played before a sell out crowc Boston College and Boston University played a bruising game. The onl problem there was a lot of goals scored and BU scored most of them. At th end of the second period, BU led 6-0.

"Be aggressive. Don't go into a shell," Coach Parlon instructed.

Steve took the directions to heart and slammed a BC player to the ice wit a legal shoulder check. The puck squirted loose and Steve raced into th offensive zone with it. He was pushed behind the net by an Eagle defensemar Steve kept digging and the defender fell down. Steve made a wrap around goa into the net and the score stood up 7-0. The guys jumped from all angles an landed on Steve.

"Geeze," Steve smiled sheepishly, "that felt great."

The guys went crazy. They raced around the ice throwing their gloves an sticks in the air. They hugged each other, laughed, and jumped up and down.

Steve found Nate and he gave him a huge bear hug.

"Man, we did it," Steve was so relieved he couldn't believe it.

"I couldn't be more happy for you if I did it myself," Nate said.

"One of the days I'll figure out what you're talking about."

The team settled down for the trophy presentation. The NCA Commissioner Stan Gordon presented trophies in all the major categories unti there were two left—the Hobey Baker and the National Championship trophies The arena became quiet.

"Ladies and Gentlemen, it's my great honor to present the 2005 Hobe Baker trophy for best college hockey player in the United States to Steve Thompson, defenseman, Boston University."

There was a loud cheer that went up from the BU side and to their credi BC chipped in with a rousing applause. Steve skated over to the trophy anc took a good look at it. It was an unbelievable piece of luck he thought and the he said so.

"To everyone that follows college hockey, they understand the talent leve that Division One College Hockey presents to the fans. It's blind luck for me tc win this. Many guys worked just as hard and sacrificed just as much.

"I'd like to thank everyone in my immediate family and my hockey famil here at BU. All of my teammates worked really hard for this title—not tc mention the support of our fans. We had a lot of fun mostly because we mixec in the straight arrows like me with the wild and crazies and we made it work We had a great year. Thank you and thanks to BC. They'll be back next year."

The crowd erupted and Steve held the trophy up over his head and th photographers went crazy. Flashes popped all over the place. He brought it tc the bench and then the big one was announced. Nate got first dibs and he skatec it around the ice with the team following. One by one, the guys got their turn. Steve felt humbled and exhilarated by the whole thing but he had to admit, it felt really good.

The NCAA had a policy about victorious or losing teams staying in the hotel any longer than they had to so they flew into Logan Airport in the early morning hours and were met by approximately five thousand crazed BU fans. The guys took turns waving and talking to the crowd. Steve couldn't believe the night he was having. It was like nothing he had ever experienced before. He wondered what winning the Stanley Cup would feel like.

When they finally got home and into the dorm, Nate asked?

"Well, how does it feel to be a pro?"

"At the moment kind of sad; we sure had a good time tonight."

"Yeah, that's what I was thinking."

"Don't get overconfident hearing this but it was great rooming with you and being your partner on defense."

"You're the best college hockey player I've ever seen and I understand you now better than I did. Some guys just have a drive to them. The thing I like about you is that you understand that's you instead of letting it eat you up."

"Man it was just plain fun. I didn't have the heart to talk to Stork tonight. He looked awful."

"Yeah, he was probably tired from the Beanpot."

"Are you just making this up or do you know what you're doing?"

"Have a little faith my boy!"

"This is the greatest night of my life."

"I wonder what winning the Stanley Cup is like," Steve wondered.

"I don't know if it will be this good."

"Really? Why?"

"I don't know. This was the first taste of winning I had at a very high level. The Cup will be second. Besides you don't have to drag yourself from practice and make yourself study until one am for a history test in the pros. I'll always like college."

"I like it but it's time to move on. There's Laurie, the Stars, and I'll finally have a real job instead of tide me over jobs. I wanted to be an adult when I was eleven years old and I got my first job selling papers. I was going to buy Fenway Park with my paper route money."

"What happened?"

"Oh! I was millions short but I bought a heck of a lot of baseball cards."

"Still got them?"

"Oh! Yeah, I'll hand them down to my kids."

"I don't think I'm going to fall asleep tonight," Nate grinned.

"We have the parade on Monday. We miss class."

"You've always missed class."

"Thanks a lot."

"I'm going to miss you're density."

"Hey, look buddy I've made it through twenty-one years with this blockhead and I'm a graduate from this fine institution and if you don't mind I would like some respect."

"Okay you can have respect."

"Thank you."

"Did you really want to buy Fenway Park?"

"Hey, I was ready to roll man. I was making thirty bucks a week in tips. Watch out because here I come."

"On a paper route***"

"It was an honest living. The only problem with it was that the ink was really cheap and it stained your fingernails, your hands, and your clothes. You were quite the mess by the end of the route but it was fun. It gave me an independence I never had before. It taught me a lot of stuff about saving and spending and it bought me my hockey sticks and baseball cards."

"You were able to see success from a paper route?"

"Not always. It always seemed that somebody had a cooler job. What I was doing wasn't cool enough. The guys who cut lawns or shoveled snow always seemed cooler to me. To me it was all I could do—not something to take pride in. I felt kind of embarrassed doing it sometimes. As I got older I never could quite figure out why. Anyway, it was a legal living and it taught me to be reliable and to do be responsible."

"Son, you done good: I don't ever think I'll meet a truer guy in pursuit of excellence as you."

"Thanks. I had a crazy dream last night and it made me think all night I'm thinking about hanging them up after Vancouver. "

"Where would you live? Dallas would kill you."

"I don't know. Probably not. I love this game."

"I took psych and that's what you are worried about—whether Dallas uses up people instead of looking out for them."

"I keep wondering if I'll put something out there—like an opinion and it will make sense and as much as they try, they won't accept it as better than theirs because they are after all human and you ain't."

"Political run?"

"No. I have this anxiety since I was a kid. I moved six times before I started high school. Your head spins and palms get sweaty. There is nothing there except dad dragged you to another place and you have to stick it out."

"No home."

"My family. They ...I mean we do things together. Those are our friends. As my dad worked up the ladder at every place, our "old friends" decided he was a rich guy and were of no need to those rich people. Now that I'll get my parents fixed up nice, they'll hate them too. Did you ever have that happen to you?"

"Sort of; Mr. Clarkson owned a small convenience store and he let my friends and I eat penny candy there and hang out if we weren't too much of a pest. One day the old guy knocks over cans of beans and I helped him picked it up and he paid me a dollar. I would hang around his place doing odd jobs and he'd help me out. Sometimes a dollar, sometimes two, and on a real good day—five whole dollars! I liked the old guy. He passed a way a few years ago and all those kids, there must have been ten of us were there."

"Man, my grandfather would be so happy. I hope he's happy wherever he is. He was a Teamster—a truck driver. He also worked on the railroad. He didn't understand me really. To him you were a success if you paid the rent and brought food home. There was a lot I didn't say to him because he was my grandfather and it's probably for the best now but we agreed that he was my grandfather and I was his grandson."

"My parents are probably most proud," Nate said.

"That's cool."

"Yeah, I think so. Incredible amount off sacrifice my parents made. They traveled with me all over the country at all hours of the morning. They bought all my equipment. Everything!"

"Same with me except I bought my own sticks; nobody touched my sticks. Do you think we'll be big stars in the pros like everyone says?"

"Until the merry-go-round stops, why get off?"

"Well, just between you and I. I think if I work really hard, I'll be able to do it. I'm glad I stayed my senior year."

"You realize we're going to be rookies next year."

"Yeah, I thought about it. Think it'll be bad?"

"Only if you screw it up?"

"What's that supposed to mean?"

"It means you put up with their garbage and do what they tell you or you whine and complain about everything and that makes them think of new ways to get the rookie."

"Yeah, I guess."

"Hey! It's part of growing up."

"Tell me about. I have to get this contract signed so I can get an engagement ring."

"My advice to you is to get the biggest contract you can because it's a rough way to make a living and it ain't going to be there forever."

"You're a fatalist."

"What does that mean?"

"What that means is you don't think that you'll play that long so, you start seeing little Martian guys under your bed. I'm going to sign a hefty contract for sure but I want to win that Cup. I'd rather have a good guy on right wing because we can afford him than some stiff who doesn't hustle."

"Hmm*** It's still a business and I've been moderately poor for the last four years. It's my turn to do all right by myself and my family."

"Well, we're going to the parade down Comm Ave and then I'll relax with Laurie. Then on Monday, I'll put a phone call into the agent's office. Finally, then I'll be a grown up. That Friday is the party."

"Yeah, I'll be interested to see a little of the hometown."

"It's kind of quiet. The place where it's being held is in Agawam. Chez Jozef is really big for weddings, proms, Bah Mitzvahs, and Holiday parties. They do a good job."

"Cool, I'm up for it."

"Oh, brother!"

"Well, gee wiz! If we ain't going to the pros***"

"You're such a hayseed."

"I am not. I am just not cynical."

"No you're not. I'll give you that. You know what I want to talk about. You're project.

"Geeze, we did it," Steve smiled for the millionth time that night.

The following night he was having a beer at Cornwall's and feeling very good. Nate crept up behind him and said.

"I got her."

"Got who?"

"Her! The one I've been looking for. She thinks I'm cute. She told me that."

"How many beers have you had?"

"I can still walk."

"Sit down. I'm not picking you up off the floor."

"What's her name?"

"Carol. Carol Johnson. She goes to Emerson."

"Where'd you meet her?"

"I was running and she was too so I turned around and ran after her. We struck up a conversation and we went to a movie tonight and she said we should go out again."

"Did you tell her you were fast becoming a drunk? What the hell's the matter with you? Shut yourself off man."

"All right! Diet Cokes from now on! The point is I actually found a pretty, sane, intelligent girl, in this city who likes me."

"Will you sit down please. You make me crazy."

Nate sat down and the waitress came over.

"He's shut off," Steve said.

"Diet Coke please," Nate smiled, "with lemon."

"Do you want real lemon on the side or real lemon in the soda?"

"Give me the real stuff please."

"Could you please just relax? Please for me."

"Man, if we didn't do it."

"Yeah, we are the best in the nation."

The waitress brought over Nate's soda.

"To the first one who will be on a team that's best in the world," Steve said.

On May 11th Steve graduated with his class. On May 12th he signed a contract with the Stars .Laurie's parents met them at the airport. On May 14th, he called BU and made sure everything continued to click like clockwork. He would get a brand new lap top with his new contract.

"I heard life is hard in Texas," Steve said to Laurie.

"It's warmer in Texas."

"Do you think they'll like me? I sort of got a handle on Boston. I heard Texas was different."

"No, they just expect you to win. It's like New York with cactus in that respect."

"What is it like from a civilian perspective? I am nervous that I'm not going to fit in—again!"

"People are pretty nice. They'll take you as you present yourself. One thing though. If you present yourself as a jerk, they'll tell you you're a jerk."

"I know we went over this but this is like a pre-test. Am I a jerk? Better yet? What causes one to be considered a jerk?"

"You know when one guy scores and then dances around the ice like a fool without jumping into his teammates arms. That's a jerk because he's not respecting his teammates."

"Oh, good! I understand that and my heart and mind accept that. However, if you were really excited, like you won the Cup with one second left. Would you still be considered a jerk?"

"Yes, this is Texas. Conservative Cowboys and their wives; by the way IBM said they still wanted to be involved," She said.

"We're going to have such a good time. That's a good thing. But just people—like regular Texans. What do they do? For stuff***"

"Football and more football—especially high school***"

"Yeah but football is only played in the fall."

"The other nine months are spent in church praying for their football team. The kids don't care they just go to the gym and play pick up all year long."

"They don't care about hockey?"

"It's coming along. More and more rinks are being built. Roller hockey is huge. It's an acquired taste but when the Stars won the Cup a couple of years ago, this town went bloody crazy."

"If we kind of rebuilt, what do you think it would be like?"

"It depends if you were rebuilding or reloading. You are supposed to reload. That's why you're here. You did study them."

"I was having a moment of self doubt."

“Well, put a sock in it, will you? You’re the best college hockey player in the land. Act like it.”

“Excuse me.”

“I was trying to motivate you. How did I do?”

“The clarinet better suits you.”

“They’re big on straight forward. Many of them live by Abraham Lincoln’s statement, “Take a position.” You may not get the slick of New York or LA but you’ll get whole heaps of honest. Plus the family atmosphere here is wonderful. I like it. I liked growing up here. My friends were my friends and they stuck bye when I snuck out of the house to drive dad’s car and he caught me.”

“How’d he do that?”

“He happened to be out for a run. It was early in the morning—about six o’clock. He comes jogging down the sidewalk—happy as a clam and I pull out of the driveway. I thought I was going to die.”

“What happened?”

“He laughed and he couldn’t stop laughing—then he grounded me for two weeks—homework only.”

“We should ask to use the car from now on. What’s really cool in Texas that we could do together?” He asked.

“Well, since we both want to go to school, we could check UT Austin.”

“That’s the school with the great football team.”

“It’s a little bit more than a football team.”

“Sorry.”

“Well!”

“I think I actually am happy in an adult sort of way for the first time in my life.”

“Yeah! But if you want to have a childish almost infantile soul mate, you can always, always enjoy my talents.”

“At what?”

“I make you laugh.”

“This is true. So the pressure is on. Say something funny.”

“I am a Yankee fan.”

She giggled.

“Actually, that wasn’t funny. I was serious.”

“That was good. I give you ten points for that.”

“Let’s get married.”

“Sure.”

“Do you think they’ll want me back?”

“Back where?”

“Hockey is kind of serious in Boston. Despite the age of jumbo jet-liners, they really aren’t cognizant of anything but the project is different.

“I’ve this mumbo jumbo act I go through every meeting to keep the team happy. I mention accomplishments from everyone's college…all kinds of stuff. We're trying to invest in better communications systems already. I mean human kind, not electronic kind. Getting the sales force revved up every day is a tough task and they're pros that do it."

"Your decisions are so business-like."

"It's funny because Brian's dad let us use his conference room for a meeting. If you had a camera, you would've died. We're all sitting in our Sunday best—jacket and tie and we're arguing our cases for ideas that would make the company better. We spent two and a half hours making constructive criticism of our present practices and didn't we agree to change 85 per cent of them."

"Did it shake the confidence of the team that you had to change that much."

"This we relied heavily on organized demographic information. Before it was a wing and a prayer approach; the team felt better and there was some general snippiness going on during the last week. Different personalities clashed. Advice became bulldozing and guys didn't like it.

"You're dealing with a lot of guys that have had success at a young age, and some of them are convinced that they are very much the guy all the time. It's killing them in some instances to admit that others on the team contribute more importantly to that given situation," Steve said.

"Do you think you can put a team together in Texas?"

"Yeah, for all my insecurities, I'm very optimistic. Thank God the Stars picked me up. It's a good organization. They free wheel around the ice. They play a fun style. I'll fit in better there. The Bruins grind it out and grind it out. I'm fast and should use my speed. Maybe the trade will be the best for both."

"I hope it's best for you."

"There is no me. There are us."

"How are you going to deal with everything?"

"Every athlete has a charity. Right? Well, mine is the museum."

"Your life is going to be a little stacked with hockey, the museum, and the magazine. What gives with me? You're going to need a break."

"We'll make love a lot."

"I had so much confidence you'd find a peaceful solution to the problem."

"It's no problem. It's fun."

"Sports Center is going to be the only TV show you watch."

"It is now."

"You need something simple."

"I chase a little black, vulcanized rubber puck around the ice. Guys try to hit me and I try to avoid them. It's just the game."

"I hope you aren't going for the complex side. "

"No, it's just so much fun. You are in a state of guilt no matter if it's college or pro. In college you get a free education at most colleges and in the pros, it's not the monopoly money they're handing out. Either way you can't miss. It's a very incredible experience to have a ten year-boy just let the dear in a head lights look when you come near. And then he fishes around his pocket for a pen. He almost cries when nobody has a piece of paper. So he sticks out his arm and says, 'Sign it! Please! Nobody will believe this if I don't have a signature.'

"I tell that it's a ball point pen. It may hurt."

"'Then sign my shirt,'" he says.

"How do we keep the kids normal?"

"They do the usual stuff around the house; dishes, and laundry bringing down. A little vacuuming on occasion; when they get old, we have to teach them how to make coffee. The newspaper won't be the problem."

"Why is that?"

"Sports page?"

"What would you do without sports?"

"I honestly don't know, maybe just working for somebody else."

"Like who?"

"Start my own business like I'm doing now."

"Instead of not as grand design***"

"No. Exactly as grand design; why even go to a school like BU, if you don't aim as high as you can?"

"Not everybody can do it. I hate to admit this but you're a genius."

"Please don't do that to me."

"Then you explain it."

"I just like having quality people working together. Sometimes we go at it but you talking about people with strong opinions that have succeeded their whole life. I've said it before. Sometimes it is quite a challenge to make your point to someone. I'm the boss and the last decision is made I make it. Sometimes the people get a little unnerved by my answer but it's in the effort to make them better."

Chapter 43

"Do you think I should take classes there?" He asked.

"I thought you were gung ho on it."

"Well, what I really want to take are foreign languages but if my business pursuits only take me inside the United States; why take them?"

"A lot of Americans don't understand that in Europe people know two or three languages. It's no big deal."

"Your reservations?"

"I'm too much of an American. My language is English. I expect everyone else to know it."

"Go to Texas and have a good time. You're such a spaz. The things you worry about."

"When we get home*** "

"In Texas***"

"Right, we can have our own place. No skipping between places."

"And to think we knew exactly what we were doing."

"Well, I did."

"I did first."

"You know about taking the languages."

"Are you wishing you hadn't said anything at all?"

"I'd go over there as a business man—not as a spy."

"Why are you telling me this?"

"Empathy my dear! You're supposed to say, 'You're too handsome to be a spy.'"

"What is confusing you?"

"It's just that I'm good at languages. They are fun to take."

"Don't tell anybody that. They'll think you're weird."

Got a quarter?"

"I think so. Call it."

"Heads!"

"Heads it is. What's it going to be?"

"I'll take at least one class of languages I guess."

"Which one?"

"I don't know? Probably Italian or French; I have bigger problems. Yes, but then I was the savior of the Bruins franchise. Now I'm the enemy."

"Yeah but if you carry it off in style nobody will notice."

"Got any tips?"

"Act innocuous."

"Well, I'm not going to act like a bull in a china shop."

"You need a lesson in Texas cool."

"What the heck is Texas cool?"

"When we get there I'll show you."

"Cowboy boots? Jeans? Ten gallon hat?"

"Now you're catching on."

"I don't think it will fit in with Boston."

"Well, I'm out of suggestions."

"I'll just wing it."

"There ain't much to do now," she said.

"Honey, I've got to meet everyone in the Stars organization from the owner to the Zamboni guys."

"Yes, but you'll be talking hockey. That's no big thing."

"Oh, really."

"What's so hard about it?"

"It's about talking chemistry between the guys, who has tendency to need a kick in the butt to get going, who is a great, intrinsic motivator, who leads, who yaks and yaks to keep the team loose and who thinks best when the heat is on. It's very complicated. You have to juggle that and more. The intrinsic motivators get me the most because they are like machines. They just go out and play but they hardly affect their teammates."

"More than lazy guys***"

"Lazy guys galvanize the team. They want to kick their butts."

"Hockey players are animals. You wear your mouth guard."

"Only eye shields, No masks in the pros."

"You're going to lose your tooth."

"Very possibly some of my teeth."

"You wear that damned mouth guard."

"Yes, dear."

His cell phone rang and it was John Franklin from IBM computers.

"Are you still planning the museum?" He asked.

"Yes, sir. I have to call all the corporate sponsors when I get situated."

"We'd like to do it."

"Well, to be honest with you, I looked around and nobody seemed very intent on quitting. I think we have to do it. BU would be ripped."

"What do you mean by that?"

"It's slang for really disappointed and angry. I didn't trade myself or ask to get traded, why is everyone screaming at me?"

"Frankly, we've been in business a lot longer than our competitors and those three letters mean something beyond a personal computer or a lap top.

They want us on BU's campus."

"Well, you are the biggest by a lot. And the commercials you do have I like."

"I'll mention that to the boss."

"Well, let me get situated in Dallas and we can talk."

"Do you want to use us?"

"Yes I do. But I'm worried about one thing. We're all in agreement that this project is good but what if we have disagreements about how it gets done."

"We let the customer make the final decision."

"What I'm trying to say is I want your creativity and experience but I want this project to hold my vision. It's important to me."

"Well, I could probably tell you a lie and say we won't have disagreements or that we'll have the same idea from time to time but mostly it's your ball. You worked with the architect major to design the building. You work with us the same way and it's still your ball. The final decision belongs to you."

"Can I ask you a question?"

"Shoot!"

"What's a billion dollar computer that does business around the globe that I know of want with an upstart with an idea."

"Well, we liked your resume however, this could be a flop."

"I can't see that."

"Good. You just passed ownership 101. You have to remain positive."

"I'm not remaining anything. I believe it."

"Good! Because you're going to have to deal with BU and they are going to want every bell and whistle they can get and you are going to have to explain to learned men that you have researched what will work and what won't."

"And there's also the matter of the budget," Steve said.

"Let, the bean counters worry about that and remember within your company bean counters and marketing people are at odds. Marketing people want to spend and that gives bean counters apoplexy."

"Yes, sir. We've been leaving that to the great thereafter. We'll have to deal with raw numbers right now. We have several companies interested in working with us. We'll be more than happy to finalize everything."

"Good-bye son."

"Through?" Laurie asked.

"I'm ignoring you only because it makes it so much sweeter when I see you."

"Who was that the Lord?"

"The point man for IBM***"

"How are you going to run things eighteen hundred miles away?"

"Well, the first thing is not to ask that question. You just do it."

"You really like Boston. Don't you?"

"Most of the time but I like seeing other parts of the country too; just to see how people live. But it's different now. I was almost a Bruin and when I have success, not only are they going to hate me, they're going to their own ownership and they don't admit that so they hate me again. I get it both ways. All I wanted to do was play for that stupid team all my life and then they don't even give me the satisfaction of one season to play for them."

"That's because you would have starred for them and they would've traded you and 'mystery insider' would leak it to the press that you engineered the trade and then you really would've got waxed."

"If they win the Stanley Cup ahead of Dallas, there will be hell to pay. I'll play on the Galapogas Islands. It'll be a new species 'toasted hockey player.'"

"So about Europe?"

"But we were having such a fun conversation. It's cool learning about other people—plus it's good business. We can trade in other parts of the world. Why not Europe?"

"You want to take me to Europe on our honeymoon."

"Don't talk about it right now. You'll spoil it."

"Would you object to spending the whole year in Texas?"

"No. It's another part of the country that I haven't seen before. It will be nice to observe and greet people. I would like to photograph some of it. But still, I'm learning more about business doing it than reading about it. I'll have to take inter net classes. I'll be on too many planes."

"What about the museum?"

"Hopefully, it comes off as planned."

"All that work."

"Easy come easy go. Start over."

"BU may like you."

"I can't do anything about that. I'm too damned nervous too worry about it actually. Do you know I'm trying out for the NHL! I'm glad for the trade because it gives me a chance to grow on my own, together with you. Boston was only ninety miles away: this is just a little farther. It's like starting college again because I have to meet everybody."

"Except me."

"You have a very quirky sense of humor."

"Yeah! But you love me!"

"Yes, I really do!"

They arrived at the party a bit early and were taken by surprise at the vast quantities of food, drink, and seltzer water that was available.

Nate dropped by for a visit.

"Laurie," he said, "Hey, Gumby."

He looked at Steve.

"He gets to play in Quebec. For Les Canadiens, Les Bleau, Blanc, & Rouge. "

"Have you had anything to drink yet?" Nate asked him.

"Not yet but I'm working on it."

"This is the last time we're all going to be together like this. You know that," Steve said.

"Yeah, I know. Damned shame. Don't you think?"

"In the future, maybe?"

"It was a fun ride anyway."

"You giving up? That's not like you!"

"Look at it already, guys are separating into different groups and they're talking to who they want to talk to. Look at us. I suggest we mingle."

"Yeah, we better. I have to make the rounds and talk to the dignitaries—being the Hobey Baker Winner and all."

"Yeah, I wanted to talk to you about that someday."

So they mingled, and they danced and they drank; they didn't eat that much but they sure did have a good time. Steve really wanted to do this again in five years and he said so, which brought a large toast from the peanut gallery.

"We have to go talk," Laurie said.

"Why? You wanted me to dance. I'm dancing. Come on. It's a one in a million deal."

"I'm one in a trillion. Let's go. "

She grabbed him by the hand and sent him down the stairs.

"Are you pregnant?" He asked her when they got outside.

"No. I have been thinking though. I have this plan. I get my MBA in Marketing because I have been listening and I like that part of business."

"Why not music?"

"I wasn't elite and I think I can be an elite in business. I'm the type of person that has to be elite or I try something else."

"And?"

"No babies until I graduate."

"Okay. Can I have them with somebody else?"

"You better not buster."

"That was in poor taste."

"Yes. It was. You're lucky this is a party."

"Always get away with as much as you can."

Rico Barrini came over, a little in his cups but not in the usual happy way. He looked really sad.

"What's with you?" Steve asked.

"This is it brother. These are the guys who won the 1996 national championship."

"Why are you so bummed out? We could've lost the national championship."

"I mean this is us. Me the lawyer to be! 'Nate the Flake' who's going to play in Canada. You Dallas! All the other guys penciled in somewhere from Germany, Switzerland, Sweden, and Finland. We bled together for this. It was the first team called a family in all my years of hockey.

"You and Nate made it that way. You let us fight at practice, you made us pass the puck to each other. What are we going to do without you guys?"

"You're shut off. Take his glass. Enough already! Listen, to me snap out of it. You have real life ahead of you man. You have a chance to be a fine lawyer. Maybe you'll even work for New York someday, as a Senator. I didn't do that to you. BU did that to you. You did that to you. You studied and you were tougher on yourself then when you had to be."

"What are you talking about?"

"When you went into the corner, you went hard. I used to hate practicing against you. You made yourself work harder in the classroom. Why?"

"Because I hate to lose!"

"No!"

"What do you mean? 'No!'"

"You like to win. I ain't never seen anybody as fired up over a teammates goal. That's what made us the best. Guys like you. The hustlers—not the world-beaters! I scored many points in my life man, and this is the first year I've been part of team like this too. We were the best because we were a family."

"Now we get to be crotchety, old, alumni who criticize every move the kids make."

"Man, I want you to make it."

"I'll do it. I'll go through law school and I'll pass the bar. I'll rip it all up."

"You'll be a great lawyer man. But there's one thing that you can help me with."

"What's that, boss?"

"Should I quit after the Olympics."

"Shut this boy off please. That's the dumbest thing I've ever heard! You play as long as you feel like it."

"Look, once you wear the jersey of your country, that's all there is. You've marched in the Opening ceremonies and exited in the closing. Beautiful! Leave at the top of your game."

"Go back to where I said, that was the dumbest thing I ever heard. Let me explain what you mean to people in this country right now. You my friend are the hottest athlete with a bit of moxie to play in the business world. You are what every parent wants their kid to get out of college. If you sell the company and put yourself out to pasture before your time, you'll go nuts! You ain't built for that man."

"I could collect as many USA jerseys as I can."

"Now, you're making sense. That's the guy I know."

"Give up another two Olympics for nothing. Now what is the purpose of that? You better stick with me man. You get some strange ideas in your head."

"Do you think they could have the Winter Games in some really cool place that we have never seen before."

"Like where?"

"Switzerland."

"You could go talk to the bankers—negotiate the takeover of the world."

"I don't want to take it over. I just want to see it."

"Me too."

Soon the party did break up and the guys just looked at each other one by one. In one hundred years, they would be kept alive by a plaque or a trophy in the case but for right now, they were a bunch of guys who wondering where to go from here.

When they arrived at the airport, a little crowd of people came up to Steve and Laurie welcoming them to Dallas. Laurie even got flowers.

"Nice," Steve said, "Keep waving honey."

"The children are so cute."

Anyway, a very long, very limousine took them to the Dallas Stars offices.

"I have been waiting for you kids. How was your flight?" Ben Masterson, the General Manager asked.

"The landing was really impressive," Steve said.

"Flowers." Laurie smiled.

"Look son, I'd like to get this done while we're in the car. I don't like the one they signed you to. It's embarrassing to this organization. You will be the cornerstone of our defense. This is what I can pay you. What do you think?"

"One hundred million over five years and a 15% stock option in the Stars***"

"Well, sir, I should earn the captaincy for that money. It's an awful lot."

"Are you afraid of the pressure?" He asked his father.

"Never have been. Still it's a long way from thirty bucks a week on a paper route. I'll play for you. I want to get my rookie season finished. I'm in a quandary about what to do about the museum. I'm stuck between Boston and Dallas. I think my knee jerk reaction to the rewrite of the contract was to go to Texas but I made commitments to Boston and besides you wouldn't believe what they are paying me. It's a lot. As soon as I get lay of the land, I can do something here. I'd like to find what's important to the community first.

Let me find a place to live and I'll fly you out here. I'm hoping to spend the off-season in Massachusetts and the season in Texas but I'm not sure what the future will be. I may stay here year round. I still would think of BU as the one that got away if I didn't go. I'm looking at International Relations. I think that would be fun. BU's job is to make it impossibly hard, which you deal with. I don't know dad. I may have to give up studying at BU—Texas and Boston don't seem to be on speaking terms sometimes. One up man ship is fine I guess but this is out of hand. I hope they know I'm not the Lord or God or anybody else. I'm just a hockey player." He wrote to his father.

And in any case if you didn't get it, I want a fifty/fifty split of our lives.

Give mom my love. Tell Tony and Anne to pack their Bags for a vacation and don't tell mom too much about this letter. She'll get worried for sure.

Guess what? The United States Olympic Committee and the International Olympic Committee have contacted me about the museum with interest. This thing will get done but it's a matter of getting the people on a team; working towards the same goal.

Steve,

In the hotel room, later that evening, Steve looked out the window to see suburban Dallas and as he did this he thought of his freshman year in Boston. He hoped he had more maturity now then when he was a kid. He was more seasoned now; he hoped. Although he was a rookie, there had to be a way off getting the veterans to listen to him instead of casting him aside. The only way he could figure out what to do was to keep his mouth shut and do his job at a consistently high level to make the veterans want to talk to him.

Although everything was optimistic because of the agreement on the contract, Steve felt it was his time on the edge—more so than in college—maybe even more so than anytime in his life ever! He lay on the bed stripped to the waist. He considered the possibilities of failure versus success. If he failed, he would go back to Massachusetts a disgrace, at least in his mind. If he went back a success, they would smile and grit their teeth and say you were on the wrong team. His third thought was a question? What if he did in fact, fail? He had never done that before—not as a Cub Scout, in midget hockey, or college. It was a very good possibility because he was playing against the best players in the world. For the first time in his life, the 100 million was making him wonder. Except a precious few, college players were all the same—watching their pennies.

He needed to get back to school. Books always reassured him on the hypothesis that if you could engage the brain everything else would go smoothly. Rookie camp started in a week and lasted for two more. Hopefully, if planned correctly and performed better, he would be in second semester at Harvard summer term. All in all he hoped he cruised through rookie camp and headed into Cambridge with a good head of steam. He had joked about getting paid in the NHL and what it would do to him. Having someone drop one hundred million dollars in your lap was an awfully humbling experience. But he had to admit it was fun.

"Hey! There has to be something we can talk about," Steve said to Tony on the phone.

"I can't believe they did it."

"Your baby with have golden rattles!"

"I'd settle for golden season tickets to the Red Sox."

"Sire, your wish is my command. How about a sky box."

"My business clients will like it."

"Oh, and you'll be miserable."

"Look, before we start fighting over money. What do we say to people now? Do you know what ridiculous situations I get into now because of this project. Some old lady comes up to me in the drug store and says, 'You're the nutty one in that company. The picture one.' With you having money, it's going to even be worse. People will want me to hit you up on their behalf."

"Use your head. Some people really do need money and then there's whatever. We're smart. We know how to get from point A to point B. We'll handle it has brothers like we always do."

"I think I'm writing the never ending story. I can't find the finish. It just keeps going."

"You're too hard on yourself."

"Mom's really worried about you. cars, money, women, new teammates who are into cars, money, women and God knows what else. Don't be most popular. BU."

"Being most popular doesn't mean we have a team full of hooligans. I met some of them. Pretty good guys in all."

Chapter 44

He called John Davis and Jack Rawlings first and they were kind of wondering if Texas would be their new home too. Jack put it most succinctly, "I didn't break my back on that cinematography not to finish it."

"Gentlemen please calm. Harvard hasn't said, 'No!' All they communicated to me was to get situated and we'll go from there. Now what we have to do is wait. I'm looking to get a three or four bedroom condo so I can turn some of it into an office. I'll be here until June because of rookie camp and then I'll be back East for the educational experience of a lifetime."

They both laughed over the speaker- phone.

"You are going to be breaking your back," Jack Rawling's laughed.

"Yes, you are. You're going to be calling me up at two am asking me if I did that," John Davis smiled.

"It's not going to be that bad," Steve said.

"Yes it is!" Jack giggled.

"I will call you when I'm in the mood."

Jack asked one thing.

"Please tell us, sir. How's does one spend a hundred million dollars?"

"It's only fifty million after taxes."

"Poor baby."

"Boys, I'm sitting in one of the grandest hotel rooms I ever seen. They know how to do it at the Ritz. Let me tell you."

"Well, you freakin' deserve it. You've been carrying three jobs for no pay and now you have your chance."

"I'm going to get the lay of the land and then see what I can do for Texas."

"What about option two?" John Davis asked.

"I don't know right now."

"Why go to BU then?"

"International Relations***"

"What the hell do you do with it?" Jack asked.

"Could you guys be a little bit more broadminded? Option Number Two."

"You're going to take it Global?" Jack said.

"I'm hoping to."

"You can go into politics with that you know?" John Davis asked.

"I need a resume. A practical, hands on resume before I think about that and like it or not I'm a Conservative Republican and what best fits my personality is work. The museum's a good start but I want something more besides hockey isn't forever. Scott Fusco played one year for the Whalers and I was really upset because he was my favorite defensemen and took his Harvard degree and went into real estate investing."

"Do you ever do anything real that a kid did when you were a kid?" John Davis asked.

"Sure, I had a paper route. I bought hockey sticks and baseball cards. Normal stuff!"

"I was talking about when you weren't working. Books? Music? Movies? Anything like that?"

"Well, the last movie I saw was *Miracle* and I thought it was great."

"You sat through a whole movie without worrying about work?"

"Why are you asking me this stuff now? We're already in elbow deep. Besides I've got to call Chris, Tony, and Lynne. Good-bye."

"Hey!"

Steve laughed and clicked the phone off.

He called Chris first.

"Hey, I'm in Texas," Steve said.

"What's going on? Is everything fouled up?"

"Right now we're in a state of flux. We have to start talking seriously with just about every sponsor whole seemed interested and see what they'll pony up. I have to call BU tomorrow and we're going through the picture session deal answering questions with the press. I hope to get some time to take Laurie and her parents out to dinner. My parents are coming in two weeks because I told them I didn't want mom crying all over the place."

"Poor baby!"

"Chagrined baby is more like it. Anyway, what I want you and Lynne to come up with a draft for Kodak and Canon discussing previous talks we've had. Harvard's going for it I know it but we have to have a plan or several plans I guess now."

"Good. We can do that. How's Dallas?"

"Dude, they put us up in the Ritz Carlton. It's gorgeous. I don't even know what I'm doing here."

"Ride it. Enjoy yourself to the max."

"Do me a favor call Lynne and tell her what the skinny is."

"No problem. I've been after her since the program started."

"Good. Because I have to go figure out what makes Texas barbecued ribs are such a delicacy down here."

"Is Laurie with you?"

"Right next store!"

"I'll see how long that will last."

"Good-bye!"

He snuck in one more call to Rico first.

"Hey! It's me. I'm in Texas."

"What's going on with the museum boss?"

"Well, I need you for something. You're going to be a lawyer so you can express yourself orally and with the pen; right?"

"That's what they are going to pay me for."

"Good, I need an overall presentation that you and I will make to BU."

"Just the two of us?"

"John Davis too but he doesn't know it yet."

"The Three Musketeers, I guess."

"Way we figure it it's a minimum one and a half hour presentation and we can't try and use filler. It's got to be the real stuff."

"How are we going to do this?"

"Well, I'm doing okay now so I'm going to buy everyone speaker phones. We'll have conference calls. Piece of cake!"

"Is it true you signed for $100 million over five years."

"It's only fifty million after takes."

"No kidding."

"Oh well, it didn't work the first time neither. Dude, it is dinner time for the wife and me. I will call you when I get a chance."

He dressed quickly and headed next door to Laurie's room.

"Let's go to Burger King," he said.

"You get that contract and you want to go where?" She asked.

"I haven't cashed it yet and I am having remembrances from my collegiate days."

"Do you want me to walk you through it?"

"Only if you walk to my room after dinner?"

"Aren't you the forward one?"

"A Whopper with cheese, large fry, and large chocolate shake; and then great … you know what afterwards. I have been eating healthy food all week. It's killing me. I have eaten more salads, chicken, and fish. I wouldn't push it on anybody."

"Do you have any idea what you just claimed to have ingested?"

"I haven't claimed anything yet. Let's get going."

"Don't eat the whole thing and I'll take you where you want to go."

"I'll just get a salad."

"No, gorge yourself. Be a pig. See if I care."

"Hey, you're supposed to be empathetic here."

"You'll see empathy dear."

"Yes, mamm."

They entered the nearest Burger King and Steve ordered the Whopper with cheese and he ordered a small diet coke.

"Cut you off at the pass did I?" She asked as she ordered a cheeseburger and a small diet.

"Hey, we're really getting married," he said.

"Let's back to the room. I need to talk to you."

"Good or bad?"

"Let's just go back to the room."

She talked little in the cab and he saw tears in her eyes. He hustled her up to the room where she promptly turned and kissed him—prying him up against the door. When she finished kissing him, he held her close.

"That was the most desperate kiss I've ever felt. What's going on?"

"I'm never going to be able to hold you."

"Please hold it. Before you go off on a rant, please, stop it. You don't hold me. You're in love with me and I you."

"I changed my mind about grad school. I want us to have a baby and I'm going to tell my parents that I want to work with you."

"I have a tough decision with me being the ahead of this company."

"What is that?"

"Look, we can't flirt in front of the troops! We have to be professional. Otherwise, it could get really messy. I am worried about Tony. I don't think he gives a damn about a book shop. Something's eating at that guy. I think he's doing what he's supposed to and not what he wants."

"Annie?"

"I think she's disappointed. I talked to her on the phone the other night. She said, he loves the baby but has abject fear that the boy will turn out like him and he doesn't want to be on a business trip when it happens.

"There is a sadness to Tony with the baby because it is almost like he's just waiting for it and he's only a baby. He has to get to his formative years for it to happen. He's got to snap out of it."

"Are you going to tell him?"

"I don't know how to. He's my brother and he's older. I followed him around. It wasn't the other way around. He's done so well. I already checked if he was jealous."

"Tony would be jealous." She laughed.

"I know, I know, I know. Let's just say for instance that his fear can be turned***see, I am greedy, I want to work with him. He has come so far and he's coachable. He's a great friend. For a crazy guy, he gives good advice. I want him with me as an ally. Let somebody else sell books."

"Tony is your friend."

"Yeah but it's different. He's my brother. That is more than a friend. We have done the stupidest things before he was sickened and we got away with them because we were young and impetuous. Tony jokes that it's a good thing he got sick, we would have got caught. He's coaching me through the lack of college thing.

"I miss it already. I thought, 'This is it. I'm never going to pick up a book again. I'm going to relax, go to Mexico, pop a couple of Corona's—relax. I've been burning the candle at both ends between hockey and the business and loving. I even missed Sports Center last night."

"What were you dead?"

"Fell asleep next to my cereal."

"How'd you end up in bed?"

"The waking up was worth it."

"Am I exonerated?"

"You're the most attractive woman I've ever seen. Stop. Let's get to bed too. I'm cold."

They made love and she smiled.

"Maybe we have a chance," she smiled.

"We damn well better have a chance," he laughed.

"I don't know what to do about this museum thing."

"This museum thing?"

"I am having trouble seeing it sell from WMASS because originally I was from there. Therefore, in their eyes everything I buy for the Commonwealth should reside there, which I cannot do because I have commitments in other areas however, there are things that I want to do in WMASS. They just have some sort of thing against Boston sometimes—not really serious and not really in play. 'Boston's rich. We're poor etc.'"

"I mean there is cool stuff that goes on there like the Big E and the Symphony Orchestra and UMASS has a bunch of events. It just isn't right what goes on Main Street. You see Springfield has one Main St. from the North End to the South End and our financial district is right dead in the middle. It's nice until about five o'clock and then most people go home. The big thing that people are praying for is the Waterfront Project to go through. That would be huge. I'm crossing my fingers and saying my prayers. "Somehow the city got old and most of the Italians, Irish, Germans, you name it moved out of the city. And it's coming along in places but some of it is just the same old same old. Forking over one government plan after another; see the problem is they don't take care of stuff. Everything that gets built for the community gets built in the suburbs because there's a reasonable chance it won't be destroyed. Still you want to be there because it is home. And truth be told they are kind of looking at privatization with the Mass Mutual Center and it worked well. The place is really nice. It's just they have to do that more often. I'm going to do my thing there and hopefully will do there's. I'm not Boss Tweed. I just want better surroundings for the place. I've got a conference call in five minutes... I have sympathy for the immigrants of the 1970's because that time was so screwed. Nobody cared about America. Everybody was me, me, me. When you're an immigrant, you're always put dead last for good and bad reasons but they didn't even have if you would learn English, you would become an American. When they got here, they got, "See how far we got. I bet you can't."

"I got news for you. Sometimes we have those here."

"I guess. It's still pretty sad though. America depends on immigrants. I didn't do glamour jobs in high. I wanted a physically demanding. I worked with Puerto Rican and they worked hard. We all goofed around a little but for the most part nobody wanted to be a slacker. We had some fun too. As much fun as you can tempering saw blades."

"Talking about girls***"

"Of course, I was so embarrassed. I would just go to church on Sunday—blushing all the way. Some of the guys were a little rough."

The phones rang minutes later and the group séance began.

"Clarence, wake up! What's going on with the presentation," Steve asked.

"Man, I think I've got it. I've been practicing in front of my girlfriend all day and all night. I've called my brother and my cousin and everybody I knew on campus that would still speak to me. I got it man. There's no way I can screw this up."

"Really?"

"Yeah!"

"Clarence, my friend, you will go far. Now, Mr. Linne, what's going on with the web site tinkering?"

"Well, it was all done but then I screwed it up again…on purpose of course but it is eighty-five per cent finished and coming a long nicely."

"Today! Hang up right now and finish it today. I will call you at nine o'clock tonight and if it ain't done, we're having a discussion."

"Really?"

"Un-huh! I know the artist world inspiration and perspiration but I need some perspiration tonight. Do the job!"

"I'll have it done by six, sir."

"Nine o'clock. Do it right."

"Yes, sir."

"Bye-bye, Mr. Linne."

"Sir, it's a lot better."

"Perspiration Linne, go, go, go!"

"Right, see you. " The phone went dead

Stork was surprisingly happier than heck on the Japan project. He was selling a lot of national pride to the Japanese and they enjoyed it to a point. He ate sushi out of politeness and then washed it down wish Japanese beer—a lot of it. After that he was one of the boys, sort of. The concept of the pictures really intrigued the Japanese, which was a sporting nation beyond baseball. He was sure that the Japanese communities of the United States would prove quite interested in the pictures from such teams as Yourimori Giants and Hanshin Tigers.

"I'm feeling good boss. I'm eating relatively healthy when I go over there. I run and there's this six, six Irish white tearing down the street, seeing over everybody. It's a picture let me tell you."

"Hey, you're doing a good job."

"Some of those guys can really hit."

"Stork, Clarence, we've been together a while. Has anybody heard from Paco?"

"He's smoking up Triple A Rochester, checking for a market in the minors. He figures 8x10's to 11x 14's. He didn't call you?"

"He probably will mail me a CD. He was miscast. He shouldn't have been an accounting major. Marketing and sales are his. The kid could be Golden for us when he hits the big time."

"Can I go home? I have to put together a not requested report. I just have some ideas that will see if we can make his thing run more efficiently."

"All right!"

John Davis and Tony were next. They were the sales team.

"Tony, what's going on?"

"Well, we're having a good idea who the market's going to be and we have several ideas about how to get the product to them but we haven't settled on where it's going to end up."

"What that means is boss, we will sell a lot to college kids. That's the good sign but the bad sign is if they start showing up in athletes' dorms, the NCAA could have a problem like that…"John said.

"Our product is just like a pair of Nike's or Adidas. We could get kids suspended. We need a lawyer who can get us a scoop on the situation," Tony finished the sentence.

"You guys work well together."

"He does doesn't get too arrogant about Harvard and I don't remind him that we keep winning Beanpots."

"We actually get along. He's helping me navigate this new girl I met. She's nice and really pretty, which throws me off. Usually I go for the skirts and they don't have much upstairs."

"And you have turned over a new leaf!" Steve exclaimed.

"She asked me out. I was sitting on the brick side walls of the library reading about demographics and then she sits next to me and says, 'Hi! My name is Dawn and we talked and she ends the statement this way,' Friday afternoon the baseball team is playing Penn. We'll go. You'll like it.'"

"Thank God for Liberalism of women," Steve said.

"Oh, you have no idea," John said.

"Before you hang up, I have to talk to you about nothing concerning hockey or the company. I just need to talk normally," Tony said.

They bandied around a couple of ideas about using the right distributors because witching hour was coming fast. They narrowed it down to doing what Brown does for you.

Tony started talking first.

“Do you know what I’m feeling lately…I mean after all those years of dying nearly I have everything that I want out of life. I have the right girl. The right baby-to-! I even have a Mustang, convertible, 5.0 engine. Do you want me to keep going?”

‘What’s wrong?”

“Every once in a while I get this feeling that—it’s all going to go away. I’ll wake up and the mental illness will be uncontrollable. I’ll lose my wife and baby. All of it; there won’t be anything left.”

“Do you really think that is going to happen?”

“Logically, no. But mental illness ain’t logical.”

“I got news for you. I’m going to you if you keep thinking this way. You sitting around moping like an old woman. Do the world a favor—just go out and live—please! I’m your brother. You’re the guy to me. I know you can do it every day.

“Annie, loves you. You should see her talking about you to people she knows or doesn’t. She’s so happy with Tony and he’s so cute.”

“Oh, please.”

“Oh, enjoy it! Enjoy! This is good stuff! What do you want to say? Whatever happens? We are family. We’re together. That’s it. That’s the end all be all of everything. No matter what happens we’ll handle it. Just enjoy the ride please, we’re working like heck for it. Enjoy it!

“The Patriots will beat the Cowboys.”

“I don’t think so they’re looking good in camp.”

“How did you become a Cowboy’s fan?”

“I was just being impartial. Of course, the Patriots will win.”

“Two years ago, I would’ve said no way. I was on the verge of giving up. This mental illness was winning. I felt I had shamed everyone. I didn’t think that I could do it and then they adjust the medication and doesn’t it feel good—my life I mean.”

“How’s your writing?”

“I keep swinging at it. I don’t watch a lot of TV. Bruins tops. Celtics sometimes. But I’m always at the computer, working on something. Annie thinks I’m crazy for real but it keeps her thin during pregnancy. If I sat on the sofa and ate ice cream with her, she’d be a thousand pounds.”

“So what do you give her?”

“Rabbit food! Carrots! Celery! Salad! Stuff like that.”

“You prepare them.”

“Excuse me, but of course I prepare it.”

“The last time I saw you at a grill was Fourth of July. You kept yelling, ‘How many hot dogs, bratwurst, burgers, cheeseburgers, and kielbasa.’ Do you think we ever recovered from all that fat content?”

“We have to stop doing that brother?”

“Can I ask you a personal question?”

"Yeah, sure?"

"Do you really want to own a bookshop? I know being a writer, it's kind of important but what about us. The team needs you. I spoke to Annie and from your brother, you cannot put that on a kid. He'll start acting mentally ill just to please you. What if the worst thing happens and he's mentally ill?

" Are you going to be alone? Like mom and pop and Laurie and I will leave you all alone. We'll help as much as we can. You can't plan for disaster man or it will happen."

"Maybe I had some misgivings about the team and the company and I didn't tell you?"

"Shoot!"

"Did you run a background check on any of these guys because I know for a fact they are going to be a problem. They want every relative on the payroll and they spend money like water. It's nice to have a young company but you have to have responsible people."

"Who and what do they spend it on?"

"Criminal or not so criminal. Some of them are just dumb and young in the city."

"Please answer the question."

"Let's just say the boys from the departments should get a speech first something along the lines of, 'straighten up and fly right or you're out.'" Some of the people push and some of them gamble. Maybe, it's just they have money for the first time but they have to be responsible and I can't say it. It's your company."

"I don't like the pushing. Gambling is stupid on wheels. People do it. They lose their shirt and that should teach them. I don't like the drugs. Why are they pushing? They are getting paid good money? I know who you are talking about. I'll fire them tomorrow."

"The kids who gamble, we'll talk to and try and explain how damaging it can be. Grandpa did that and no matter what he always had his money to go out and lose and he always had a story about it. I wouldn't gamble with him and he got pretty mad. That was the only fight we ever had.

"I'll just tell the guys, I am not a money tree. I pay you fairly and hopefully, you can be responsible. If we have to, we bring in a budget analyst and trace where there money goes. So much saved and so much spent etc. We are young, and we shouldn't be lopping off heads unless they deserve it but at the same time we don't reinforce bad habits."

"You keep saying we."

"You noticed that."

"Tony, I want you to finish our story. It's important to me. I want to read it in a nice quiet setting. It must be that way for a best seller."

"You think? My book too!"

"You know why I like what I read so far?"

"I need moral support. Fire it up."

"I liked the fact that you documented what it was like to have the joys of mental illness."

"What are you talking about?"

"It's your personality. Instead of burning with anger, you laugh at it. But when it's really against you, you fight, you push yourself to do better at work and you love Annie and the baby some more, maybe even that when it's bad, you don't lose your morals. That makes the character a human being. I don't care what you say, mental illness is not a defense.

"You told me yourself that the medicines are not a morality pill. Yet when you went off the meds, you somehow beat the evil influence into the ground. You're a good man Charlie Brown."

"Charlie Brown's a sad sack."

"Are you in a mood tonight, or what?"

"My game ain't right today. Did you ever wake up and think, this day is going to be it and then swing and miss at whatever you swing at."

"What are you talking about?"

"At work I clashed with my boss over a point in the rehearsal of our presentation for next week. I told him that the client was going to laugh us out of the building. It got pretty hot there for a while. If he had any reason to fire me, it would've been then. But he didn't. he actually bought me a beer after work and I told him.

"You're some whippersnapper telling people who have been in the game for at least ten years. 'I just don't get,' he said."

"Madison Avenue prepared you for Madison Avenue. You don't run demographics in this town. You go to the coffee shop or to Friendly's and you shoot the breeze with people. Talk to them—not down to them. You hang out. A cup of coffee takes an hour to drink and you mingle. People reveal themselves that way."

"And?"

"He said, 'I'm thinking about Madison Avenue again. My wife and I have discussed it and we like the action of New York. I've been getting my resume to send out.'"

"Maybe it's best for both. Who knows, we could be going down Times Square and checking out the sights so we could see him and his wife."

"You're not thinking a business deal?"

"Maybe in the future on something but for that day, just hang out him."

"And I thought you were a cold, hard business man."

"Only ninety-nine point nine per cent of the time***"

"For like three hours, my boss was a real guy. He showed the baby pictures and everything. I was very impressed. The babies were cuter than him."

"I was better looking than you when we came out of the shoot."

"I had fuzz on my head. That's all."

"It spread."

"I came for your advice and you're ragging me?"

"I was just pointing out the truth. I was handsome forever."

"What are you drinking in Texas? Besides it's the tortoise and the hair thing. I'm better looking than you now."

"You're lucky you're my little brother."

"Will you stop calling me that please? You can't say that in front of the baby. Are you crazy?"

"Okay, I'll lay off."

"Thank you very much."

"I have to go. You are going to send the E-mail?"

"The one to the guys from 'over there***"

"Yeah, it's about time, we're almost an entity. We're stable so far."

"Do it!"

"I'll call you tomorrow."

"Later on?"

So Steve sat down at his computer and typed out a letter to the troops 'over there.' Wherever 'over there' was.

Ladies and gentleman! From twenty-two year-old hockey player who by all rights should be over there with you. In addition to playing hockey for the Dallas Stars, I'm fortunate enough to know people who have supported in my dream. Like most of your life, it's classified. But I promise you that when you come home, you'll understand what the American people knew about what you did for them.

I want you to understand that you can come home and understand that Mickey Mouse is important to your young children and for the older children, wives are just as important. It's a matter of what you were fighting for. Yourself, your family, your country and the possibility: that peace could exist in such a troubled area of the world. From a guy who was regular guy, to a man of some importance and a millionaire almost instantly, your effort in the most trying of times has lifted my spirits to a new level.

The military's friend always,

Steve Thompson, #7 Dallas Stars.

Graduate of Boston University

"Come to bed!" Laurie yelled from the bedroom.

"Yes dear."

"What's going on?"

"I have to talk with the wonder triplets."

"You usually like them."

"Oh, they're the team in Europe in Scandinavia. But I'm afraid we're fighting Americanization. Those guys are getting blow back from their own people. They're afraid we'll start changing customs and stuff—make things different you see."

"Don't they know their own people change things?"

"The point being at least it is their own people. Peter Blute was so mad fighting with his brother, he slammed the phone down and said that was enough. He hasn't talked to him in a week. "

"There isn't anything more frustrating Pemo said than introducing a new idea and have it kicked away because it came from an overseas training ground. They're regrouping though and going back out there, partly because it will benefit his home country and partly because he sees insidious hate underneath just enough of them to make him nervous."

"Over sports pictures?"

"You know, it was such a peaceful dream. You go in and you see as a child sees it—'It's a small world,' at Walt Disney and you grow up and they hate each over national colors, school uniforms. Just the ordinary, average acceptance by people who tolerate each other; It would kill to say I would've with BC—admittedly—but every time I went up there I thought the place was beautiful, so who knows?"

"It's not the money anymore is it?"

"Not in a situation like that. Obviously you have to understand their culture a bit. You can't go over and lose yours yet: you don't want to make an enemy of them because it's a simple matter of respect. They have ways that aren't yours and won't ever be but we have ideas that are different them sometimes."

"So why go?"

"The way I figure it, if you have one or two people that can be there incase all hell breaks loose maybe we can get less people killed. I'm not after changing Sweden's uniforms. I want to see the world, not to break it to the fist."

"You would have been weird in Texas too."

"It's starting to break but I would like to be there. I'm going to draft a letter to each of the three and they can present it to their various obstacles."

"Geeze, do you know how much faith I've spent on God in the last few months. I'm going to have to call on him again."

"Well, he's there for us. That's his job."

"I wonder how he puts up with it. You're talking about a company that wants to produce memories for people and they are positive yet, the guy shooting has a different camera than you so you won't buy it because he used the wrong damned camera and he likes the shot. I was totally amazed by people who saw me shooting a Canon and were convinced the people who worked for my company were being betrayed because they didn't use Nikon—like evil spirit stuff. We were bad in college but these were grown people."

"Life is funny?"

"Why God puts up with it is beyond me? Instead of noticing the beautiful, historical events of the city or country, they find some reason to find a cutting remark in their bag."

"You ever hear of jealousy knucklehead?"

"Man, that was something the old man didn't tolerate. If my brother or said something stupid like that—boom! Go to your room and don't come out until supper."

"How long did it take you to wise up?"

"A couple of times, that was it."

"I've never seen brothers so close."

"We don't know what to do with each other now. We eat and talk on the phone at the same time. I've ruined more ties talking to him."

Chapter 45

At five o'clock in the morning, Steve was on the phone yammering away with the head of Swedish hockey. The President of the Hockey Federation in broken English, and Steve with absolutely no Swedish; Steve said.

"Where do you think I'm going to get the photographers from?"

"Well, it could be adventurous American College students…They cause trouble."

"Fine! We'll get middle aged, family men from Sweden. Do you have any of those?"

"A few, are you always this rambunctious?"

"It's five o'clock in the morning. I forgot my coffee."

"Well, go have a cup we'll talk."

"Okay! Now we're cooking."

"You have to understand us… in WWII we were neutral…nobody told the Germans. After sixty years things are relatively peaceful. Nice, little, fishing villages. Good medical plan, great fish. Three hours of sun light in the winter. We just want to find out if you are going to push us out of our own country."

"Sir, I was talking to my wife last night and I was confused and maybe a little hot headed. I was angry because my guys didn't convey the message that I wanted to see the world not break it to the fist; ours or anybody else's."

"I like hockey. That's why I'm doing it. Maybe after my playing career is over, my wife and kids can get over there for a few weeks and I can fire away with my camera. Photography is fun man. I don't make a Federal case out of things when it comes to that."

"You need more coffee. We will work together. I have made many friends in the organization over the years. We will do it."

He hung up and ran into the bedroom.

"Hey! Wake up!"

"It's six o'clock in the morning."

"I just got off the phone with Sweden. I spoke to Per Gutterson. He's a legend in Swedish and world hockey."

"You spoke to him for an hour."

"We were negotiating like two kids over a Yaztremski card."

"I thought you were a Yankee fan."

"Yeah!"

"He approved."

"He said we'll work with you. I feel like Donald Trump. This is great!"

"Do you really have to go to practice today?"

"You like the house?"

"Crash Davidson wants you to call him."

"I'm burning up those minutes."

"How much do you think it caused to call Sweden?"

"First of all, it's a write off and second of all, do you know who plays in that league?"

"I'm from Texas!"

"It's Sven Bjornson, he's the best defenseman in the draft. He's so good he plays like me."

"If Dallas could get him…"

"We'd be freewheeling over the ice."

"Are you going to get him?"

"He'll be gone in the top three."

"Where will you draft."

"Hope fully right at the bottom -26. The last spot reserved for the team who wins Lord Stanley's Cup!"

The phone rang and he smiled.

"Hello," he said.

"Hi! It's Rico."

"I'm in bed."

"Alone?"

"I could say something but my wife wouldn't like it."

"Well, you know. She could be doing something."

"What's up?"

"I need a favor."

"What would that be?"

"I sort of need a business reference for a clerk ship at a law firm."

"Is this sort of a law firm?"

"Butkowski and Moore. They are really deeply into corporate law. It's a good firm to be in, a lot of solid accounts with clients who have been there many years."

"You most definitely have the recommendation. So that's puts in you in new York without partying that much. Are you going to survive."

"He said I'd only be working fifteen hours a day. There's still time when there's still girls."

"You should Dallas," Steve said.

"It's too bad you are almost married."

"I call her my wife all the time."

"I'm going to get married but there is time and space for everything."

"The amount of skirt in town is just to abundant to believe."

"Really… you'd never in all our lives… believe it."
"Look, my friend. If he needs to call me then, by all means."

Chapter 46

The wedding was two weeks away and Steve was trying to stay out of the way.

"Hello?"

"Go away," Laurie said.

"What do you mean go away? It's breakfast time. We always eat breakfast at the same time together."

"I'm looking for a wedding gift for you."

"The bride's not supposed to get the groom anything. It's a computer magazine."

"That's because there are computers in it."

"For us."

"No for you."

"Why?"

"So you can e-mail every night from the hotel. "

"So it's like a night light."

"'One if by land two if by sea***"

"You don't trust."

"Nope, it's not that."

"You're going to spend $3,500 on suped-up super-duper model lap top from Dell because you want me to super killer from the planet mars."

"I want pictures. You're lucky enough to go to these places. I want pictures."

"Are you serious? Do you know how cold Chicago is in February?"

"Do you know the educational value of a professional athlete's life is?"

"No."

"They have the opportunity to see the Liberty Bell, Old First Church, The Golden Gate Bridge, well, a myriad of places. The St. Louis Arch is a good example. You can see the people of this country and that is worth the price of admission in itself. So I expect you to learn this thing and e-mail me pictures."

"Yes, dear."

"Please!"

"Let's go back to bed. It requires physical exercise to think."

"Eat you English muffin first."

"We're not having sex?"

"I think there's peanut butter and apricot on your mouth when you kiss me. Now finish up. Time's a wasting."

"I'll double up the peanut butter, it's crunchy."

"Quickly please."

Afterwards, she lay in bed and put his robe on—looking out the window.

"I have an idea," he said.

"I didn't smell like peanut butter, did I?"

"We have a party."

"I think we do well."

"Anybody who's really officious in the office?"

"Why?"

"I could play subservient jock all night and get him/her going really good."

"So we're planning a party?"

"Season's almost here. Why not?"

"We'll invite the 'Turks.'"

"The who?"

"The 'Young Turks.' We're kind of like misfits because nobody took Political Science in college. There's five of us. We just kind of get along."

"How far are you away?"

"About five minutes."

"I have to do the tea thing. Good-bye."

"Roll down the sheets."

"All this work to do; Do you know I played a contact sport tonight?"

"Hey, buster I offered you my body."

"Good-bye!"

So he made the tea. She tasted it when she came in.

"Good. The bed?'

"All turned down."

"You still want to finish your tea?"

"Maybe, how did you get so cynical about politics."

"Leaders I don't mind. Politicians anger me. They are for the people until right after election day. Than it's all: not bad for a guy from Camp Muckawuck, Gooberville. I made it to the big time. It's all about them. They forget that they work for me. Not all of them of course but it must be the water in Washington. They seem to get out of touch six months into office."

"Do you think Franklin is worth his weight in salt?"

"I think the guy passionately believes in Texas and the people here. And I think he believes in the American dream if you do it the right way."

"You're honest and you work hard."

"And you'll move up to whatever level you want to settle at."

"Yeah."

"That's us."

"What if you are extremely frustrated because you made a mistake on the ice you haven't done since high school?"

"I think we should we should go to the bed and discuss the problem; converse a while. You can take of my clothes. I can take off yours and whatever happens after that we are both consenting adults."

"I think that should clear up a lot in my head."

They made quiet, love and then she fell asleep in his arm. Even he wondered why he was so cynical about government service. He was an educated from a good school. Well, he was from BU, which was a very, good school with talent and ambition running high. He had been in Dallas about half a season now and did notice differences in the two cities. Boston's look at Government was built on the right and obligation to protest, while Dallas stood by traditional family values. He fell asleep with unresolved issues.

In the morning, he checked his e-mail while Laurie slept.

Hey it's me! Dad!

Am looking to come out in January when things slow down at work. Working like crazy here now though; not much more than proud of you.. If you have any questions about the baby, call the boss. Annie and William Steven Thompson are doing fine. 8.3 lbs.

Tony is beside himself. He was watching the hockey game and all of a sudden everything went upside down. The nurse ran in screaming, "Mr. Thompson, Mr. Thompson." They scrubbed him up and sent him in. They did it. The two of them did. Born 8:37 p.m.

I'm very proud, relieved, and happy to be Grand Dad but boy, was I wiped out. It was like you guys but I'm twenty-five years older. Give me some time before you and Laurie, well you know.

Dad

Dear dad,

Do you people believe in cell phones? Couldn't you have called? I would've caught a plane to Logan! Anyway, I'm happier than heck for the both of them. However, Tony needs tickets for the Ranger game on the twenty-fifth. Are you coming? Let me know. I'll have to play horse trader to get more tickets.

I'm going to call him right now.

Later,

ME

"Hey! It's me!"

"Do you know what time it is? It's six o'clock in the morning."

"Hey! It's your fault for letting your wife have a baby without me."

"Do you know how much sympathy I have for you?"

"What the hell did you name him after me for?"

"Because, I said we should."

"Do you know what Aunt Alice called me when I was a kid—little Stevie Winwood. Do you want your kid to go through that?"

"Steve Winwood, is a protégé. You should've been proud."

"Then she called me Steve Shutt when I started playing hockey and that was no good because he was a Canadian. You can't be from Massachusetts and be a Canadian fan."

"We were talking about my baby?"

"What's it like, man?"

"Geeze, I'm spent. What a night! We go rushing off to the hospital. It was a disaster. Both of us forgot everything they taught us in Lamaze class. The doctor's yelling, "Don't worry about a thing! Everything will be fine! Everything's all good!"

"It sounds like...Well, I can picture the whole situation without a problem. How's your mental illness?"

"It sucks! After the project was completed, I kind of went into a slump. The voices started bothering me more regularly but luckily the past week, week and a half I've been holding my own."

"Well, what are you doing for work?"

"I'm still with the consulting firm in town. Working on an international sports photography museum certainly looks better than working in some nondescript retail position. I feel like I'm utilizing my BU degree like I was working for you. Now all we have to do is wait for the Big Dig in June.

"What do you do out there in Texas when you aren't playing?"

"Today we're going to UT Austin. It should be cool with all the kids there."

"Dude, you're twenty-one years-old."

"Yes! But I'll be a Master's degree candidate. That's serious business. I'll have to act serious now."

"Explain exactly what you are going to do now?"

"I don't know exactly what I'm going to do yet?"

"Do you know you're paying for this?"

"All right! Please shut up about this."

"Are you perchance doing something like joining ROTC?"

"I don't know if I can trust you."

"Why?"

"Because you'll shoot your mouth off over sharing beers with somebody and you'll say something stupid like, 'hey, do you know what my youger brother's doing?'"

"Try me."

"I would like to finish my novel and get it published."

"You are the man!"

"No. I'm not."

"Yes. You are. You are the man!"

"Okay! I'm the man."

"When are you going to do this?"

"Well, I went into the hot streak at the beginning. I wrote and wrote and wrote then, I cooled off, saying this will never get published. The funniest thing happened after that. I had a good voice and it said, 'Hey, what's with the book.' It kept after me for days, weeks and finally I took pen to paper again. It was the first time I ever heard a good voice. I figured maybe it was God."

"Boy, you're a load. You'd think for five minutes you could be happy."

"I am very, happy. But thing is I need projects to keep me happy. I need to be working."

"Do you realize that when your little personal sweat shop: you could be travelling with Laurie?"

"She has a fellowship to Rice. She's starting in September."

"Because of the, 'I'll do it for a while job and see what happens.'"

"Yeah, life is funny."

"Let's say for instance we work together like we did on the museum?"

"So you are all in?"

"Yes. You're my brother. Of course."

"All right then."

"What do you want me to do?"

"Sit on your hands for right now. Don't tell anybody?"

"I can't tell Rico and the guys?"

"No, not yet. I have to batten down the hatches and get through grad school first. So do you."

"I have to do what?"

"You my friend have to pick a graduate school."

"I thought I told you I wasn't going to grad school."

"Are you breathing?"

"Aw, come on, are you serious?"

"Did you or did you not ask? 'What can I do?'"

"Yeah, but…"

"I'm paying for it."

"Why? We did the museum?"

"Because we don't know everything in the book yet***"

"Do you realize I have a baby and a job?"

"Tony, do you know how much I make for a living. Quit the job."

"Then I'd be exactly in the position I never wanted to be in—living off my family."

"You're being very difficult about this. What is your problem?"

"I'm having a problem with the whole money deal. You pay for everything, school, books, clothes, car insurance, car payment, and fun money."

"You're the first recipient of the Steven D. Thompson Scholarship. It's not like you aren't going to be working."

"Would you mind if I looked at UMASS? That wouldn't be too

expensive?"

"Why don't you come to Texas? We'll have a good time."

"Like for what?"

"I don't know. There's UT, Rice, SMU, TCU, and A&M. Oh, there's also Texas Tech. I'd rather have you, Annie, and the baby out here."

"And mom and dad?"

"I'm working on them."

"What do you have planned?"

"I can't really tell you in complete detail right now because I haven't been through school."

"What are you going to major in?"

"Of course, BU has some of the best shooters in the business. This situation is good for me from a number of standpoints. My fiancee is happy, the exposure to another state and business culture is good, and I'll be able to make some friends here like the ones I left in Boston."

"What about Springfield?"

"I'm trying to hook up with the Basketball hall of Fame to do a sort of promotional night sort of local news stations—live—maybe 8-11 open to the public."

"They're the best."

"Yes they are. "

"Ain't you the operator?"

"Son, this is America and it's the land of opportunity. You make the most of your opportunity."

"We'll go see UT but I am from Massachusetts. When I fly in, should I book a hotel?"

"No. You can stay in my place."

"Can I book a hotel?"

"Hey! That's terrible!"

"I'm booking a hotel."

"There's a Marriott about ten minutes from here."

"Good, I can cook my own breakfast."

"Dude, you eat a fried egg and a English muffin when you cook."

"That's because nobody can get the over easy part right. The fancier the hotel the more screwed up the egg gets."

"You're cracked just like an egg."

"I'm serious do you know what an over easy, over, egg meant?"

"I'm can't believe we're having a conversation about this."

"An egg is an egg is an egg."

"You're an egg head. Just bring your camera. I'll get you into practice and you can some of the guys. How's the story coming?"

"I like it. It has a lot of me in it. Before I was very conscious about my mental illness so I wrote stories about people without it; now, this one has a piece of me in it so it's easier to feel the characters. I think I'm going to find an agent when it's finished and try to get it published. And the funny thing is, I really looked back at my life because of the writing and I realized that we had a good time in America."

"Good for you. That's the spirit! I want to experience America but understand Massachusetts is home."

"I learned thing in those hospitals. If you're still breathing, you have a chance."

"How long has it been since you've been in the hospital?"

"About one year, six months."

"That's good. That's very, very good. Graduate School is going to be tough."

"I have a second life. I handled being marketing manager for the project. I'll handle this."

"All right! Look I have to shower and shave to get ready for the big square dance at UT."

"The big what?"

"Look they do that down here. Don't make fun of it."

"I'll call you this week."

Laurie and he walked around the UT campus; just too get a once over. It was an outstretched campus with many students in one kind of various motions or another. Steve had been away from BU about a year and the kids looked so young. He was very embarrassed to think that he could think like that. A couple of guys in Dallas Star outfits came racing up them asking him for an autograph and that started it. They all came and they all had pens being in college so Steve signed and Laurie tried to keep the situation under some control.

"Thank you! Please! One at a time!" Laurie would yell.

That lasted for close to two hours.

And then wedding day arrived, Steve woke up at 4 am with the worst feeling in his soul. He was very nervous. In the middle of the Texas heat, he downed a cold beer. It was eighty-five degrees already and then he sat on the edge of the sofa in his boxer shorts and t-shirt. He looked at his watch and wondered when high noon was coming.

It wasn't that he was reluctant to get married but he was frightened—not so much of the ceremony either but of the responsibility that came with it. In his race for the race on the ice, he felt terribly awkward telling himself that the company was for his unborn children. In truth it was for him because he liked it. There was no other way around it.

At nine o'clock his mother called.

"How are you doing?" She asked.

"Only one beer***"

"You drank a beer!"

"At four o'clock in the morning."

"Did you sleep last night?"

"Sort of?"

"Should I come over and make you breakfast?"

"No thanks, "

"Cocoa Pebbles?"

"Yes, mother. Cocoa Pebbles with chocolate chips."

"I'm coming over right now."

"Why?"

"Because you have to relax***"

"Having your mother in your house on your wedding day will not calm a person down."

"No more beer."

"Okay but please, for 'life, liberty, and the pursuit of happiness,' relax, have an orange juice and please if you must read a book."

"If you aren't stone sober at that wedding today, I'll kill you."

"I, excuse me, had one beer."

"I hope you know that she is your friend."

"She's sort of my friend."

"What does that mean?"

"Well, we're more than friends mom."

"I know but could you just fake it for once."

"I will see you at the wedding, good-bye mother."

Steve kept looking around the church during the wedding ceremony. It was packed and there was more lined up out the door.

"Would you please not do that?" She said.

"I think we're going to need to relax."

"We?"

"Yes. We! You're nervous too."

"You're not helping."

"You want to start?"

"You go first."

"Okay!"

They walked down the aisle, arm in arm, with smiles beaming.

"What do you think?" He whispered.

"Lots of people!"

"You nervous yet!"

"I heard the rice stings."

"Congratulations."

"For marrying you," she giggled.

"For carrying it off so well***"

"I don't have anything left and the reception hasn't started yet."

"Mrs. Stevenson, I know how you feel. I got out of bed that way."

"Smile and wave; here's comes the party."

A tremendous amount of people parted off to the side as the rice rained down on them.

"It does sting," he said.

"I told you."

"They climbed into a white limousine and he smiled.

"Now what he asked?"

"I don't want to mess up my dress."

"I'll be gentle."

"Come on, please?"

"We could mess around with the bar?"

"Can I make a Virgin Mary?"

"Two. Make mine extra hot!

They ended up at the reception hall and it seemed to be packed more than the church.

Steve was immediately joined by his brother Tony: the best man. And they collided into a big bear hug.

"I thought I was going to have a heart attack," Tony said.

"Why it went beautifully? Right?"

"I was so proud. I thought everything went—now as a special surprise. We've got the boys from the hood. There they are. The old gang from East Longmeadow High***"

"How'd you get all ten of them here? This is great. I thought we had lost them. Hey! Ladies and gentlemen! This is it. We're out to have a little fun tonight so, if you haven't proposed to your girlfriend, please do it now. We are all over the place tonight. This is a great time and I hope you all stay a couple of days. Laurie and I can show Dallas to you.

"Frankly, you'll love it. First guy I want to talk to is the guy with the camera. Mr.Whiteside. How the heck are you?"

The night went on like that. In the midst of entertaining guests and encouraging friendship and good feelings, Steve and Laurie must've danced with every guest they could get their hands on.

"Hey," he said, "Do you want a soda?"

"Please, this is crazy but good!"

"No. I'm crazy but good. You're getting a soda."

"Diet."

"Yes, dear."

So he went over and picked up two diet cokes from the bar.

"Let's go sit down." She smiled.

"Boys, will be boys," he smiled.

"What?"

"There you all go. Charley Brown and the boys! Let's go see East Longmeadow, miss."

"It's Mrs! now. And who do we go see first?"

"All of them."

"Okay."

Steve offered to pick up the tabs on the hotel for the guests staying in them. Everybody laughed that night and that's all that Steve would remember in the years to come. A lot of old man jokes later the conversation came around to struggling and succeeding. Steve was asked how could he do so much? What was his secret?

He answered truthfully.

"I just liked the idea when I was sixteen and I let it lie for a while to the point where I conversed with other people and learned a lot from the pizza meetings about loyalty and courage of your mates. It's taken for granted in sports and that happens all the time. That's not true. I've played with some of the most selfish guys ever.

"But then I got to college and Coach put a firm hand to anyone who wouldn't pass the puck. It's very much nature I think. I think a guy can come from the most trying of circumstances and win. My brother Tony here is the guy I look up to. He's the guy that made it all the way back from nowhere.

"He's the guy who made me work harder because he worked harder than that. Success equals work and work is a great equalizer. There's some school of thought that you should struggle—just to find out how good you are. As to whether or not I agree with that, that's we have training camp.

"I would like to say one thing. This was better than the previous visit. Both sides were a bit embarrassed I think. I have a lot of money now and that's good and bad but most of it goes right to the company. I like that so far. I don't know what success is really. Live to your capabilities and enjoy yourself along the way. I figure that's success."

Chapter 47

Steve's cell phone rang at about two in the morning.

"You have got to be kidding," Laurie smiled.

"Had too much champagne did you?"

"My head hurts. Don't bother me."

"Hey, it's me!"

"Hello?"

"It's your brother you idiot."

"Where are you?"

"I wanted to say Hello."

"Okay, you said it. Go to bed."

"Don't be a jerk. I need to talk to you."

"About what?"

"My medication."

"Take it and go to bed."

"My nurse practitioner wants to lower the lithium and I don't want to do that."

"Why? What's her reasoning?"

"She just says I'm doing really well and it may be good to try it because the side affects may be less. I don't want to."

"She's the nurse. That's why you go to her.

"Yeah, but look at how great I'm doing? It makes no sense. Why screw around?"

"You have final say, right?"

"I have control to a degree what they put into or take out of my body. It's a real temptation because the side effects suck eggs. You gain weight, your hands shake, diarrhea, it makes you wicked thirsty, you feel sleepy all the time, and blurred vision. Yet, I'm in ten pounds of my playing weight for high school football. I don't want to screw around. I really don't want to cross swords with her because she's my friend but you have to look after yourself."

"How adamant is she about it?"

"She told me three times that she was 100% sure that it was the right move."

"Why now? I have a new baby on the way and as joyous as that occasion is, you get nervous."

"Wouldn't it be great to feel less side affects?"

"It would be fantastic but losing your marbles along the way is not a good thing."

"Come on Tony. She's your nurse."

"I think she's moving too fast on this one."

"Okay, I'll back opinion."

"Thanks, man."

"You tell her you are a manager in the company."

"Why did you give it to me then?"

"Because you're the best we have now."

"Should I be worried about my job?"

"You should be worried about doing your job and what half a pill reduction is going to do to it."

"What lacks in my game in your opinion?"

"You're a great manager and you know what. You stick to your guns on this. Because I firmly believe this because if you trust her and she trusts you then you'll make your point without losing your temper."

"I must be subconscious. I wasn't aware."

"I think because of your situation, you have the best traits of leadership of any of us. You have the ability to see inside a person when he's down and instead of kicking them, you have a way of motivating them to be the best they can at that assignment. You're a natural. However, you have got to understand that we have been in college in nearly eight years together. We have to get in touch with these kids. We're going to be drawing for a young talent pool. Get it?"

"What do you think about my little experiment?"

"You know. I had it all planned out. Now I want to go to college! Again!. Okay, I'll go. But can I pick my own?"

"Where are you thinking about going?"

"Back to BU to study international relations***"

"Are you sure? Because you've already seen Boston; I figure you may want to see stuff. I know you. You like going out there."

"I think I've found the correct place to knock that chip off my shoulder. I liked the place before had some anger toward it, come full circle and now I want to see if I can love the place."

"You knew what major you were taking," Steve observed.

"Uh-huh!" I think if you should not put too much pressure on yourself, you'll do fine. John Davis called. He said to say 'Hi!'"

"Can the man use a cell phone or send an e-mail?"

"Dude, he's been hiking in Paraguay since school ended. He just got back."

"Maybe I jumped the gun."

"A little***"

"Chris Davidson is in graduate school. Right?"

"He went down south to George Washington. He's studying International Relations to go with his business MBA."

"He's got a lot of untapped talent that kid. If he ever gets wheels under him, he's going to be a player."

"What do you mean? Untapped talent? He did good work for us."

"He did but he still has doubts about his abilities sometimes. Somebody has to be there to pump him up. You want to see him get more and more confident on his own."

"I bet he does."

"Me too! Taking the plunge to go to graduate school is definitely a positive step. I like it for him."

"What does he want to do?"

"Work on Wall St. He wants to study international markets like the Japanese one. He's a smart guy."

"He could get us Japanese baseball tickets."

"You sponge."

"Yes, sir."

"Tony, are you worried about the mental illness? With the medication change?"

"I'm kind of worried about it. The job, the baby, and worrying about you. Like I said. You wonder if you can get it back if it doesn't work and I decompensate however in three or six months when we have the decision in full: will you make it all the way back? I'd don't like this going off the medicine stuff."

"Why?"

"Understood, are you afraid?"

"Yeah. You know how it is when life really starts going well, your voices start going crazy and telling you all these "wild and crazy guy" scenarios. That people particularly women, particularly Annie don't want to marry some nut. They want a man and a man doesn't take medicine. I've heard that I'm being used as a medical experiment. All kind of very stupid but very possible life paths I can take because of my fear of doctors or my fear of medicines or my fear of the side affects."

"So are you going to ask her to keep status quo."

"Carpe Diem. I don't mind if I have to put up with the side affects because I have time on my side. The doctors and scientists and companies like Merck, Pfizer, and Johnson & Philips, are working hard to create new and better medicines and they are but like anything good it takes time."

"I don't know what to say. I wish I knew what to say."

"On goes the battle but we're winning the war. It's a war of attrition. You push and fight and scrap just like going into the corner. The mental illness pushes you. You push back."

"How?"

"You see somebody on the street, you say hello. Or you see someone reaching for something at the grocery store and you help him/her. Just do little normal stuff. Because what it tries to do is take that away and make you feel stupid. I mean if they were people, you could kick them.

"What possessed her to think like that."

"Because when I was young and stupid, I told her I wanted the least medication as possible, theory being I would retain more control over my personality with less drugs. Dumb! Uneducated but she bought it. I'm going to tell her I like it the way it is. I don't want to mess with it."

The next thirty games were a study in how teams use the trading deadline. The Stars took a chance on a young Russian forward named Vladimir Lanonov for Brent Price, a forward with talent but a reputation for being soft in the corners. They also unloaded many of their perennial all-stars in the minors for draft picks. The whole feel of the organization was going young.

Lanonov fit right in as the third line, left wing. He was barely twenty and spoke little English.

"What?" He spread his arms wide as he pulled his jersey down as he was tagged for slashing. Steve pulled him aside.

"Go sit down. We need you. Comrade. Do you understand?"

"Dah," the speedy forward said.

"What the heck were you doing on the ice?" Colin teased Steve.

"Every time I tried to get off the ice, the puck came near me."

"You had a five minute shift."

"I had to keep Thunderball from killing the referee. "

The Stars tied St. Louis in St. Louis to clinch first place in the division and overall home ice advantage throughout the playoffs because they finished number one in the NHL—even ahead of mighty Detroit."

The champagne poured in buckets over people's head's in the locker room.

"Hey, knock it off!" Colin yelled, "We are a team that plays together. We pay the price together and we enjoy together but most of all we win together. And we have more winning to do. We've gone through training camp. We worked out the kinks. We brought new guys in for old guys that didn't fit our system. We are the best of the West and the best of the East but without that Cup nobody will remember. We would've blown a perfectly good season. Let's not get too cocky gentlemen or we'll be the best of a bunch of nobodies pretty damned quick."

"Hey Colin, this year is our year. You go home and worry too much over it. You'll get gray hair," Roberge smiled.

"The baby of the bunch is right. We're going to have a good time tonight and then we'll be back at it in two days."

"Look, if you guys show up at my doorstep dead drunk and passed out to the work. I'll have the coach cut you. This is the big leagues. You act like you want to be here. You are representing Dallas and you're making a damned fine living at it. No shenanigans."

"All right, we'll watch ourselves but how sweet it is," Steve grinned.

"Overall champs!" Atkins hollered.

"We are just so cool," Steve smiled, "Lord Stanley come to papa. This sure is fun."

They went to a rib place and partied all night and Steve amazed at how close the guys had become since training camp. Nobody drank too much but for an eleven thirty at night a lot of ribs disappeared. They had a good time and several guys signed autographs for the waitresses and whoever else was brave enough to come near the scavengers.

"Damn, if this ain't a good night," Colin said.

"Texas has good barbecue," Steve agreed.

"Solve me a riddle."

"Sure."

"Why would the Golden Boy of Boston not go back there and study at Boston University?"

"They have the best photojournalism program that I know of. It's not like I'm going to kill myself. It's one or two classes."

"Are you aware that you live in a free country? You don't need papers or anything to go home or you can share homes, whichever you prefer."

"People get kind of grabby and they don't respect your plan in life. I have to have the right set of circumstances as much as the reputation of the school."

"Once you become a commodity, that's the way it is."

"Truth is, I really miss Boston in its own way but on the other hand we're having such a good time here, I could take both majors here and be happy. It's like they don't have airplanes and Logan closed down. Now, to be honest with you, some of Harvard's more elite have their nose out of joint because I said I liked it here. That would mean putting cowboys and red necks ahead of them and their paralysis by analysis way of life.

"Now there are others at BU that see it as an opportunity because in the next thirty years we're going to have to do something about energy. We have scientists in Massachusetts and we have oil in Texas—simple. "

"Do you think of normal things like the game of the week?"

"I just thought that beyond the basest of human emotions; I gave you 'What's in it for me?'"

"Well, heck I guess you did."

"I like both places."

"Like I said; It is a free country but you'll have to explain to me. Why were you a Yankee fan?"

"Well, my grandfather got sick and he was a Yankee fan so I would talk to him about baseball and about the Yankees. I kinda got to following them and they kept winning so I figured life was good as a Yankee fan. So when he passed on I was the only grandson he had so I became a Yankee fan sort of in my grandfather's honor."

"It better have been a story like that."

"Are you a Red Sox fan?"

"Absolutely?"

"Why?"

"Because they finally freakin' won."

"Wait a minute! You're a Red Sox fan because they won. What do you do when they lose?"

"I watch the Blue Jays."

"You fair weather fan you."

"Listen to the guy talk."

"If the Yankees lost one hundred and sixty-two games a year, they'd still be my team. If the Sox lose three in a row, you're in Toronto."

"I have a high demand for success."

"Cherry picker!"

"This summer I'll take to Skydome. We'll have a good time."

"I'm going to be studying."

"Where?"

"I don't know yet. I'm going to do some heavy duty negotiating."

"With who?"

"Not with who but with my photography. I have to shoot a lot to get my talent up to where it should be."

"I have a question for you."

"Shoot."

"What if you go to the point in your career, where the company was going well and you were playing hockey?"

"And?"

"What would you want to do?"

"I'd pick my predecessor of CEO and just shoot. Get a regular old press pass and shoot."

"Some people say you can be more than that."

"I'm twenty-two years old. I don't get it. If people want me to do this or that, shouldn't I have experience first?"

"You can have too much experience."

"I have too many photos to take."

"Two artists in the same family!"

"We were joking about it the other day. We went into to college to find a trade and we ended up artists."

"You know where should go to photograph. Ellis Island; as a Canadian I was moved by it. As an American, you would see America from the Industrial Revolution on."

"Pretty impressive."

"You should see the doctor's office and surgery. I'd swim back to the old country before they got a crack at me."

"Chicken."

"Damned right."

"My mother's family came through P.E.I. Prince Edward Island on a fairy boat—a long time ago."

"My great grandparents came through Ellis Island—three times—they kept lugging stuff back from the old country. Do you know they had the presents to set up a college fun for their kids?"

"When did they come over?"

"Let me see. My Great grandfather passed on when he was 94 and that was a few years ago. Now. my grandparents are 73ish. My great grandfather came over when he was twenty-two. So I say about 78 years ago."

"Where from?"

"England."

"Religious freedom?"

"Yup!"

"You're kidding. About being English!""

"It's English for Tomassini. He didn't want his grand children to run numbers in the streets so he changed his name. Everybody knew he was an Italian but he worked as a bell hope in this hotel in Manhattan for umpteen years and to be honest with you. He loved the place as if he had owned it. He saw people from All over the world. That's partially my desire to learn more about photography; to go around the world and photograph.

"You have to understand, to some of the Italians I met, we had to have conversations about my families value on that stuff and our version of the Golden Land. My grandparents weren't rich but come Sunday we were all at the house together for supper and my grandfather drove it into us. 'You learn English to be a good American,' and people may say other things but because my grandfather said it, it became a badge of honor. It' too bad he missed this."

"Did you feel that you were giving up your Italian Identity."

"We didn't even notice. We always had Italian Christmases, and Easter, birthdays and so forth. We were just Americans first. It didn't bother us. We never thought about it. My grandfather told me about Joe Dimaggio, Yogi Berra, but there was one guy that was his favorite. Vic Raschi, 'The Springfield Rifle.' From Springfield, Massachusetts where my grandfather had lived all his life and he cursed the family by being a Yankee fan! He was such a nice guy too!"

"There's something out there…What's going on?"

"Some of our conversations got kind of loud."

"About?"

"It gets kind of serious about Red Sox and Yankees. Why do you do that kind of stuff?"

"I bought some of it but I don't buy all of it. I just want to be a good role model for kids, if they deserve it. They act like little animals then what can you do but if they're polite kids, shoot the breeze with them for a while, make them feel good. Sign an autograph. It takes what? Five minutes of your time."

"Kid, if I don't like you."

"We're going to win this championship."

"So what does that mean?"

"It means I have to write one great letter to Getty with my proposal."

"Are you serious?"

"Look man I didn't break my back for my BS not to be aggressive with my idea."

"I don't think you need to go to grad school."

"Do you think it'll be a whole lot of practice for nothing?"

"Do you have any idea what you just said?"

"I guess. Maybe not! I've been thinking a lot about Getty lately. I'm going to take a shot."

"Now from a guy who doesn't know about anything, it sounds like you have a good idea."

"Yeah, it does."

"What's Laurie doing in all of this?"

"She's waiting for my conclusion so we can get to work. I'm going to take a gamble to see if Getty will want to work with us."

"Well, God Bless you."

"This is so cool. I have had this in my head since I was sixteen. I don't feel like I'm such a coward now. I am not kidding anymore."

"Dude, you smooth talked BU into the museum project. They said they'd share."

"I didn't smooth talk them. They wanted it."

"This is the real test if I can form a coalition between American Sportsview and Getty International. I don't really want to go head to head with them because they are a major contributor to many media outlets and their base country is the major ally in the world. Sometimes you have to pay attention to politics."

"You're thinking about something else."

"Yeah, back home. I don't know what they'd think of me."

"Why's is that? You're an American success story."

"The team's doing the right thing. Just do the work and it will work out."

"Well, See, where I come from, we're supposed to be seconds to Boston and I exacerbated the situation by going to BU instead of UMASS. I didn't want to be a second. Now success has taught me working on the museum project that these kids can play anywhere. If there's one thing I'd say to the WMASS contingent, it would be thank you. I always got very uptight when it was put to me, 'Success like that isn't for people like us. It's only for people with money.' Money helps but it isn't everything: You've got to have the juice."

"The juice huh?"

"Absolutely. Did you ever see that movie *Stand by Me* with Morgan Freeman? He was walking round the high school of kids that didn't count and inspiring them to do better. He'd say, "Do you have the juice?" That's where I picked it up from."

"I saw that movie. He was one hard man."

"Yeah! But they won."

"Look, I have to go home. The wife should be calling any minute now."

"Yeah, me too. I have work to do."

"I can't even believe you're the same kid that showed up in August."

"All right; why?"

"I didn't know the bonus baby was a mogul."

"Yeah, well it hasn't happened yet."

"Be aggressive."

"Yes, sir."

"Would you please not call me, sir. I'm not in the army."

"I could call you mamm."

"Wet nose."

"Hey, see you at practice tomorrow."

"Ten o'clock. Be there with bells on."

"Yes, sir."

"Ah!"

Steve had a more expensive handset for his cell phone in his car than the car was worth.

It was ringing like crazy too.

"Hey, it's me boss," a voice came clearly over the speaker.

"Abe Simon, how is life in New York City? Have you seen Rico?"

"Yes, on both accounts. Rico, is whittling his little fingers to the bone in law school and I'm giggling."

"What's the scoop?"

"We're working on some plans for some new marketing techniques. They are a little more sophisticated."

"Meaning?"

"We're trying to piggy back them with other projects like the Hall of Fames, and the Photography Museum when it gets finished. We want to show the magazine is just what the doctor ordered when it comes to credibility."

"All right. Look, do the world a favor. Go out with your family—relax. I can tell you are stressed. It's a great idea to be honest with you boss, I'm more excited than stressed. I want to work 24/7 until we're satisfied."

"And by the time that's over, you won't know what satisfying is about. Take in a show or something. That's an order."

"Yes, sir."

"Good-bye and good luck. Start at nine am on Monday and if you're in that office this weekend I'll fire you. I have spies. Do not sit in your apartment and eat Chef Boyardee out of the can like I saw in *The White Shadow* and devise marketing schemes. It is better to go in Monday fresh. So just enjoy yourself."

"Can I go to a Rangers' game?"

"You're asking me permission?"

"Well, you play for Dallas."

"If we didn't have any other team in the league, who would we play against?"

"See you later boss."

Just as Abie hung up the phone rang again.

"Hey, hello from New York, It is Rico," That came through the cell phone just after he answered it.

"Hey, are you graduated yet?"

"No. Not yet. There are so many girls here. I've been through four this month."

"What did you call me about?"

"Essentially nothing! How's the company coming along?"

"Things are happening fast. Like a bullet through an apple."

"No kidding. Is there anything I can do for you?"

"Does the NIT mean anything to you?"

"Oh, Yeah! Who do I talk to?"

"I don't know. Find out."

"You guys really are going ahead with this."

"Yeah."

"Geeze. I'm astounded in a good way. You're more brave than anybody I'd ever seen."

"Well, if anyone does it, it's Tony. He's played to win all his life and knows what it's like to lose. He's like a large bear slamming himself up against a tree to knock it down for the pine cones he wants for food."

"I'm sure he'll appreciate that. Look I'm sorry I haven't called. New York has been New York. It's been a riot without the chaos. I study so I can stay here."

"No sweat; I've been busy myself. You sit down at the computer and you plan for an hour and it takes maybe all night."

"I know the feeling. Law school has been really enlightening. It makes you and pulls you towards morals and ethics. You can tell the washouts right away. On my very first day, I voiced my opinion on the matter to a couple of them and from then on they sat in the back."

"Really? What a shame! What a terrible, damned shame! What's the matter with, man? Your opinion counts just as much as the next man."

"I feel kind of awkward there. Like, I don't belong somehow."

"Why?"

"I feel like I'm the dumbest one in the class."

"You're the dumbest one in your own head. You're plenty smart. You get in there man. Raise your hand."

"The third or fourth time I went to raise my hand, I just froze."

"Why?"

"There is this beautiful Italian girl in the front row—not like the usual air heads that I go out with. She's bright and she's tough. She squared off with the prof on the women's right to choose issue and she buried him. She made an argument and everything."

"Are you telling me you go home and practice how to ask her out."

"It's not that bad yet but it's getting there."

"Just ask her you moron."

"I'm planning it."

"What's that saying, 'People don't plan to fail. They fail to plan.'"

"Look, I just want to let you know that I wanted to check in. Hang in there brother. She's mine. I'll just have to do it like a gentleman."

"See, you brother. I'll give you a call in a couple of days."

On the way back from Alfredo's, he called Tony.

"Hey, It's me," Steve said.

"What's going on?"

"Look I decided to take a flyer on Getty. I'm working like heck trying to compose a letter. Plus I think they might have an interest in the way we do things. I've always liked their management style."

"Which is?"

"They want the best photography in the world to be shown. That's good enough for me. We'll work on the numbers later."

"What about UT?'

"It was gorgeous. Spent an hour and a half signing autographs and I'm a rookie."

"You really think we can make this thing work."

"Is that pessimism or awe?"

"I don't know to be honest with you."

"Look, I can't start hiring and bring people in from the project if sitting around muddling. You will be the marketing manager—besides me the most powerfully positive force in the company. If you don't believe in this project I'll get somebody else."

"Hey!"

"Hey! Nothing! You are my brother and I love you. You're doing great Just relax more. You're not going to end up on the scrap pile. You know what want you to do. Think about where you were to where you are now. Keep moving forward. Don't think about the past. You worry so much. I have neve seen anyone like you."

"Can we get down to business, please? What do you want me to do?"

"Start making contacts amongst the group that worked on the project. Easy, low pressure stuff; until you hit John Davis. Hammer him. Pump him up. Get the juice going. He's sometimes too much of a realist. He uses his Harvard brain to see walls instead of ladders. He's a good guy but we need to juice him up every once in a while. How's your mental illness?"

"I'm beating it into the ground. Destroying it actually!"

"Yeah! But are you happy?"

"Doing this you mean?"

"Partly?"

"Dude, my wife's downstairs holding our first child, we're doing something people write books about. And the Sox are just around the corner. Things are sailing."

"Great! Keep it right there for the rest of your life."

"Thank you for interrupting me that rudely."

"Good-bye."

When he arrived at their condo, he went into his room and pulled out his file on Getty. He went into the TV room and found her sleeping. He jabbed her in the ribs quite playfully and she fell off the sofa.

"Jerk!" She said groggily.

"Wake up! I need some PA thinking."

"Do you want to go to bed with me tonight or what?"

"Yes. Actually I would. However, I have an assignment for you."

"Which is?"

"I want you to take the same information I have and write a proposal to Getty."

"You're going with Getty?"

"Yes. It's the best move."

"What are you going to do with my proposal?"

"Compare it to mine. We have two weeks before we get it going."

"Wow!"

"Very important that you take this seriously***"

"Do you realize I gave up a Fellowship to Rice for this?"

"All right, that was a stupid comment. I'm just nervous. I want it right."

"You'll get it. Don't worry."

"My biggest concern is financing. I have to figure that out."

"At $20 a share we should do okay. It's going to take a little praying though."

"Maybe; in the business we're in it may not be that big of a jump."

"I think that you'll get a lot of interest with the college kids and sales may be really solid."

"If you, had a choice between sales and marketing, what would you chose?"

"Definitely marketing, a lot of creativity within a team environment defines a good marketing department."

"Well, I'm not going to change what you are because you're good at it. If it makes you happy, do it."

"You could probably do that too."

"This is so much fun. I'm not going to lose out to a financing problem. There's got to be a way of pushing it through."

"You have heard of banks?"

"Yes, but that is a last resort."

"Who's the finance guy?"

"Rob Williams from BU: He works for Fidelity. He sort of moonlights for us! He's a smart guy."

"You're worrying about way too many things tonight. You know what you should do? Buy the car tomorrow. And after you buy the car, call Mr. Williams."

"Really?"

"Yes."

"I was thinking about a Ford 150."

"A pick up truck; You live in a condo."

"It's Texas. I'll fit right in."

"Hey, look pal, it could be the whole Texas scene. I'm your brother, I understand these things."

"So, am I and I've only been here since last summer."

"I haven't seen you get a Cowboy hat yet."

"I need the truck first."

"Good man."

The following Thursday he was having lunch with the Governor.

"Governor Franklin, I know you've heard this before, but what I'm proposing will be good for the country and the world."

"You cured cancer and didn't tell me."

"Not as great as that but still great."

"I'm curious."

"What if I told you certain defenseman from Boston University who was traded to Dallas for business reasons has business of his own to discuss?"

"Discuss it."

So Steve told him everything he had so far and the Governor nodded a couple of times and finally he said.

"It's definitely viable."

"Governor, can you do anything?"

"Business helping business would probably be better than Government at this time, because we could offer a tax credit to businesses that help start ups like yourself. They'd get it all back on Uncle Sam and the state of Texas. What are you looking at?"

"Four million."

"And your stock price?"

"Twenty dollars with forty-eight shares left."

"Bring it up to twenty-three."

"Yes, Governor."

"Lunch has turned into dinner," the Governor smiled.

"I really appreciate your help?"

"When did you come up with this idea? It's great."

"When I was sixteen—in high school!"

"You haven't waited too long. "

"Sir, I need your other opinion on something. Graduate school?"

"Yes. You can play. I understand the need but you're flying as it is. Let it ride on the project and don't get nervous."

"You really like that truck. Don't you?" Laurie said over breakfast the next day.

"Yeah, I though about getting one of the smaller but I want the big one. What do you buy for babies that are big and clunky?"

"Cribs and playpens!"

"See, all that stuff can slide right in the back and when you have people in the cab, nobody is yelling at each other because people are close to each other. I'll pick you up after practice and we'll come back with a truck."

Well, they came back with a truck and a car. He bought the Ford and on the way through his dealerships, he found he found a very hot, navy blue Mustang. He was so wild and crazy about it that he called his father.

"Dad, I need help. I just spent sixty thousand dollars on two vehicles."

"What were they made of gold?"

"They're so cool. I picked up a Ford 150 and a Navy blue Mustang GT. It's a rocket ship."

"What color is the truck?"

"Fire engine red, definitely!"

"You are kidding."

"Actually, no."

"I could here a great big sucking sound from my checkbook."

"Wait until you buy a house."

"Dad? The best thing about our money is that we're sinking it into a winner of an idea. This photography thing is going to hit huge. We're going to have a lot of fun. Right now it's just a Massachusetts, Texas company but I want it to grow."

"I've seen more people who have made it in America than the other way around and most of the people I met cared about their community so I say."

"I think, I'm going to have the most fun time in the whole world."

"Just be careful in that rocket ship, all right."

"Okay. I understand. I felt so good today. We accomplished so much."

"I bet you did."

"When you get out here at Easter we'll give you a ride. It'll be cool."

"Now don't go nuts with the money. Relax for a bit. Enjoy your new toys but don't be foolish."

"Yes, sir. Dad, it was good to talk you. I've been running in about a hundred directions since I got here."

"Look there's two theories in life that I've heard. 1. After work you should come home, watch TV and relax or 2. You should do what makes you happy. "

"Enjoy it. You are ambitious. So what? Just do it with morals."

"All right?"

"Graduate school?"

"Oh, yeah!"

"What if you did something like went for a ride?"

"Yes, we might."

"Two is definitely better."

"I got hit right in the side of the head with the puck the other night. Maybe that has something to do with it. Did mom see it?"

"No. I would've heard about it all week."

"What do you think about me as a person? Am I good for it?"

"You better be. Why?"

"I'm relying a lot on friends new and old for advice and somehow it's got to come back. Most of them will want it monetarily; some have so much money they wouldn't care if you gave them a million dollars. Some friends are a little gun shy and don't know what to say. It's, 'Man, I went to high school with you.' It's not derogatory but it's incredulous and I can't blame them because it's incredulous to me too. I had an idea but who could've thought?"

"The important thing is that you did."

"Honestly, the first meeting at Cappo's in Boston, was so funny, I didn't know what I was doing or how to do it. I just kept talking."

"Look dad. I promised I'd take Laurie out somewhere."

"Where?"

"Just going to drive and see what happens. My last drive in the Mustang before it's tripped to the junkyard."

"They didn't want it?"

"I couldn't blame. I lost them right when I said I drove to Texas. They flew out of the sales room."

Chapter 48

"Well, Bessie, this is our last road trip together. Please make it back to the house tonight." Steve prayed silently.

"Are you having a séance over there?" Laurie giggled.

"I was praying miss."

"For what?"

"For this to be turned into a magic carpet: that can be subdivided, and exchanged evenly for my two new automobiles."

"Keep dreaming."

"Yes, I know. Oh, well, what do you feel like eating?"

"Doesn't matter*** Let's drive."

"They ended up at a family owned Mexican restaurant way on the outskirts of the city. It was clean and the food was good. It was obviously a family place.

"Hey," The waiter asked, "Aren't you Steve Thompson from the Stars?"

"That's me! This is my fiancee Laurie."

"Senorita."

"Can I get a camera. I'll be right back."

"Sure kid."

"Pictures," Steve leaned over the table and winked at Laurie.

"Come one gather round, bring in the family."

There were five of them.

"Hey, wait a minute. I don't even know your name," Steve said.

"Pedro. Pedro Marques. I watch you guys all the time. You will win the Cup I think."

Pedro introduced his family and they lined up for photographs.

"Hey, tell me something. Did you like the food?" Pedro asked.

"Yeah, sure. It was good."

"Whew! We just got a new cook last week. The other guy quit. The new guy is a little hit and miss sometimes but he is a good guy so we work with him."

"Are you going to college?'

"I made it to TCU on scholarship."

"Good for you. What are you going to study?"

"I don't know. Liberal Arts for now as college is a long way away from this place. I just want to work at my grades and find myself. Find out where I fit. I took this test and it said manager or leader in some respect."

"Good for you."

"We'll see. Look, I've got to jet. My hombres are coming to pick me up and throw me in the shower so we can chase girls."

"That is healthy. One hundred American Red Blooded healthy! Don't you think so honey? I pursued you!"

"Finish your tequila. Pedro. Don't listen to him. He ran me over coming out of the student union."

"Yes but you didn't hit the ground."

"I did too."

"What's Boston like?"

"Well, in the summer it's really nice. The weather's great. I can't say this anymore because I'm engaged but the girls are outstanding. In the fall, it's the Patriots and Boston College football. In the winter it's just about everything. And then from spring until God mercifully puts it to an end, there's the Red Sox."

"They did win once."

"I'm a little demanding. I'd like them to win twice. It'll probably take another eighty-six years."

"Well where were the Yankees?"

"I hate to say it. I'm a loyal fan but they really sucked eggs. Wait until we go through whole baseball season. You'll understand what I mean when I laugh and cry with those guys."

"Thanks for the picture. Bring the guys. We are always open it seems and we love the Stars. We don't love the Yankees so much. I gotta go and chase chiquitas."

"If you catch one you better be careful, or you'll be a papa before you know it."

"Yeah. I know."

They back to Dallas with take home packages from the meals.

"Breakfast tomorrow," he smiled.

"Burritos for breakfast," she smiled.

"Absolutely! I think they gave us more food because the packages fee heavier than they did with just plates."

"Did you leave them a good tip?"

"Of course, what do you think I am?"

"You're cheap."

"I'm not cheap. It's an old college thing. Hey, I've tipped in change before."

"Do you have any idea how much money you make?"

"No. It doesn't seem real. I spent $60,000 on two cars: I almost had a hear attack."

"Well, wait until you start writing checks for expenditures on the company. Then you'll see sticker shock."

"Avarice rears its ugly head."

"Capitalism rears its promising head. Look, I'm going to call my agent after I get this little note to Getty and see just how much capitalism I can do in the off season. I have a feeling I'm going to need it for this little business venture."

"Can't we just be normal people? You can photograph want you want to photograph in Texas and Massachusetts. Heck in Texas, you've made friends with the Governor on down."

"I think I'm dead."

"Why?"

"I have too many friends in too many different places."

"That's not dangerous, honey. That's smart."

"No. Actually it isn't because everybody wants to give it the old college try for their own college basically using the same theory you used. 'Come on, our school is a great place, come on out. You can photograph. You don't need all that travel. You can be home with the kids. Blah! Blah! Blah!"

"I don't know why I'm saying this but and?"

"It's the in between stage. Do you want to do what you want to do or do you settle. Don't ever repeat that because if you tell a friend that his offer is a settlement, he could get very offended."

"I understand in order to see your friends on any regular basis, you have to go big."

"That's what I guess they'd call it."

"Can't you just enjoy life?"

"Challenging yourself is enjoying life."

"I just want you happy."

"I want us happy."

"Why? Don't I sound happy?"

"Come on Laurie."

"I'm afraid you're going to drop dead when you're fifty."

"That's the crazy part of it. When I set down and watch TV, I feel more stress than when I am participating in my life. The funny thing is I've always been like that. Even if I wasn't excellent at what I was doing; at least I was trying. This however, I have a chance at being excellent at what I'm doing. If we do it together, it'll be a lot more fun. If you don't mind, would you put up with me please?"

"Do you really find me valuable?"

"I hate to ask. But In what capacity?"

"As a wife!"

"What kind of question is that?"

"Well, you're so wrapped up in this business…"

"Stop it! Enough! Stop! Have you been reading those dumb romance novels again?"

"Sometimes they sound real."

"So aren't Batman cartoons. Does my car look like the bat mobile?"

"Maybe it would be better if I asked questions?"

"Fire away. I'm open to anything at this point."

"Other women?"

"No."

"Sex with me?"

"Great."

"Ok! I'm done."

"The sex part. Really, I meant it."

"You chauvinist."

"Hey! You were impressed the first time."

"Jerk."

"I'm kind of confused. Did you want me to say it was too slow or something? Well, I had to hit you with a bulls-eye. It was on the tip of your tongue."

"You know, sometimes when have the right answer, you should just shut up."

"Why teacher?"

"Well, when you grow to be a man son, your wife will explain it to you."

"So everything's good."

"Yeah, you were right. Fink!"

"So we should probably go home and make love. So, we can disperse stress."

"That's a good way to say it."

Chapter 49

"I want to know this fixation you have with graduate school."

"It's important to me because it's the goal I set for myself when I was a freshman."

"And?"

"And it's tailored to my needs now if I can explain it to the powers that be at BU."

"How are you going to pull that off?"

"Are you being a cynic or is there a constructive end to the question?"

"Answer the question and you'll find out?"

"You're afraid of another woman. Since we've known each other, have I even joked that you were second best to anyone."

"What I'm pulled between is two homes. One here and one at BU. UT is really great but I miss the East Coast a lot. There's a terrible amount of gifts both offer. I don't want it to look like I'm racing out of Texas on an airplane as soon as the season ends to go to school in Boston but on the other hand. BU is only summer semester. It's like playing hockey in August."

"You not worried about going or coming. You're worried about upsetting people."

"That is it in a nut shell. See, in college we had the opportunity to take a couple of friends to the Big E on a weekend before the schedule started. Here's is great. You can go to Cowboys games and we can go to Arlington for Ranger games. I'm going to be working too hard not to have a break. Working 24/7 7 days a week is not a good thing. I know this rationally but my head is still telling me I'm a quitter. I just will have to take languages at UT at some other point in my life. I can't do it. My head will go splat."

"I just want to go and have a great season every year, hopefully win the Cup and get my degree so it can help me run the company. And by the way, if we want to sneak out for a Saturday afternoon to go do what married couple's do in Boston or Dallas then we should do it. Running the treadmill is fine as long as it isn't forever."

"I love it when you make manly decisions."

"I just really like you."

"You don't feel like a failure or anything?"

"No, actually I find you to be very comforting."

"No! No! No! I meant do you feel like failure?"

"I was trying to dodge that. I will take the classes at UT—just later. Short answer is, 'No, I don't feel like a failure.' You just need some time to be yourself."

"And your photography?"

"My company; It will go along if I do the job. It's important I do it on this schedule because I have friends on the East Coast that will be concerned if I go of to Texas and let's say, never come back. That would be very, very bad."

"You are kidding?"

"It 's what as known as the 'grandma affect.'"

"It smells like the money effect."

"Sometimes but you can get by that. It's the other nutballs that I worry about."

"You are too funny."

"I'm a realist."

"Yes! But I live in Texas now, Cowboys, and cactus, and rocks. The occasional hurricane too!'

"So?"

"I don't know what the big deal is. We're all in the same country."

"What are you talking about?"

"Look, I've already cleared it between Governor Franklin, God, and Governor Romnan."

"So what does a liaison do?"

"He writes a couple of papers and reads them in the Kennedy Center or somewhere."

"Do you like politics?"

"Are you asking me if I'll run someday?"

"Sort of."

"Sort of yes and sort of no. I have a lot of learning to do. I think I'd have the hardest time with the whirlwind 50 states tours in 25 hours kind of a thing. I like my way to see America better."

"Which is?"

"Take your camera all over the place. Then you can see people as they are. In twenty years you'll have prints from all over America. You will really see the American people. Besides your President should look like your father—not your little brother. You'll know how important an AA team from Iowa is to their community. You'll know what the Bruins are like to Boston. It is important that on Martin Luther King Jr's birthday, you can see the campus that he studied on. That happens to be mine."

"We also have Howard Stern."

"Yeah***"

They laughed.

"Do you have as much fun doing this as I do?"

"I like looking after you. Do you have any idea what a wreck you are in the morning?"

"Can we make love now?"

"Not yet!"

"I'm going to delegate authority."

"Meaning?"

"I'm going to call Tony and explain to him that I am busy for the evening and that he should field all the calls himself. We are actually going to have a night in."

"You are going to make love to me."

"Yes, mamm."

"Right now***"

"Yes, mamm."

After they made love, he said.

"Listen, I think we can have a really good time. That's why I'm pushing for this so hard."

"Why don't you think it is fun? But you never had doubts about accomplishing the enormity of the task. I don't know if that's good. When you start investing your own money it is going to be real."

"Laurie, I have to lead. I could have the worse possible day ever and I have to get the troops involved and feeling good. I have to get the troops in sync and feeling that they are going to have an outstanding day. I could have found out I'd go bald tomorrow right in front of God and everyone ring the bell for New York Stock Exchange. You still do it.

"Let's say, someone in an honest effort, really screwed up. What you do? Fire the guy or the gal. Work with them to correct the mistake. Find out how egregious the mistake is. You have to be part motivator, part Reverend, part coach, teacher, motivator, and part Vince Lombardi."

"What I'm asking you is that you do not see too many walls."

"No. I was like that once and it sucked eggs. I know I have the talent to push this beyond the ordinary bounds of an established company. From playing on the Junior National Team, I have friends in USA Hockey. The logical step is to ask them who to talk to in the United States Olympic Committee. Then you go to the NCAA, pro leagues, junior leagues in Canada. Like Ronald Reagan said, "The sun always shines in America."

"I get nervous because you're involved."

"You get nervous because you see me travelling alone in an airport and some feminine creature comes zipping up to me asking me if I could light her cigarette."

"You're a jerk."

"I am not. You're always last! You put yourself last in everything and that's not right. You make yourself crazy and it scares me."

"Well what would you do in New York or Chicago alone in your room at eleven o'clock at night?"

"I'd call you."

"You're making points fast."

"Oh, I'm a point maker."

"We're taking our honeymoon two days after the season ends."

"As long as we get married because I want to have babies as soon as possible."

"Four."

"You upped it one."

"Well, you said four would be nice."

"I was just joking."

"Too late you're stuck with your suggestion. I like it and I'm the boss in that department."

"We can show them how to photograph."

"Yes, I guess we could."

"Imagine the Australian open, the Italian basketball leagues, or God forbid our own country."

"Do you realize we're in bed?"

"Miss, we can make love in all those countries."

"You see the bright side of everything. Don't you?"

"If I were to say, please tell me what your most romantic Easter gift you need, want, or have to have, what would it be?"

"I would like a trip, well, a long weekend to Vancouver. I want to see that mysterious land of Olympic Gold."

"I thought I was bad."

"I'm serious. Sometimes I think you only play in the NHL is to get a chance to at playing for Team USA."

"Don't tell anybody. But the only reason I play in the NHL is because it's fun. I don't worry about work ethic because that's necessary or you'll get killed. I don't care about holding up the reputation as the Hobey Baker winner I don't even worry about the money for my company. Although, it is all part of growing up; I am going to renege my statement. I'm having so much fun. I may play as long as the body holds out.

"I had all these rookie fears when I got here. Now, I'm learning the league and that's good. My teammates are a bunch of guys that know they have talent but they're not stupid about it. They aren't arrogant. Mostly, you'd like them over for a cookout when the weather gets warm. I learned a lot about management style from coach already."

"We should relax more."

"We should. When it reaches seventy, we'll have a cook out with the team."

"We need a house. A spacious one."

"That would mean commitment."

"Don't start. If you turn into one of those, you'll never know what hit you."

"Yes, I am doing the house thing in my mind myself. Do you want modern or something?"

"I want one of those big, Mexican villa deals with the certain kind of Mexican, shingle type thing roof."

"Dog or a cat?'

"No animals."

"Why?"

"They aren't messing up my house."

"So I get all the blame!"

"You really aren't that bad accept for the morning. You stumble about a lot. And you leave your socks on the floor."

"I will be more careful."

"You know, I don't really want one either but I thought for sure you would."

"I'm allergic to them both."

He laughed.

"I'm serious. Look, my nose would drain and I couldn't kiss you."

"No animals. Forget the animals."

"Just relax. Everything will happen."

"Miss, if I was relaxed one day in my life, I wouldn't know what to do with myself."

She hit him with the pillow for emphasis.

"Hey!"

"Hey! I'll give you Hey!"

"Miss, we probably shouldn't talk business after making love."

"You're much to optimistic about life. There's no reality to it."

"Miss, I grew up in a small town and it was okay to dream for a Mercedes, a Jag, or BMW. A nice house in the suburbs was good too, which really isn't a bad thing but what if you have a dream like Henry Luce, or Bill Gates, or Warren Buffett. Did that make you a bad guy? Am I a bad guy?"

"You're a bit high strung."

"I can't help it. We…you know and I get to see Nate tomorrow night. We go to Montreal. It's a very different idea that I had and I didn't know how to present it. It was hard for me to get out. Olympic Games seemed so grandiose but it's not that far away anymore and we may win—unless Canada gets really upset."

"How can you be such a grounded flake?"

"I don't say much to the outside world. You are a rookie so you're supposed to keep your mouth shut. Tony has a better story than me anyway. He's hesitant about talking in the press because he is afraid that people will laugh at him and won't take his position seriously in the company. It's bad enough his brother hired him. It would be worse for him to say he got it because of a mental illness scholarship."

"What about you?"

"Me. What's so special about me? Look at the way I dress on off office hours. Polo shirts and jeans: Big Deal. Please don't put that put that in the guys heads. On the team or the company; why work as I do to not dress the way you want or enjoy the people you want to. For at least one season, I am lucky. I see guys together and girls, working and sacrificing their time to get the job done and it's because they respect me. They do it because Steve Thompson is important to them. And they're gifted too."

"Have you talked Chris Davidson back yet?"

"We have an agreement. He gets paid as consultant to probe new markets and the political atmosphere in that country. I hate to say this because people are getting down in South America and it is poor beyond poor but someday baseball fields will replace poppy fields. You never lose touch with people. Hopefully things will change down there."

"I didn't know you liked baseball that much."

"Baseball is my favorite game right up until hockey starts."

"They respect you and like you because of the statements you make; because you are willing to back them up. "

"I gain strength from my team on the ice and in the conference calls. Do you know that of all the things we've talked about since the company was initiated, I've grown into the man I thought I could be when I was sixteen."

"Hockey didn't do it for you?"

"Hockey's kind of a regression. I play like heck but I never grow up."

"I just have to get used to the man in you. When you were in college it was sweatshirts and jeans. Now it's suits almost every day. You grew up over night."

"Yes! But how must I remind you I dress when I'm home."

"Well, in today's world."

"What am I?"

"You are a guy that if he had his druthers would provide a picture for every elementary school child in every hospital and every school in Texas. Maybe, Massachusetts?"

"Definitely!"

"I work really hard but that's what you're supposed to do. That's a given. I think about Tony and me and why he has it and I don't. I have to drive away in the desert alone sometimes to get all the anger out of me.

"My brother however, is past the anger and he's focusing on fighting and beating the disease. He likes to call it a medical condition. I don't call it much. I failed him a couple of times as a brother after he was diagnosed.

"A bunch of us were going, so I asked him along. He came and didn't say anything all night. He froze and afterwards I got mad and yelled at him. He was always there with five bucks to buy a soda or something. I thought my brother was a pretty sharp guy and I really ripped for not talking and he went up to his room.

"I didn't understand what he was really fighting against."

"And the other time?"

"I wouldn't take him out anymore because he embarrassed me."

"I think Tony has more confidence in you now."

"I still carry it with me. He could be so normal and then when he'd get around a crowd of people, he'd stand in the corner and watch the party go by. The voices used to be very bad and sometimes they still are. You can tell when he's mad at them. He looks like Bobby Knight on a bad day."

"What do you do to help?"

"I pull him off into a corner and introduce him to three or four people. Before he was married, it was great. Three or four girls and he's happy. That's one thing he had over me. He could and can talk to the ladies. Annie saved him from a life of jigiloism."

"Tony: sweet little, innocent, little Tony."

"He was an ace with the girls before he got sick ad then. You know Tony. If every letter isn't perfect on the contract and the 401k doesn't read right etc… The man ain't getting married. He's neurotic—not to mention crazy."

"How could he be so hot with the women?"

"He is a writer. Chicks dig that."

"After he got sick, he lost confidence. He couldn't take care of a family and he had to rebuild. Thank God for Annie. Just a remarkable lady! Fun to be around but very much tough enough to tell him to snap out of it; Life is ahead."

He lay in bed for a long time that night and he rang the cell to his father's number.

"Hi!"

"How did you survive fatherhood?"

"Is she?"

"Not yet, we're hoping to conceive on our honeymoon or after, whatever delivers the most fun."

"If your mother, ever heard you talk like that."

"I brought the subject up. I really want a son."

"She wants a girl."

"Yeah, of course; we're just going to find out if he/she is healthy. That's it. I bet everybody in the locker room a hundred bucks it would be a little Stevie. Besides, that's natural. Your older brother takes care of the younger sister. Or he teases her beyond end."

"Well, the first thing is to understand that you are at the mercy of them. No matter where you go. No matter what you do—especially the girls. Boys you get some hockey equipment and they are all set. Girls burst into tears. I've seen it. Man, there isn't anything like it. You make them mad and the water ducts come on. It scares me to death."

"You're not helping to day."

"But seriously, even with the agony of Tony's condition, there is a tremendous amount of genuine friendship that develops between a father and a son—especially when the sons grow up and understands the world as a man does."

"Dad, I'm a professional hockey player and sports photographer. I haven't grown up yet. What happens in a years' time if we have a baby."

"You asked for one."

"I want hand to hand combat—day to day stuff."

"You'd lose."

"I can't lose to a two year-old."

"Look, enjoy the kids. You work like a demon and you keep telling yourself that part of it is a family business…yet, your children are unborn. Please remember that this is America and they may want to do something else."

"I know. But they won't have to go anywhere for posters."

Chapter 50

The next night he was in Montreal. During pre-game warm up, he found ate Williams.

"Why haven't you been e-mailing me?" Steve asked.

"Man, I've been really busy. New girl."

"You?"

"Thanks a lot."

"Hey! E-mail me. I want to talk shop with you."

"Oh Lord, what do you have going on now?"

"Come on now. Don't sound so fatalistic."

"You and you're wild plans."

"Aw, come on it'll be fun?"

"Give me a hint and I'll think about it."

"You don't trust me."

"Dude, fifteen thousand people are here."

"We're on the ice!"

"Tonight. After you lose, go home and write me an e-mail."

"You're still the same insolent little puss bucket you were in college. You on't tell me."

"Later."

"You better keep your head up tonight."

"I'm offering something really good so shut up already."

"Hey, ladies are you two having séance. Let's get going," Al hollered.

"E-mail me."

"I will."

The game was fast, the Flying English, Frenchman, Swedes, and Fins were ack in full force. They even had a couple of Yanks thrown in. It was up and own with a curl in the middle, race around hockey. The goalies were tested nbelievably. The mouths on the ice were running just as fast, which was good ut because of the language barriers nobody understood each other, which was lso probably a good thing with what was coming out of those guys mouths.

It was definitely a highly refined Olympic style game with very little enalties and an incredible amount of speed. By the end of the third period, the eams tied 4-4 and Montreal lost the shootout when its biggest star Pierre Martin hit the post.

"I'm definitely going to e-mail you now!" Steve laughed.

Nate grinned as they shook hands.

"If you weren't my brother, I'd kick your butt."

"You going into politics?"

"Heck no."

"How's Dallas treating you?"

"More than fine. I'll fill you in on the e-mail."

"We've both been busy."

"No apologies necessary. It's a good idea. Just hear it out and think about it."

"You know I got it?"

"What?"

"The whole damned thing; the Rhodes Scholarship, the hockey career, and the girls—all of it seems to fit together too. That's the weird part."

"Well, run with it. Enjoy yourself. It's not like anybody gave it to you."

"I have a flight to catch."

"I'll go home and write you an e-mail. Swear to God."

"Don't swear to God. That's not nice."

When he got to the locker room, most of the guys were half dressed.

"I thought you were going to ask him out on a date," Al grinned.

"We baby sat each other through college. He was my defensive partner. Quite a screw up with girls back then but the boy seems to have his action ready now."

"I'm sure that's what you were talking about. Are you going to bring him in?"

"I value his opinion either way. I'll just tell him and see what he thinks. He's kind of useful. He's a Rhodes Scholar."

"Wow!"

"You see how hard that kid studied in college—up until two or three in the morning every night. He worked hard. Plus the guy's just gifted at life. He's not one of those individuals who were an egg-head. He can go to a ball game and have fun—just to enjoy himself. He's my brother: I guess."

"Came on, we better get in the shower before there's no hot water left."

They showered, dressed and jumped on the plane. First they went to Ohio to play the Columbus Blue Jackets. And then they would be flying them to the coast for the Florida teams—the Panthers and the Tampa Bay Lightning. Then they would go home to Dallas.

"Hello!"

Steve grinned as they got into the hotel room and called Laurie on his cell phone.

"You won," she said, "How did you win?"

"We held our composure. It was against us tonight. We hit five posts in the first period. Nobody panicked and we played through it."

"I'm working on my paper."

"Me too! This place has wireless so I'm going to patch in Nate and see what's been going on. It was good to see the knucklehead again."

"He was your friend."

"He is my brother. He was a real class act after he lost though. Real gentleman! BU man all the way."

"What are you doing for the rest of the trip?"

"Columbus, Miami, Tampa Bay; I'm going to be working on the company and see what contacts are to be made in these areas of the country. I'm going to look for different avenues, like Nick Bolliteri's Tennis Academy."

"Shouldn't you be concentrating on hockey?"

"Miss, there's a whole lot of down time in between games. Either that or I can spend my free time in a bar…never mind, I almost said something stupid."

"I hear no evil, speak no evil, see no evil."

"Thank you. Montreal almost really whipped our butts tonight. The thing that is frustrating is that we weren't awful, they were just so fast. The league is going speed. I have to work on power skating this off-season. We gotta figure out a way to contain teams like that in the future."

"Well you can't do it tonight. So stop worrying about it."

"Yes. Mamm."

"Call me tomorrow."

"Will do."

They won two of three only to lose to 2-1 to Columbus in a shoot out and darn near getting killed by Coach Mickleman for not hustling against a young, incredibly enthusiastic team.

"You idiots think you are the best team ever. How dare you put forth an effort like that? Good, hard working, people pay good money to see us play. And you sucked eggs. You weren't even a decent junior team tonight. If you don't straighten out in the next two games and WIN THEM, you will be eternally in my skate marathon until you drop. Got it? With the fear of God instilled in them, they went out and thrashed the next two opponents and they all kept their mouth shuts on the plane hoping that Coach Mickleman didn't notice they were there. The Coach was still upset at the Columbus game.

He got home and collapsed next to Laurie.

"Can't you just 'Hi!'" She mumbled.

"We're twenty-four grown men and we stood out on the Dallas Ft. Worth area tarmac and got yelled at by coach Micklemen for a half an hour. He even yelled at the assistant coaches. He said and I quote, 'You're winning on talent not on hard work, and then Chickie Smalls our third line center got himself fined five thousand dollars for laughing. That made it all worse and we stayed another fifteen minutes. In dress shoes and overcoats, the dust coming out of the desert, we felt like idiots."

"I'll take you to bed and we'll get warm."

"We better get roasting."

After roasting each other most of the night, they fell asleep. The next morning an early practice was called and it was a part of damnation.

"I'm going to die," Chickie said at the end.

"Shut up or you'll get us more."

"If you guys want to do this all day, keep jabbering," Coach Micklemen hollered.

Nobody said a word.

"If you want to be punished like children, you guys keep screwing around."

Nobody said a word again.

"Go home, do your thing and then be ready for the Flyers tomorrow night."

Steve physically was sore as he jumped into his brand new truck.

"What are you doing with a truck? Ranchers have those," Colin said.

"I have to see a man about a horse. Tomorrow I can give you a ride."

"Dude, you all better."

"You what?"

"Buddy, if you're going to drive one of those around here. You better learn to say you'all."

"Great. Just what I need an ethnic stereotype."

"It's a means of survival."

"I'll keep that in mind."

Steve zipped out of the parking lot and headed home with business on his mind. When he arrived, He started making phone calls. First he called Chris Davidson and got a positive response.

"Heck, I'd love to do it. I think that it would be a challenge and I learned so much the first time. My mother used to drag me to Junior Achievement when I was a kid. I can't help but say it was a wise decision and I'm glad she stuck it out. What do you want me to do first?"

"Well, you're the first person I called and if all goes well, I can fly you out here for the week and stick you in a hotel, it'll be a working vacation. We can turn the ordinary into the extraordinary."

"Same as the museum."

"Something like that."

"Man, you're just full of plans."

"I'm trying to get Getty to allow us to cross market our name with theirs. It's just a wild scene right now because they somehow found us. We weren't expecting it and now we're scrambling to get it done. It's good scrambling but we're still scrambling."

"You better get an attorney. When those contracts start flying round, you going a legal signature."

"You're pretty smart for a music major."

"I took business for a minor."

"Yes, you did. My mistake."

"Tell me about Getty?"

"They are the biggest and the best in the world and it also happens that they reside in the staunchest allies home that we have, which is nice to know."

"And photographically."

"I consider myself an accomplished photographer but I would have to say to make their organization, I would have to shoot three times as many images to make the cut. They are that precise and that demanding and the funny thing is, you don't even mind it because you are representing the best in yourself and the company you work for."

"What if we get off to a hot start and guys and gals get noticed by other firms like *Sports Illustrated* and they leave?"

"It would be awful from a personal view but terribly worse if we froze like a deer and didn't move forward by finding new talent. You're right. I didn't think of that for five years. Why have you heard of any grumblings?"

"Just rumors really. Lynne has an offer from an Italian basketball club as a team photographer. She's trying to convince her parents that, she won't be ravaged by drunken Italian Sailors in Venice."

"No kidding."

"That's what I hear."

"She's a very good photographer. Why don't you have her call me."

"I can handle it!"

"Please…for me. How's baseball season?"

"Three news articles are already done. I liked them. I'm going to try and write columns next. What is everyone else going to do?"

"Lynne would examine Italy as a prospective sight if she stays with us. Rico would get us a law firm. John Davis would see what Germany and France are up to. Peter Blute is trying to get an in with the Germany Athletic Association. Lars and Pemma are juggling articles in Scandinavia. It's a pretty eclectic group. Different they are professionals and they do their job."

"What about China?"

"I don't know. There copyright laws aren't exactly standard. It's a big country with a lot of people. It takes some exploration and questions by us. They have to accept the questions without losing face and we can't go in there like we own the place. We'll be riding rickshaws in the streets. It's very delicate dealing with the Chinese. You just don't say I want a piece. They talk for four hours for four minutes.

If we can get them on our side, it will be interesting in a good way. If we both act like we're in the losers and users club, we could be in trouble."

"I'll get some information on them.What's with Stork?"

"I'm going to call him after you. Man, have you changed. How's GW?"

"The basketball team's having an off year but other than that I like it. The girls here all have an agenda. They want to marry the President."

"So run for President, what do you care?"

"No, that's not for me."

"You took International Relations."

"To study and write books. Not to run for anything."

"Did you catch any agenda seekers?"

"I'm working on a brunette. She's in my Global Economic Wellness class."

"Pay attention in the class junior. That can help us gain bank notes for the loans when the time comes."

"I'm on board man."

"Good. But I really have a ton of home work."

"Go get him Ace."

"Hey, are you awake?" Steve called Stork.

"I am now. What's going on?"

"Good I ask you a little inconvenience?"

"Could you cover Japanese baseball for us."

"I'd have to learn how to speak Japanese."

"Yeah, that's the catch."

"The things I do for you. Why Japan?"

"The Yankees bought their own team! It's the new rage in baseball and people will want pictures. Look, I'll do something to smooth it over. You seem like you're enjoying the experience."

"Actually, I am. Baseball out there is a different game. They all run. Of course they have to go through boot camp to make the team. What language are you learning?"

"I don't know. I can speak pidgeon Spanish but that'll have to be touched. Spain was considered for the Olympics. They didn't get it but who knows in the future?"

"What's with you and learning the language?"

"It's polite and it's easier to learn the culture that way."

"Okay, I'll do my job and part of me will even like it but there's a large part of me that says, 'I like English.'"

"Dude, you're going over to their country."

"Okay! Already! You sold me. I'll do it."

He called everyone else and they were in. All in! What encouraged Steve is that they were excited about it. Many laughs were taken sometimes in arrears but all were real. It was good to talk to the team again and it was good to have that old college atmosphere back. He checked his e-mail and there was Nate.

Hey, it's me.

What's the big state secret? Send it now or I'll be really upset.

Nate

Nate,

Look, you're either going to go for this idea or you'll think I've flipped.

Remember when we were under grads desperately seeking our chance at the real world? I spit out every once in a while a pseudo plan for a photography company. Well, I'm going for it except it's going to be a magazine. I got some of the team from Massachusetts and we're going to find some of the people from Texas. I would need a man up North of the Border and to be honest with you, you're the only guy I can talk to in the English language without somebody shoving my head into the boards.

Please respond ASAP

Steven

Chapter 51

They had the cook out the next weekend and the families filled the tiny backyard.

"I told you we needed a house," Laurie grinned.

"You don't want a house, you want the Ponderosa."

"We'll get a modest mansion."

"I thought you wanted a ranch?"

"Watch the burgers and dogs, will you please!"

"Hey! My buddy what's going on?"

Tom Jackson's ten-year-old raced up to Steve.

"Big man! You re the guy!"

The boy smiled.

"How many days until school is out?"

"Twelve days. I'm going to junior high school next year!"

"You are the man!"

"Yes I am!"

"What do you want? A burger or a dog?"

"A cheeseburger."

"Do you want real cheese or that fake diet cheese?"

"Give me the real stuff."

"All right. Here's a toasted bun!"

"Mom said not to go to close or my buns will get toasted."

"Okay! Ketchup, mustard, relish, and onions are over there. Go get 'em killer."

It was a good cookout. The guys relaxed finally amidst a torrid push for the play-offs and the Finals. They conversed all night—talked about their child hoods growing up playing hockey; talked about their child hoods just growing up. They relaxed, had a few beers, ate their fair share of the summer's best and enjoyed just living for a few hours. The high pressure, dangerous world of hockey was something that every player craved yet it could be a downfall like flying experimental planes or being a test pilot.

"Hey, man, that's for inviting us. It was a damn good party. The missus and I have to take the Wonder Twins home and get them to sleep," said Ja[illegible] Hoekstra, a speedy little center said.

"Hokie, you come by anytime. Are you ready for the finish?"

"Yeah, are you?"

"I want just want to win the last game of the season."

"Well, maybe I'll get a can of Coke."

"You're the best damned rookie I've ever seen."

"Prague will see the Cup. I'd bet anything on it."

"Nice! Back home in the summer?"

"The kids treat me like a rock star. But sometimes my wife and kids get away with our friends and do goofy stuff like take the kids to the movies and stuff."

"Was it bad? Communism?"

"Yeah. It's weird because nobody wants to talk about it. It's like it happened. Let's move on with Democracy."

"Once again thanks from my family to yours."

Hockey season became a pole position chase between Philadelphia, Detroit, and Dallas. The players were saturated in information about the other team's progress. Steve's best defense against all the madness was to bury himself in his work. He worked on his letter and he was pleased with it.

"Lay it on me," Laurie said.

"I sort of forgot about ladies sports. I have to retool it."

"If the shoe fits, wear it."

"The funny thing is, there's UCONN ladies hoop right down the road and I watch them on CPTV all the time. How could I forget that?"

"Because you're a hockey puck!"

"You're not helping me."

"I won't tell anybody."

"That's reassuring."

Steve called Tony.

"Hey, it's me." Steve said as he held Laurie close to him.

"I'm in bed with my wife, this better be good."

"Hey, I am too. Look, I need to talk to you. Is it really a bad time?"

"Make it quick please."

"Tomorrow the letter will be done and I'll send it out by Friday."

"You're seriously going through with this."

"Doubting Thomas?"

"No, just shocked that you would have the guts to do this. Do you know what this entails?"

"Half of me does. The other half is kind of winging it. How are you feeling? Do you think you'll be ready for the meeting?"

"As it stands now, very well; the same lousy voices come up but I push them away. It's the way it is. My mood swings are beaten. I'm sure of that. They haven't bothered me in years. My writing has been coming a long though. I like it. Hey, I heard you went and spent $60,000 on wheels.

"It's stupid. The voices are popping me up and down telling me I don't need my medication anymore because things are going so well. It happens all the time. When things are going well, that's the worse time. My voices say all kinds of things. Then when times suck they try and finish the job."

"So what do you do to combat this?"

"I imagine drop kicking them over touchdown at Notre Dame."

"Are you kidding me?"

"Nope!"

"And it works?"

"Sometimes it doesn't and then I get mad. Then I think of Annie and I feel really embarrassed so I stop. Don't tell this to the guys but I pray a lot. They may think I'm sort of holy roller/sky pilot."

"That usually works."

"Yeah, that's about it."

"Deal. How's the baby maker?"

"The baby likes books. She flips through magazines all the time."

"What happened?"

"The baby maker elbowed me in the ribs."

"Put her on."

Everything was all good for a while and then Steve asked what to do about a baby gift.

"Steve, we're the same people you were in college. You don't have to go spending your money on us," Annie said.

"Look, how do I explain this? I like spending money on you. Is there anything you need?"

"No."

"Annie, everybody always needs something."

"Come on Steve. You know me. When I need something, I'll ask you. Ask him about his father."

"Put, my brother back on the line."

"Hello?"

"What's with you and the old man?"

"He cornered me about graduate school and I told him that I was going. It was kind of cut and dried but he was kind of like he was feeling me out like he was trying to decide if I could really look out for myself."

"I don't think he has even reached that point with me."

"It's good though. It's not like dad wouldn't let me out of his sight or anything but it's kind of cool to let the air out of the balloon."

"I'm glad he trusts and am really glad, he didn't yell at me."

"You owe me one Boss."

"I want to talk to Annie," Laurie said.

The girls spoke quite seriously about plans for the future and whether or not the family would move out to Texas and the answer was for now, "No."

About two seconds after they hung up, Al called.

"Hey, Chief," The big defenseman said.

"What's going on?"

"I'm in need of a truck. Where'd you get yours?"

"Clarkson Ford just on the outskirts of town. The guy with the somewhat dignified commercials that bring 'People to the road.'"

"Man, I can't believe I'm helping you with the company. Speaking of which is there anything I can do."

"How Italian are you?"

"You are going to come up with a good explanation for that."

"I mean. Do you speak the language fluently."

"Clear as a bell."

"Good. You take your genius knowledge and find out who's in charge of what in Italy and then we'll come back and take notes and draft a letter explaining who we are and what we do."

"Do you ever stop thinking?"

"Yeah. When I'm at a Red Sox game!"

"Now that's not nice."

"Che cosa fa?"

"Mezzo Mezzo?"

"Why?"

"The wife thinks I'm going to run myself into the ground because I'm working so hard."

"And?"

"I just tell her te chiamo (I love you)."

"You are having fun."

"Huge! Like I said I went to Soo U; an opportunity like this for a guy like me. Huge!"

"Between your wife and my brother's with babies—It's a wild thing!"

"I'm going to have to get lap top. Any suggestions?"

"I've used IBM all my life and they've been great. Pick the one that suits you. If you want Laurie gets to the web site every month. You can check it out"

"You don't understand what Junior Hockey is up North. The OHL is the pros for many whom can't get to Toronto or Buffalo. We just are the best thing all winter. We're forty below weather and these people come out. We had 6,500 o 7,000 people come out one night and it was 35 below. They sucked down all the hot drinks by the first ten minutes of the first period."

"Stop being so in awe of other people. Just freakin' talk to them. Don't sell them anything in the first minutes. Shake his or her hand…Just rap with them about their hobbies. Their kids in school! The Stars chances this year! Anything! Relax them. Shoot the breeze with them but don't shoot yourself in the foot."

"That's why I'm here. What do you think selling is? It has to be more than being nice."

"I don't know. The way I figure it. 'What goes around comes around.' If you're trustworthy to a person and you're honest, I think the customer appreciates it. They may not buy from you that day but they'll remember you the next time and they'll probably take a handful of business cards just in case. There are guys that get one order because they are slick and full of it. But they will never get that second order."

"Honest and trustworthy***"

"My dad told me that people who aren't trustworthy couldn't tell someone telling them the truth if you hit them over the head with a 2 x 4. I don't want to be like that. I don't want to be another wise guy."

"I've met some Italians they were pretty normal. Not like the smart guy gangsters we're supposed to be."

"Look, I don't think of you that way. You're a member of our team. That's it. And that has good and bad in it, I realize but at least it's honest."

"We could try and get the bad out.

"Well, look, between you and me. You're square with me. I'm not in anyway have any moral delusions that you're a bad guy because you're Italian."

"Look, my mom and dad are coming down from the Soo. My mom makes the best, fried dough. She stuffs some with anchovy's. It sounds gross but it's really good. What don't you and Laurie swing down Sunday night about six-thirty—seven o'clock?"

"What kind of beer should I bring?"

"No alcohol. Just brownies or something; I don't want to do the drinking bit."

"Fair enough—in the off season, will you do something for me?"

"Yeah, sure."

"I'll pay for it. I want you to take a public speaking course somewhere. At Soo U or somewhere."

"You think it'll work?"

"They've been known to."

"You're going to hire me."

"Look, as a friend, I'll tell you it looks good but as a professional, you have to do some stuff."

"All right. I want to be qualified. Fair enough."

"I think you can do it. Take the class somewhere. Enjoy yourself doing it because I took one in college and we had a blast.'"

"Thanks brother."

They hung up and Steve decided to recede from telling Laurie all of what they talked about. They quietly went to sleep around eleven o'clock. Steve had practice the next day and then it was his time to put the finishing touches on his letter. Then it was done and he had no excuse not to mail it so he did and now the big wait began.

Danny Mark called on the way home from the Post Office.

"Hey, my brother is coming in from California. Do you want to go for a beer or two tomorrow night?"

"Yeah, sure, I just don't want to break up the brotherly reunion."

"Hey, no problem! He wanted to meet you. I was kind of wondering if I could go back to San Diego and help you in some way."

"What does he do for a living?"

"He's a head hunter."

"Outstanding! I'll definitely talk to him."

"He's been doing it for six years."

"He wants to Stay in Diego."

"He kind of doesn't have a choice. He's in the Navy stationed in the Jag corps at Coronado. He's a lawyer who wanted more for himself he started a Headhunter business. He's been judging personalities and people for years. He's an ultra sharp guy is married with a boy and a girl. He never leaves the Navy even after hours. He does everything by the book."

"Well, mission accomplished. It would be nice if the West Coast liked us. I want to go easy on this just so we don't lose the accounts. Tell him to go over it Navy style. And we'll sit down and we'll flesh out the candidates together. Tell him thanks from a respectful citizen."

"About me! I'm just kind off looking for a business to get to on the side. I don't know if I'll commit to it. "

"Well look at it this way. The only thing I want from you is an honest effort. You take those courses that I talked about with that I talked with you before. If you find yourself going through the motions, we'll have to sit down. Not everyone can be a photographer. It's a very demanding mental application. However, I know you're a good leader. Maybe management suits you better.

"Don't get discouraged. I mull things over a lot before I make a decision to hire people. I think you're a winner. I just don't think you know own strengths yet."

"I'll see you tomorrow. Thanks. Hey! If my kids want to go to college in the Continental United States, they're going to BU."

"That's Democracy for you."

"I'll see y'all tomorrow."

The phone rang.

"I just ripped up half of Hamburg," Peter Blute said, "You better be right bout this."

"Look, you learned English. That's half the battle."

"In German, my father just ripped my head off. He was so mad that I passed that job up back home in Berlin."

"You'll make money." Steve smiled.

"He thought I went to college to be an engineer. An engineer is a nice safe job in Germany. That's where you can set yourself up for life. It's all good."

"And you are in trouble."

"He told me if I'm not a success, don't come home for Christmas."

"Are you serious?"

"He'll cool off. I'll send him Rumpelminze."

"What about you? Are you ready?"

"Well, the Sharks want me to play out the year in Worcester. It's hard to concentrate on what I am sometimes—a hockey player or a sales guy. There's been slim picken's for free time to do the manly thing and chase girls. My teammates think I'm an idiot."

"Don't fill your dance calendar every night. Just go out like a Worcester Shark."

"Really?"

"I wanted to hire you. I didn't want you dead by the time you were twenty-five."

"Cool. You should've heard my father. 'If you want to play hockey, you come home. You can hold a real job then.'"

"You could always tell them you were having fun."

"I don't think he would've understood that at the time. My father, once he gets an opinion in his head, he's furiously made other people to be aware that they should be somewhere else."

"Look, if you want out?"

"Look, so far, I've three interviews by *Der Spiegel* so far because of my association with you and the Sharks. I'm having the time of my life and that you have said to be a gentleman around the ladies: I'm ok. The leg around here is pretty good–a couple of nice restaurants too!

"The thing about is that I'm into the financial shows, because for the minors you get paid a good amount so you don't want to fritter it away. You want to learn what to do with it. In some respects, I'm like my father."

"Well, I hate to break this up. But what are your gut feelings about a minor league division?"

"I'm still observing but it's like anything else. The winning teams draw and that affects everything from soda concessions to souvenirs. I don't know if there's enough of a middle class that goes there with disposable income to do it. Yet, if we succeed at the big league level first*** The product identification especially with guys who have climbed up the ladder may push this to a higher level."

"What the heck were you an engineer for?"

"My dad said if you're going over there, you're going to be an engineer. It's a nice, safe job. I was eighteen. Who was I to argue?"

Chapter 52

The next day after a long practice filled with complicated diagrams and lots of sweat, Danny, his brother Joshua, and Steve went out to lunch and had a very deserved cold one.

“”So how did one get into hockey living in San Diego?” Steve asked.

“Well, I lived in Minneapolis and my dad got transferred California about five years ago, so I always off to college at UMD. I visited during the summer and liked it like who wouldn’t? So, now it’s kind of like: I have money. This is cool.”

“Josh?”

“I don’t know where he came from. None of us are athletes. He’s a freak of nature. But he’s a good brother.”

“I tell him to say things like that.”

“If you don’t mind my asking? What’s your claim to fame?”

“I’m an analyst for a local TV station concerning the stock market. Nothing’s better than having a chance at being here seeing your brother playing in the National Hockey League. He’s been working his rear end off, running, jumping, lifting, and praying to get to where he wanted to go and now he’s there.”

“They talked for about an hour and a half about hockey, women, and hockey.”

The general consensus was that Steve was nuts for marrying this early. Steve shyly smiled at that and said simply, “She’s the only girl I could run over by accident, not be embarrassed, and ask her out in the same shot.”

“Well God bless you brother,” Danny smiled.

“We’ll win the Cup,” Steve said.

Clarence left him a phone message saying, “Call immediately.”

Steve called immediately.

“What’s going on?” Steve asked immediately.

“Who is this?” Clarence asked.

“Please call immediately. Guess?”

“Oh, Hi! Boss!”

“Did somebody die?”

“Is it true you’re going through with that company?”

“Yeah.”

"Well, I want to be involved."

"Clarence to be honest with you: I don't need an architect."

"My cousin Lawrence is a big shot with his advertising firm in New York and is tepidly interested. Do you want his name?"

"To be honest with you, I'd rather look local first."

"Dude, it is Madison Avenue. Do you want his name?"

"What firm is he at?"

"Kingston and Hutchinson. "

"How long?"

"Eight years."

"Do you have any information?"

"He gave me a bunch of stuff. I need your mailing address. Are you afraid it won't sell to the good old boys because he's black?"

"If he's good enough, he can play anywhere. If that's the first thing out of his mouth, we can't do business."

"Understood, can I have the address?"

"Sure. Here it is."

"I wanted to thank you for the job you did for us once again. It's a good building. People should enjoy it immensely."

"I was so nervous making presentations to all these important people. Drawing it up was easy."

"I'll be back in the summer. I'm not going to grad school so it's part business part social. We could go out and hang out."

"My buddy has gotten us an apartment in the South End."

"No kidding. Why?"

"Because it's one less scuzz ball in the apartment we rented. The neighborhood is getting better."

"Man, just be careful. Don't be hanging around at one am on the streets. It's still a tough section. Getting you shot would not be a good idea."

"You sound like mother."

"Kids today. You teach 'em. You worry about them and they still test your patience."

"How should I take that?"

"Look, I'll call you. We'll go out. We'll hang out."

"Good enough. See ya.'"

Chapter 53

The next two series against Phoenix and Detroit were masterful exhibitions of play off hockey. Between the skating, stick handling, passing and body checking the networks loved it because the ratings were huge. The best thing about it for Dallas was that they won both series and advanced to the Stanley Cup Finals against the new kid on the block—the Carolina Hurricanes. The glory of it all came from the wherewithal and spirit to make champions.

"Is there anything I can get for you?" The stewardess asked Steve.

"How about a nice, cold Coors?"

"Soon enough," she smiled.

He closed his eyes on the plane back to Dallas. The Detroit series had taken it's toll. He had taken a shot off the left instep of his boot and he ended up hopping to the bench. It still didn't feel better—almost like being brought down to a lower player's level.

"We won! Lighten up!" Colin grinned.

"I was enjoying the piece of quiet I could snatch from you animals. Relax man. We're in. If you celebrate too much, it means you were surprised. You gotta be cool. We are the team. Screw Carolina."

"You aren't used to drinking. Are you?"

"How mellow am I?"

"Does slinky mean anything to you?"

"Do I look like Botox?"

"That would be a step up. How many have you had?"

"Three."

"Curses lad. Enough!"

"Hey! Don't take my beer! What are you doing?"

"You aren't driving home. I don't want my project wrapped around a tree."

"I was only kidding. See, I'm happy as a lark."

"You're still shut off. Now join the party."

"Will this plane fill up if we all go to the back?" Steven asked.

"You went to Boston University. Didn't you?"

"Un-huh!"

"I'm writing a note to the Dean of Admissions asking them politely what they were thinking?"

"I graduated with a 3.5. Eat my dust."

"There's a certain amount of intestinal fortitude I need to have a conversation with you."

"We're playing in the Stanley Cup Finals."

"I know. Makes all those games worth it?"

"Oh, yeah."

"Come on."

❧

Steve followed the Captain into the party. Where the veterans all poured whatever alcoholic beverage they were consuming onto his head. They ruined an $800 Italian cut suit. And he didn't even care.

They had one day off before the games began so Steve took Laurie out to dinner in North Carolina; to Shenanigans a famous rib place. They had incredible fun with the waiters and waitresses over the outcome of the series.

"No, sir, I do believe we have you this year. The 'Canes are coming around."

"No, no, no this is the Stars turn to shine. We own that Cup."

"We beat you in the regular season."

"Do you want a tip?"

"Oh, yes, sir. Another beer."

"Where do you go to college son?"

"How did you know I went to college?"

"It's stamped on your forehead."

"I'm going to be a senior at Duke. Management major. With an towards grad school but am not sure yet."

"Duke. The Duke Blue Devil!"

"That's us."

"What are you doing waiting tables?"

"I don't know. But I'm having fun at it. I'll get a job. I might as well have fun now."

"You like sports photography? And by the way, what is your name?"

"Clark Johnson, III the only one of us who isn't an Esquire."

"Do me a favor: take my card and here's another one. Write down your e-mail. I think I may have found a job for you."

"May I ask what?"

"I'm establishing a sports magazine and I was wondering if you were interested. We need good people down South."

"Well, sir I don't believe in spontaneous combustion but if explain it to me a little better over the e-mail, I'll give it serious thought. It sounds intriguing."

"Good, real work can be fun too. Just for the record, I like Duke."

"Well, teach you with some sense up North. I can work with anybody except North Carolina on game day. The other 363 days a year they're okay."

"Well, that's good to know."

"Thanks for the opportunity. Stay for as long as you want. Season hasn't started yet. It's mostly the locals. When you're ready, I'll take this up."

The next night he was on the ice.

The Carolina Hurricane's had their collection of talkers.

"Hey, you college boy!. You think you can beat us in our house."

"You guys are a one season wonder and you know that. Shut up you baboon."

"Hey, boys tonight is our night? These guys ain't nothing—even the light show sucks! Come on now," Steve tapped the pads of Big Al, Colin, and then himself.

"You guys all in?" Steve asked.

"We're here little brother. Don't you worry about that?" Al said.

Joe Spano came skating through.

"Come on now boys, we're all in now. It doesn't get any better than this."

"Everybody huddle up," Colin hollered.

The Stars brought themselves in together.

"Whatever we've been through together since training camp, this is what brought here. We have to put aside our differences and play like champions. We have to play like blood brothers for seven games. We have to play like warriors. We have to play like friends.

"They beat us by one lousy point this season. You play like you are capable of and we'll win it in four. We are the best of best. Let them be the best of the rest. Stars on three. One-two-three! Stars!"

They were an angry bunch of hockey players after Steve got sticked in the face and required five stitches to close. The 'Cane got a five minute major and the Stars picked up a goal on the extended power play.

"We need you for the series. Don't do anything stupid out there," Colin said at the period break.

"Oh, they'll remember me. I have my ways."

"Just don't do anything stupid."

"Yes, sir."

"I'm going to come down on you like a ton of bricks," Steve said to the guy who sticked him. And they did; the two players waged a personal war—banging at each other and slashing, elbows flying. It was quite dangerous for a while until Steve scored on a slap shot and was cross-checked from behind. The player was called for a blatant penalty and thrown out of the game. The Stars won the first one 2-0.

"I'm going to kill him," Steve said, "Wait until Game two."

"Look, Zorro if you don't stop screwing around we'll lose you for the series. Where did you learn that stuff in college?"

"What stuff?'

"The stick work you idiot. You looked like a surgeon out there."

"He deserved it."

"I can tell already: the league is going to review this game and they're going to call every freakin' call for a month of Sunday's tomorrow night. You'll be in the bin all night. I've been in this league long enough to know. If you don't cool it, I'll cool you. We're in this to win the Stanley Cup championship—not to play pond hockey."

"All right, All right. You're right."

"Nice goal."

"That was a lot of fun."

"Well, you have three games left. Did you here from Getty yet?"

"They are tentatively examining the author of the work and his background and the viability of the idea."

"What does that mean?"

"Shut up and hold on."

"Well, that's them. At least they didn't say 'No!'"

"It would be really cool if it worked. It would just be like one of the divisions at GE or General Motors. If we can finance it ourselves, that would be an extra bonus. The press is coming in."

"They're going to want to talk to the goal scorer."

"It was a team win. Johnny had to pass me the puck. Please don't tell people I need the press."

"Just don't act like a jester and you'll be all set. Here they come. Good luck?"

Someone had gotten wind off his strategy to build the company. He didn't expect this so he had to back peddle.

"To be absolutely honest with you, we don't know yet. It started out as kind of a hobby thing and it grew. Right now we're looking at the feasibility of it coming off. There is a very good chance that it will occur and I will have a real job. Mostly though we have a few areas of demarcation that have to be established and adhered to."

"With who?"

"At this point, with legal considerations to be sensitive to we'll have to wait until I can give you that answer."

"So you have a whole bunch of nothing right now."

"No, sir. What we have is a dream and that is worth a million dollars."

"Bigger than this dream***"

"They work in conjunction with each other."

"Do you realize what you're alluding to, if this comes off. You're a magnate."

"This is America and if anything thing, I want to inspire kids to go after their dreams. I think I'm a guy that has worked hard and has a gift. Anybody want to talk about the game?"

A few questions hung around but not many. The buzz of the evening was on the company.

He went straight to the hotel room to meet Laurie and then after her kissing her deeply said,

"I'm going to catch the e-mail."

"You've got to be kidding me. That's it."

"I hate to say it but I have work to do."

"I'll have you know that I have the letter from Getty."

"You're not joking."

She took the 9 ½' x 11' manila, paper envelope out of her carry bag.

"I didn't your mind on it during the game."

"Please let me see it."

She handed it over.

He opened it carefully and read the hole three pages top to bottom.

"We have an invitation to discuss the matter further at their London offices June 16-25th. When are we getting married."

"You know, it's a wonder I don't kill you. It's July seventh then the honeymoon. You do have your Tux."

"Hey, I have my tux and I got the band. My duties are over with."

"Back to reality—nine days that we'll be having discussions. How many can we bring?"

"Five. First class tickets British airlines."

"Better get to that e-mail."

Hi! It's me Nate!

I read your proposal and it's interesting as heck! To tell you the truth I wiggled around and then bought an IBM. I was very excited but now a few questions. Would I have to stay in Montreal for twelve months because I do miss Boston? Also, am learning to speak Francophone. My girlfriend is teaching me. She makes me go into the local shops and practice. I feel like an idiot but it works.

I like to be involved definitely and I see a tremendous opportunity here with QMJHL, colleges like McGill University and other looks and no touches kind of places. To tell you the truth, I didn't know what to expect I got called up. But the people here who are demanding like you've never seen before over their hockey team are really for the most part, really nice people. They drink more wine than anybody I've ever seen.

One other thing is stopping me and that's our personal relational relationship. We've known each other for six years counting the Junior National teams. I consider you a good friend. If work changes that, then it may be worth it to hire someone else. On the other, if you, in clear conscience, can act like the slave driver you are, and get away with it by whatever rules of safety they have up here then we should get along fine. I'm not really worried much else than that, especially if Getty is all in.

Nate.

Nate,

Hi! It's me Steve! Look, I hired you for your analytical ability as much as your sales sense. Your friendship with me only influenced my decision to the fact where I knew you were a hard word worker and a stand up guy.

Hot off the presses. Five of us are welcome to join Getty's intelligentsia for a nine-day summit in London. It is June 16th-25th. I would like you there for your insight and as aforementioned analytical ability. Please consider and I'm sure they'd be impressed that you speak flawless English.

Steve

Hi! It's Chris!

I think we're expanding too fast. Stay in North America. Get a good base and push into Europe and the Far East. We can break it into as many Zones as we want. We still need great quality photos from photogs. We also need to pay them, which is a minor deal. Chief, I'm giving you the best information I have with the emotional even keel that I can muster. I think everything you want is possible in time if you start establishing goals now. If they ask you to come, then you sit down and talk business. If they demand you come, then you can have a little fun with them because of you want to be in the same place.

The promising places in any order you wish to place them are: England, Italy, Germany, Greece, France, China, and Japan. Don't forget Australia.

I don't think they'll fall like dominoes. Every since the EU came together they've discovered capitalism.

Set three and five year goals. If we get there faster nobody would be happier than me but reality is reality. And it's better to get the home folks behind you first.

Chris.

Chris,

Call me on my cell tomorrow at eleven o'clock.

Steven

❧

The phone call came.

"Hey, it's Chris. You just got me between classes."

"Look, buddy. I like most of your ideas but we have to tailor them to the troops in a more positive like our projections should put us in London by 2008. Or Italy can be launched on the same date 2009. Etc.etc. We always want to be some place and we're always networking because to facilitate the networking process makes it easier to initiate other solutions to the challenge. You did a good job on the research but just don't hit the panic button. Take a step back. Relax. Right now we have 48 shares to earn financing for this operation. Now, we have to set a price that is as high as we can get because this operation is going to need it."

"Who's going to buy the other 52 shares?"

"You're talking to him."

"Are you serious?"

"That's why I'm not in Boston. I had to push for the big contract."

"Geeze, you've got stones."

"It'll work."

"That's why I'm here."

"Once again to reiterate, just take it easy try to find a viable plan to take the next step. Nothing's impossible. We just haven't figured it out yet."

"All right. Now I understand. By the way, on June 16-25th we have been cordially invited to Getty's London offices for a nine-day summit to see if we can make this work. We'll be flying British Airways—first class."

"Are we going to have any chance at the girls?"

"I imagine."

"I'll start packing today."

"Speaking of which. How's school?"

"I'm working a lot. Because of this project I'm, leaning a lot of my papers toward business proposals for fairly developed countries. It's an interesting angle to look at because most people concentrate on developing countries. There's a lot of immigrants' descendents in this country with ties to the homeland. Some of them are really old but some aren't."

"Well, look I've got to go win me a hockey game tonight. I really respect your opinion but we have to be as aggressive as the Lord lets us. Push, push, push—fore-check all the time. At the very least, we can merge with *Sports Illustrated* because I really think America is ready for this idea. I'll talk to you later. Keep the e-mail coming."

"Yes, sir."

His father called next.

"Dad, we won."

"I watched the game. What's going on?"

"I'm trying to engineer this deal with Getty, and I'm looking hard at possibilities in which we can go with it. And, I have this proposition I'm rolling over in my head."

"Sounds vague so far***"

"I want sports galleries like hard Rock Café's or Planet Hollywood's throughout the North America and maybe Europe. How arrogant does that sound?"

"It's not arrogant. I don't know quite what it is but where did you come up with this?"

"Well, I was thinking about art being able to go to the MFA anytime I wanted practically. I saw a blurred line between sports photography and art. So I thought who had done it differently. I want it appealing to young, active families. It's not a bar to get drunk but to socially have a nice time. And they'll be Pictures everywhere. For sale of course, like a real gallery, and a room with the history of photography from the used in the Civil War to develop prints to the most sophisticated digital photography. What do you think?"

“At what point in time do you expect to be married. Like with children?”

“Dad, don’t take this wrong. Laurie and I have a unique relationship. We like being around each other twelve hours a day. That’s just at work. We talk at dinner. It’s nice. As hard as we work, we’re practically always together and I don’t even ask her to make coffee. We are friends. She takes care of me in more ways than you know. Whatever I need, she knows. The best part of both of us is that we are accomplishing stuff but it’s never competition that gets out of hand. We’re together.”

“Yeah but can you really be sure that you’re happy?”

“What?”

“It seems to me amongst your goal extraction, you don’t have time to just sit and watch a ball game. You’re always upset that you aren’t there shooting it.”

“I can’t go against nature dad and I don’t think Laurie can either. She can play a mean clarinet too.”

“Well, don’t do it if it ain’t fun.”

“Understood—where’s mom?”

“Right here!”

“Mother.”

“Yes, dear. Are you getting enough sleep.”

“No.”

“Do you eat right?”

“No.”

“Good. How’s Laurie?”

“She keeps me floating.”

“Well, I didn’t want to say anything.”

“But…”

“Listen. Mr Universe here! Could you please take some time and relax.”

“Mom, I feel good when I work. It’s like relaxing because I’m working towards goals I have in my own life. Laurie is the same way. You have to understand. As soon as I declared myself a professional photographer, photography suddenly became work. Who’s idea was that? It’s so much fun! I’m the only guy in the world that has two professions and no work.”

“Well, your father can’t come this year. He’s piled on at work. We’ll be out in the summer.”

“Good. We’ll follow you home. I’ll show Laurie the digs and then we’ll go to the Berkshires. I want to see Norman Rockwell’s Museum. Laurie wants to see Old New England and the Basketball Hall of Fame. She wants me to take her on the roller coaster at Six Flags.”

“You’re afraid of heights.”

“What a fool is for love! What can I tell you?”

❧

Several hours later, Steve took his regular shift on Carolina’s home ice to beat the Hurricanes. Carolina had many Euros on their team so there was a lot weaving and dodging and cutting at center ice. Frankly, Dallas didn't care what they did at center ice, as long as the neutral zone remained frozen to the opposition. That meant hustling back and hammering them at the blue line. They did this well through two periods and then things got bloody.

Jimmy Franklin, a late season call up hit Vladimir Lananin in the mouth as the 'Cane forward crossed the blue line. Lananin, on the way down lost his edge and his skate sliced open the back of Franklin's leg. Jimmy yelped in pain and crumpled to the ice. The pile on began as players started throwing hay-makers all over the place. Meanwhile the trainers were trying to get at Franklin who was bleeding all over the ice. If the referees could've cancelled the game, they would've. In any event, Colin won the game breaking ice on a shoot out. With the 1-0 win, the Stars we're going home with three games in hand leading 2-0 against the hottest team in the league.

On the plane home, people just mostly slept they were either halfway to the Cup or halfway to thee biggest blown opportunity ever. Laurie sat next to him.

"Why aren't these guys celebrating?" She asked.

"We won in a shoot out. Those are blind luck. Carolina's furious. Franklin's out. Overall we broke even no matter what the score. Don't worry about it. It's this team's style. We get awfully serious in an awful hurry when we need to examine our personal games for the greater good of the team."

"So what are you thinking of."

"I've got to put some enthusiasm into use; throw a big check, make an end to end rush. I have to figure something out. I have to impress upon them that our defense is impregnable and contrary unsubstantiated rumor that it has died out offense pushes forward."

"You're a rookie."

"I'm a twenty million dollar a year rookie. They didn't pay me that to stay on the sidelines."

"You're first rotation, first power play, and first penalty killing unit. I think they're getting their money's worth."

"Look, kid. Let me define it in the simplest terms. My performance—just like the rest of these guys—is defined by us winning the Cup. Luckily, we have the tools and the juice to do it. "You remember Herb Brooks, 'You were meant to be here.' He used to walk around and tell the players. We have it and we know it. The problem is so doesn't Carolina. They aren't going to roll. We have to beat them."

"Are you going to miss the off-season?"

"In what manor?"

"Working with the kids; you'll be in a boardroom with the rest of the suits."

"I know this sounds extraordinarily weird. But I like the boardroom. I like calling the shots after it has been examined from a million angles. I like helping people understand the world of athletics, the passion, the pain, the joy that people experience either playing, coaching, or watching the game. It's fun."

"Right now, I think of tomorrow night. That's it."

"You're a strange one Mr. Grinch."

"Always have been but I hid it from you because I wanted to impress you."

"And now that you have me."

"You get all of it."

"Which means?"

"This is me. This isn't the sixteen year-old kid that was afraid that people would laugh at him if he suggested such a thing. Instead of trickle up economics or trickle down economics, it's a combination of both. Even when I'm on the road, I'm measuring different factors and possibilities and they all point green light. At the beginning I look through it with the most jaundice eye—just so I don't get caught up in my own enthusiasm."

"This is fun for you—Talking like this."

"Does that make me a nerd?"

"I don't think particularly."

"I love Bill Gates. He said, 'Be nice to nerds. They may be your boss someday.'"

"You're not a nerd."

"Don't go that far."

She laughed.

"You're a head case is what you are."

Chapter 54

Game three was in the Stars house and during warm ups, Steve pulled Joe Spano aside.

"Look at that!" Steve said in unabashed awe.

"If that ain't Lords Stanley's cup, look at it," Joe said.

"What are you two joker's looking at?" Colin asked.

"Look at center ice," Steve said.

"Well all be."

He quickly gathered his guys on the blue line.

"You get a good look, gentlemen. It's all those guys, all those years ago. Mighty Detroit has fallen so it's ours to claim. It make take forever and a day to get someone to remember the 2006 Stanley Cup Champions but we will know, our friends will know, our families will know, and most importantly every single guy who has laced up skates for us this year will know.

"Imagine taking it home to your town and signing autographs this summer. Imagine having your name engraved on the Cup. Your place in history! Forever the best in your occupation for one year…."

Steve didn't listen to the speech from then on because he knew the Stars were going to win both games and they did 5-1 and 7-2. When Steve and Laurie arrived home from the celebration, they showered separately because they both smelled like various kinds of alcohol. Steve came out dressed in jeans and a Stars T-shirt. And Laurie wore a spring dress.

"We get to bring it home?"

"What?"

"The Cup. We get to bring it to our high school."

"Really."

"It's tradition."

"Like Christmas."

"Yeah, exactly."

"I think you're going to need a bigger building."

"Like?"

"The Mass Mutual Center."

"You think? Are you serious?'

"Yes, most definitely. After all these years, you're a hit."

"That many people are going to come."

"How many high schools and colleges do you have there?"

"Yes but will they all come."

"If they do you'll need a bigger building than that."

"It would be nice. I'm not objecting but it's still weird."

"Are you saying, one guy with one Cup can make all-that ruckus."

"You must believe like you did when you were six and anything was possible."

"I've never claimed be an adult—ever and the company not withstanding—it is important to understand that's why I succeed. Instead of jealousy the Good Lord gave me the gift of giving. That meant compliments. I practically have, 'Good for you tattooed on my forehead.' If you get excited about your teammates accomplishments other good things will happen. If you want to be jealous, there are just other places you can work. We have a good group of people here because we are a team and we the most fun letting each other each other know every once in a while… but we never get malicious and we never get stupid."

"What happens if this thing becomes a fortune 200 company and you're working ninety hours a day?"

"I'd bust myself from President and CEO down to staff/photographer/ consultant."

"This is something I've never saw before. A bunch of college kids who can't even get along on the ice, form a company over pizza and Cokes at a local restaurant…"

"No! No! No! It's a pizza shop."

"Excuse me it's a pizza shop. Then you come to Texas and reconnect with the East Coast with out missing a beat. Am I correct?"

"Absolutely, wouldn't want to interrupt. Go ahead."

"We are in the midst of something great for America here. I can feel it."

"I fight the challenge every day of just parking myself at a college and photographing and going home at 5:00 o'clock at night. It's easier but there's some pull out there telling me to go ahead with this. I like the people and the motivating and being the guy they go for with questions.

"Still as an artist, there are times when I just would like to shoot."

"I bet. Yet, it's yours now. You can't go away now."

"There is absolutely nothing as cool as a still picture."

"You're a good boss. People call you the Chief behind your back. It's not disrespectful. They just know you're the go-to guy."

"I'm glad we're married."

"Of all the things that you do in your life, I'll be there for you. Just talk to me. Keep an open line of communication with me. Don't be afraid to reach out there. Heck, it's so difficult to get out there, there's less warm bodies to bump into. Go! Do your thing and don't be afraid."

For the next month they were in Europe—enjoying it immensely. They saw as much they could on any given day then they went back and saw it again. It was an incredible ride, the history mixed with modern life that just went around the history. They had fish and chips in Trafalgar Square and cannoli's in Rome. They saw Venice, and Milan and Rome coupled with Tuscany.

Their last night in Italy they ended their honeymoon together in the quiet of thee summer sun.

And then they woke up.

"Were in Italy," he said.

"Surprised?"

"I didn't expect to be known as a hockey player. They do jump around a lot if they think you're important."

"I think we have test marketed your company."

"I expected some flack from the common people I guess."

"Why?"

"Because, I do different things from them."

"Most people admire you. Stop trying to turn it into a class war."

"The whole trip has been amazing. I had some lady ask me to sign her cheeseburger wrapper in McDonald's in Turin."

"Did you like England?"

"Very much. The people aren't half as cool as they are portrayed. They are proper though. You don't mean to offend because it's their country but it's kind of different from back home. It's a little more formal back on the Isle. It's nice though. I like it. I wish we could have caught that soccer game in it's entirety. "

"I wasn't going to sit in a hotel room and watch a soccer game. I love you dearly but no."

"All in all it was a really fun vacation. I have no complaints. The people treated us great no matter where we went and with my ten-word vocabulary in Italian, I could order coffee and espresso. What more can a man ask for?"

"I think Rico wanted to stow away in your suitcase."

"Yeah. But he is a smart kid and he has been to Italy. He knows the people. They are his own. Do you think we should change the language to Australian?"

"Honey, it's a honeymoon. And that's one thing he and I don't share. He's Italian and everyone knows it. Everyone thinks I'm English. Besides, they communicate differently than I."

"Meaning?"

"The thing is I'm English."

"Yes?"

"So do it."

"I just may. Let's go catch the bus."

"You know something, when our baby is born, it's going to be able play soccer like an Italian, baseball like an American."

"Do you think pure people go on vacations to other countries?"

"Yeah, sure."

"Do you think they enjoy it?"

"They must. They keep going."

"Boy, I hate that. My children will treat people with respect."

"My mother will straighten them out and then dad will get them."

"My problem is. I like people. If you're standing in a museum and you just strike up a conversation with someone. You learn so much."

"My grandfather was not a formally educated man but he knew life. And he taught Tony and I that. He said you will enjoy life a lot more if other people were involved in your life. Now, we enjoyed that but we were different—both of us. I think Tony will be a writer some day and he'll come to Italy just to his wife and children the pictures and he may just go to England too.

"I was thinking. Maybe, if you'd want to follow me around Canada to the OHL."

"What's the OHL?"

"The Ontario Hockey League. They are the junior circuit."

"I have to come. I'm your PA?"

"Yes but I asked and wasn't that nice?"

"You do have friendship appeal. Do you know that?"

"Look, we're going in the summer. The weather is fine."

"I'm sure we'll enjoy ourselves."

"Will we come back?"

"Oh, yeah!"

Back home in Dallas, Laurie looked at him.

"Nice?"

"Yeah."

"What's on your mind?"

"Look? Italian Red and some preparations for zeppoles in the fridge; 'Congratulations! You're in up to your neck now. Eat and drink hardy. You'll need it.' Signed, the Spanos."

"Do you think it will be that bad?"

"You have to understand Joe. He has a wry sense of humor. He wants kids from us by next training camp. He told me when we were married."

"That's putting pressure on me I don't like."

"Joe's the other brother I've never had. I was well on my way to becoming one of the top ten rookie goons when Joe straightened me out. It was probably worth ten minutes of ice time a game. I better call him and say thanks."

"We better."

"Yeah but he's my buddy I get to talk first."

"Okay but I get to talk."

"Yes, dear." He rang him on the house phone."

"Ciao, che cosa fa."

"Joe. It's me. I can't speak Italian."

"Which me would that be?"

"The one that just got back from his honeymoon***"

"Shouldn't you be elbow deep in zeppole dough? And don't forget the wine. Very good vintage."

"Joe you've been in the league three years now right?"

"Second round, Vancouver B.C. Went from the Lions ball boy, to NHL star if I do say so myself."

"When you left B.C. for your first training camp, what did your friends from back home think? Were they happy for you? Did they think you were a jerk? What was it like?"

"Mostly, every kid wants to play in the NHL in Canada. You have nothing like it in the United States because you have so many sports. You know, you play and you practice and you try and get the most out of yourself because somewhere in the back of your mind, you don't want the guys to laugh at you.

"It's a little tough now, with the guys in the minors. I've been in the league three years now and this was my best year yet and they're still slogging away down there somewhere. I'm lucky. I work hard but I'm damn well lucky. I know that."

"My situation is different. It's like I'm in a museum everywhere I go back home. People look at you but they are afraid to come up to shake your hand. I'm not them anymore. It's very strange."

"You have to force the issue. Go up there and shake their hands. What do you care?"

"Be careful of beginning to think that way yourself. Because you'll pull away and look arrogant; he more people you meet the less hard up you'll be. Just mingle."

"It's odd seeing the guys now. Most of the guys I hung out with are in the financial district. There are 'workin' for a livin''" like the song says."

"I think I'd like to be in the front office someday when playtime is over."

"I'm having so much time having fun with the company, I don't know when playtime will end."

"All right, one question. I played with the Toronto Marlies and studied one year of Business MGT. I did pretty well only because I was desperately afraid that I wasn't going to make the pros. I did okay mind you. but it was more panic I guess. I'm thinking about going back to University of Toronto in the summer."

"I recommend college."

"That was quick and brief."

"Look, Toronto is a cosmopolitan city. You should have a lot of fun. Why are you going to Canada? You can do it at UT?"

"You Americans only think America has national pride. You are so mistaken."

"Fair enough. I'll tell you one thing. We're going to have fun next year. Here, the wife wants to hang out with you and yours for minute. Good luck in

Toronto. Can you pick me up a baseball cap? I'll pay you back. I just collect caps—as many as I can."

"Now, there's one thing that we talked about."

"Which is?"

"My name."

"Which will be?"

"Let me tell you the history behind it. My granddad, Giusseppe Tommasino came to this country on the boat with his mother when he was three. His father had come earlier looking for work. He found some on the docks of New York City. A tough place, my grandfather was promoted to police after three months on the job. He broke his nose four times in fights before Nana gave him the hook.

"The family decided to head inland and ended up in New York City. They ended up in Manhattan. He was really strong and they hired him as an escort as what they called him in those days. He had limited English the first couple of years and worked very hard to improve it. He wanted his citizenship badly. And so didn't mama.

"He really loved that hotel. He stayed there thirty-five years. Had three kids with his wife and to my knowledge never went home to anyone but his wife. He would play baseball with us. Because of course the Yankees were the town all summer back then. He was amazed that we skated so well. He was big and had weak ankles."

"He sounds like a great guy."

"Nothing against my dad—I was scared of Nono because he was a bear. The guy was huge and I asked him one Fourth of July what made him an American."

He smiled and said.

"'You learn good English. You become an American that way.' I was four or five and that made a huge impression on me. He also told me, 'Always be a gentleman.' And he meant it. It's too bad I had to grow up to be a hockey player. I almost made it."

"You'll wear Tommasino on your back next year."

"Yes. I will. Number 7 too. It wears well across the shoulders. Don't you think?"

"How do you think we'll do next year."

"We can win for a while with these guys. I've never seen such hustle in all my life. They are extremely talented and extremely motivated. They are the best and they let me tag along for the ride this year but I have learned and I will play my game at their level next year."

"When are we going to have the baby?"

"Let's start tonight."

"Aggressive."

"I can play it any way you want it."

"Why didn't you marry an Italian?"

"Why didn't you marry a white guy?"

"Don't get so defensive. It would just be nice to know."

"I couldn't really. I just spoke to you and it was so easy on a personal level. I am a really by the numbers guy and I figured I'd get married when the big money showed up. I would have my portfolio and my Ira's along with Equity on a condo. Financially I would be in order. I could take care whoever it was going to be with me. It turned out to be you and everything went a little too fast I think."

"You're telling me this on our honeymoon."

"I'm sorry, we didn't wait."

"Wait for what?'

"The thing everybody's supposed to know about."

"You never abused me."

"If I did, my father would've cut my hand off."

"Not physically or mentally, but the privilege; I always felt loved with you. That's why I didn't marry a white guy."

"Oh, that ought to go over big in Midland, TX."

"I really hate that part of you. Do you know how well loved you are here after one season. Half the kids want to play hockey and the other half have signed up for Junior Achievement."

"If we were struggling at $25,000 a year and paying of loans so we could go to grad school, would it be the same?"

"Maybe we'd have to put off children a little longer but we'd make it."

"Yeah, I think we would. Want to kiss me."

"Yeah sure!"

"One more thing; I was scared to death of your parents because you were who you were in your own right."

"Well, I was the perfect child."

"That goes notwithstanding. Yet, I could just see, 'Here's comes the judge being played and me walking to the gallows.'"

"You should've been there when you had the talk with dad outside. It would've made you sick, 'What a nice boy! What a young gentleman! How proud, yet without arrogance.' I had to tell her to stop."

"I still feel weird around dad."

"No kidding. You say, 'Yes, sir!' more times in one conversation than any boy I've ever seen."

"So about the babies."

"We should start tonight."

"Right. Okay, I'm game."

The End

Prologue

When he arrived home to Dallas via home at Logan, flying over home in Western Mass, he considered the name change a lot.

"You know my grandfather never made a big deal over it. Maybe he liked it. I could be going against his wishes."

"Are you embarrassed?"

"No, of course not, I have Italian friends. I just don't want to be forced on a loser's talk show sitting around with fat old ladies for an hour discussing their lives were changed by me changing their name. Do you know how much business I can do in an hour?"

"So keep it the same."

"I feel my grandfather would be disappointed."

"What do you mean?"

"If I said it out loud, maybe it's best that I keep it the same. I don't know."

"Please, a little more information…"

"The Italians will hate me again. The ones I told growing up hated me. They called me a sell out. So I just stayed with the English guys. Now, I'm going back the other way and am going to catch it from the English guys."

"I don't think so."

"Why?"

"You lead to well. People respect you. They know you are an honorable man. You can do business because people can trust. You putting ideas with China and they're Communists. Go figure! You have the ability to help people and they know it. Do you really think I wouldn't be with you, if your name was different?"

"I don't know. That's what I've been talking around."

"I'm severely disappointed. I like you. I trust you. I think you're a workaholic and I severely think that you want your company to fit into the United States game plan—policy and everything else wise. I see you running for office someday."

"Let me tell you something kiddo. It won't be for a while. There's more pictures to take—more articles to write and maybe I'll take a crack at a novel. Besides, your President should look like your father not your little brother."

"President?"

"If you're going to swing, swing hard!"

"What about Tommassini?"

"I like it. The only thing is the autograph. I'll have to learn to sign a new name."

"You aren't going to change, right?"

"People change as they go through life."

"What does that mean?"

"You just do. Unless you're a rock head! Opinions get changed and people gain an understanding of you in the middle and at the end when they have didn't really understand you at the beginning."

"You really think this is going to be a big deal."

"The lease for the new office came through."

"Good, we can clean your home office."

"No. No. No. That's mine. I will still have to work there and I want everything the way it is."

"Why?"

"It's comforting."

"There you go, lighten up it'll be fine."

"I see people as Americans. White Americans, African Americans, Italian Americans, etc. I still know the 'Pledge of Allegiance' and I haven't said that since I was in the first grade. In any event, I'm Italian American and you're white."

"You're going to ask me this now."

"I'm not asking. Some people think that we're screwing up the gene pool."

"We're not bad people. We're not even medium people."

"I love my country even though I do business with a lot of other countries. They think I've gone native if I respect their customs. It's a sign of conformity and weakness. Let me tell you something even though I'm dead set on it yet, I'm pretty sure I need religion. Being blessed by the Pope has some affect on you. I don't care who you are. What if he's different from me in the final analysis of who I am. Do I hate him?"

"You're all screwed up about something and I want to know now!"

He laughed.

"I'm serious," she giggled.

The home of my ancestors brought so many good memories back and some bad ones To be honest with you, the guys who were buddies from back home who were Italian were big enough to teach me about the world at least through Italian eyes and they were all successes.

"Other kind of people taught me other stuff. And that's our neighborhoods were safe. America is the best because of that. Obviously, you'll have disagreements sometimes but the fights and gangland stuff is controlled and kept to a minimum.

"You know we have the same thing in Texas. Some people say it is better to have one type of person in a certain area. Other people say no, you need different people to balance each off."

"I just want to be good. I want to make consistently good decisions. I've met a lot of nice people in this world and they were different from me. They were even Yankee fans. We may be classified at first. I don't what they're going to call us. I'd like to be called a full fledge American. I have my driver's license and everything."

"I don't know. I never really relied on race much. I hung out with the kids on the block. Waved to their parents," Laurie said.

"Me too! I delivered papers to all kinds of people—including the mayor. I liked him a lot. He gave me a fifty-cent tip. God, I don't want to get on a news show and talk about my ethnicity. That is for family and friends. I'm good at what I do. I don't have to finagle to get a job. Heck, this company may actually go somewhere."

"You're talking to China. You are going somewhere."

"We should have a big party, when we go home. We should invite friends from Boston, Springfield, Texas and just enjoy the people we work so hard for. What the heck? My last gasp before I get back into training."

"I'm glad your head is clear."

"Me too! Let's go home."

❧

There was a lone message on the answering machine when he arrived home. Luc Favre, and up and coming winger on the Stars had left a quick message to let call back.

"Hey, it's me!" Steve said.

"I have a question," the other rookie said.

"Shoot!"

"Mon ami, how many times do I have to tell you. Frenchman don't shoot—they pass."

"What's going on Ace?"

"We will be playing for the Cup next year again."

"You will be first line next year."

"Do you think?"

"Maybe. Hey, where'd you play your junior hockey?"

"Laval."

"No kidding. Happening team."

"I think that everyone in French Canada wanted to play for them after Raymond Bourque."

"Have you calmed down yet?"

"Next week I get the Cup."

"Back to St Laurient's."

"The whole town's going to be there—all ten of them. Great people but not many."

"What's your question Ace?"

"Well, should I go back to school or not. These guys are throwing money at me next year and I don't know what to do with it. I'm thinking about going to an online school for Finance and finishing class work on the plane and stuff. I hate flying anyway."

"What are you going to study?"

"Finance but do you think it's worth it?"

"I don't know. I never took on line before. If it was a scam, the government would crack down."

"I think so too. I may do it."

"For what it's worth school was always good for me. I think it's worth it."

"I'm nineteen years-old. I can' even get a drink at a bar. I have to do something with my spare time. My fiancée is in college at St. Michael's in Vermont and she's been bugging me to go back to school. I think I am. I'm pretty sure."

"Do it. You're ninety-nine per cent convinced."

"I'm French. You don't understand. It takes a bottle of my father's best. And a loaf of pattisierre to figure this out."

"Watch the bread, you'll end up a porker."

"Hey, what's it like being married?"

"We're doing the baby stomp."

"Huh, Huh, Huh! I think the little monsters were bon chance. Au revoir."

"Later on my friend."

His phone rang several minutes later.

"John Davis here. How was the honeymoon?"

"Well, we took a ton of pictures and loads of souvenirs were bought. We did so much walking, I had to buy an extra pair of sneakers."

"That's it?"

"Look, if you ever get to an English soccer game, find a way to get to the commissioner or whomever and get a press pass so you can shoot. I saw a Manchester United game. Great!"

"What about Italy?"

"I liked the Venice the best. The gondelas and so forth. Laurie liked Rome. She flipped when she saw the Swiss guards and everything. It was definitely humbling to be there. Over so many years it's there. Understand?"

"I have a huge problem. Well, it's not really a problem. It's more like an opportunity. I have been offered full professor ship at Harvard upon completion of my Masters in May—to teach Entrepreneurialship no less."

"Selfishly, I need you. You're our right arm on the East Coast. You're great with customers and you work within a team mentality. I can see why your so valued. Let's say I sweeten the pot and give you another $25,000 to stay."

"I'd rather have it stocks. This thing is going to fly huge. I know it. But I like Harvard."

"Geeze, you admitted it."

"Are we talking as friends?"

"Um-hmm!"

"I say this with all do respect. I came to Harvard pretty okay financially. My dad was paying for it. I saw a lot of people scrambling with financial aid and stuff. I learned a lot and had a really good time too. Yet, this need to give back, I don't know if I'm cutting it to the quick too early. Maybe I work for twenty-five years and accumulate some assets. Of course you give back along the way but you have your big score in the end."

"Jack, twenty-five years would put you at forty-eight."

"I was born a man of leisure. I took philanthropy."

"I respectively decline this appointment yet, want to continue my close association with Harvard University and Harvard College as a guest lecturer."

"Think it'll work?"

"Yeah. I get the same response from several Profs. Sports? What do you mean? We'll have to show them."

"I just helped shoot down an appointment at Harvard."

"Yes, you did."

"It's just too funny how we ended up, huh?"

"Hey, look buddy, we are beginning a journey that most people can only dream of."

"Anything you need?"

"Well, don't take this the wrong way. We should broaden our horizons a bit."

"I just want to get good at what we're supposed to be good at first but wha do you have in mind?"

"In three years, I want to be put in charge of the art photography wing o our program."

"No kidding. At what point in time were you going to go to Harvard?"

"Well, it was an either or…"

"It sounds like a really good idea tangentially yet, I'm a black and white o paper kind of guy. Keep typing."

"Yes, boss. I'll have it for you in a month. You're going to be working your butt of all summer."

"Weight training starts tomorrow."

"What'll you all doing for Dana's birthday."

"She likes quiet. I am going to cook my famous old Grouse and prim rib and then walk Fanueil Hall where I will get unbeknownst to her ou engagement ring."

"You're going to get a whole prime rib."

"No dummy, we're going to go and spend a weekend at the Westin and b engaged. I've sent out red flags to everybody's parents and they all came back. think the only one who doesn't know is her."

"Do you really think you can do it?"

"The marriage or the business?"
"I'm telling you, sometimes they're one in the same, John."
"She likes me. We can talk about stuff."
"One month."
"Yes, sir."
"Congratulations, John!"

The End

CPSIA information can be obtained
at www.ICGtesting.com
Printed in the USA
LVHW081302241221
707105LV00019B/259